Richard B. Kimball

Undercurrents of Wall-Street

A Romance of Business

Richard B. Kimball

Undercurrents of Wall-Street
A Romance of Business

ISBN/EAN: 9783743382749

Manufactured in Europe, USA, Canada, Australia, Japa

Cover: Foto ©Andreas Hilbeck / pixelio.de

Manufactured and distributed by brebook publishing software (www.brebook.com)

Richard B. Kimball

Undercurrents of Wall-Street

OF

WALL-STREET.

A ROMANCE OF BUSINESS.

BY RICHARD B. KIMBALL,

AUTHOR OF "ST. LEGER," "ROMANCE OF STUDENT LIFE," ETC.

"Mislike me not for my complexion."
MERCHANT OF VENICE.

NEW YORK:

G. P. PUTNAM, 532 BROADWAY.

1862.

M'CREA & MILLER, STEREOTYPERS.   C. A. ALVORD, PRINTER.

Pelatiah Perit,

PRESIDENT OF THE CHAMBER OF COMMERCE,

IN THE CITY OF NEW YORK,

THIS WORK IS DEDICATED

BY

THE AUTHOR.

CONTENTS.

PART FIRST.

PART SECOND.

PART THE LAST.

UNDERCURRENTS OF WALL-STREET.

"Beneath heaven's genial sunshine everywhere
Is heard the utterance of the human heart:
Each in his language doth the plaint impart;
Then why not I in mine?"

CHAPTER I.

INTRODUCTORY.

On Saturday afternoon, the sixteenth day of October, 1858, something extraordinary occurred to change the dreadful routine of my life. I cannot now recall it without a sudden quickening of the pulse. Then it rendered me for a time nearly insensible.

On Saturday afternoon, the sixteenth day of October, 1858, the postman brought into my office a letter for me, received two cents, and departed. Before I state the contents of this letter, I will give the reader some account of myself. On the said sixteenth day of October, 1858, I occupied an office—no, I had "desk-room" in a basement office, No. —, Wall street. I was a note-broker; no, I was not a note-broker, but a sort of Man-Friday to several note-brokers and to several note-shavers, men well-to-do in the world, whose property consists in cash in hand, and who, spider-like, repose quietly in their dens and suck the marrow out

1*

of hard-working men—industrious, laborious citizens—unfortunate devils who have not much credit at the banks, and who are in consequence, like other unfortunates of another sex, forced upon the "street."

At the date aforesaid, I was a jackal, tender, runner, pilotfish, satellite, serf, toad-eater, or any other humiliating phrase you choose, reader, to employ, for the respectable class of note-brokers and note-shavers just referred to. Do not suppose I was in love with my situation. Do not suppose I was not keenly alive to the disgusting office from which I could not escape. Day by day, when wearied and worn out with incessant toil, and humiliated by varying but never-ending exhibitions of coarseness and arrogance, I would go to my home, resolving never again to expose myself to these, the sight of two daughters grown into womanhood—two motherless daughters—and a son, nearly grown to man's estate, and dying gradually of consumption, would send me back the next morning to the "street," meek, sorrowful, submissive. How did I come to this?— How, gradually, from the enjoyment of wealth and "fashionable society," and friends without number, and what are called the "delights of social intercourse," from influence and consideration—from all, in short, that is deemed desirable, and highly respectable, and absolutely the thing; how, I say, gradually did I come to pay two dollars a week for "desk-room" in the basement of No. —, Wall street?

It is no new story—it is the old story, scarcely with variations. I am sixty-one years old—almost sixty-two. In 1837 I was a leading importer of silk goods in this city. I lived in what was then a very fine house in Broadway, a little above Bond street. I visited Europe frequently—on business, it is true; but my tastes were refined, and my education good; for, although destined to a commercial life, my father, who took a wide and liberal view of what was required for an accomplished merchant, had sent me to "Yale," where I graduated respectably, and from whence I entered a counting-room. These European trips, therefore, were not thrown away on me. My wife sometimes went with me, till the care of young children prevented.

The crisis of 1837 swept over the entire country like a tornado, and it carried our firm irretrievably under. I was in the very vigor of manhood, and I laughed at calamity. I only felt the stronger to resist and to conquer. Just as soon as we could discover the extent of the disaster, I set to work to clear the wreck and to prepare a statement, so that I could put a clean sheet before our creditors, offer to them all we had, and request a discharge. But our creditors were not to be found. They in their turn had gone down, had made assignments, had no power to give discharges; all was blended in a general insolvency, a universal ruin; and so our firm made an assignment, like the rest. I was not discouraged. I occupied myself, for a time, in aiding the assignee at our old counting-room. We still had our house as before; it was the inheritance of my wife, and I felt no shame in living in it, since I had surrendered every dollar's worth of my own property to the assignee. Soon I discovered that it was a hopeless task to endeavor to make any thing out of our bankrupt estate. What should I do? I could attempt no business in my own name, and I saw no hope of relief from thraldom. A man in the prime of life, full of energy, and courage, and resolution, to be chained hand and foot, and kept in perpetual bondage!

About this time, my friend Russell remarked to me (Russell had, through his wife, come into possession of a large fortune, consisting principally of unincumbered real estate in the city, and did nothing but look carefully to the collection of the rents)—Russell, I say, remarked to me, in his cool, supercilious way: "I tell you what it is, Parkinson, there is no necessity for a man's failing—none whatever. Just look at me, now!" At that moment I was in a very bitter mood, and I am afraid I cursed Russell in my heart. I do not know, but I think I have hated him ever since, for in after years, when I used to walk wearily past his house (I saved sixpence by not riding), I saw him stepping into his carriage for an evening drive, glossy, and sleek, and full fed, sometimes—God forgive me—yes, sometimes, between my close compressed teeth have escaped, as if spontaneously and not to be repressed, the words—"damn him!" I mention this because I do not believe, with some, that poverty tends to subdue or improve the evil in our hearts; if it does, why, looking thus at Russell, in his fine, open landau, did the gall so rise and overflow?

Well, two or three years ran away. We had preserved an outward semblance of our old life. Friends had not absolutely dropped off. I had no rent to pay, and my wife knew how to economize. But every now and then visions of the wolf began to haunt me. It was only the head which appeared, thrust through the door into the parlor, exhibiting the slightest possible curl in the long, sharp mouth, disclosing two pointed ivory fangs—disclosing, but for an instant, two pointed ivory fangs, and then quickly concealed, and the head as quickly withdrawn. My GOD! reader, do *you* know by experience any thing of the sensations produced by such an apparition? Do you know what it is to have a wife who clings to you, quite safe in her protector, and young children who look to "papa" as to OMNIPOTENCE?

At last the year of Jubilee was announced. A general Bankrupt Law! Men's faces brightened with hope. Hurried congratulations passed from lip to lip. Hands were grasped with an almost unnatural fervor. Jubilee! release from bondage! joy—joy over the whole land! Yet Russell, who, with all his care—with all his close, sharp, persisting management—had, now and then, been victimized, as he called it, by an unfortunate debtor, who, his security having failed, was found wanting on the last quarter-day— Russell, who had sometimes foreclosed a mortgage, and taking advantage of the depressed state of things, had bid in the property for one-half its value, and thus obtained a decree over against the once happy possessor of a comfortable home—Russell was, as a matter of principle—oh! yes, wholly as a matter of principle—opposed to the general bankrupt law! opposed to any relief for the thousands and tens of thousands who, indebted beyond the faintest hope of retrieve, were suffering the torture of despair. But Russell's objection to the law—on principle, mind you— fortunately had but slight effect on the happy applicants for its favor. I was among the first to take advantage of the Act. I met with no opposition, and in a short time I was free.

This was early in the year 1842. I now cast about to decide what I should do. I concluded not to embark in the old business. I thought it would be easier to renew confidence, and make a credit, in some other line of mercantile affairs. This was perhaps an error, because I had been thoroughly educated to that particular branch, and I should have much to learn in commencing on another. Looking back, I think that pride lay at the bottom of this; pride, because I could not at once start on my old footing; pride, that many younger men, who had commenced since I had stopped, were already so much in advance of any thing I could undertake. I did not understand this, then; but now I know myself better. At the same time, let it be understood that, in New York, five years comprise almost a business generation. I had been laid one side, and shelved for just five years; and now, when I was preparing to start again, I had to compete with a new race of merchants, younger, keener, fresher than the race who had gone under. This did not alarm me. I had confidence in myself, and I preferred to encounter those who exhibited intelligence and activity in affairs, rather than the incompetent and stupid. After considerable reflection, I resolved to commence a wholesale grocery business, which should include, from time to time, legitimate operations, sometimes in cotton, sometimes in produce. I started with a cash capital of twenty-five thousand dollars. Fifteen thousand of this my wife insisted on raising by a mortgage upon the house we lived in. Five thousand more was contributed by my mother; it was about the portion to which I would be entitled on her death, and she urged me strongly to receive it then. She was old, she said, and had no longer the wants nor the wishes of younger folks. I took the fifteen thousand from my wife, and the five thousand from my mother, with some misgivings. It was my only chance, though; what weakness to refuse it! A friend—a tried, thoroughly tried friend—a college mate, who was possessed of large means, lent me other five thousand, without security, and with a declaration that, in event of misfortune, he would not permit me to treat it as "confidential."

Behold me, then, with twenty-five thousand dollars in cash, with a junior partner who put in three thousand dollars, and who was brought up to the business, and favorably introduced to me by the old and experienced firm of Powell, Weatherby, Keep and Company—behold me, on the first day of January, 1843, in a fine, spacious store in Front-street, my flag once more to the wind:

Charles E. Parkinson and Company.

There was great joy on that first day of January, 1843, at our house in Broadway, a little above Bond-street. An open house it was, and many were the New Year's visits my wife received, and many the visits I made. All the gloom and hope deferred of the past six years were forgotten. The three little folks—my two little girls and my one little boy—partook, without knowing why, in the general hilarity.

.   .   .   .

I found on setting seriously to work at my new business, that I had every thing to learn. My partner proved to be an active and intelligent young man. He knew the routine of the trade well, and although he sometimes assumed more than was becoming a comparative youth, I cannot say that he took advantage of his position; nor am I aware that he ever violated the rules of our copartnership. He made two or three pretty large bad debts the first six months we were together, which had the good effect to lower his self-confidence, and to lead him to me more frequently for advice.

With the best possible management, the thirty-first of December, 1843, found me, after deducting family expenses and interest money, with a small inroad made on the capital. It found me, however, in good health, with strong courage, and a competent knowledge of my business, no longer dependent on my junior for advice or suggestions. There was one drawback quite unexpected. On commencing business, I felt myself fairly entitled to a first-rate commercial credit. Frequently through the year, I discovered there was some mysterious influence working against me. I would be on the point of closing some advantageous operation, which required the giving of our acceptances for considerable amounts, when the parties would return, after a little, and regret that they could not enter into the arrangement—that they found they could not employ our paper as they anticipated, and so forth. Now, I had reason to know that we stood well at both the banks where we did business, and further, that the officers of both these institutions did not hesitate to speak favorably of our firm when applied to. What could it mean? Was there a snake in the grass—a secret foe—a disappointed creditor, perhaps, of 1837? After mentioning these facts to an old friend, and after his puzzling a good deal over it, he suddenly exclaimed: "Parkinson, how do you stand at the Mercantile Agency?" "At what?" said I, not exactly understanding him. "At the Mercantile Agency," he repeated; "what I call our 'Commercial Intelligence Office.' I don't know-what we should do without it, though sometimes they do get a little astray there; but they are always ready to correct mistakes." My friend's suggestion struck me as a very probable one, and I wondered it had not occurred to me. I requested him, therefore, to obtain a report of the standing of our firm at the agency aforesaid. He procured it the next day. It read as follows:

"CHARLES E. PARKINSON AND COMPANY (Charles E. Parkinson and Edwin A. Rollins). Wholesale grocers, respectable house, in fair credit. Established 1st January, 1843. Parkinson was importer of silk goods prior to 1837, and failed. Took the benefit of the Bankrupt Law. Unacquainted with present business; put in twenty-five thousand dollars. *Nearly all borrowed* ($15,000 from his wife's estate), *and which will probably be treated as confidential, should he fail.* Keeps house, and lives expensively. Rollins, unmarried man, about twenty-five, brought up to the business in the concern of Powell, Weatherby, Keep and Company. Puts in three thousand dollars. In trade for the first time on his own account. Firm doing large business. Mem. (July, 1843): said to have made some heavy losses. Mem. (August, 1843): Rollins drives a good deal on the road. Supposed to own a very handsome turn-out."

I read this *ex-parte* judgment with mingled surprise and indignation. Scanning it with more scrutiny, a second and a third time, I was forced into a train of philosophical reflections. After all, the Mercantile Agency had stated but

the truth, that is, mainly.   It was the *inferences* drawn from
the facts which were so damaging.   Yet the inferences were
natural.   One could not accuse the "Mercantile Agency"
of any malicious *intent*.   Yes, the inferences were natural,
but mind you, reader, they were FALSE.   And I had been
suffering for a twelve month from what was really a cruel
and a slanderous statement.   The fifteen thousand dollars
raised by mortgage on my wife's house, was absolutely
given to me for capital.   No evidence of indebtedness was
taken, no recognition of it on our books, otherwise than as
cash belonging to and put in by me.   The debt of five thousand dollars to my friend was, as I have before stated, actually placed, by a positive understanding, as an ordinary indebtedness.   The statement that I had made some bad debts
was true; but it did not add, what was more essential, that
the senior partner, myself, was a strictly business man, and
had gone through his first year in a new line, with little
loss, supporting his family meanwhile, and gaining a thorough
insight into affairs.   Again, poor Rollins came in for a sharp
hit, in the way of driving a fast team.   Now, Rollins was
really economical.   He lived with and supported his mother
and some younger brothers, and his habits were unexceptionable.   It so happened that a wealthy cousin of
Rollins's, who did drive a pair of good horses, went out
of town for nearly all the month of August, and told R. he
might exercise his team while he was gone, if he liked.—
Rollins had informed me of this, and I believe he enjoyed
his drives for about three weeks, and resigned his "turn-
out" without regret on his cousin's return.   Here, again, the
Mercantile Agency had stated a fact, and with it a *false in-*

ference. However, now that I saw where the difficulty existed, it was easy to remedy it. I called at the office of the "Agency" with two influential business friends—"undoubted" names—and went into an entire explanation. It was satisfactory. The statement as to my capital, "nearly all borrowed," was erased, or, rather, a new statement was prepared and entered on the books, quite clear and to the purpose. Poor Rollins's inexpensive drives were no longer marked against him. In short, our firm stood "right" on the books, and we were thus well advertised. We had no longer any difficulty about our "paper;" indeed, we now enjoyed all the facilities to which a good credit entitled us.

And here permit me to digress a little in order to say a word about "Mercantile Agencies" generally. The system has been greatly elaborated since 1844. Complete method has been introduced through all its branches, and a most unique and surprising skill is displayed in the information obtained, and in the general characterizations. The enemies of the system complain that it produces an espionage worse a thousand-fold than that under a European despotism; that no circumstance of private or domestic life is safe from the prying, eager curiosity of these keen investigators, who are paid well for gleaning; in short, that the whole affair is a shame and a scandal to a free country. On the other side, it is retorted, that no honest man fears to have the veil drawn aside which may conceal his minutest acts; that such a man courts investigation, and claims to be judged by it; and that those only are opposed to the plan who suffer from having the truth told of them. Now, my view of the question is not based on either of these hypotheses. It seems

to me that the mischief lies in another direction. The
agency undertakes to give information by which subscribers
can form reliable judgments of a merchant's responsibility,
and so forth. This is very desirable, and if the agencies
accomplish this they certainly render a service to the commercial community. But the truth is, we do not form an
opinion of an individual so much from certain absolute facts
we hear of him as from his *general reputation*. Every man,
every firm, every incorporated company does, in some way
and by some sure process, after a time, acquire a general
reputation—good, bad or indifferent—for which one would
be puzzled to state any reason or cause whatever, but which
is true in ninety-nine cases of a hundred. So well settled
is this, that our courts, when a person's character is under
investigation, will not permit, in the first instance, questions to be asked except as to *general* reputation. The
agencies, with the best intent, doubtless, busy themselves
with picking up circumstances. A merchant rushes in and
reads the record; he thus goes to an *ex-parte* tribunal, where
reputation is manufactured out of one set of facts, instead
of into the world, where currents of opinion flow free, and
where truth and error have a fair field for contest. If any
one doubts this, let him look at the "record" of four merchants out of five who fail, and he will find that these merchants took especial pains to keep that record fair. My
opinion frankly is, that these agencies have their growth in
our great desire to save ourselves the trouble of forming an
opinion, so that we readily welcome one manufactured for
us. It is very convenient to be told off-hand what really
nobody can ever know—whether a merchant is "good" or

not; and I believe our agencies would come badly off to-day in a series of libel suits, one-half of which should be commenced by their patrons for too favorable statements, whereby those patrons lost their money; and the other half by the subjects of mercantile criticism, whereby such subjects lost their credit. I refer to what is got together and reported about our city merchants. As to the reports recorded in the city of the standing of people through all the towns and villages of the United States, I reject them as generally the preparation of one man (in each place) who is biased one way or the other, so that he returns an opinion either much too severe or much too favorable, and by which the merchant here is quite sure to be misled.

To return: I had no further reason to complain of the "Agency." They told the truth about me, and drew no disagreeable inferences. Indeed, after a while they began to exaggerate my position, for on the day I failed my record stood as follows: "First-rate house. Credit A 1. Thoroughly up in their business. Large capital: said to be at least a quarter of a million. Reported to have cleared over fifty thousand dollars the last season on produce. Very cautious operators."

Not to anticipate. The year 1844 was for us the commencement of a new season of prosperity. With great assiduity and great watchfulness the firm retrieved the losses of the previous year, strengthened its credit, changed some important details in the mode of conducting its business, and gradually settled on a prudent and safe basis of operations. From that time we took position among the "leading merchants."

The years 1845 and 1846 passed very happily; yes, very happily, because prosperously and without drawback of any kind. To become once more a man among men. To encounter an acquaintance, and meet his scrutinizing look with an air of conscious strength and stability. To feel that you are no longer exposed to the humiliating sympathy of "friends," or the silent triumph of enemies. To be assured that you form again a part and portion of the activity which supports and moves the world; that you are of consequence in it, and recognized accordingly, recognized by old companions with whom you used to engage in various affairs; many of whom sincerely regretted what befell you, and honestly rejoice in your re-appearance in the business arena; who shake hands with you with a smile, and a look as much as to say: "I knew you would come out all right. Glad to see you here." To pass from the dreary stupor of inactivity to fresh, hopeful, energetic action; to plan and form combinations; to feel yourself gradually and surely gaining ground; to enjoy the healthful happiness of an ascending scale; to get on, to prosper, to again grow rich, and find every thing around you cheerful; to witness "troops of friends" returning to range once more under your banner, with many apologies for absence, and so forth—apologies which you receive very amiably (as if you had never felt bitterness of heart, and gangrene, and hatred on their account); which you not only receive amiably but excuse, making due allowance for human infirmities. [You forgive, and your misfortunes are forgiven, but see to it that you repeat not the offence, lest a worse evil overtake you.] To pass through all this, rising meanwhile till, like the man of

Uz, your possessions greatly exceed their former proportions. Well! life *is* worth something at that. How agreeable to have money; how pleasant not to be forced to calculate! How charming for us, the favored few, few by com-
parison, to express a wish for what we desire, and lo! it is
supplied; to plan out new pleasures, and enter into their
enjoyment; to find all things practicable, all things yielding; to encounter smiles and approbation everywhere; to
find every avenue smoothed for our approach, every path
made pleasant. Why not? Why should not these things
be desirable and acceptable, and very enjoyable?

So in the midst of business successes and social delights,
was ushered in the notable season of 1847. Some, perhaps,
who read these pages have cause to remember that memor-
able year. To such the index, "1847," will not be viewed
without emotion. Nay, to those who date from it the beginning of, to them, a period of misery and misfortune, of
blight and calamity, of stagnation of soul and withering up
of energy—leaving them walking nonentities, collapsed and
dwindling gradually away, instead of living, enterprising
beings, to such do the figures "1847" appear spectral; and
when seen printed here, will cause a shock like that produced by some fancied apparition from the dead. . . .

Thus, as I said, with much joyousness and merry-making,
amid Christmas festivities and gayeties and frolics, came in
the crisis-year. And I will proceed to explain how I happened to be paying two dollars a week for desk-room in the
basement No. — Wall-street.

CHAPTER II.

A CLOUD ON THE HORIZON.

On the first day of January, 1847, the financial condition of these United States was "most satisfactory." So said leading bank presidents and directors in the coteries to which they severally were attached; so observed the prominent members of the Stock Exchange, conversing daily between the "boards;" so echoed the principal merchants. Eminent bankers talked soothingly over their sherry of the "remarkable prosperity of the country." With the second bottle they demonstrated how we were now beyond the reach of panic. The resources of our land were so great, so various, so extraordinary, and its extent almost illimitable. Such room for development, for the employment of capital, which could never fail in returning its legitimate increase. No, thank HEAVEN! we were at last on a sound basis, and none but the most reckless need fail in any lawful enterprise.

Russell, too, was of the same opinion.

There was not even a speck in the commercial horizon giving token of the storm which was so soon to burst. Only it began to be ascertained that the failure of the harvest in Great Britain (which had been for some time known) was even more deplorable than at first reported; and, with the blight of the potato in Ireland, there was threatened for that unfortunate isle the visitation of the Angel of Death in the shape of FAMINE! But to most people this served as an additional argument that *our* prosperity was founded on a rock. We should find, at high prices and gold for payment, a market for all our surplus breadstuffs. Some, unappalled by the terrible calamity which threatened a friendly nation, chuckled over the news brought by each successive steamer of the great rise in the prices of food; while with all there was an ill-concealed satisfaction at the existing condition of things. But there were others who shook their heads, and said such condition was unnatural; that affairs could not go on ruinously for any length of time in England without re-acting forcibly here, so intimate were the relations between us; besides, they said, an unfortunate state of affairs in one country is *never* beneficial to another country with which it has a close business connection. These individuals were set down as croakers; people who were behind the age; men with antiquated stage-coach ideas. The great majority of moneyed men declared that the country was in a most pros-perous state, and accordingly it was generally so accepted.

To come to my own affairs. The position of the firm of Charles E. Parkinson and Company, on that same first of January, was essentially and absolutely a sound one. The year after I commenced business anew, my mother died. The five thousand dollars I received from her proved, as was anticipated, to be about what I was entitled to from the estate, and thus that was settled. I had within a twelvemonth repaid my friend the five thousand dollars borrowed from him. It was indeed so much in reduction of our capital, and the money to us was worth much more than

2

seven per cent; but something whispered to me, "Pay it!" and I did so. Strange to say, many years later this circumstance proved to be the final turning-point in my earthly career. Since we began, our capital had increased from the sum of twenty-eight thousand dollars, as the reader will recollect, to one hundred and thirty-eight thousand seven hundred and sixty dollars in stocks and assets, after deducting all probable bad debts and what the firm owed. In other words, that was our "balance-sheet." This was certainly doing well; at the same time we had acquired the reputation of having made still greater gains, so true is it that "to him who hath shall be given."

I was one of the few who were not carried away by the excitement consequent on the great rise in all species of produce. I believed when, stimulated by the high prices, the north of Europe began to pour in its large stores of grain, that a reaction must take place, especially if the coming season in Great Britain promised well. For this reason I did not permit myself to be tempted into a speculative course, in which my neighbors were clearing large sums rapidly. In April and May the financial distress in England, and distress from hunger in Ireland, were very great. An American government store-ship, loaded with provisions, was sent to the relief of the Irish people, thousands of whom were dying from starvation. Still were we on this side prosperous; still taking in gold for food at high prices; still counting on more gold at higher prices. About the first of June these prices came to a stand-still in Europe. From the ports in the Baltic rich granaries were shipped to the British Isles, the harvests promised well, and the potato appeared to be without blight. We were then carried into the summer in the midst of a great speculation in produce; with falling prices in Europe, and purchases and contracts maturing here; grain shipped to a tremendous extent, bills drawn heavily against it; bankers, ancient and honorable firms, breaking all over the Continent, all through England, Scotland and Ireland, till the panic there reaching its height, the market here became utterly depressed, and bills of our best houses were floating about in all directions, offered at enormous rates without buyers. Then was Wall-street one morning taken suddenly aback by the refusal of some of the largest bankers in London to honor the bills drawn on them, of an old and leading house here! What confusion, what consternation! It was all a mistake: oh! certainly a mistake! A matter of precaution only, till the arrival of the next steamer, then all the bills would be protected, all accounts arranged, and every thing be put right. Just wait for the next steamer.

The steamer never arrived!

But if the firm of Charles E. Parkinson and Company did not speculate, what had it to fear? Reader, you know little of commercial affairs if you suppose in times of general financial distress it is possible for any house engaged largely in business to escape unscathed. Quite early in the season I attempted to act with great prudence and circumspection. I came to the conclusion that such were my then business relations with correspondents in the South, we should undoubtedly meet with large losses. I was prepared to accept this as the "fate of war;" for my gains had been large. During the summer I was applied to by a leading banking-house in Wall-street to make purchases of large quantities of grain for foreign want; these were to be made through the West, and I was to charge a certain commission, and receive in payment bills drawn by this banking-house, on Baring Brothers and Company, in London. Nothing appeared surer or safer. The produce was to be consigned to the Barings, and since that house stood so high, and the drawers themselves were so undoubted, I did not consider it a risk. For all that, I stopped short in this arrangement before the parties had finished buying, and left them to select another agent. This was in consequence of the disheartening news brought by every steamer. Resolving not to make another business transaction, I joined my family, who were at Newport, in order to enjoy some relaxation. I enjoyed but little. Week after week brought intelligence · more and more gloomy. I determined not to prolong our stay, but that we would all go to town the first of September, instead of my going in alone. I cannot say I experienced any presentiment of coming evil. I do not know why, but I wanted my wife and children around me.

On Wednesday, the first day of September, in the afternoon, we reached our handsome house in Broadway, a little above Bond-street. How pleasant it looked; that dear, happy home! By evening we were comfortably installed. The next day I was early at my counting-rooms. Affairs were threatening, but I maintained a courageous self-reliance. I believed, although I might be considerably damaged, that I should weather the storm. Rollins, who had greatly improved in sagacity, and now become an experienced merchant, was untiring in endeavoring to carry out my suggestions. Things were no worse than I expected to find them. Rollins had anticipated one or two very important steps which I had proposed to take, and with a favorable result. I had occasion to go that morning to Jersey City, with reference to a number of storage receipts, about which some question had been raised, and I told Rollins that I should not return to the counting-room, but would go directly home, having many little matters to look after at the house, and I requested him if he had any thing of importance to communicate, to call in the evening. I transacted my business, and reached my house with spirits much improved, and my courage a good deal exalted. The children welcomed me with great glee as I entered. Mamma had invited two or three of their own age to spend the evening with them. Besides, young Havens was coming;—Miss Alice, my eldest, was nearly sixteen, and did not appear vexed at this last announcement, and I was expected to contribute toward the entertainment. I smiled with a father's pride and joy as I beheld the glowing countenances around me. There was nothing which whispered to me that the atmosphere was loaded with fatal intelligence. How happy was I in my unconsciousness!

At dinner we were all animated. I partook with a relish of our own cheer, and was gladdened besides by a bottle of generous wine which the old cellar had held for many a year. My return home, a favorable business day, the cheerful voices of my wife and children, a good dinner and the fine old Madeira wine—all combined to produce a comfortable and confident state of mind. "We will weather it yet," I exclaimed aloud, with a complacent nod.

There were some young people gathered in the parlor in the evening. They had danced a quadrille; they had talked and laughed. Now Alice was requested to sing. She seated herself at the piano and began one of the gems from Norma. The music was particularly adapted to her voice, and as the tones floated through the room I was gradually carried away by the *abandon* of the air. Insensibly I closed my eyes to enjoy it.

Just then I heard the door open; the servant pronounced: "Mr. Rollins, sir." I looked up. Rollins stood before me. He was very pale, but otherwise apparently not disturbed. He betrayed no unusual excitement. "I want to speak with you a moment," he said. I rose and walked with him as far as the pillar which separates the parlors, and leaning against it, I waited for him to speak. Alice, meantime was continuing the song from Norma.

"Have you heard the news?" he said, in a low tone.

"What news?" I replied.

"The Caledonia arrived this morning. We have her advices by telegraph. Barings have refused acceptance of Wise & Co's bills.

"How many with our indorsement must be still out?"

"At least seventy thousand dollars."

Alice was finishing the last strain of that delightful air. With the last strain I beheld fading away like a dissolving view those beautiful velvet carpets; vanishing the fine sofas, and the soft couches, and handsome furniture; gone, the rosewood piano; gone, the choice damask and silver; gone, the luxurious board, with the old wines and delicious *liqueurs:* and the house, our HOME—lost is the house; recorded against it is that mortgage for fifteen thousand dollars and interest, the value of property depressed, and we in the hands of a prompt creditor. Oh! why had I not paid off that mortgage? Oh! why? Wife and children; yes, wife and children remaining—but to suffer what discomfort, what unhappiness, possibly what destitution!

Not one quarter of a minute had elapsed since Rollins's answer, "At least seventy thousand dollars," yet, behold, how much had rushed through my heated brain! I turned, for I felt a soft hand on my arm—it was my wife.

" Charles, what is it?"

"At present, nothing; only I must step out for a few moments with Rollins."

" Papa, papa, where are you going? Come back! You are always running away!"

CHAPTER III.

WILL THE STORM BURST?

HAVING gained the street, I proceeded with Rollins to our counting-room. There we remained till long after midnight. I went carefully over all our assets. After I had left in the morning a telegraphic dispatch had arrived announcing the failure of another heavy house in New Orleans with which we had business relations, and which at that time was largely in our debt. Under the shock of the astounding news from Europe, Rollins did not think to mention this at the house. "It never rains but it pours," said he with an air of forced cheerfulness as he handed me the dispatch. Rollins even then had no idea of the extremity we were in. He had learned to trust to me implicitly, and I believe he considered me beyond the reach of catastrophe. Therefore, when after several hours of careful investigation, I said, "Rollins, the firm is INSOLVENT," he looked at me with an air of amazement.

"My dear sir," he exclaimed, "why do you take such a gloomy view of our position? I am certain the next steamer will bring intelligence that the Barings have accepted those bills. Read that," and he handed me the journal containing the foreign news. I did read as follows:

"Corn bills to a large amount, drawn by Wise, Dreadnought and Company on Baring Brothers and Company,

have been refused acceptance by the latter house, in consequence of the heavy fall in bread-stuffs. The friends of
Wise, Dreadnought and Company have interposed to prevent the return of the bills, with the hope of arranging for
their acceptance before the sailing of the next steamer."

"Surely," continued Rollins, "it is not possible that so
powerful a house will have their bills sent back. It is a
temporary derangement only; besides, if the bills do come
back, they will protect them : they *must* protect them to
the extent of their entire means, and we shall not suffer."

"The house of Wise, Dreadnought and Company," I
replied, "will stop payment in a week, that is, on the arrival of the next steamer, and they will not pay ten cents on
the dollar —— "

"How can you say so," interrupted Rollins, "with no
data whatever before you ?"

"Look at that!" was my reply, pointing to another paragraph, which stated that at Limerick cargoes of Indian corn
had been offered for their freight and no takers. "But," I
continued, "all surmises are idle; let us prepare for the
worst; meanwhile, not a token which shall indicate the
least weakness or fear of the result on our part. I think it
best, however, to tell you what we must, in my opinion,
come to." Rollins would not listen to the idea, and we
shook hands at the door of our warehouse, our routes homeward lying in different directions, with the understanding
that we should meet early next morning.

Since I quitted my house, clouds had gathered, a storm
had commenced, and the rain was falling, with gusts of
wind sweeping through the streets. I had neither over-

2*

coat nor umbrella. The last omnibus had gone up. Not a carriage on the stand before the Astor. I was left to make head against the tempest on foot. Ordinarily, exposure on such occasions braces one up to a fine degree of physical resistance, and produces rather an agreeable sensation than otherwise. But on that night I was supported by no such stimulus. I tried to rally, to bring my manhood to bear against the blow that was falling; I could not. Suddenly it seemed to me as if I was weighed down by a prescience which could not err, against which no resolution was sufficient. I was cowed by it. The enemy were upon me, and my hour was come. To many who undertake to read this history, the account of my experience will present no feature of interest whatever. Such will be very apt to turn over the page in search of matter more attractive. But I feel sure that, with others, what I narrate of myself will find a sympathetic response in their own memories. *They* will accompany me as I walked that night slowly homeward through the rain. Fifty years old; recollections of the past swelling within my breast; a heavy weight—that weight which poor humanity *must* sooner or later take on itself and bear—oppressing my spirit; walking slowly homeward a bankrupt.

"CHARLES E. PARKINSON AND COMPANY,
BANKRUPTS."

I read the letters glaringly displayed as I passed along. I read them above, below, around until my head swam and I reeled, walking with difficulty.

How little do the majority of the world understand the sensitiveness of the merchant as to his credit, of his keen appreciation of the sacredness of a business obligation, of the horror which oppresses him at the bare thought of " suspending." How little is known at times of his desperate struggles to sustain himself; of his days of incessant application ; his nights of sleepless anxiety; his agony at the approach of the fatal moment when he must submit to the first protest.

My wife came to the door, for unconsciously I had reached home, had mounted the steps of my own house and rung the bell.

" I thought you would be caught in the rain," she said, cheerfully, " and I have every thing dry, quite ready for you. But you are soaked through and through," she exclaimed, anxiously surveying me. " How is this ?"

" There were no carriages to be had, and I had some ways to go."

" Never mind," she continued, " you are safe back. I began to be anxious about you, it is so very late. But I have a good supper ready ; there is still a fire in the kitchen, and you can have something warm if you like, or a bottle of your old wine—which shall it be ?"

" Let it be the wine ; the Scripture says it ' cheereth GOD and man.' Let it be the old wine."

Soon I had effected an entire change of garments, and was seated at the table. With the sudden strain on my nerves and brain by the untoward news of the morning, and the evening's work, I had become absolutely exhausted in mind and body. I ate with the voracity of a famished man, and emptied the bottle of old Madeira. The food and wine had their usual effect. The stomach fortified, a gleam of hope lightened my soul. When I had finished and paused, quite satisfied, my wife came close to me and laid her hand affectionately on my shoulder, and said: "Now, Charles, tell me."

I raised myself quietly from the seat, took her hand in both of mine, and with something of my old courage returning, I said, not in a tone dispirited, but with a degree of self-reliance, yet kindly and almost gently, so as not to break it with too much abruptness: "Our firm will have to stop! I fear we are insolvent!"

"That is bad news, indeed," said my wife, without a shadow passing over her face; "bad news, to be sure; and how it torments you! But why, after all, should it cause you such agony as I see it does? Remember what you have done already; and you are young yet, in the very prime of life, and I feel certain it will turn out better than you now think."

Precious comforter!

CHAPTER IV.

DISASTER.

I SLEPT soundly.

When I awoke the next morning the sun was shining in at the windows. I opened my eyes under a complete oblivion of what had occurred the previous day. I suppose an eighth of a minute passed in this happy forgetfulness. Then, sudden as a flash of lightning it came swiftly, smiting my heart, crushing me as with a sense of some fearful, undefined calamity—a *doomed* sense of impending evil. Gasping for breath, I sprang from my bed, unable to bear the agony which had seized on me. I descended to the breakfast-room. The cheerful voices of my children greeted me. They were so happy to get back to their dear home again. Oh! yes, indeed, and various were the plans of enjoyment already formed for the coming season. My youngest, as I entered, was singing with great animation:

> "Oh! I miss you, NETTY MORE,
>   And my happiness is o'er,
>   And a spirit sad around my heart has come;"

and Master Charles ran up to me, exclaiming: "Papa, what do you think; I met Johnny Satterlee on the side-walk this morning, and he says his father has failed, and they are going to sell their house and move into the country. What did his father want to fail for, papa? You wont fail, will you, papa?"

We spent a silent half-hour at the breakfast-table. Then I quitted my house and hastened to the counting-room. We read of the nervous consciousness of guilt, and how the criminal, still free, fancies as he walks abroad that all eyes are upon him. It was so with me that morning. When an acquaintance saluted me in the street with the usual free and hearty greeting, I felt self-condemned before him, as if I were sailing under false colors. It seemed as if I ought to say: "I perceive you know nothing about it; but, sir, I am insolvent." On the corner of Broadway and Wall-street I met the President of the Bank of Credit. He stopped to shake hands with me, and inquired the news.

"You will have some pretty severe rubs, I apprehend."

"I suppose so," I rejoined. "What do you think of the situation of Wise, Dreadnought & Company?"

"To you I will say they are in a very bad condition. I presume you are interested, but I hope not largely."

"Too largely for it to be agreeable. Good morning."

A little farther on I encountered Russell—the last one in the world I should have wished to meet. I discerned him a long way off. As he approached he looked at me, as I thought, with an inquisitive, prying gaze. "How are you, Parkinson?" he exclaimed in his tone of vulgar complacency. "Rather stirring times with you produce gentlemen, eh? I suppose *you* are all right. Mind, it wont do to speculate—I always said so. I always stick to my legitimate business (collecting his wife's rents) and I don't fail."

He passed on. As I turned the corner of Wall and William streets I heard the voices of two persons in conversation behind me. I caught the following:

"Wont Parkinson be a tremendous loser if Wise's bills do come back? Can he stand it?"

"Well," was the answer, "he had a good many of those bills; but I tell you, his house is firm as a rock—could lose seventy-five thousand dollars and not feel it. I happen to have confidential means of knowing they are worth a quarter of a million."

In my intercourse with business men on 'Change, I found the mercantile community greatly excited, discussing the probabilities of the acceptance or rejection of Wise, Dreadnought and Company's bills; for on it turned not alone the fate of Charles E. Parkinson and Company, but of the old banking-house of Wise, Dreadnought and Company itself, and with it of hundreds of other firms or individuals.

An old-established banking-house! What associations of stability and strength gather around its name. How the senior member is regarded as he moves along the street; how polite are bank presidents; how obsequious bank cashiers to him. And yet that man and his " house" may have been actually insolvent for years, sustained entirely by CREDIT—by the value which habit, prescription and confidence have attached to his signature! In that year of our LORD eighteen hundred and forty-seven, one eminent London house stopped payment, and it was ascertained on examination that the concern had been bankrupt over forty years. Others failed whose statements showed that for several years at least, they had been absolutely worth less than nothing; each member all that time living in purgatory, hoping each season to recover the lost ground!

[Reader! whoever thou art: whether seated on some luxurious couch within reach of the satin bell-cord, which shall summon a servant to do thy bidding, a woman fair and beautiful, knowing not the sense of the word ADVERSITY, having at command *all* which thy heart desires; or some successful banker, or a well-to-do merchant or broker, hear me. Ye know not what a day may bring forth! Hear me! —*me* who in Wall-street for long, long years have suffered agonies indescribable, who have experienced there all that can belong to the lot of man to undergo, as much certainly as humanity can bear—hear me, I repeat. The record I indite is genuine; and in this history of mine, called by my editor "The History of Charles Elias Parkinson" (the history is true and the name assumed), I shall lay bare what transpires in the business routine of New York. I shall speak of evils which are potent and pestilent therein: I shall visit the counting-room of the merchant, the office of the broker, the cabinet of the bank-officers, and touching them on the shoulder, shall say, I am not in your power; I am about to tell what is true about myself, and in so doing, I shall not spare you. Now to all—the fair woman, the sleek man of wealth, the banker, the broker—I proclaim the fact, that there is nothing which should make the position of any one of you assured for the coming day.]*

I suffered the torture of eight days' delay, during which time I could form little idea of what would transpire beyond

---

* What appears in brackets has been interlined by Mr. PARKINSON himself in the editor's original MS.

my own conviction of an untoward result. At last I called on Mr. Wise, hoping to ascertain something. He was not in, neither was Mr. Dreadnought. The junior partner, however, assured me he *hoped* all would end well; but there was something in his manner which gave the lie to his words. I was determined to see Mr. Wise. After calling several times I did see him. I repeated my question as to the probability of the bills I held being protested. The answer was still more vague and uncertain than that given by the junior partner.

"Mr. Wise," I remarked, "at what rate will you settle these bills with me on the supposition they have not been accepted ?"

"I could not think of so uncommercial a transaction," he replied.

"Mr. Wise," I retorted perfectly calm, "*as* a commercial transaction I will take seventy-five cents on the dollar, protect the bills and release you."

The color rushed to the face of the banker till it was crimson. A composition offered to their house: the great house of Wise, Dreadnought and Company !

"I repeat I cannot listen to a proposition so out of the common course."

"Mr. Wise, I will take *fifty* cents !"

The banker, thus bearded, made a motion toward his cashier's desk, as if to close with me, but checked himself and replied: "Mr. Parkinson, Wise, Dreadnought and Company have not stopped payment; if they do not suspend, they certainly will not permit you to lose through them: and if they do stop, you yourself must acknowledge the injustice of their selecting your house and settling with you on an imaginary basis before a correct one has been ascertained."

It was my turn to blush. I looked at Mr. Wise and I saw by his troubled eye, and a certain nervousness which, while he had sufficient self-control to repress, was in a degree manifest, that he was suffering from an agony of spirit much stronger than my own.

" I am wrong," I exclaimed with some warmth. " You must make allowance for my critical position —— "

" And for *mine*," interrupted Mr. Wise.

" I see it ALL," I answered ; " good morning."

I returned to my counting-room. The steamer would be due the next or the following day. It was a New York boat, and the news would not be anticipated by telegraph. To me it was now of little consequence. My interview with Mr. Wise had settled the question about the bills. It was time for me to put my house in order; to see as near as possible where I stood. That had been my labor ever since I came back from Newport; but every mail from the West and South changed the aspect of affairs, bringing letters still more disastrous. My correspondents too had speculated on my credit, and had managed to deceive me as to the extent of their operations. I say, I returned from Wise, Dreadnought and Company to my counting-room, and endeavored in brief to ascertain what if any thing was left of the one hundred and thirty-eight thousand seven hundred and sixty dollars which on the first day of January of that same year stood to the credit of our concern as capital. My failure in 1837 was so much a part and parcel of the universal bankruptcy of the land, that I never realized in its utter and extreme extent the chagrin and mortification of stopping payment. In a general calamity there was a salvo to wounded pride; besides, I was at that time of an age not to be cast down or discouraged. The crisis of 1847 was more special; sudden indeed, involving a large portion of the community, but after all not so extensive, so prostrating, so *excusable*. Therefore when I sat down to examine what had become of our one hundred and thirty-eight thousand seven hundred and sixty dollars, I appreciated fully for the first time in my life the force of the assertion: "*Riches take to themselves wings.*" What had become of our capital? that was the question. Of regular business debts due to us I had made in our inventory a liberal allowance for losses. Here my account was not diminished. Quite as much had been collected since the first of January as I had calculated on, but we had suffered severely since then, by the failure of two of our best customers, whom we regarded as undoubted, and trusted to a large amount. Their paper had been discounted at the bank, and would soon commence to mature, and would have to be protected. Other debts which I still considered good, required indulgence. Some of these notes were also under discount, and for present emergency were of no more avail than if the makers had suspended. On this scrutinizing examination, this boiling down of assets to ascertain really what was available, I felt more forcibly than ever that in such a process, all that one *owes* must be counted as so much against him payable in gold, and what one *owns* must be valued only at the amount at which it can be converted *into* gold. This is one secret of the mysterious melting away of a man's means on his failure, and consequent loss of credit. So long as he is pursuing his business career his assets are valuable (because available) to him for their face ; he knows how to use them to advantage, and to nurse what requires attention. When he stops, every thing tells against him ; his weak debtors take advantage of his position, doubtful debts become bad, and many good ones doubtful. I say I never *felt* before the truth of these self-evident business propositions, until looking carefully over my affairs the real state of things stared me in the face. The seventy thousand dollars of Wise, Dreadnought and Company's bills would all be back on us to take up within three weeks. *Several thousand to-morrow or the day after.* Lewen and Company's notes coming due Saturday must be protected. Ellwise and Company must have an extension or go to protest : discounted also. So must Dexter. Liscombe and Company had consigned to us a large quantity of gunny bags, on which we had advanced our acceptances for not quite three-fourths of their then market value. This article had fallen with the grain-market, and was almost unsalable at one half of the original invoice, and Liscombe and Company had failed. With all this against us I felt that we might push through with entire loss of capital doubtless, but with a business position unscathed were it not for the blow at our credit consequent on our transactions with Wise, Dreadnought and Company. Our two banks I knew would not sustain us in face of the failure of that house, and unless we were largely, very largely, sustained, we were gone.

Rollins had left, too well satisfied that there was no hope

for us; I had requested him to go to my house to dinner,
and say that I should not be home till in the evening. No
one remained at the store except the porter, who used to be
in my employ when I was a successful silk-merchant. I
bid him light the gas. I went resolutely over the figures
again:

Seventy thousand dollars with ten per cent damages,	$77,000
Lewen and Company,	11,300
Tigho and Lenan,	13,700
Liscombe and Company, gunny bags,	5,600
Other bad debts (at least),	17,000
	$124,600

One hundred and twenty-four thousand six hundred dollars nearly a dead loss, beside depreciation of stock and
complications with correspondents. The slight per-centage
which ultimately might be paid could scarcely be taken into
account. Again, this sum was not only lost to me, but that
amount being nearly all under discount and all going to protest, I had the sum to raise in cash from my assets if I would
preserve my credit, and that within a few weeks. I knew
it to be impossible.

I sat half an hour, my head resting on my hand; my
thoughts busy, very busy. They went back to the period
of my childhood. I am not a native of New York. I
came here from Rhode Island when I was a young man.
My early associations therefore are not of the city. My
early friendships not here. I had no family ties here, for my
wife was herself from my own native place. We had

grown up together, and had journeyed through life in the closest sympathy. Thus, although I had a large circle of friends and acquaintances, yet I had not for protection the shield of FAMILY CONNECTION, which is so potent when adversity overtakes one. I often used to think of this, and almost envy the lot of those who were surrounded by parents, brothers, sisters, cousins : a network of relations firmly woven around them.

So I sat, my head resting on my hand, revolving the events of my past life. Thinking of my boyhood: how active and fresh was my boyhood! of my father and mother. How, after a life of honorable usefulness, they had gone to their rest. My father's salutary counsel sounded in my ears once more. I heard afresh my mother's tender advice. Well, I had worked hard. The battle of life had been a sharp one, and I had lost. I rose and looked into a mirror which was placed over the mantel-piece. There is a way of doing this quite different from the ordinary habit. Instead of the complacent or important or scrutinizing air employed ordinarily when before a glass, for the purpose of adjusting the dress, or confirming a satisfactory opinion, or looking after some little obstruction ; I say, instead of this, go before it and regard *yourself* there. Ask the question : " Watchman, what of the night?" "Oh! there you are, met at last! what have you been doing, what *are* you doing ? Dare you two look each other long in the face ?" Thus, you see your SOUL gazing out at you through the two eyes. In this manner standing up before the mirror I was regarded by myself. There was a man who looked much older than fifty, whose hair was becoming very gray and thin. Care, anxiety, weariness, were exhibited in the brow and over the countenance. Said the soul out of the glass:

"Well, my companion, at last we have come to this, with worse before us."

"Do not be severe: do not regard me in such an awful manner," was the reply.

"You have not used me altogether as you should."

"Neither have I spared myself. Do you remember how pleasantly we used to gaze at each other when we were young?"

"Yes; I do remember."

"Let us try to be young again."

"Impossible."

Was it indeed so? Never to be young any more! Never any more to have a fresh, joyous, impulsive feeling! From this time forward to be chained to adversity till death should release me! Then I thought how I had omitted, of late years, to cultivate the *morale* of my nature: that part which should survive misfortune and calamity — my *manhood!* I had been too much carried away by the material success of the past four years. I had placed too much value on becoming rich. Yes: I began to see it. Then I thought over the list of my friends—what would they say when they heard of my failure? What would every body say? How could I look people in the face? I, who was regarded as so "undoubted:" whose credit was "good for any amount." Wouldn't folks eye me curiously and exclaim: "There's Parkinson, whom all the world thought so good. What a burst up!" By a strong effort I seated myself and tried to bring philosophy to my aid, and en-

deavored to regard my position calmly. But I could not be
calm. A nervous feeling had possession of me. I rose again,
again I looked in the mirror. I was startled by seeing the
figure of a man reflected in it. I turned and beheld Williams our porter. I have already mentioned that he had
served me in the same capacity when I was first in business.
He was about my own age, and had by honest attention to
his duties brought up his family comfortably, and besides
placed quite a sum in the savings bank. He was remarkable for honesty, and was a very conscientious member of
the Methodist Church: the trust we reposed in him was
great. He was a favorite at our house, and my children
really loved him. In short, Williams had identified himself
entirely with us. This was the man whose reflection in the
glass caused me to turn."

"Mr. Parkinson," said Williams, "I have no right to say
it, but I see you are in trouble. I wish I could help: I know
I can't. But there comes a time to every body under heaven
when it does 'em good to hear a friendly voice; and my
voice is friendly, Mr. Parkinson: it *is* friendly."

I took the man's hand in mine and pressed it warmly. I
could not speak. Williams continued:

"It isn't for me to give counsel, but if things be going
wrong, I say if they *be* going wrong, Mr. Parkinson, take my
advice and don't make a beggar of yourself. It's no use.
Nobody will thank you for it. 'Tan't honest nor just to
your wife nor them young children. I know what you
would say about your property belonging to the creditors.
Now I try to think right and to be honest myself, and I
don't allow that any man has any lawful right to make a

pauper of himself, because then he has no power to help himself or any body else. If you want to pay all off, you mustn't put yourself where you can't earn any thing. There was poor Mr. Hazlewood who failed last year. You remember the auction at his house; he would have every thing sold; then he took a small tenement at Harlem; he died last Monday; broke his heart; tried to get into business again; couldn't get credit; those who used to sell him said: 'We have got our pay, we won't risk any more.' So it clean broke his heart. I attended his funeral yesterday; leaves a wife and six children. GOD knows what they will do."

"Thank you, Williams, thank you. We shall see, and endeavor to do for the best."

"Don't think me too plain-spoken," said Williams. "I couldn't help it, it *would* come out. Shall we lock up, sir?"

The good creature did not want me to stay any longer in my dismal solitude.

"Yes; lock up, and bring my letters to the house early in the morning."

"If those bills should after all turn out right!" I said to myself as I walked up the street. The very thought caused my heart to beat quick. It was a glimpse back into the heaven from which I had been thrust out.

CHAPTER V.

ATTEMPTS AT COMPROMISE.

THE steamer was in. Wise, Dreadnought and Company's bills returned. A panic in Wall-street. A card from Wise, Dreadnought and Company announcing that they deemed it best to suspend, from prudential motives, hoped it would be but temporary, and so forth. Some were led by it still to have confidence that the house would go on, but I knew it was only to soften the fall. I had passed through my panic. Now that the blow had fallen, my spirit had recovered its natural tone and vigor. I was no longer cowed by a slavish apprehension. I had gone to protest. None but the merchant, proud and sensitive of his credit, can properly appreciate the intense agony which reaches its acmé as three o'clock approaches, after which, when all is over, comes a sensation of relief and relaxation.

I had determined what course to pursue. Looking carefully again and again at our exact situation, it seemed to me if I could have the control of my own affairs I might possibly pay our debts in full, of course with the entire loss of our capital. I determined therefore to prepare a clear statement and submit it to my creditors, and after showing them exactly our position, to request them to take seventy-five cents on the dollar, reasonably extending time for payment of that sum by installments. I would add my honorable assurance to all, that if my life was spared it was my intention to pay the whole.

If you would test the different natures and dispositions and temperaments of men, go around among a set of creditors seeking for a compromise, either on your own account or for a friend. After preparing myself carefully, I undertook the task. I had first to overcome with nearly every one the idea that I was worth at least a quarter of a million, and where was it? It was a *prima-facie* case of some improper or reckless management, for the "mercantile agency" reported me worth that amount, and it was very accurate authority. It never occurred to these good people that here was an instance where the mercantile agency was *not* accurate. However, I will not say that this proved a serious impediment. My accounts were very clear, my course of business legitimate, my conduct irreproachable, and these did carry conviction along with them. I was frank, too, in stating that I hoped to save something to work with beyond the seventy-five cents offered, and I believed it was better for my creditors as well as for myself that I should do so, because if forced into an assignment I feared our assets would scarcely realize fifty cents.

With the necessary documents prepared I started on my visit to the various creditors. The president of the Bank of Credit assured me of the favorable disposition of the directors, and bade me rely on it there would be no difficulty with them. The president of the Bank of the World said nearly the same, but in a tone rather more guarded. He would submit our proposition, and he believed it would be favorably acted on.

I then went to Longstreet and Company, a large tea house, who held a considerable amount of our paper. This house I had known less of than any other with which I did business, although we had been extensive purchasers from them since we commenced. Their dealings with us were always conducted with a degree of formality peculiar to the senior partner, and I dreaded more to go in and state my errand to him than to any other of my creditors; so I thought I would relieve myself by going there first. I found Mr. Longstreet in his private office. He received me, I fancied, with more ceremony than usual. As I proceeded to state what I wanted, his manner relaxed. He drew up his chair to the desk where I sat, and went patiently over my statements, asked some pertinent questions, and finally adjusting his spectacles with much precision, he took the document respecting the composition, and quietly affixed the name of his firm thereto, and handed it back to me. Then he said: "Mr. Parkinson, our house are satisfied with the manner you have done business, and I wish you success in getting through; if we can render you any assistance let me know." I left the counting-room of Longstreet and Company with a light heart. What courage those quiet words of old Mr. Longstreet had given me! How much might I expect from personal friends if almost an entire stranger had treated me in this handsome manner!

I went next to Chapman and Terry. I had not much intimacy with them either. Here both partners were in; both expressed great surprise. Did not understand how it could be; thought I had a quarter of a million to fall back on—every body said so; couldn't afford the loss; every man

must look out for himself; did not believe much in signing
off; thought I ought to get the banks on first, and so forth.
I was despairing of making any impression on such people,
for they declared they had not time to look over my statement, so I said: "Well, gentlemen, I will call again when
you are more at leisure." Oh! as to that, they were as
much at leisure as they were likely to be these times; better
make a finish of the matter, and have no more bother about
it; and thereupon Terry took the paper out of my hand,
ran his eye hastily over it, nodded "all right" to Chapman,
and without more ado scrawled rapidly the name of the
house, and handing it back, said: "Good luck to you, Mr.
Parkinson; get through as quick as you can, the longer you
delay the more trouble there will be. Besides, we want
you for a customer. Good day." As I stepped into the
street my heart began to warm toward all the world. This
effect was produced by the success of my two interviews.
I could have hugged in my arms that formal old gentleman,
and could have jointly and severally embraced the firm of
Chapman and Terry—rough, grumbling, petulant, generous-
hearted fellows that they were. Fortified with these two
important signatures, I called on several other merchants
with whom I had more or less difficulty, some taking a day
to decide, some wishing to see other creditors, some signing
off at once. There was a Mr. Oilnut, whose office was in
Wall-street, to whom I paid an early visit. He held our
note for eleven hundred and fifty dollars. He was a rich
man who invested most of his ready means in commercial
paper, and had purchased this note only a few days before,
and after our credit began to be weakened, at the rate of

three per cent. a month, trusting to information which he thought sure as to our unquestionable ability to go through.

Mr. Oilnut received me with an extreme of courtesy—deeply regretted our *temporary* embarrassment. As to his little affair, he presumed we did not intend to include it in the list to be compounded with. I must recollect he had paid cash for it—hard cash.

"True, Mr. Oilnut," I replied, "but in so doing you made a much larger profit than the merchants who are my creditors, and at the rate you can buy notes now, you will lose but little by taking seventy-five cents on the dollar."

"Tut, tut," said Mr. Oilnut, blandly, "you are too hard on us. Cash in hand, Mr. Parkinson, cash in hand people must be expected to give value received for. You can't pay an invoice of merchandise over the counter, nor a bond and mortgage, and not always good stocks, but cash in hand—*that* we must have quick returns for, and re-a-son-a-ble profits."

"And do I understand you refuse to sign off?"

"Oh! no, my dear sir, not absolutely refuse, certainly not. I was merely explaining to you the difference between my position and that of your other creditors, that's all. Besides, the note I hold does not mature for two months, plenty of time to arrange for it. You wont find me an unreasonable man, God forbid. You had better get all the business debts on first, and then come to me, and ——"

"But this *is* a business debt, Mr. Oilnut."

"Well, well, we will not quarrel about terms; call again, call again, Mr. Parkinson. You will find me disposed to accommodate you."

Thrice I repeated my visit to this man, receiving each

time more encouraging assurances, with a suggestion that I should get such and such a name on before applying for his signature. On my last interview, having procured the name which he had the previous day requested should be obtained before he was ready himself to sign, I found Mr. Qilnut more bland, more sympathizing, more uncertain than ever. On due consideration, he did not think he should be called on just then. His opinion on the subject had undergone some modification—a *slight* modification. He pledged me his word as a gentleman and a man of honor—and he felt that I would appreciate *that*—that he would not cause me the slightest inconvenience, not the slightest. He begged me to go on precisely as if this note was not in existence; when it was perfectly convenient I would arrange it, he knew I would.

By this time I saw plainly it was Mr. Oilnut's intention to be paid in full, and on the day his note fell due. The scoundrel hoped before that, I should be once more in active business and could not afford a protest.

"Very well, Mr. Oilnut," I said (for I was now thoroughly indignant), "I see your drift, and had you told me plainly the day I first called on you, that you declined to sign off, I would not complain; as it is, permit me to say to you that I despise your conduct; and since you have appealed to me as 'a gentleman and a man of honor,' I will add that in my opinion you are neither."

"My friend," returned Oilnut, quietly placing himself between me and the door as I was going out, "my friend, do you volunteer that as a piece of information?—if you do, it is stale: I have heard it before. Good morning!"

"And has such a wretch any soul?" I asked myself as I walked along the street after leaving Oilnut's office. I had taken my first lesson in misanthropy: more was to follow. Could this be the Oilnut who had such a nice daughter; who was a leading patron of the opera; who affected the fine arts; who had dined at my house; attended my wife's parties; interchanged visits with us generally?

As I did not wish to follow out such a painful train of thought, I went to the store of Mr. Goulding, a personal friend of mine, who at the same time was a creditor to a large extent. His family and mine were very intimate; we attended the same church, in which he was a leading elder; our business relations had been always most agreeable, and particularly advantageous to his house. Mr. Goulding had been absent in Charleston ever since our suspension, and I looked anxiously for his return, because I considered him a judicious adviser, and one warmly interested as a true friend in my welfare. I knew he had come back the day before; so I hastened, after leaving Oilnut's, to call on him. He was quite alone in his private room. I was surprised to discover a certain embarrassment exhibited on my entering. He begged to be excused for a moment; was absent a quarter of an hour at least, and asked pardon with great formality on entering. All traces of the friend had vanished from his demeanor. Heavens, what a change!

"Very sad news, Mr. Parkinson," said Goulding solemnly, as if he were condoling with me on the loss of my wife or child; "very sad. I suppose you will be able to pay all? But it will break you up: yes, I foresee it, it will break you up."

I was struck dumb, actually dumb. For a minute not a word was said. Then Mr. Goulding continued:

"Mr. Parkinson, we should consider all these misfortunes as a direct chastening from the LORD. Doubtless your worldly pride has been too great; you have had too much confidence in your own strength. The unsanctified heart, Mr. Parkinson, must be brought by affliction to a due sense of dependence. I have long felt that you have too much neglected the things which belong to your peace."

During this harangue I was slowly recovering my senses. I felt like one bewildered, but I strove to retain my courage. I said to myself, I am nearly through; both banks have decided officially to accept my proposition. Oilnut to be sure must be paid in full: so my creditors themselves say. Two or three others take time to consider—courage! So, with a long-drawn breath and a settling myself out of my old position as this man's friend and a settling myself into the position of regarding him as somebody hard to deal with, I responded: "Mr. Goulding, I have no doubt you are right as to my short-comings, but you do not understand the exact position of my affairs at present. In your absence I have made great progress toward procuring an extension, on the basis of paying seventy-five cents on a dollar. Nearly all have signed, and I come now for the signature of your firm."

"My dear sir," said Goulding, "we cannot afford to make such a loss. You owe us over four thousand dollars. In justice to my wife and children, I must decline."

"But our long and intimate friendship," I exclaimed; "surely for a thousand dollars you would not sacrifice me!"

3*

"A pretty idea, to expect to pay your debts one part cash one part friendship! No friendship in trade! that is my motto, Mr. Parkinson," was the coarse reply. "But, Parkinson, I tell you what it is, if you will agree *privately* to pay me in full, privately you know, and secure the *whole* by a mortgage on your wife's house, why, there now, I will for once waive a business rule and let friendship sway me from my duty; yes, I will for old acquaintance sake — I declare I will. Besides, I will sign the paper, and I will go to Screwtight and Company, and to Gripeall, and put you through there. You see I know where the shoe pinches. By George, you will be as good as new in a week, and we will be friends again, Parkinson, and visiting together, and all that: and you will go on just as ever. Will put you right too with the ' agency,' only, you know, shan't expect to sell you at first: you understand, not till you get all straight again."

Reader! if you are, or have been in business, have stopped payment, have asked an extension, or have sought to effect a compromise, *you* will appreciate my situation and will follow me in this narrative with a degree of interest; and so will *you*, lady, who are the wife, mother or sister of some such one. You, too, young man, who are clerk for a merchant or banker or broker, or other business establishment, may and should find a useful lesson in what I indite. *It is literally what happened to me.* Read it as a true experience. Tell me, each of you, what was my duty under the tempting offer of Mr. Goulding? It *was* tempting. By accepting it, I secured the services of an adroit and influential merchant, and it probably would insure the success of my plans. It was only paying him a thousand dollars more, secured to be sure, beyond peradventure—for my wife's house could not fail to bring four thousand dollars above the mortgage. Do you wonder I hesitated? I did hesitate; but the image of HONEST Mr. Longstreet rose before me; Chapman and Terry, too, I saw with their bluff but genuine sympathy; and other creditors who trusted me, all of whom had signed on condition that the rest should join on the same terms. Perhaps I made a mistake; but in the hour of my greatest need and misery, I never regretted it. I REFUSED, peremptorily refused Goulding's offer—peremptorily but calmly, nay, mildly. I had still hopes to bring him to my views. I explained to him how I could not honorably accede to his request; that I believed I should pay *all* in full, and that at an early day, and so forth.

It was of no use. He was like adamant, and I left him; as it was late in the afternoon, I went directly home. I had nearly finished my dinner when there was a ring at the door, and a servant announced that a man wanted to see me. What was his name? The servant did not know; the man refused to give it. I felt nervous; so, directing him to ask the person into the library, I hastily finished and went in to see him. I found, seated in an audacious, self-possessed posture, a large, coarse-featured, self-sufficient, overbearing looking fellow, perhaps thirty years old, with heavy black hair and whiskers, and insolent swagger and domineering air.

"This is Charles E. Parkinson, I presume," he said in a coarse, loud tone.

"It is," was my reply.

"And I am John Bulldog, attorney-at-law!"

CHAPTER VI.

JOHN BULLDOG, ATTORNEY-AT-LAW.

HE rose as he spoke, and confronted me!

I stood quietly waiting for him to speak.

"Is this," said he, "your signature?" producing a note which he held up for my inspection. I took it in my hands. It was for ten hundred and sixty-five dollars and thirty cents, payable to my own order. I recognized it at once as one of the notes given to Goulding. The name on the back had been carefully erased, but I was certain it was one held by his house, from their habit (which has since become almost universal with merchants) of having all notes drawn to the order of the makers.

"Yes; this is my signature," and I handed the note back to Mr. Bulldog.

"Are you prepared to pay the note?"

"No."

Whereupon the fellow drew a paper from his pocket, which he reached toward me. I took it. It was a "declaration," entitled on the back:

"NEW YORK COMMON PLEAS.

JOHN BULLDOG
vs.
CHARLES E. PARKINSON and
EDWIN A. ROLLINS."

I looked at it for a moment. "I perceive," said I, "this suit is on a note we gave to the house of Goulding and Company."

"All right," said the attorney. "Now you will understand, Mr. Parkinson, it belongs to me, and it's I who have sued it. Motives of delicacy; Goulding your old friend, and so forth; you comprehend," continued Bulldog with a leer. "Having brought my action on this note, I demand of you that you apply the furniture in this house, not exempt by law from execution, to the payment of my claim. I demand further, if the furniture be insufficient, that you apply the sugars and teas, and other merchandise in your store in Front-street, to the payment in full, including costs, charges and expenses. Do you consent or refuse? I want an answer."

I did not know what to make of this extraordinary proposition. Instinctively I felt that there was something breeding below the surface.

"Well!" said Bulldog.

"I will consult my counsel and give you an answer to-morrow," was my reply.

"That wont do," said the attorney, "I have made a demand and I want to know what you have to say to it."

"You have heard all I have to say this evening. I repeat, to-morrow I shall consult my counsel, and you will then hear from me."

"Look here, Parkinson," said the creature, coming nearer to me, "are you green? Don't you know me?"

"I do not."

"Don't know John Bulldog! By —— you've got to

know him, that's all. You had better believe that. Come now, I can't tell why; but damn it, I would rather you should listen to reason. I know who your counsel is. I know Norwood.   He's a damned fool; a good lawyer enough with no common sense, and that makes a damned fool any time. Look here, will you? Just listen to what I have to say. I tell you you've got to pay me the four thousand and odd dollars you owe me, *me*, you understand. You an't dealing now with Goulding. *I* own those notes. Now, Parkinson, this sort of business is new to you: I see it is, so I think it worth my while to explain. I am an attorney-at-LAW, and mind you I go *by* the law. I don't know why, but I feel somehow inclined toward you, and by —— I will save you if you will give me a chance. Only you *must* pay these notes. By this time you have found out that Goulding is a damned sneaking old hypocrite. Now, fix up this busi-. ness, engage *me* to get you through, and I will have you on your legs in less than a week. I tell you that you had better not hesitate. Screwtight and Company and Gripeall, are both my clients; you know how much you owe them; you know whether they have signed off or not. Retain me and you are all right there. For one thousand dollars counsel-fee, I will put you all hunk. Damned if I don't. Would like to see any of these chaps oppose you then. But if you don't do it, Parkinson, I, who know, tell you that you are a gone case. By —— it's so."

At that moment I felt something pulling at the skirt of my coat. It was my youngest child, a little girl four years old. She was looking at Bulldog with wide-open surprised eyes. Just then his glance fell upon her. Strange to say, the wretch still had twinges of conscience. I heard afterward he had a wife and two children. He started as if seized by a sudden and acute pain; he turned quickly away, then recovering, he laid hold of my arm, and said with another horrible oath: "By ——, Parkinson, come this way. You are in the hands of a man who never gives out. Once more I tell you pay Goulding's debt; you *must* do it. *I* own it, and that's enough. I believe I am getting to be a damned fool: damn that little child, send her out of the room." For little Anna had followed, and was again pulling at my coat. "Parkinson, let me take hold of you, and put you through. Now then! 'tis the last call. What do you say?"

Up to this moment I had not spoken a word, since replying to his formal demand. Now I looked him steadily in the face. I knew it was all over with me. But my blood was up. I opened the door. "There," I said, pointing to it, "quick! or ——." There was a desperation in my eye before which a coward would be sure to quail. Bulldog walked out of the house without a word. Yet I knew what would be the consequence: knew and accepted it. So taking my little one by the hand, I returned to the parlor.

"Any thing wrong?" was the first question.

"Oh no."

Then we had a pleasant evening. The children were very happy.

CHAPTER VII.

A DIGRESSION.

AND blessed be GOD for all that children enjoy! Did you ever think of it, how independent they are of circumstances? How the children of the poor are as happy with a penny toy, with a bit of broken china, a rag baby, or their mud-pies, as the offspring of the rich with their endless variety of playthings, selected with so much care from the most expensive shops? Do you know how ready children are to find enjoyment in any condition, with a contentment and a cheerfulness which grown-up people may indeed envy? . It is not till they become acquainted with the conventionalities of the world, and find they lack what is most important in the world's eyes, that discontent creeps into the heart, and dissatisfaction takes the place of this blessed state. Thus it is not the thing itself, *but our consideration of it*, which has on us so extraordinary an influence.

Strange to say, looking back to what was most oppressive, most agonizing, in our change of position from wealth to poverty, I recall distinctly the fact that it was the thought of my children which most afflicted me. There was that in their young natures which in this connection touched me to the quick. It displayed such entire reliance upon their father. *He* was stronger, *he* was better than anybody else. *He* could not suffer defeat nor discomfiture. Never. Where *he* was, there was safety. Even now I recollect the confident grasp with which little Anna held hold of me as she gazed with instinctive apprehension in the eyes of Bulldog. Perhaps—who knows?—it was her presence which moved me to act toward the villain as became a man, which prevented any compromise with successful knavery.

I repeat, it was the thought of my children which most touched my heart when I reflected upon what was about to happen. Their innocent and guileless faith; the shock which it would receive; the impossibility of their understanding all about it; was it unnatural; have you yourself never experienced any thing like it? Whether you have or not, I declare these feelings at times oppressed me almost to madness. Yet how unconscious were *they* of causing me such pain.

But I digress, and if you cannot sympathize with, will you not at least excuse my devoting a few paragraphs to those little beings, of whom our Saviour said: "Of such is the kingdom of heaven."

CHAPTER VIII.

THE ASSIGNMENT.

I REMARKED that after turning Bulldog out of doors we passed a pleasant evening. It was so. I understood perfectly that it was in the power of Goulding to prevent my carrying through the proposed compromise, and I saw he was determined to do so unless I paid him in full. I had resolved not to do this. That settled in a manner to preserve to me my self-respect—and self-respect is a tower of strength —I was perfectly calm. Yet when I stopped to reflect on Goulding's course, I confess I was astounded. It really was not for his interest to sacrifice me. Evidently, however, he acted on the principle of making sure of every dollar. His doctrine was, "A bird in the hand," etc.; "Never risk what is certain for what is uncertain." He was confident of being able to compel payment or security for the four or five thousand dollars we owed him. If he gave up twenty-five cents on the dollar, besides granting time for the balance, he *might* lose even that balance. This was the narrow reasoning of a sordid, narrow-minded man. Yet this course had carried him successfully through many disastrous seasons, and made him rich. In every situation and by all classes Goulding was considered a safe man. Not content with standing high in financial circles, Goulding took stock in enterprises which he believed would entitle him to admission into the kingdom of heaven. He subscribed largely to charities. He was an elder in the church; and generally present at the Thursday evening prayer-meeting. For several years he had been the active superintendent of the Sunday-school. The clergyman sought his advice; and in any matter under discussion his counsel was apt to prevail. His family assumed a good deal of fashionable display. His carriage was an expensive one, his horses thorough-bred, his coachman in livery. He used to say how much his heart was foreign to such things, but the women were to be considered, and if it gave his wife pleasure, why, after all, it was harmless enough. This was the man who could employ such a creature as Bulldog to ʻharass and distress me.

And this Goulding, who by the way is a type of a pretty large class, was he really unconscious what sort of person he was? Did he honestly believe he was travelling the road to eternal life, that he really had safe assurance for passage into the next world? I am inclined to think he did. That is, the part of sanctimonious hypocrite had been so long played that it had become a second nature. He had probably learned to thoroughly deceive himself. So that, should he read this history, and it is probable he may read it, he will be very apt to exclaim: " Why, what had Parkinson to complain of? It was a fair business transaction. It wasn't for me to pay his debts. Didn't he owe the money? Business is business."

.   .   .   .

What misery, what trouble, what distress, what anguish one human being will cause another! Is it true that the goddess Nemesis never tires, never intermits her unerring pursuit, surely reaches her object, and always at the appointed hour? According to my observation and experience, those merchants who are most severe in driving debtors to the wall, most extortionate in their demands, most unsparing in their prosecutions, generally go down themselves in the long run. But there are striking exceptions to this stern rule of compensation. Goulding has not failed. He has retired from business with a large fortune, and is employing his capital so that it brings in handsome and safe returns. An odor of sanctity surrounds him like an atmosphere. I see his name often on public subscription-lists. His family have attained a high social position; all things flow smoothly with the man who employed Bulldog to visit me that evening. To whom is chargeable the breaking up of my business, the loss of the little which might have remained to my wife, the misery and destitution of my family, and my own personal torments. All things flow smoothly with him!

When, O Nemesis! is the appointed hour?

.   .   .   .

I lost no time the next morning in calling on my counsel, Mr. Norwood, of the law firm of Norwood and Case. Notwithstanding Bulldog's sneer, this gentleman held an eminent position at the bar, and commanded the respect and esteem of all. Mr. Case, who was associated with him, was a shrewd, quick-witted, energetic young attorney, of honorable instincts, and a high sense of what became his profession. With Norwood I had been on terms of great intimacy for more than twenty years. Minutely I stated the whole affair with Bulldog (I had previously conferred with Mr

Norwood about my matters, and he knew the progress I was making in my efforts for a compromise). When I had concluded, there was a profound silence for a few minutes. Mr. Norwood appeared to be in a brown study. Presently he said: "The fellow seemed to lay stress on his *demand*, did he?"

"Yes."

"And he specified certain articles he desired you to apply to the payment of the debt?"

"Yes."

"My friend, I am very sorry you have fallen into the hands of this scoundrel. Members of the bar are undecided what course to take with him. As long as he infringes no law and no rule of court, what can we do? I know all about him. He undertakes to collect doubtful debts by bullying his victim. There is no species of petty persecution which does not embrace a violation of the statute which he does not resort to. The result is, that RESPECTABLE MER-CHANTS employ him to manage what they call their hard cases, or when they wish to appear in the background. Now I know that Burnham and Prince are the regular counsel of Goulding and Company, persons of the highest respectability, yet you see they call in Bulldog for their dirty work."

"But what can he do?" I asked.

"That is what I am coming to. He can do nothing except give you a great deal of annoyance, by which he hopes to wear you out and compel payment of his claim. He has doubtless something in view in making this demand. As to the legal result, give yourself no uneasiness about that.

What is to be dreaded is, that he will obstruct you in getting through with your compromise. But stay a minute." With that Mr. Norwood stepped into another room and called Mr. Case. The latter entered, bowed to me, and said to Mr. Norwood: "I have but a few moments, as I must be at the Hall at eleven o'clock."

"You are better acquainted with the tricks of Bulldog than I am, now let us know what he is driving at with Mr. Parkinson;" and he briefly described my interview.

"I can tell you," said Mr. Case, promptly. "Bulldog brings all his suits in the Court of Common Pleas, where he has managed to obtain an extraordinary control in all matters of mere practice. I don't mean to say any of the judges are corrupt, but the fact is, he has actually got the upper hand of Calcroft in particular, before whom he manages to bring all his motions. It was only yesterday I endeavored to get a 'snap-judgment' opened which Bulldog had taken against us after promising one of our clerks *verbally* to give us another day to plead. The young man was to blame in applying for further time to him instead of the Court, and, as you know, no verbal stipulation is binding, Bulldog entered judgment, and laughed in my face the next morning, for being so credulous. 'Case,' said he, 'you never need be afraid of me so long as you keep yourself within the RULES. My advice is, to turn that clerk out of your office and get a better one in his place—he's green.' If it had not been in the court-room I should have knocked the fellow down, I was so enraged. Yesterday I made the motion to open the judgment, and do you believe, so completely is Calcroft under Bulldog's influence that instead of vacating the judgment and indignantly reprimanding him, as was once done in the Superior Court, he only consented to let me in to defend on payment of costs, and allowing the judgment to stand as security!"

"But, Mr. Case," said Norwood, "smiling at the way his junior was carried off by his interest in his motion, "you forget that it is Mr. Parkinson's affair we have now to consider."

"Oh! I understand about that. He tried it on with Lewis. Very annoying, though. Bulldog contends that after he has commenced such a suit, and made such a demand, on failure to comply he can bring the case within the provisions of the act to abolish imprisonment for debt, and TO PUNISH FRAUDULENT DEBTORS. Of course he can't do any such thing, but he gives one a world of trouble."

Mr. Norwood took down the second volume of the "Revised Statutes," and turned to the one hundred and seventh page. "There," said Mr. Case, putting his finger on section four, "Bulldog claims that a refusal to apply property to the payment of a demand against which the defendant admits there is no defence, is *prima-facie* evidence that the defendant, in the language of the act, '*is about to dispose of his property with intent to defraud his creditors*,' and for which a WARRANT OF ARREST ISSUES! What is worse, I am told that Calcroft is inclined to sustain this construction; at all events, he has issued warrants to my knowledge, on affidavits prepared by Bulldog, when he knew just what the facts were. The question has never been tried, because the parties will be only too eager to settle in some way, and escape from the custody of the sheriff before it becomes known they have been arrested. For my part, I have made up my mind the only way to get along with Bulldog is to fight him hard and strong, and if necessary to administer personal chastisement. He is a cowardly bully, and it is a disgrace to the merchants of the city that such a creature finds employment." Mr. Case here looked at his watch and made a hasty exit. Mr. Norwood smiled as the former went out, and said: "Case is still smarting under that snap-judgment, but really it is quite as he has described it. Now to your affair. Plainly, I think he will be ready in his attempt to arrest you early in the week, and you were judicious in coming directly to me. One thing first—you decide not to buy him off?"

"I am settled on that point."

"You are aware this will force you into an assignment?"

"I am."

"Well, then, go to your counting-room; prepare schedules of your liabilities and assets as soon as possible. If any thing special occurs, send at once for me. I shall be either here or at my house."

I took leave of my friendly adviser and went to Front-street. I had not been long there before "declarations" were served on me: one at the suit of Screwtight and Company, one by Gripeall on notes of our firm already protested. Rollins had been already served, and when I told him what we had to expect the poor fellow was greatly depressed. I endeavored to encourage him. I said this was nothing but valuable experience to him who was just beginning his business life; he must think of it as such. With me it was another affair. At my age recovery was difficult.

In the afternoon I conferred with some of my largest creditors; they all sympathized with me, and some offered to call on Goulding with the hope to influence him to change his course. Among these was Mr. Longstreet. The interview was a protracted one, and it was fruitless. I never learned the particulars; but I know the next time the HONEST man met the HYPOCRITE he passed him without sign of recognition. As for Gripeall and Screwtight, they were under Goulding's influence so entirely that application to either would be useless.

Before I went home that night we had made our assignment. Late in the evening it was finished and executed at Mr. Norwood's office. Thus I was forced to dispossess myself of a large estate. For I was not willing such men as Goulding, Gripeall, Screwtight and one or two others, should receive their entire claim by prosecuting, to the detriment of more honest and indulgent creditors. The course taken by Bulldog was ingenious. Through his influence with Judge Calcroft he would be able to procure a warrant of arrest for me on the ground I had failed to comply with his demand. It is true such a course would not ultimately be sustained, but the warrant once granted we would be forced to give bonds that we would not " *assign or dispose of any property with intent, or with a view to give a preference to any creditor,*" etc. Could this warrant be served *before* the assignment was actually executed, Bulldog felt assured he could worry us into payment. Indeed, we would never be out of his clutches while any thing remained to plunder.

In my assignment, after providing for a few confidential matters, I divided all among my creditors equally. I was

4

greatly tempted to leave Goulding out. But I thought the revenge would be an ignoble one. So he shared with the rest.

Once more all was gone! 1837–1847. Ten years out of the marrow of my life! And I was swept back, to begin where I had left off ten years before. No; that was impossible. I could never begin *there* again. Never were those years to come back. I had to repeat my circumstances with ten years' less vigor and vitality. There comes a time, often before we actually perceive any diminution of health or strength, when we experience a loss of confidence in our power to do and to achieve, to endure and to suffer; when we are tempted to bow the head and say: " Enough! let there be no more strife." It is the first sign of decadence, a mournful sign ; this drooping of confidence, so much more appalling than any physical failure of the frame.

It was Saturday evening when we accomplished this. It was with a sense of relief that I thought of the next day as one of rest. It was many years since the Sabbath had seemed to me so desirable. Before I reached my door I was endeavoring to accustom myself to what had now taken place. The execution of the assignment was a death-blow to any immediate plan for getting into business. While I was energetically employed in attempts to carry through a compromise, I never stopped to contemplate such a result. It had come, and I already began to devise some method to make the best of it.

Step by step we become accustomed to what happens. Gradually pushed from one stand-point to another, we learn to submit. Wonderful is the power of adaptation in man;

to climate and temperature, to every kind of food and clothing, to every variety of habit and condition and circumstance. Give him sway, and he is a very lord paramount!
tyrannizing over his fellows, attempting things unnatural
and preposterous, wasteful and ridiculous. Important and
self-sufficient, he shows it in his look, his walk, his gesture,
his surroundings. Let the hand be put forth against him,
and does he fall, does he wither into insignificance? No;
he adapts himself to his new state. He discovers that his
former condition was not propitious to a high moral and in-
tellectual life. He sees things in a new light, and his opinions alter accordingly. Misfortune still pursues him. Instead of crouching, crushed and humiliated, he stands up
and proclaims aloud that it is only in adversity the true
powers are developed. Press him down harder and closer
until he is in positive extremity; he boldly defies the god
of this world, points triumphantly to the next, and wel-
comes what shall come *there*; averring that only as a so-
journer he has tarried here; never claiming a residence, he
desires none, for he will soon leave for *home.* Verily,
strange is the power of the soul!

CHAPTER IX.

AN INTERESTING DISCUSSION.

"PAPA," said Miss Alice, after we had returned from church in the morning, "what do you suppose is the matter with Harriet Goulding? She scarcely spoke to me as we came out. I was rushing up to catch hold of her, but she looked so strange that I hesitated, and she passed on before I recovered myself. What can it mean?"

"I presume it is on account of a business difficulty I have with her father."

"Is that it?" exclaimed Alice with spirit. "And so that's what Harriet's friendship is worth. I wish I had known it before, we would have seen who would have been the first to put on airs. I hope I shall meet her face to face in the street to-morrow. How I will cut her!"

I laughed.

"You would not laugh, papa, if you knew how intimate we have been, and how glad she was to see me when we came back from Newport. Well, because you owe her father she treats me so," and tears of vexation stood in her eyes.

"My dear child," I said, "you must accustom yourself to this. It will not be Miss Harriet alone who will fail in cordiality. It is very probable that many young misses, whose fathers I don't owe, may exhibit similar caprice in their friendship; not perhaps so abruptly as Harriet has done, but in a more polite way, and with a gradual diminution of civility."

Alice burst into tears.

"My dear daughter, I am sorry to grieve you; but the time must soon come when you will begin to experience the effect of what has happened to me, and it is best I should talk to you about it. With Harriet Goulding it is simply the exhibition of her father's feelings; with others, it will be the natural result of our change of circumstances. You cease to belong to your set when you cease to do as they do. Should we move to Philadelphia, we should not expect to receive morning visits from our friends here. And when we move away from our customs and habits and houses, it is not in the natural course of things that we shall continue to receive visits from those who remain. They do not desert us. We desert them, and we must not be vexed if they do not run after us. But, my dear child, there is nothing in this to sadden or discourage you. We will be happy, for we love each other; and wherever we are, we shall be sure to find some who are congenial and friendly. We must not be misanthropical, nor permit ourselves to be soured by exhibitions of wickedness. The good exceed the bad in numbers and strength; let us thank GOD that they do."

I was interrupted by happy sounds from the next room. They proceeded from little Charley and Anna, who were singing together one of their Sunday-school hymns to a charming air, partly taken from music which would hardly be considered sacred. I listened with a new pleasure, quite ready to agree with the learned divine who pressed certain operatic strains into the church service; for "Why," said he, "should the devil monopolize all the good music?" I listened. These were the words as they fell on my ear:

> "To do to others as I would
> That they should do to me,
> Will make me honest, kind and good,
> As children ought to be."

I had never been what is called religious. I went regularly once on Sunday to church, but was not a member. I cannot say I had any habit of prayer, although I was a conscientious believer in the truths of our sacred religion. I suppose I had heard my children sing their little hymns hundreds of times, yet never till that day was I impressed by them. A sweet solemnity took possession of me; and when they had finished, tears were in my eyes. Alice saw it. She hardly understood my emotion; but rising, she came, and putting her arms around my neck, she kissed me and said: "Dear papa, do not fear that we shall be unhappy whatever shall befall us. We will all try to make your cares lighter, and no one can rob us of our love."

I pressed my daughter to my heart, while now the tears flowed freely down my face. I rose and walked up and down the room. "Miserable hypocrite," I said to myself, "you are claiming for yourself to-day an exalted religious feeling; say rather it is a morbid sentimentality arising from disappointment in business. Hallo! stop that! Be a man. Do not insult your MAKER with this cast-off performance. Wait a while till things go smooth with you; then, if you want to be pious and good and all that sort of thing, you can have the opportunity." Shocked by this sudden revulsion, sufficiently depressed by recent events, the idea that feelings which I regarded as sacred, were nothing but a phase of low spirits, threw me back on myself again. Alice was still in the room regarding me with painful solicitude. *There*, I said, in the society of your family, in the honest determination to bear what comes with courage and with fortitude, in the sifting the chaff out of yourself, and preserving what wheat remains for the harvest; that is a better work, just at present, than indulging in a sentimental whine over your sins."*

The bell rang. Presently the servant announced Miss Stevenson. She was a frequent visitor at our house—a superb piece of God's handiwork in flesh and blood. She was an orphan at this time; twenty-two years old; in possession of about ten thousand dollars a year; with exquisite taste, and both amiable and accomplished. The world had for her a daily succession of delights and joys. There she stood, her handsome face exhibiting that fine polish of the skin, that delicate, rich surface which only the best possible *keeping* will produce. The hat was faultless, so was the rich camel's-hair shawl which she laid aside after my wife came in, displaying a faultless shape, set off to best advantage by her dress, which exhibited minute without any painful attention to detail. Every possible appliance which the sug-

---

* We think Mr. PARKINSON unnecessarily severe with himself. That we neglect to turn to God for support until other sources fail, is no evidence that our feelings are not sincere. Although it seems ungracious to seek our MAKER only after every earthly hope has perished; still this is just what HE tells us we may do. Doubtless, with many their feelings will not stand the test of returning prosperity. But we have always felt that, whether genuine or not, they forcibly illustrate man's recognition of a HIGHER POWER.—EDITOR OF MEMOIRS.

gestions of a refined, luxurious taste could furnish was supplied. All told of wealth, rich comforts and ease in one's possessions. As I looked at her, I was recalled to the world —the bright world, with no burdening cares, no anxious forecast into the morrow. What a seductive type of it was before me.

Miss Stevenson made a long visit. She was sincerely attached to my wife. She did not appear to be affected in her friendship by our change of fortune. I handed her to her carriage, a beautiful open barouche, with well groomed horses, a coachman in neat livery, with a *pose* on his box of absolute self-satisfaction; all in all, complete in every appointment.

Just then a bare-footed girl, ten or twelve years old, with ragged dress, torn hat, no shawl, no cloak or other protection from the November wind, passed by. She paused with careless hesitation and cast her eyes on the fine young lady in the carriage. She was not a beggar, this girl; but she stopped, as I have said, perhaps in some degree fascinated, or perhaps in a mood of bold or idle curiosity. I do not suppose it occurred to her as it did to me, to ask what has made this fearful disparity between two young people. Is there nothing wrong in a system where such disparity exists? Or is it only error in our hearts which makes a good system work badly? Has that charming, amiable young woman any right to sit in that carriage with half the world suffering around her? and so forth. These thoughts, trite and familiar to the philanthropist, had rarely been entertained by me, and now were evidently called up by the immediate contemplation of my own misfortunes.

When the young lady in the carriage caught sight of the

bare-footed wretch on the side-walk, she exclaimed quickly:
"Do speak to that poor child, Mr. Parkinson, and see if she
does not want something."

The "poor child" evidently understood the remark, for
she turned abruptly and proceeded on her way.

"Speak to her, *do*," continued Miss Stevenson.

I called to the girl. She stopped and looked at me with
an independent air.

"This lady wishes to know if she cannot help you," I said.

"I don't want any help," was the abrupt reply as she
started on.

There was nothing more to be done, and Miss Stevenson
directed the coachman to drive on.

In the evening my wife and I sat together, and endeavored
to take a careful survey of our situation. It was gloomy
enough. The semi-annual interest on the mortgage for fifteen thousand dollars would be due the following week. We
could not pay it, and a suit for foreclosure would be the
immediate result. For the holder, Mr. Glynn, was a prompt
collector. The carriage and horses belonged to my wife, at
least so we had always considered; but Mr. Norwood intimated a grave doubt as to the legal point. The fact was, I
had been in the habit when I was in business before, of
appropriating a certain sum for the rent of the house, precisely as if it belonged to a stranger. Not that my wife
really kept a separate purse; but she enjoyed, and so did I,
the appropriating of this amount to certain expenditures
which, although not absolutely necessary, are yet continually
incurred in every family of competent means. If a new
shawl was to be purchased, or a piece of plate, or a birth-

4*

day present made, or if some unlooked-for circumstance, like the marriage of a friend or some public festivity, involved the ordering a new dress, this fund, under the treasureship of my wife, was drawn on. It was thus made a source of much happiness, and it was with pleasure I recommended the habit on starting in business again; on a smaller scale to be sure, for first had to be deducted the interest money, and only the balance between it and what would be a proper rent for the house, went to make up this purse. Our horses and carriage were sold on my first failure. After I resumed business, my wife laid aside the rent-money to purchase a new establishment. Only at the commencement of that very year had she gained the necessary sum. And it was one of the petty annoyances consequent on my present reverse, that it should come so soon after this special event. Now, it was considered doubtful by my counsel if my wife could avail herself of this property, or the proceeds of it, as against an uncompromising and active creditor; such men, for example, as Bulldog was acting for.

Since that period an effective law has been passed by the legislature of the state of New York giving adequate protection to the separate property of married women; a tardy but most necessary acknowledgment of their rights.

The making of an assignment was forced on us so suddenly—the change in our prospects from the expected successful compromise to this untoward step, that I had had no time to decide what was to be done in detail. I had a right to count on some sort of an attack from the enemy on the following day. What was it to be? Thinking it over so much annoyed and irritated me. It seemed as if we had been extravagant in keeping a carriage and in the order of our household, and so I told my wife, in a querulous tone (as if I had any reason to complain of her!) and I went on in the strain that men are apt to pursue under similar circumstances, and which is a species of littleness in our natures I never could account for.

"The fact is," I continued, "we have not been economical enough; we have lived too fast. There is Alison now, who came from the other side with a petty agency for spool-thread; he pays this day but six hundred dollars rent for his house; lives frugally, and is already one of the heaviest commission merchants in the city. No, my dear, we have been going on at too fast a rate altogether."

"Charles," replied my wife, "I do not like to hear you speak in this way. We have *not* lived too fast. If we have lived in a measure expensively, it has not been a wasteful or a heedless expenditure. Tell me, would you like to be such a man as Mr. Alison? Would you wish me to be like his wife? No, there are habits acquired along with the mere labor of accumulation that no wealth can compensate for. It is true we have lived generously, and I am glad we have. We do not carry about with us cramped-up, narrow, sordid natures, such as utter devotion to gain produces. Besides, Charles, be honest: tell me, were our household expenses the cause of your embarrassments? Had we lived on one half of what we did, would it have made any difference? No, indeed. Really, then, you have had the advantage of Mr. Alison, because you have lived as became a gentleman, and you cannot be robbed of what you have enjoyed, nor of its liberalizing influences. If Mr. Alison fail, what has he to look back on that can give him the slightest satisfaction ?"

I smiled, pronounced my wife in the right, asked pardon for my ill-timed remark, and then the discussion of our prospects was resumed.

Another important question was about the furniture in our house. Originally it was purchased by my wife, and the insurance on it as well as on the house was in her name. But a large proportion had been changed by substituting new articles, as the old got out of repair, and which I had paid for. The furniture was doubtless at the mercy of the first creditor who obtained a judgment against me. Bulldog had commenced the first suit, and *his* would be the first execution.

"After all, Charles, is it not best to propitiate this man ? He offers on certain conditions, which are not impossible, to carry out your plans for you. Look at it deliberately. On the one side, absolute pecuniary ruin, and whatever that shall entail; on the other, a return to active business—successful business—with the power sooner or later to pay all your debts, so that all will fare as well as this man you have now to pay. Ought you not, for the sake of your family, to accept this means of extricating yourself?"

"Do *you* think I ought to accept his proposition?" I asked.

"I do not know; I will not say; I cannot decide. I only ask you to reconsider your decision—to carefully reflect before you finally reject his offer."

"I am inclined to think *he* considers it final after the summary way I expelled him from the library," I said, unable to repress a grim smile of satisfaction.

"Such a miserable wretch is insensible to insult."

"I suppose so." And thereupon I silently canvassed the matter over again. I permitted to rise before me the picture of a happy household, a prosperous business, position, friends, social life—all these to be retained. The reverse of the picture a dark, unfathomable blank. Only secure Bulldog's influence with a thousand-dollar fee—an extra thousand for Goulding—that is all. "Be not righteous overmuch; why shouldst thou destroy thyself? Think of the sea of troubles you will enter on to-morrow!"

Was I base enough to compound a felony? Could I live out of the wages of vile iniquities? Would I pay a premium for highway robbery, theft, picking of pockets, subornation of perjury, whatever else was low and vile? If not, what had I to do with Bulldog?

"My dear, I have decided!"

"Well."

"No! a thousand times no!"

"You have spoken as becomes my husband. Charles, I *did* waver. I hesitate no longer. You are right."

Thus deciding—thus supported in my decision—holding my wife's hand, we silently renewed the pledge made to each other at the altar many years before—"*for better, for worse.*"

CHAPTER X.

THE ARREST.

I WAS in the act of putting on my coat the next morning, after breakfast, preparatory to going to the counting-room, when some one was announced as wishing to see me. His name—for he considerately sent it in—was Bellows. As I had no acquaintance bearing that appellation, I asked the servant what kind of looking individual Mr. Bellows might be.

"A very pleasant-spoken man, sir, was the reply; "seems a civil, nice person."

"Ask him in."

"I did, sir; but he said he only wanted to speak with you a minute."

My wife looked at me with apprehension.

"Very well, tell him I will see him directly."

"Charles," said my wife, "I am afraid this is some fresh trouble."

"Well," I replied, "if it be so, the sooner it is met the sooner it will be over." With that I proceeded to the hall, where Mr. Bellows was waiting.

My servant was right. I saw a well-dressed man, with a pleasant expression of countenance, not more than twenty-five or thirty years old, who bowed politely as I approached. The brief time I had to form an opinion of him from his appearance baffled any conjecture. Evidently he was not in what is called polite society, but he exhibited a peculiar case of manner which few possess who are not accustomed to it; in short, he appeared perfectly at home as he stood patiently waiting for me.

" Mr. Parkinson ?"

It was thus he desired to be assured of my identity.

I bowed.

" I have some papers here which I wish to hand to you," he said, in a tone so bland that a by-stander might have thought he was inviting me to a wedding. Thereupon he took from the breast-pocket of his coat two documents, which he presented to me. Yet, although his errand seemed concluded, he showed no signs of leaving.

" You are ——"

" A deputy-sheriff."

" Walk in for a few moments till I can look at what you have given me." And Deputy-Sheriff Bellows politely accompanied me to the library. Despite every effort to be cool and self-possessed, I was not at all so. I looked nervously over the papers in my hand, and could get no further than " *City and County of New York, ss.*," before I found myself re-reading this apparently harmless statement of a geographical position. I raised my eyes to the officer, and in the expression of his countenance I thought I discovered a look as if he would say: "Pray don't take the matter so hard, it wont amount to much." So I thought I could not do better than follow up this interpretation by asking him to tell me what was the object of the service.

"Sheriff," I said, "will you please explain this matter, and say what you have to perform?"

"It is a warrant under the Stillwell Act," said the officer. "You will have to go before the judge, and bail must be put in. My duty is to take you at once before Judge Calcroft, but you will of course want to see your counsel first. I will accompany you wherever you wish to go."

He would accompany me. That was really very kind, very considerate; but a queer sensation came over me when I stood there for the first time under ARREST. A strange, odd feeling it was that I could not stir one step without this man, in any direction. His very civility—a kind of patient good-nature—while I really appreciated it, actually gave me a more forcible idea of the situation I was in than any discourteous or illiberal course he could pursue. Had he, in a bluff, harsh manner, demanded I should go instantly with him, I should not have felt half so much the force of that *warrant* as I did when the officer, wishing to put me quite at ease, told me to take my time, he would accommodate himself to my movements as far as possible, while I knew he was destined to be my companion, *nolens volens*, till released from his society by order of the proper tribunal.

"You say bail is to be put in?" I inquired.

"Yes, if you wish an adjournment. I don't suppose you will be ready to go right into an examination."

"Bail," I repeated to myself. And I began to cast about for friends who would under such circumstances be ready. If you have never suddenly found yourself in any emergency which required the guaranty of two names with yours to enable you to walk out of your own house free, let me ask you to stop a moment and consider whom in such case among all your acquaintances you would apply to for this service. Possibly the names will not embrace those with whom you are most intimate. You will be much more apt to select some old-fashioned, considerate individual, on whose judgment and experience you depend to take a just view of the necessities of your own requirements. Perhaps you may be surprised that on a careful marshalling of friends you find so few whom you feel you can rely on to go with you on a "bail bond."

In my state, I was greatly embarrassed to decide who to ask ; for I was in no condition to return the favor ; and a large proportion of those I called friends were the last I would request a service of this kind of. Here was a test. After considering a time, I could think of no one except my counsel, Mr. Norwood. I would tell him how I was situated, and ask him what I should do. I was but a few minutes revolving these matters, while the officer sat waiting. In sharp times we think fast and much. I found myself taking a new admeasurement of most things under the sun. Many of what I considered fixed ideas, began to change or melt away like dissolving views ; others, quite faint before, became firmly established. It seemed, *apropos* of myself, as if every thing in the world had broken loose and was driven hither and yon, helter-skelter, while preparing to form again in regular place. That morning I think I began, among other things, to appreciate the sense of the term LIBERTY. I am sure I never did before. Now, when I was absolutely under the control of a man who could say, "You shall not rest there; you shall come here;" even if such control was to be but temporary, I learned a practical lesson of its sweets.

I thanked Mr. Bellows for his patience and told him I was ready to go, and we proceeded to the office of Norwood and Case. I bade the children good morning as usual. They suspected nothing, although Charley stared at the officer a little as we passed out. My wife was in her own room.

As we walked along, he seemed inclined to enter into conversation.

"This sort of thing can't hold," he said. "It has been tried on before, but the parties have always settled. I don't believe Mr. Norwood will advise *you* to settle. For my part, I would like to see the question tested. I don't approve of such doings. It's a great mistake if people think we care to execute such a process as this. Not at all; and· although Bulldog brings a great deal of business into our office, I never want to find one of his cases in my box."

Before we reached Mr. Norwood's, my conductor became very communicative, and I learned a good deal from him about Bulldog which the reader is in general sufficiently acquainted with from what I have already said. It was in fact a full confirmation of Mr. Case's statements of the actings and doings of the creature.

Fortunately I found both Mr. Norwood and Mr. Case in their office. Soon I was closeted with the former, Mr. Bellows manifesting an entire absence of responsibility as soon as he saw me in the hands of my counsel. I exhibited the papers, spoke of the situation of my furniture and of my horses and carriage, suggested that in due course Bulldog (that is, Goulding) would first obtain judgment and execution.

"We must block them there," exclaimed he. "This is private property, and I cannot put it on the Company's schedule; but in fifteen minutes I will draw a short assignment to protect any private debts you may have. I named several, and in a very short space of time the document was prepared and executed.

"There; so much for that," said Norwood. "Now I am at leisure this morning, and shall insist on going on with the case.

"But if we do not get through," I said, there is bail to be procured."

"I will take care of that," was the reply.

So we all started for the "Hall," where Judge Calcroft was sitting in chambers. He looked half ashamed on seeing me, for I had a slight acquaintance with him. At the same time Bulldog entered, he having been duly notified by the sheriff of our appearance. As he came into the room he spoke to me in a loud voice, "Good morning, Mr. Parkinson," as if nothing disagreeable had ever occurred between us. I scarcely nodded in return.

"I suppose, Mr. Norwood, you wish to enter into the ordinary bond to plaintiff and take an adjournment."

"Not at all," replied Mr. Norwood, who was all the while busy writing. "We controvert under oath, as you shall see presently, and are ready to submit to an examination."

"The devil you are," said Bulldog, who only wanted to gain time till his judgment could be obtained, and meanwhile have me bound not to make any disposition of my property. "Are you aware, sir," he continued, "that this examination will take up more than one or two, or even three sessions?"

"Bulldog," interrupted Norwood, "you are too late; my clients made an assignment on Saturday. Now," continued my counsel, "just swear to that before the judge, and we are ready to proceed."

"Bulldog was furious, but he could not help himself. He consoled himself, however, by subjecting me to a long, and what seemed a very impertinent examination, until the Judge said he could sit no longer, and the matter must of course be postponed by order of the court. I was forced, therefore, to put in the required bond, and Bulldog had thus the satisfaction of, in one sense, carrying the day by his perseverance, aided by the countenance of Calcroft, who it was too evident was in a degree under his influence. The affair was thus concluded, and I may as well observe here that I heard no more of it. Bulldog, seeing we were determined to meet him boldly, and finding also that he was too late to throw any obstacle in the way of an assignment, failed to appear at the adjourned day, and the case was dismissed.

As we were leaving the court-room Mr. Norwood asked me if I had given the sheriff any thing. I said I had not. "Hand him five dollars," he whispered. Going out together, I took occasion to follow his suggestion, thanking the officer at the same time for his politeness. Mr. Bellows took the money without the least hesitation, quite as a matter of course, remarking, however, as he thanked me, that if they (the officers) were confined to their legal fees it would be impossible for them to live and support a family; that they endeavored to treat those whom they were required to arrest with as much courtesy as possible, consistent with prudence; and so we separated.* Thus I acquired some practical insight into the sheriff's department, and also got a glimpse of both sides of the legal profession—one very honorable, one very base.

I have been thus minute in chronicling these circumstances, because it is my design to record just how, in this crisis, a selfish, bad man was enabled to destroy my plans and cast a blight on my prospects. Examples like mine are not infrequent. The business world suddenly misses one of its active members; a few questions are asked, a sympathetic ejaculation of "poor fellow" uttered, and the current sweeps by and he is forgotten. But the one left high and dry does not forget. Wistfully he looks after his comrades, who are energetically pursuing their various avocations, from which he is debarred. He, so lately a prominent actor among them, is now absolutely powerless. He can neither buy nor sell. He cannot perform a single business transaction requiring the use and possession of property. His name is not worth the paper it is written on. He knows it, and he *feels* it. It is idle to attempt to make an advantageous purchase. "Six

---

* Mr. PARKINSON's account of his first introduction to Deputy-Sheriff BELLOWS, and of his intercourse with him, is a very natural one. The sheriff's deputies in the city of New York are generally civil and obliging in the discharge of their duty, and the openly receiving of a gratuity for time spent in accommodating a party under arrest, in visiting counsel and finding friends, is not improper. We have known several instances where an officer has been offered a handsome fee to induce him to arrest a defendant at an unseasonable hour and hurry him to Eldridge-street, which was peremptorily refused. Cases to the contrary may have occurred, but not within our observation.—EDITOR OF MEMOIRS.

months' credit," to him, means "cash on delivery;" and he
dare not even at that take the smallest article in his own
name. And why? Because his creditors, or some one or
more of them, refuse to release him. They declare that he
shall remain in bondage. They hold him enslaved. He has
a will and a hope, and much energy; they destroy all. He
has a family who depend on him—these are beggared. He
turns in every direction to find some gleam of ,light, and
finds none. And the world is impoverished to the extent of
the loss of this man's labor and industry. There is but one
true course when an individual *can't* pay his debts, and that
is for his creditors to *release* him and let him go to work.
When a man is down he should be helped to rise; return
him to the world, to his position, and so save him.

It is but just to the merchants of New York to say, that
as a class they are indulgent and liberal toward those who
are forced to suspend. When convinced the debtor is honest, they are apt to take the first offer, and let him go on
with as little delay as possible. But there are, at the same
time, a good many such men as Goulding, who manage by
one plan or another to secure payment in full, or push the
unfortunate debtor into inevitable bankruptcy. I wish I
knew some method of reaching these people. As I have
remarked, most of them do fail themselves eventually, but
a portion grow fat on what they thus wring from the unfortunate and despairing. Even now I can scarcely restrain
the expression of a solemn curse which rises to my lips
when I think of Goulding—Goulding, not Oilnut. Shaver
and sharper and unscrupulous as he is, Oilnut would not
have arrested me. He would *manage* to secure payment in

full, but not brutally, nor with legal violence. The reader must therefore have patience while I go still more into the detail of my misfortunes, showing how gradually I was forced *down*. It will be seen that by the action of Bulldog I was compelled to make an assignment of the household furniture, and horses and carriage, which really belonged to my wife, but for which legally she was not protected. Here was the commencement of the break-up. For in a few days there would be obtained three judgments against me in favor of Bulldog, Screwtight and Company, and Gripeall; and the assignee would be forced to act. As I attempted to look this state of things in the face, a sense of *horror* would sometimes overpower me. Sell our furniture! Leave our house—my wife's house—purchased with the money left to her by her father to insure her a home independent of the vicissitudes of business. Wretch that I was to take her money and lose it; and I had reproached her for our expenditures. Nearly seventeen years in that house. The children all born there. Every room hallowed by some happy association. Was there *no* help for this? *Was* it really to be? Perhaps I was only dreaming. At the last moment relief would come from some quarter. Yes, relief *would* come. During the day I managed to drive off the thick black brood; but at night, after a short and unrefreshing slumber, I would wake; and oh! the agony which during its silent watches held possession of me until the morning broke, and I hastened to rise. I know of no species of suffering which compares with *this*—no affliction, no pain, no trouble. There is no resisting it. No armor of reason or philosophy is proof against it. Long afterward, when I had descended to my position of chronic misfortune, GOD was merciful to me, and I could sleep. Now this " chief nourisher" was denied to me, and in its place I encountered those dark fancies of the night which few will fail to recognize who have had their season of calamitous reverses.

CHAPTER XI.

AN AGREEABLE DISAPPOINTMENT.

DAY after day ran by. Affairs went on in the world's old routine, quite irrespective of my situation. Our assignee was quietly at work, winding up as fast as he could what had been placed in his hands. Rollins had been employed at my suggestion to aid him. In December judgments were duly entered against me in the three suits I have already mentioned. The law at that time (it has since been changed) provided for a delay of thirty days before execution could be issued—a short respite for which I felt thankful. On the first day of December, Mr. Glynn sent as usual for his semi-annual interest. I wrote him a note stating my situation and saying that my wife intended to dispose of her house, and asking of him some indulgence. I received in answer the following:

NEW YORK, *December* 3, 1841.

" MR. CHARLES E. PARKINSON :

" DEAR SIR : I have your note of yesterday, and in reply would state, that, considering the unexpected disarrangement of your business affairs, I shall postpone any application to your wife or yourself for interest on your bond and mortgage for fifteen thousand dollars until the first day of

5

June next, unless you should earlier have disposed of the property. "Your obedient servant,

"E. P. GLYNN."

Here was another pleasant disappointment. Mr. Glynn was looked on as a close, severe man, prompt and exacting. And he was so. But this proved him to be also considerate and just. The world frequently sets a totally wrong estimate on such men. They may have begun life soft-hearted enough, but after a while experience teaches them that in money matters they cannot rely on one promise out of ten which, is made to them, except it is put in a business form, and made subject to business penalties. And so these persons become sharp and strict, and apparently uncompromising; when, should a proper occasion present, they show a conscientious feeling at the bottom.

Well, here was ample time for us to dispose of the house. What a relief! blessings on Mr. Glynn! For from the surplus which the sale of it would produce above the mortgage, was our only hope for the present. We expected to be able to dispose of it for twenty-five thousand dollars; since property in Broadway was fast increasing in value, and on and adjoining the spot where our house once stood, stores are erected worth almost a fabulous price. I breathed with a lighter heart after receiving that letter, and I began now to calculate what was best to do should we succeed to our mind in making the sale. Mr. Norwood was consulted about the furniture. He was my wife's trustee, and, let me say here, from first to last our firm, substantial, undeviating friend. *My* assignment of furniture embraced only certain valuable articles which I had myself purchased; and, since we had determined to fight Bulldog and his crew, as Mr. Norwood well remarked, we should be careful to leave no loophole for the enemy. So he went to work to make all secure before execution should issue.

Our carriage and horses Mr. Norwood sold to a client just then in want of a neat turn-out, and at a fair price; and he afterward sold most of the furniture mentioned in my assignment to an acquaintance, who after the sale permitted us the use of it for the present. This was my friend's explanation, and I trusted the whole matter to him. In this way, as I have said, the days ran by. Those judgments coming nearer and nearer to execution, when the war would be commenced, and doubtless carried on with vigor.

CHAPTER XII.

THE HOLIDAYS.

CHRISTMAS was approaching! Christmas with its sparkling frosts, its cheerful merry-making, its round of pleasant visiting and interchange of gifts and happy congratulations. This was to be our last Christmas in the old home. How should it be spent? In sackcloth and ashes; or bravely, joyously, as of yore? I declared for the latter. My courage was getting back to its normal condition. "There shall be a Christmas-party for the children and a Christmas-tree, and open house on New-Year's. Neither sullenly nor sorrowfully will we look toward our new condition, but with hope and resolution. Come," and I led my wife into our parlors and planned how it should be as we walked up and down.

> "'HODIE mihi:
> Cras tibi.'

"Do you understand me, Florence? 'tis a scrap from my college days. It is the *carpe diem* of the philosopher. You remember that painting in the Gallery at Munich? Well, we will illustrate that. Seventeen years *here*. Brave old years—gone, sealed up for the judgment. GOD willing, we will remain in this house till May, and *then* we will close its history and depart." My wife shuddered slightly, very slightly, yet I perceived it. I looked in her face and saw that she did not enter into my cheerful plan. But she said nothing, and I did not tell her I noticed her emotion. Soon she began to rally; she assented with alacrity to what I proposed, and we both set to work to carry out the preparation for those holidays.

And with entire success. The Christmas presents were purchased, the children's party was fully attended, the tree loaded as usual. Two or three invitations we accepted ourselves; and so long as the gay world perceived no difference in us, we discovered none in it.

Only *I* noticed (no one else could) that my wife went through all this as some appointed task, enduring not enjoying; but the children did not know it, and I was glad of that.

New Year's! It passed with us to all appearance as the New Year's of the previous year. The accustomed visits were received, and I made the ordinary round of calls. The day was fine, and the spirits of every body elastic. In one of the streets I encountered Bulldog. We brushed closely past each other. I did not notice him. He, however, nodded familiarly, exclaiming: "Going it while you're young, eh?" At the house of a mutual acquaintance I met Goulding. He seemed disposed to bow as my eyes fell on him; but he recovered in time, warned by a look, full of contempt, that there could be no recognition between us. Oddly enough, coming out of another house I was stopped by Oilnut, who seized my hand, and in his softest manner asked how we all were, declaring that on that day we must forget any little misunderstanding; I smiled in spite of myself, for I had never nursed my wrath against the man for acting out his

nature, and I was thinking of the ridiculous way he answered me when I last left his office. So I laughed, but
made no remark, and we both passed on.

  . . . .

When this first day of the year was over, the visits all
paid, all received; the children in bed, Miss Alice gone to
her room, while the gas still burnt brightly through the fine
parlors, over the *debris* of the entertainment that strewed
the tables, I stood before the fire, looking around on the
scene. My wife came toward me from the further end of
the apartments. Putting both her hands around my neck,
she looked an instant in my face, and burst into tears.

Without a word I placed her gently beside me, on one of
the sofas, where, leaning her head on my shoulder, she sobbed
like one broken-hearted for many minutes. Gradually she
grew composed. Then she raised her face, and taking one
of my hands, she pressed it convulsively against her heart,
and with much effort she said: "There! it is over; it *would*
come, Charles, and I could not help it. I feel well now."

There was no need of words between us. In that struggle of the spirit she was not unconscious of her husband's
sympathy. Any assurance of it would have jarred that
delicate chord which encircles united hearts. I knew but
too well what she had passed through in that brief quarter
of an hour. I knew but too well that, as a mother strains
to her breast in a last embrace a child embarking on some
returnless journey, so she with all the sorrow and anguish
of a lost love, had taken leave of the dear and happy and
unreturning *past*, and even now had made ready to meet
the gloomy prospects of the FUTURE.

CHAPTER XIII.

SIMPKINS.

Two weeks afterward I sat in the counting-room, no longer *my* counting-room, looking over various papers, and examining various accounts; when a person entered whose face was familiar, but when or where I had before seen it I could not remember. I was not long, however, in recalling the features of Deputy-Sheriff Bellows. I wondered if I was again to be placed in duress by that amiable official. Before I had time to speculate on the subject, Mr. Bellows had approached, and begged to speak to me in private. We withdrew to a corner of the room, where he exhibited what he called an "execution," and told me that although he regretted it had fallen by the rule of rotation into his hands, I must be aware he was forced to do his duty; to which reasonable statement I assented without remark.

"I am directed," continued he, "to levy on the furniture in your house. I came first to acquaint you of this, thinking you might be able to arrange it."

I explained to him that a portion of that furniture had been held by Mr. Norwood, as trustee for my wife for many years, and that the remainder did not belong to me, and that he would certainly run a great risk in attempting to hold the property.

"You forbid my making a levy, I presume?"

"Oh! no. You must do as you see fit. I only acquaint you distinctly with the fact that it is not my property you will levy on."

"Just so; and I meant as much by my question. I will call on Mr. Norwood, and if he makes the matter clear, as I suppose he can, we shall require to be indemnified before we proceed further." Thereupon Mr. Bellows took leave of me.

I saw nothing more of him for a week, and was beginning to congratulate myself on the easy disposition of the matter, when one morning, just after breakfast, he came to our house, accompanied by a man whom it would puzzle any body to describe. It was difficult to determine whether he was twenty-five or fifty-five years old, whether he was an idiot or a philosopher, whether dressed shabbily or like a gentleman, whether knave or saint. He kept a step in the rear of the sheriff; his eyes neither raised nor depressed, but with an utter absence of expression directed toward an imaginary point at the extreme end of the hall. He did not turn to the right or left, as I advanced once more to greet his leader or companion, as the case might be.

Deputy-Sheriff Bellows looked concerned and distressed when he saw me; he looked nevertheless like a man who had a painful duty to perform, and had made up his mind to go through with it.

"Very sorry, Mr. Parkinson, but the sheriff has been indemnified. Wouldn't act till he had a perfectly fire-proof bond, then he was forced to. No use saying any thing about it. It's disagreeable, but it's a part of our business. I am obliged to remove this property or put a man in charge."

He glanced as he said this to the mysterious personage near him, who while shifting his position—a sort of pantomime "Here" to the sheriff's imaginary roll-call—never took his eyes from the supposed object far off at the lower end of the hall.

A cold sweat stood on my forehead. A pain shot through my heart. To be turned out of doors with no warning of the coming blow! I saw the fatal red flag of the auctioneer; I beheld the furniture carted off in every direction, and we left homeless, if not at the moment houseless. How I feared lest my wife or some of the children would open the door of the parlor and learn what was going on.

Mr. Bellows came to my relief.

"Better go at once and see Mr. Norwood," he said.

"What's to be done meanwhile with your friend here?" I asked.

The officer doubtless appreciated my anxiety on that head, for, considering a moment, "Simpkins," said he, "you have not been to breakfast, I dare say."

"Not *yet*," answered Simpkins.

"Very well. Perhaps, Mr. Parkinson, you will allow the man to step down stairs and get something to eat, and," (turning toward this strange specimen), "Simpkins, you can sit a while, you understand, till *relieved*."

Simpkins again shifted a leg, but kept his eyes at the favorite point. However, when the servant appeared at my summons, Simpkins fell into single file, and followed him below, while the deputy bade me good morning, and I started off rapidly for Mr. Norwood's office.

I was forced to wait two hours before he came in.

5*

Meantime, singular as it seems, I was chiefly employed in speculating as to the movements of Simpkins. After breakfasting to his mind (for I had told the servant to feed him well), what would Simpkins understand his duty to be, considering that he was "in charge" of every thing in the house? Would he be content to sit quietly in the basement, or would he think proper to mount to the parlors, or perhaps, like a sentinel on duty, perambulate the house from cellar to garret? Would he explain to the servants? Should he encounter my wife on his peregrinations, would he explain to her? Would he frighten the children? In short, what *would* he do, or what might he *not* do? So curiously does the mind run on trifling incidents while under some severe and painful process.

At last Mr. Norwood arrived, and I hastened to give him an account of what had transpired. He was much annoyed for the moment. But he soon recovered, and said : "I perceive we must fight these fellows. What a piece of base humanity that Goulding must be ——"

"Bulldog," I interrupted.

" Bulldog !" impatiently exclaimed my counsel, " why, he is infinitely less degraded than his employer. Bulldog is an open, undisguised bravo, who tells you what he means to do, and tries openly to accomplish it. Goulding is a covert, cowardly knave and hypocrite, without one redeeming quality."

Mr. Norwood checked himself in his severe harangue, stepped to the other room, and was closeted for half an hour with his partner. Coming out he said : " We will take care of this matter. You can go to your business without further solicitude."

"But that person 'in charge?'" I asked.

"Shall be *dis*-charged, and that speedily," said Norwood with a smile. "We will see to it, let me assure you," he continued seriously. "Your house shall be relieved of the nuisance. Attend to your affairs as usual, give not another thought to this. Good morning."

I learned afterward that two separate suits of replevin were commenced against the sheriff and Bulldog jointly. One of these by Mr. Norwood, as my wife's trustee; the other by the gentleman who had purchased and paid for a part of the furniture, which he permitted us the use of. Mr. Norwood himself procured the necessary bondsmen, and in short acted the part of friend as well as counsel in every particular.*

When I went home to dinner the coast was clear; that extraordinary personage, Simpkins, whom I half expected to encounter near the hall-door, had taken his departure. Mr. Bellows having called, Simpkins had followed him away much after the manner of a well-trained dog.

A very great relief this; but now I begun to taste the fruits of my recent misfortunes. We were retaining a precarious foothold in our house by the forbearance of Mr. Glynn and the friendship of my counsel. Money for daily expenses began to be necessary. Questions of curtailment in the household were raised—of dismissing some of the

---

* The action of replevin is brought to recover the possession of any "goods or chattels" which shall have been wrongfully taken. The plaintiff in such action, on giving the required security according to the statute, is entitled to a "writ" commanding the proper officer to cause said "goods and chattels" to be delivered to him without delay.

The sheriff having taken actual possession of the furniture in the house by putting Simpkins in charge, it was necessary to resort to this action to recover it for the owners.—Editor of Memoirs.

servants—of economy in our wardrobe, which included the important point of making visits, attending parties, and if of attending, then of giving entertainments. For the sake of our children, my wife thought it worth a struggle to retain our place in society; but after a little reflection she saw how impossible this would be. Embarrassed as we were by a cruel litigation, from which there was no escape, the small funds which I had thus far provided from private sources beginning already ominously to diminish, we commenced to count, as we never before had done, how much each servant cost per month, and to scrutinize the bills of the grocer and market-man. We were, in truth, *on allowance;* the enemy besieging us. Whence were to come supplies? No more *visions* of the wolf: he was domesticated within doors: hungry, gnawing, sullen—not fierce. In verity, what was I to *do?* How keep alive my wife and children, how clothe them, where to lodge them? "Oh! you forget the handsome surplus your wife will have on the sale of the house." Yes, for the moment I did forget, looking as we sometimes do entirely on the dark side. Well, there is a prospect there, a *sure* prospect, I may say. Delaine, the real-estate auctioneer, tells me the property can readily be sold in the spring, and for its full value. I *did* forget the house. So, girding on the armor again, [Hope! Energy! how often the heart sinks, and how often it is renewed by these!] I addressed myself to the important subject of occupation for the future.

CHAPTER XIV.

FRESH COMPLICATIONS.

SOMEBODY sent me, a few days after, a copy of the *New York Evening Post*. In it was an advertisement with pencil-lines drawn around it. It ran as follows:

" Sheriff's Sale.

"By virtue of three several writs of execution to me directed and delivered, I will expose to sale at the vestibule of the City Hall, in the city of New York, at twelve o'clock, noon, on Saturday, the twenty-third day of March next, all the right, title and interest of CHARLES E. PARKINSON, which he had on the twentieth day of December, 1847, or any time thereafter, of, in and to the following described piece or parcel of property."

Here came a description of our house, and at the end of the advertisement was the signature of the sheriff.

The blood rushed to my brain as I read it, really without fully comprehending its import. The first impression was, that all was gone—the very ground we stood on swept away. I had received so many shocks, and in such rapid succession, that absolutely my nervous system was affected by them. On looking through the advertisement again, I perceived that it was *my* " right, title and interest" which was to be sold, and which, of course, any creditor had the power to sell under execution. If I *had* no "right, title or interest," then the creditor would take nothing by his motion. What, therefore, had I to fear? Much, considering who was di-

recting this crusade against me.   It was easy to make the
sale, easy for the party to purchase my interest, and take a
"sheriff's certificate" to that effect, easy to record this, so
that on my wife's attempting to sell the house, there should
appear a cloud on the title, and then a certain sum forced
out of us for removing it, or the sale prevented.   That was
clearly the plan.   These fellows know how sensitive capital
is—how cautious men are as to title when making a permanent investment in real estate.   Even to-day, Delaine asked
me if the papers were all straight with respect to my wife's
house.   He hoped to sell to James, the commission-merchant,
who had realized a large fortune by dealing in "prints only,"
and had retired, and was making investments in city property.

I put the newspaper aside as my wife entered the room.
It seemed as if it would be cruel to acquaint her with this
new move of our adversary.

For, within a few days—I was slow in acknowledging it
to myself—I had perceived that my wife's countenance exhibited a degree of pallor which it never bore before.   She
had, when not in conversation, a care-worn, weary look.
The sound of a sharp, hacking cough frequently fell on my
ear.   It was owing, she said, to a severe cold taken some
time since, from which she had quite recovered, except this
occasional tickling in the throat.   That was all, really, it
was only in the throat.   I was ready to believe this.   It is
a blessing, sometimes, not to be clear-sighted.   Even delay
in becoming so, we should be thankful for.   The goodness
of GOD permits us to be blind sometimes, that we may not
discern too closely the future.

· However, I did feel sufficiently anxious about my wife—sufficiently observing of her languid appearance—to withhold the advertisement which I had just read. This was the first instance since my failure, that I had omitted to mention to her any special subject of annoyance. My habit was a selfish one, perhaps; for it was a relief to tell her; a relief to hear her pleasant, loving voice, rich with encouragement and hope in reply. But there was a stop to it now. Here the road grew more difficult. I dared not take my companion with me. I must travel it alone. Good-by, my wife, to that close confidence which permitted me to recount to you even matters the most harassing. How the children are playing over the house, scampering up and down. Why not? What have they to do with difficulties, reverse of fortune, debt and embarrassment? Their time is not yet. Even Alice does not appear to be any the less happy, and she is really almost a young lady grown. Well, if I can manage to live; why, I will bless GOD for that. Even to *live* is a joy; somebody says so. [Somebody not in debt, nor in extreme bodily pain.*] A nice little house, a steady occupation; charming evenings at home. Books—ah! I have not looked often enough into my library. I will brush up my classics, revive the memory of college years, help to educate the young people, and let the noisy, busy, driving world sweep on. And I repeated to myself some lines which were part of a favorite poem:

> "Ambition's lofty views, the pomp of state,
> The pride of wealth, the splendors of the great,
> Stripped of their mask, their cares and troubles known,
> Are visions far less happy than thy own.'

* Interlined by Mr. PARKINSON in the original MS.

In this manner I endeavored to get rid of the unhappy impressions produced by the sheriff's advertisement. In this manner I endeavored to reconcile myself to what I saw must come, and make the most out of a new situation. And with success. I was not only cheerful, but I did much to raise my wife's courage, which I perceived (she did not) was gradually giving way under these repeated trials, while she no longer enjoyed that firm, elastic health which is so necessary to enable us to cope with misfortune.

. . . .

We have to encounter the inevitable nature of things. Were I inditing a romance, how agreeable it would be to record the triumph of honest dealing over trickery and fraud. How easy to give the pleasing particulars of the defeat of Bulldog in the several harassing cases brought against me, and the utter discomfiture of Goulding, Screwtight and Gripeall. How satisfactory, as in the old fiction, suddenly to introduce the wand of the magician, one wave of which should demolish all my enemies, and another wave restore me to position and wealth, provide for the happy marriage of my daughter, place the younger children on the same charming road, bring again the bloom of health to the cheek of my wife, and recreate for us all the hoped-for happiness of life. Thus illustrating those pleasing, and by no means difficult theories, which the writer of a novel generally feels bound to sustain.

I have no such task before me. I fear, indeed, I have to weary the reader with what will almost seem a repetition of untoward circumstances.

Not to go into any further minutiæ of my litigation with

Bulldog, I will observe that, after a while, attending to it got to be with me a special occupation. In fact, in one way and another, it kept me busy nearly all the time. For the creature maintained a perpetual round of perplexing motions, examinations, etc., etc., while I, determined that the man who had caused my financial ruin should not reap any reward from it, vigorously resisted every fresh attack, and with the aid of my counsel generally baffled the foe. But how dreadfully damaging were even my victories: how destructive the contest to all my hopes. The advertisement of the house by the sheriff soon attracted the notice of the real-estate auctioneer, the one who was attempting to sell it for us, and greatly damped his energy of action; for James, who was thinking seriously of making the purchase, was not willing, he said, to take it, if there was any dispute about it. He did not wish to contract for a law-suit. Then the report was busily circulated that the title to the property was defective: thus it acquired a bad name, and my hopes of a sale were daily diminished. At last I found the only course was to call on Mr. Glynn, and request him to foreclose his mortgage, and thus put every question at rest.

Meantime I began to make preparations for quitting our home on the first day of May. We resolved to go far "up town," even to an extreme point, where a small house could be rented for a moderate sum. Economy was the great object.

The poor are entitled to commiseration, and sympathy and assistance, but the *reduced rich* require much the larger share. They hide themselves in misery away from their former intimates; they are oppressed with recollections of past happiness, and with apprehensions of the future; the children withdrawn from school, the daughters portionless, yet unfitted to earn for themselves; overtaken by destiny; divorced from their circumstances; compelled to toil without hope, and to exist without aim; with settled habits of luxury, to be obliged to live in a manner the most meagre; with constitutions adapted by long use to comfortable modes of life and easy living, to be deprived of them, and plunged into the opposite extreme. Ah! reserve some portion of your sympathy for the reduced rich.

.   .   .   .

In one of my excursions house-hunting, early in April, I found a small dwelling which I thought would suffice for us. The rent was three hundred and fifty dollars, and the neighborhood not disagreeable. With a considerable degree of satisfaction I proceeded homeward, intending to ask my wife to go with me to see it. When I arrived, she was not in the parlor, and Alice told me that mamma, not feeling well, had gone to lie down. With some trepidation I hastened to her room.

CHAPTER XV.

FLORENCE.

THAT sudden awakening to the truth—that instantaneous perception of what has long been directly under our notice unrevealed—the veil lifted—the sight quickened, and lo! we stand aghast with terror at the discovery.

. . . .

We think we can bear no more when under the weight of a great calamity; but we *can* bear more always while we live (*afterward* it is our consolation that the weary are at rest); we can always bear more, but we might not be able to sustain too great a load of anticipated trouble. Therefore I conclude this occasional dullness of vision, this absence of apprehension, to be a wise and beneficent provision of GOD's providence. But the time *comes.* We pass rapidly through the struggle, and then accept the fresh burden.

My wife was lying on the bed when I entered the room. I approached her.

"Charles, I do not feel as well as usual."

It was enough. For now regarding her with solicitude, I saw what I wondered I had not perceived before, that she was much changed. Her cough sounded sepulchral. She said her side pained her so much she was forced to lie down. I sat on the side of the bed and took her hand within mine and gazed in her face. It was the most unhappy

moment of my life. She saw my emotion and smiled.—
"Do not look so anxious," she exclaimed. "It is only a
fresh cold I took last evening which gives me this pain;
otherwise I am perfectly well. Now, pray do not be foolishly anxious; you will make me imagine myself ill."

I rallied, and attempted to speak cheerfully; but presently I left the room and sent for Dr. Chadwick, our family
physician. He came promptly, and said it was a slight attack of pleurisy. He did not appear alarmed, made the
usual prescriptions and went away. The next day she was
better, and soon she was able to leave her room and come
to the table as usual. But my attention was aroused. I
watched my wife with an anxiety that I cannot describe. I
saw that her cough grew more harassing, that her strength
was diminishing. I recalled the fact that her mother died
of consumption, and one of her sisters; although till now
my wife's health had been excellent, and she had never exhibited the least tendency to this insidious malady. Trouble
had brought on weariness of the spirit, and the enemy had
entered by the weakest side.

I began to pray earnestly. I would retire away by myself and on my knees implore God to spare my wife's life—
only her life. Strip us of all we had; leave us utterly des-
titute, but take her not away. Merciful FATHER, take her
not away from us. The failure, the subsequent misfortunes,
the vexations and miseries which followed, what were these
now? Give us the most humble home—the meanest abode;
let me live and earn her support by day labor, but let her live
too. Is this blow to be added to what has come on me? And
I strove, agonizing—yes, agonizing in prayer to God.

It was of no avail, not the slightest. I called on our clergyman—a good man, a good, pious man, I believe—and I
begged him to pray for the recovery of my wife. I know
he did do so sincerely and earnestly, for he was impressed
with the desperate energy of my appeal. It did not serve
any purpose. Florence was worse each succeeding unpleas-
ant day, and she did not rally much in the sunshine. I felt
bitterly. It seemed as if GOD had singled me out to vent
His vengeance on. Why did he not practise on that hypocrite Goulding?—on Goulding, who, if my wife died, would
be really her murderer. I was in a horrible state of mind;
I shudder now when I look back to it.

In this way the season advanced into the month of April.
I was doing every thing in my power to prepare for the
first day of May. On that day we were to leave our house
for the one I had rented " up-town." I had endeavored to
conceal from my wife that I entertained any apprehension
with regard to her health. The physician was always
cheerful. I essayed once or twice to ask him his opinion,
but the words died on my lips without utterance. My bitterness of feeling was in no degree softened, indeed I think
it increased daily. I had discontinued my prayers since I
saw they were not to be answered. I felt as if I did not
care what GOD did with me, now that the gates of death
were to close on Florence, for she seemed, since she became
so weak and delicate, to be the young girl I had wooed in
our native village many years before. A tender and a
youthful expression overspread her features. Looking at
her, I would ask myself: " Is *this* the promised end ?" And
I would go aside, not to pray, but to shed tears of anguish

—tears which hardened my heart instead of relieving it, and led me to feel that I was ready to " curse God and die."

All the while I attended to whatever was necessary for me to do—to wit, the various suits of Bulldog, occasional meetings with our assignee, and consultations with Mr. Glynn as to the foreclosure of the premises we lived on. I endeavored to induce him to purchase the house; but this he declined to do, not wishing more property in real estate. He consented, however, to permit the house to be rented for one year, without interference on the part of the purchaser under the mortgage, and would also accommodate me as to the time of sale and in any other matter which should not impair the security. By selling under the mortgage, all possible dispute as to title would be removed, since a deed on the foreclosure would dispose of any question under the sheriff's sale by Bulldog; at the same time, since the buyer would know that the property *must* come to the hammer, he would not be likely to arrange in advance for its purchase at a sum certain, preferring to attend the sale and bid for it.

I said I attended to my necessary business. I did so mechanically, without the slightest interest in the work. I said mechanically, yet with that species of energy which indifference to whatever may happen always produces; with a singular forecast and shrewdness too, begotten of the same cause. I was moody, it is true, and at times harsh, but I had no more perturbations. The appearance of the sheriff with a dozen warrants of arrest, or the placing of a dozen keepers inside my house (except it might come to the knowledge of Florence) would not have stirred my blood to an extra pulsation. I took a species of grim delight in encoun-

tering Bulldog and sternly looking him out of countenance.
The fellow was not lacking in knowledge of human nature.
He perceived I was at bay, and he wisely took care not to
expose himself unnecessarily. He kept on, nevertheless,
with the steady prosecution of his various suits and counter-
suits, but he no longer attempted any personal annoyance.
I believe I have stated that Goulding was an elder in the
church we were in the habit of attending. Indeed our pew
was directly in front of his. Latterly I was careful to be
at church regularly, that I might, as opportunity occurred,
catch his eye and disturb him by my contemptuous expression. I would sometimes take pains to stop as we were
leaving the church and speak to a mutual acquaintance with
whom Goulding was already conversing, and enjoy his retreat on my coming up. Once I saw him going into the
"lecture-room" to attend the Thursday evening prayer-meeting, and I followed him in and took a seat beside him—a
front-seat, such as he loved to select. Presently he was called
to lead in prayer. He attempted to go on in his usual glib
and unctuous manner, thanking the LORD for all His mer-
cies, and following with a recital of a fearful catalogue of
sins, of which he claimed to be guilty (had he been accused
of committing the least in the list, he would have resented
it with fierce indignation), and triumphantly vindicating his
right to be esteemed before his MAKER as the chief of sin-
ners. I perceived, however, that Goulding was considerably embarrassed by my presence. It was evident that while
he was praying. some peculiar magnetic relation was springing up between him and the man seated next to him—myself. He was not now in his counting-room dictating terms

which should cause no matter what amount of distress and sorrow, but in the house of GOD, where his *rôle* was to be sanctimonious, exhibiting the calm serenity of a Christian character: dear, wise, good Mr. Goulding. Now, to have the man he was so wickedly persecuting, and whom he was resolved to destroy, present at an exhibition intended for his own peculiar audience: not only present, but evidently by special design, in close proximity; a critic on his words and sentences, an utter disbeliever in their sincerity; this had the effect, as I have said, to establish between Mr. Goulding and me a magnetic relation; and in so doing, displaced his relations with the listening saints around the house. Goulding *knew* I was saying to him in my heart: "Hypocrite! who devourest widows' houses, and for a pretence makest long prayers." He stammered, he became confused; he prayed that "Satan might *continue* to have dominion over us." That "we all might have our portion in the lake which burneth with everlasting fire!" The audience, though solemnly composed to worship, began to prick up their ears; a few turned their heads toward their elder, who was evidently wrestling in prayer and apparently getting the worst of it. Goulding became more and more confused, plunged from one bog to another, until he was forced to wind up in much confusion and in a profuse perspiration, before he had completed half his usual performance. For the first time in his life he had made a failure, and I enjoyed his discomfiture.

I have no doubt the reader will consider this either a puerile or a wicked exhibition of my nature. Doubtless it was both. But, I repeat, my design is to give a literal account of what occurred, and to show precisely into what a state of mind I had gradually fallen.

.   .   .   .

I felt ashamed—I hardly knew why—as I went home. Should my wife ask me where I had been, what would I say? However, with the satisfaction I enjoyed in witnessing Goulding's perturbation, I did not allow that to disturb me much.

When I entered the parlor, Florence was reclining on the sofa quite alone. She welcomed me as I came in with unusual tenderness.

" Will you hand me the BIBLE ?" she said.

I did so.

" May I read to you ?"

" Do."

She read a portion of the address of the ALMIGHTY to Job, commencing: " Who is this that darkeneth counsel by words without knowledge ?" When she had finished, she begged me to sit near her. She took my hand, held it in both of hers, looked anxiously in my face, and said: " Charles, here on this spot and at this time, we must not, O Charles ! we *must* not make any mistake. It *cannot* be, with loss of fortune, of home, of friends, you are also to lose your faith in GOD's goodness and justice and love. Then, indeed, all is lost. I have regarded you, my husband, of late with trembling; I have watched you anxiously until your very thoughts are clear to me. In what you have passed through I have been unable to give you any aid, except the little my sympathy afforded. Now, it seems to me that I shall no longer be useless; now I can endeavor

6

to dispel those unnatural thoughts which are breeding around your heart, which will produce blight and gangrene and death. Oh! no, no! You shall *not* cast off your only hope. GOD be praised, I still live to *compel* you to come with me — your Florence. You will not hesitate. You would never desert me, should dangers and terrors and death threaten; you will not desert me now when I lead you where you shall find peace and joy."

My wife continued to plead eloquently that I would dismiss all bitterness of feeling and not permit my misfortunes to pervert my moral nature.

I heard her in silence.

. . . .

There is a wayward element within our bosoms compelling us to hold out moodily against the entreaties and prayers of those we love. It is a portion of the "ancient leaven" still undigested, which has for its essence, "I am the spirit which ever *resists*." It has wrecked many a soul, and grows more potent where apparently there is least opportunity or reason for its existence. It becomes hardened and obdurate under kindness, like flint under entreaty, nursing itself with the devil's own nutriment, indifference and scorn.

While my wife was addressing me so tenderly and so eloquently, I felt this spirit gradually taking possession of me. I was quite conscious all the while, but it was the consciousness of one oppressed by nightmare. I so far controlled myself (strange to say), as to resolve while I was exhibiting these wicked manifestations of the evil one, that I would yield in the end. But to do this became harder every moment.

At last Florence paused, discouraged, despairing. Clasping her hands tightly together, she sat and looked at me mournfully. Then resistance was at its height; for presently I saw the young girl who had stood beside me in the village church one bright June morning — saw *only* her. The moisture gathered in my eyes; the devil's wand was broken, and I exclaimed: "Pshaw! what has been the matter with me, Florence; quite beside myself. There, I am sane—sane! GOD bless you, Florence, and whatever befalls us, let HIS name be praised."

The spell was dissolved, the gangrene cut out, the plague-spot eradicated, and I saved—saved, it is true, to live on under intense suffering a life of wretchedness; but never forgetting there is a GOD who *reigns*, and never distrusting HIS wisdom or providence. All this was the work of Florence—her last work, her last loved work.

CHAPTER XVI.

PREPARATIONS.

I SUCCEEDED in renting the house to a good tenant at a fair price, with the consent of Mr. Glynn that it should be sold subject to the rights of the lessee for that year. This would keep the interest on the mortgage paid, and leave something toward our support.

The person who took the house had himself failed in business three years previous, and was my debtor for about a thousand dollars. He had made a respectable compromise, and I had been among the first to sign off. His affairs had taken a successful turn ; he had made money fast, and was now, as he thought, able to take an expensive establishment.

The habits of our countrymen are a mystery to Europeans. Among the latter exists always a horror of coming to want, or, as the French express it, *de tomber en misere.* The first thought is to provide some income, be it ever so small, which shall be certain and permanent. They look with amazement on what they term our reckless disregard of the future, and wonder at the lavish expenditure of persons who have no receipts beyond what they earn from year to year. As is usual, both are right, both wrong. There is not in this country, owing to the innumerable opportunities for getting on, based on its fresh and varied resources, the same necessity for that careful and provident provision for the future which exists in the old world. Here a young man, well educated and in good health, and of ordinary capacity, feels no need of capital to enable him to rise. All he requires is honesty, activity and perseverance. We all understand this, and it makes us less thoughtful of what is to come. Unfortunately, it does more: it makes us thoughtless, and too often reckless in money matters. It leads to various extravagances, which produce strong contrasts from year to year in the fortunes of our ever-shifting population. But there is a salutary result at the bottom. PROVIDENCE makes no mistakes. Although we subject ourselves to the criticism of that prudent philosophy which teaches

"A PIN a day, a groat a year,
A penny saved is two-pence clear;"

still, let it never be forgotten that the sanguine and the restless are a *necessity* in a new country, and indeed are natural products of the soil. It is the sanguine and the restless who make a nation great. An old business community are not competent critics of the new. While Wall-street would not be content with the slow and steady gains of 'Change Alley, the latter regards with horror the precarious tenure with which here our money-kings hold their wealth and sway.

It was, therefore, with no feeling of surprise that I found Mr. Williams an applicant for our house; nor yet with any feeling of jealousy or chagrin. We both had had our struggles, and were about to change places. Something more than that, to be sure, since I was not in the favorable position of being freed from embarrassment. As it was, I experienced no heart-burnings nor foolish regrets. It was true it occurred to me that there was due from Williams over three hundred dollars. Ought he not to pay it? I had released him, but how far was he morally bound? This is a question which has been a good deal mooted. There are those theoretical moralists who do not entertain a solitary practical notion, who hold that a man is bound to toil all his life for the purpose of attempting to pay a legal debt in full. Now, I admit it is most agreeable to be able to do so; and when it is done it is very apt to be heralded by a flourish of trumpets, and a proclamation of how the honest man has paid his hundred cents on the dollar, and interest, although he *had* been released! It will be discovered, I think, on investigation, that those who have done this had an abundance left after making payment. Sometimes this is done out of policy, often, doubtless, from a feeling of pride, and often, it may be, from a conscientious sense of duty. My own opinion is, that when in the chances of trade losses honestly occur which render a compromise necessary, this should be absolutely as well as legally regarded as final. Every merchant in his time releases a large sum to his debtors, and in the long run things are pretty equitably balanced. I do not believe any reader of mine who happened to take advantage of the general bankrupt law of 1841, feels it to be his duty to have toiled laboriously since then to pay up old scores. Neither is it a good policy in affairs that he should do so. The Hebrews understood this, and it led them to provide a year of jubilee. I recollect, some years ago, one of our merchants, whose name is still associated

with all that is upright and honorable in commercial dealing, and first in enterprises of benevolence, was said, a long
time after his failure, to have paid all his obligations in full
with interest. He was an acquaintance, and I felt sufficiently intimate with him to ask if this were so, and I learned
that he had a partner at the time, and subsequently, after
getting again into successful business, had paid *his half* of
the general indebtedness in full. Really he was not only
legally but morally bound, if bound at all, to pay the whole ;
he had taken one of many views of the subject, and it does
by no means disturb my own theory of the hazards, the
philosophy and the morals of trade.

I quickly discarded, therefore, any latent idea that Mr.
Williams, because he was now doing a prosperous business,
ought to volunteer payment of the balance of his old debt.
Practical application is the true touchstone, and with this I
felt content to let Mr. Williams pass in honor " scot free."*
The lease was signed, and nothing remained but for him to
take possession on the first of May. Mr. Norwood endeavored to make a sale of my wife's furniture to him, for most
of it would be inappropriate in our new abode ; but in this
he was unsuccessful. Mr. Williams had already considerable of his own, and for the rest Mrs. Williams wished to

---

* We feel bound to defer in a measure to Mr. PARKINSON's opinion of the moral or
honorary liability on a discharged debt, in view of his large experience, and the attention he has devoted to the subject. We admit it is presented in a new light, and conscientiously presented. But we confess it disturbs our nerves somewhat. We have
been accustomed to regard business obligations as always binding, and the act of grace
by an indulgent creditor as no way morally releasing the debtor. Perhaps we did not
sufficiently take into account the fact that matters of trade are founded on conventional
rules, having for their basis a wise and liberalizing policy.

Again, if free pardon obtains under GOD's dispensation, it need not be inconsistent
with man's method. It is, however, a question for the conscience of each individual,
and thus we take leave of it.—EDITOR MEMOIRS.

purchase new furniture. The carpets, however, he would take.

I walked up and down over the house, endeavoring to ascertain by what arrangement of certain articles in our new abode I could preserve a semblance of our old home. I am not only greatly attached to localities, but to specific things—a chair, a table, a book-case, for example. In my heart is associated with such objects the scenes and incidents which have occurred during their occupation. It is hard to part from what use has made us familiar with; add to this the thousand little occurrences closely connected with one's *household furniture.* Here on this sofa your little ones have climbed about you; every piece of porcelain reminds you of happy scenes around the table; the arm-chair—what a history in the arm-chair! Are these not all friends, mute, it is true, but pleasant to the sight, happy in the memory—the very lares and penates of your home? Think of an auctioneer rudely taking up one of these dear objects, exhibiting it to a gaping crowd, and urging with professional volubility an increase of offers. There, he has seized your wife's pretty sewing-chair—a little beauty, a birth-day present when expense was not thought of. It is passed around among a curious crowd; various remarks are elicited; you can hear yourself abused for your extravagance. Big, coarse Mrs. Easton, who weighs two hundred and forty pounds, undertakes to sit in it, and is vexed because the chair is too small for her; for by her own account she was crazy after it. Then a joke is perpetrated, and the sale goes on. All this is not very pleasant to a sensitive person, who loves to cherish his associations, and who makes his surroundings dear to him as a part and portion of his daily life.

My reflections were something after this sort as I walked musingly over the house. I did not call Florence into the consultation. Why? I did not dare confess why; but I found myself selecting many little things I knew were no longer of use to her, but which were dear to me because she *had* used them.

I had previously consulted with Mr. Norwood as to what and how much the law permitted me to hold.* I had read the generous list prepared by our law-makers, including "all necessary pork, beef, fish, flour and vegetables actually provided for family use; and necessary fuel for the use of the family for sixty days," etc., etc., etc., and which concludes with a later and more humane provision, exempting

---

* To that portion of our readers who reside within the charmed precincts of well-invested wealth, who are "gorgeously apparelled, and live delicately"—to whom the idea of a restricted want would be a novelty—we present a curiosity in literature, to wit: an extract from the Statute Book of the State of New York, which specifies what property is exempt from levy and sale under execution. Sincerely do we hope they will never be forced upon a more intimate knowledge of its contents than the bare perusal will now afford. It will be seen these provisions are intended to favor those who dwell in the country, where favor is less needed than in town. A poor man in the city of New York would find some difficulty in keeping a cow, ten sheep, two swine, and the necessary food for them, albeit the law permits him to do so. We think some compensation should be provided for residents of cities, by way of additional items in the exempt list, as an offset to these indulgences to the country.

PROPERTY EXEMPT FROM LEVY AND SALE UNDER EXECUTION.

1. "All spinning-wheels, weaving-looms and stoves, put up or kept for use in any dwelling-house.

2. "The family BIBLE, family pictures and school-books, used by or in the family of such person, and books not exceeding in value fifty dollars, which are kept and used as a part of family library.

3. "A seat or pew occupied by such person or his family in any house or place of public worship.

4. "All sheep to the number of ten, with their fleeces, and the yarn or cloth manufactured from the same; one cow, two swine; the necessary food for them; all necessary pork, beef, fish, flour and vegetables actually provided for family use; and necessary fuel for the use of the family for sixty days.

6*

" in addition" one hundred and fifty dollars' worth of articles. Whatever should be the result of the litigation with Bulldog, I had a *right* to certain specific things, and this certain amount in value in furniture besides. With what could be legally held by my wife added to it, our small tenement would be neatly furnished. All the furniture I owned and had assigned, would be sold at auction, together with such belonging to her as was thought inappropriate. Reluctantly in my mind I yielded this and that, retaining at the same time that and this by some such process of association as I have just spoken of. Descending again to the parlors, I caught sight of my wife going out of the dining-room, so as to escape to her own apartment without observation. I knew very well that she was about to lie down and did not wish to attract my attention.

.   .   .   .

I received a letter the next day from the owner of the house I proposed to occupy. It was courteous in terms, but conveyed to me his decision, that he should require security for the rent. This was only reasonable, but it galled me nevertheless. I whose note a little before was so "undoubted;" whose paper was considered, in the present parlance of the street, "gilt-edged;" who received the congratulations of bank officers and wealthy financiers for my

5. "All necessary wearing apparel, beds, bedsteads and bedding, for such person and his family; arms and accoutrements required by law to be kept by such person; necessary cooking utensils; one table; six chairs; six knives and forks; six plates; six tea-cups and saucers; one sugar-dish; one milk-pot; one tea-pot and six spoons; one crane and its appendages; one pair of andirons; and a shovel and tongs.

6. "The tools and implements of any mechanic necessary to the carrying on of his trade, not exceeding twenty-five dollars in value."

A subsequent section, in addition to the above articles, exempts "necessary household furniture, working-tools and team of any person having a family for which he provides, to the value of not exceeding one hundred and fifty dollars."

eminent success in affairs, to be called on to give security for three hundred and fifty dollars! That was only eighty-seven dollars and fifty cents per quarter, and security wanted. Well, was that not a fair indication that my future landlord, himself a shrewd man, taking all things into consideration, had decided that *the chances were against my paying him his rent?* Therefore he asked security. This conclusion was not more encouraging to my hopes than the demand itself was to my pride; but it was idle to resent it. Necessity is a great leveller. If I was to have a roof over my head, I must comply with the conditions. "Beggars must not be choosers."

Who would "go" my security? That was the point. To whom could I apply? Out of all my friends, out of all those dear "five hundred," who had enjoyed the hospitality of my house; who had begged me to command their services on any and every occasion, to any and every amount; who would be security that I would faithfully pay eighty-seven dollars and fifty cents each and every three months for the space of one year?

Echo answered, " *Who!*"

What nonsense, such reflections! Those friends of yours took you as you *were.* No clause in the articles provided for your bankruptcy; before, it was fair "give and take," now it is all on one side. You might command them, to be sure, but they expected to command you as well.

Once more I had recourse to my counsel, once more Mr. Norwood proved a friend in need, and freely became my guarantee.

The lease was duly executed, and Mr. Norwood readily

accepted as surety. The rooms were measured for carpets, the hall for oil-cloth, and various orders given to be executed before the first of May. Next came the preparations for the auction. The day fixed was the twenty-seventh of April. The auctioneers were the well-known house of A. A. Lee and Company. The list was carefully prepared; the reserved articles selected; those sold to Mr. Williams marked off, and a correct catalogue printed. Already had advertisements appeared in the daily papers, of the magnificent sale of household furniture at No. —— Broadway, which should take place on the twenty-seventh day of April. The description was in the best style of Lee and Company, and all the concomitants worthy the name and fame of those accomplished auctioneers. A few more days, and all would be going, going, gone!

CHAPTER XVII.

DEATH.

THERE was no auction at our house on the twenty-seventh day of April. No moving out of it on the first day of May. A darkened chamber, a woman wearing a professional air of solemn solicitude near the bed, careful footsteps, voices scarcely above a whisper, loving countenances mournful, despairing, were tokens that some one "appointed to die" lay on that couch, and that the time drew near.

The motions and counter-motions with Bulldog were no longer pressed; adjournments were consented to without question; delay granted on either side. For in that hour none were so hardy as not to acknowledge and pay respect to the approach of the destroyer.

It was sudden and swift. Another fresh cold led to acute inflammation of the lungs, and death was to follow. It is not my design to attempt to portray my anguish those few days, nor how, watching by the bed-side of my wife, I beheld her sink and die.

There are some of you who know what it is to hold the hand of the one most dear to you, and watch the feeble pulse, and while in your grasp to have it flutter and stop. It is a fearful moment, first filling your soul with awe and terror before the fountains of the heart can be loosed, and grief come to your relief. The history would be impressive, but could convey no *new* impression.

It was past the middle of the afternoon, on the third of May; a pleasant day with warm sunshine and a balmy atmosphere. I returned to my wife's chamber, having been absent perhaps a half-hour. She asked me to send the nurse down stairs, and to tell Alice to leave the room for a few moments. My heart beat violently, for I knew Florence designed to take a last farewell. I did as she desired, and sat down by her side; it was the last scene of the drama, commencing with that pleasant little party in September, when—I am foolish to recall it: let it pass.

"Charles, *it is coming*, we have little to say to each other, for our whole life has been rounded from day to day by love. I leave you; I leave you to encounter misery and degradation, and what shall seem disgrace, but through all you will preserve your integrity, and at the last there will come a season of repose. GOD permits me to see this, and to tell you, O my husband!" . . . . After a pause she continued: "I have one request to make;" her voice trembled. "Keep them together. Keep them *all* around you. Promise me—you will not separate."

"Never! while I have life, never!" I murmured. . .

"Kiss me: call the children!" . . . .

She died that evening.

CHAPTER XVIII.

MOURNING.

"THE dark sail shifts from side to side,
The boat untrimmed admits the tide,
Borne down, adrift, at random tost,
The oar breaks short, the rudder's lost."

I NEED not tell the reader how, the morning after my wife died, I rose with a feeling of utter insensibility and indifference to all that was transpiring. It seemed as if the world should stop in its daily avocations, and I could not realize that its machinery was in motion just as ever. I recollect going into the hall, and mechanically opening the street-door, and gazing out on Broadway. The sun shone glaringly. Why should the sun shine any more? Omnibuses and carriages of every description rolled noisily along. Why were they not silent? Business men were hastening to their several offices and counting-rooms. How useless! People of various conditions would stop and exchange cheerful salutations and lively pleasantries. Did they know *she* was dead?

So entirely do we color and shape externals out of our own profound egotism.

This period is generally a brief one in the experience of the mourner, especially if we be forced quickly back into the current from which we were withdrawn.

After the funeral—we buried my wife in Greenwood—

my thoughts turned by necessity to my children. For a time, however, I found it impossible to summon the least energy or resolution. My situation is best described by the lines I have placed at the head of this chapter. I was nerveless, purposeless, regardless of the present, and without the least care for the future.

This season too has its limits, and even if, unlike my own case, we are not roused prematurely by stern necessity, the feelings gradually get into their former channels; the world which we regarded with indifference and disgust by degrees presents itself with the old charm, and we find ourselves returning its smile and friendly greeting. Soon we forget the poignancy of that grief which held so complete control over us; and lo! again we walk abroad, subdued somewhat by our sad experience, somewhat more timid perhaps in view of future possibilities, but wedded firmly as ever to our old habits, enjoying our old delights, eager in our old pursuits.

There is something more melancholy in the transitory nature of our mourning than in the affliction which causes it. Deep grief, while it lasts, lifts us above all earthly considerations, and we feel self-reproached when first forced to admit any returning sensibility with regard to them. Yes, it is a melancholy idea that we must come *back* after accompanying the loved spirit part way on the journey heavenward.

But is the short period of our mourning humiliating to human nature? Does it indicate that it is capricious and unreliable? I do not think so. It would be impossible to live in this world of ours and carry around always such sharp grief. We may indulge in a tender melancholy, softening in its influences, and do our duty manfully, but it is providential that the season of intense sorrow is but short.

So it was not very long before I became engaged as determinedly as before, resisting or attacking Bulldog and Company, fully resolved that if I were wrecked they should not benefit by the disaster.

Mr. Williams who was to take our house was very considerate of our situation. While my wife was ill, he sent me a message begging me not to have the least concern or solicitude about not being able to give it up on the day. Mrs. Williams felt that a few weeks at a hotel would be an agreeable change. When all was over, he called to condole with me, and insisted I should take time and have the auction on the premises, just as I had previously intended.

I now attempted to address myself vigorously to the task of fitting up the new house, and arranging for the sale of furniture in the old. I had promised Florence not to separate myself from the children. Indeed I could not have done so if the pledge had not been given. They were now to be my only solace; for them alone I now was to live and toil. Alice appeared to grow suddenly into a woman; she was thoughtful, tender, sympathizing. Sometimes I loved to believe that the spirit of my wife had communicated to her that maturity of feeling which was now so congenial and companionable. Little Charley and Anna were yet too young to grieve. They cried when their mamma was carried out of the house; they knew they would not see her any more, but in a day or two they were playing about quite as usual.

CHAPTER XIX.

THE AUCTION.

AGAIN, in the daily journals appeared the advertisement of Lee and Company, announcing the " splendid" sale of household furniture in Broadway.

I was subjected to not a little annoyance by the calling of several female *friends* to ask about certain articles of furniture. Each was desirous to have some trifling memento of their dear Mrs. Parkinson. One fixed on a centre-table, another selected a fauteuil, a third a tea-set, and so forth. Their purpose in coming was to inquire if, under the circumstances (since they were desirous of procuring these several objects *merely* as souvenirs, having really no use for them whatever), I could not consent that they should take them away before the sale, and (delicately put in) at a nominal price. Mrs. Amelia Vanderheyden assured me it would give poor Mrs. Parkinson, could she but know it—and perhaps she would know it—so much satisfaction to have that particular piece of furniture in *her* possession ; it had always been a favorite with her, and on one occasion (and she was eloquently minute in particularizing when, how and where) my wife had actually proposed to present it to her, but she (Mrs. V.) was really ashamed to accept it, because she had just been praising it so.

I had but one answer to give to these disinterested souls,

and that was, that I had no control whatever over the furniture or the sale. I must refer them to Mr. Norwood. Whereat I was subjected to certain polite but distinct innuendoes of "how soon husbands were apt to forget their poor wives' requests, and slight their well-known wishes."

There was a very fine grand-action piano among the articles to be sold; the same instrument on which Alice was playing when the news arrived of the protest of Wise and Company's bills. I had paid only the year before nine hundred and fifty dollars for it. Mr. Norwood told me a friend of his stood ready to pay six hundred dollars, and would bid to that amount if it was thought necessary to sell it at auction, which he decided was the safe course. The day before the sale, Mr. Chandler, a merchant who claimed to hold me in very high esteem, called, and in a very condoling. patronizing tone said: "Mr. Parkinson, motives of delicacy will prevent my attending a sale which is the breaking up of the establishment of an old and valued friend; but, to relieve your mind about a pretty expensive article which will hardly find a purchaser, as times are, I will say I have left orders with a person to bid off your piano at four hundred dollars.

I thanked Mr. Chandler a little bluntly perhaps, but gave no information that he would probably find a competitor at the sale.

"You know, Mr. Parkinson," he continued, "pianos are a drug, a perfect drug; yours, though a good one, would not bring over two hundred dollars, I dare say; but it is worth four hundred, and I give you my word I shall bid that amount, irrespective of competition. [He *did* bid up to

six hundred and ten dollars, and it was struck off to Mr.
Norwood's friend at six hundred and twenty, much to the
chagrin of Mrs. Chandler, who had vowed she would have
it.] Again I thanked this delicate-minded and generous
man, and shortly after he took his leave.

. . . .

"My friend," said Mr. Norwood to me the evening before
the sale, "do you propose to be at the auction to-morrow?"
"Certainly."
"I shall not consent to it," he replied. "The children of
course are not to be here, you are all ready to leave; the
other house quite prepared; I know almost as much about
the property as you do. I will be present, and shall not
permit too great a sacrifice. I invite myself to breakfast
with you at seven," he continued, "and I invite myself to
be your companion and escort to your new house."

I knew how much there was disagreeable in store for me
at that auction, but I thought I might be of service there,
and I had decided to be present. I was easily persuaded
to yield to my friend's advice, since he went on to descant
upon what I should encounter.

"You will see there," he said, "every lady who knew
your wife, with her daughters and nieces if she has any,
roaming curiously over your house, and into every nook and
corner. Your library and your breakfast-room, so pleasant
in your recollection, will be invaded by Goths and Vandals.
Women who make it a business to attend all auctions everywhere over the city, will throng the halls and staircases.
Men who go expressly to crowd among the women will
help to add to the confusion, and——"

" Enough," I exclaimed.

. . . .

The small house up-town had been neatly but very inexpensively furnished. A cheap piano was purchased, a very good one, for two hundred dollars. Alice had herself superintended the arrangement of the furniture. She displayed extraordinary energy, and I found myself taking an interest in every thing before I knew it. We had engaged a good-natured, serviceable Irish girl to do " general housework." We were to have no other servant. Alice could not attend school any longer, but Charley and Anna were to go to a respectable day-school. Alice and I had planned it together, and we had carefully calculated expenses.

The morning came. Mr. Norwood arrived, and we sat down to our last breakfast *there*. It was eaten rapidly and in silence. Soon the carriage and baggage-wagon were before the door; what remained for us to take, was speedily removed. Mr. Williams had, on my recommendation, engaged our man, since he had employed none before. I had procured places for the other servants. Nothing more remained for us to do in our handsome house; we stepped into the carriage, the wagon followed, and we were soon entering our new abode. Then Mr. Norwood shook my hand, and praised Alice, and said a pleasant word to the children, and left for the auction. He had done every thing for me—made every arrangement. He had gone carefully over the estimate of the furniture which *I* could hold. Without any regard to the replevin suit, he had made such selections from my wife's furniture as we thought suitable, and which now belonged under the trust to the children.

He had taken the responsibility of the sale, and was furnishing the necessary funds for carrying on the several suits in which I was involved. After an intimate acquaintance of fifteen years, he proved on the closest trial a *friend*, and I pay here this humble tribute to his memory.

The morning passed in unpacking and arranging. The day stole quietly away. The children appeared just as happy in the new house as in the old, and Alice enjoyed the satisfaction of making all comfortable by her careful oversight.

I did not quit the house that day, and it was not till late in the evening, after the children had retired, that a mournful home-sickness took possession of me. I had separated myself from my social life; a necessary act, but a severe one. I felt stricken with a sense of desolation. Presently something seemed to whisper: "Cease your foolish repinings and regrets. *Pass down into that class, and accept your condition!*"

END OF PART FIRST.

UNDERCURRENTS OF WALL-STREET.

PART SECOND.

> "The strawberry grows underneath the nettle;
> And wholesome berries thrive and ripen best
> Neighbour'd by fruit of baser quality."

CHAPTER I.

THE LOCALITY.

ON the front of Trinity Church, looking down Wall-street, should be inscribed in large letters :

> "The rich man's wealth is his strong city."
> "The destruction of the poor is their poverty."

To no locality on the habitable globe are these sentences more applicable. Every transaction relating to money, from the "legitimate" discounts by the banks out of the offerings at the ordinary meetings of the board, to the shaving of a fourth-class piece of paper at the rate of "a quarter of a dollar a day for a hundred dollars" (a favorite standard price, and a favorite way of putting it, as less calculated to shock the nerves than plain, blunt "quarter per cent. a day," which by the way is only ninety-one per cent. per annum, or thereabouts); every movement of the stock-market, every transfer of property, every auction, every operation by the brokers, whether in bonds, bills, stocks, goods or merchandise, but confirms the fact of the economical advantages of wealth and the expensiveness of poverty.

Our sympathies are often tried by the recitals of harrowing tales of pauper life, or of the miserable beings who wear out a degraded existence in mines and collieries, and shops and factories. Some delight to picture these scenes in all their horrors, possibly not exaggerating in the account; and many of our popular writers have entered the field with success. If they could experience ten years in Wall-street they would dispose of their present stock in trade, and eagerly seize on this. There exist in that street those who suffer more than the pauper, and the men, women and children in the mines and collieries, and shops and factories, for they have sharper sensibilities, and keener appreciations, and a more vivid despair. The overworked wretches of the manufactory have, it is true, no possible chance of release, except by death. Physically they sink to a very low scale, worn down by hard labor, bad shelter, and a stinted diet. But intellectually there has been no descent, and ignorant as they are, they may enjoy the consolations of religion, and be comforted by a faith which affords the prospect of a happy rest hereafter. But the Wall-street "operative" has *fallen* from position of some kind into *his* awful serfdom. Well educated, with respectable associations, with perhaps a refined and interesting family at home, who have no conception of the desperate shifts and expedients he habitually employs to feed and clothe them; tied with the cord necessity to the chariot of the rich, employed to gather gold for them, and swell their triumphs; with the power of reflection and appreciation, and a consciousness too : his condition is infinitely the worst. He must learn all the tricks of the street; the how to lie and cheat and swindle, so that it will not *legally* be lying, cheating and swindling. He knows that he is degrading his nature, yet he has no opportunity to stop even for one moment to regard himself. He sees glimpses of green fields, and clear skies, and a pure moral atmosphere away yonder, but he has no time to visit them. Perhaps at last, with a growing sense of injustice toward him from some quarter, he becomes desperate, steps over the delicate line drawn by the law between moral and legal crime, and is sent to the penitentiary by his patrons, whose dirty work he has done so long ; or, his moody nature taking another direction, he commits suicide, and is reported in the morning papers with the comment, " no assignable cause for the commission of the rash act."

There is another class equally, nay, more entitled to our sympathies. It is the class who from day to day, and week to week, and month to month, and year to year, labor unceasingly for money; who think of nothing else, who care for nothing else, who have no other idea. Whose lives outside of this are a blank—are idiocy. To hoard up cash, to force the last piece of coin from the unfortunate, to calculate every possibility, to press every advantage, to make every sacrifice—for gold ! The miserable individuals first described are not irredeemable, for they have not lost the attributes of humanity. They are conscious of their position, and where there is consciousness there is hope. But these last are beyond the reach of every human influence, and

7

have nothing to expect in the future, unless it be a "fearful looking forward to judgment." But I must not anticipate.

Wall-street is a short and somewhat irregular avenue, leading from Broadway to the East River. The numbers of the buildings reach only to one hundred and twenty. The lower part is devoted to houses connected with the shipping trade, auctioneers, cotton and merchandise-brokers in every variety, including liquor-brokers, wine-brokers, segar-brokers, and so forth. As we advance up the street, we encounter an array of insurance companies, fire and marine, innumerable lawyers' offices, and an occasional bank or banking-house; with more merchandise-brokers, and occasionally a shop for fruit, cigars and confectionery. Approaching William-street we enter the vortex, and behold a palatial array of banks, more insurance companies, more lawyers' offices, a multitude of brokers' signs of every kind; stock-brokers, bill-brokers, collection-brokers, money-brokers, all sorts of brokers, from the leading houses down to the curbstone "operator," known as the "hyena," or "Bohemian" of the street, and now crowded out of Wall around the corner along William-street to Delmonico's.

Approaching Broadway we escape in a degree from the oppressive flurry, and find again something of the commercial atmosphere, mingling with that of money-bags, stocks and bank-bills. At the top of the street we encounter Trinity Church, with its magnificent spire, practically announcing: "Thus far shalt thou go, and no farther"—in this direction; a striking illustration too of "The nearer the kirk, the farther frae grace."

But we can do no justice to Wall-street by any simple

grouping or attempt at concise characterization. Its advantages for a universal mart are incredible. It is Lombard-street, Threadneedle-street, Old Broad-street, Wapping, the Docks, Thames-street and the Inns of Court, combined. In it is the Custom-House as well as the Exchange. It is a good dog-market, cow-market, and bird-market. If you want a pair of horses, and any description of new or second-hand carriage, wait a little and they will be paraded before you. You will find there the best fruit, and the finest flowers in their season. If you would have a donkey, a Shetland pony, a Newfoundland dog, a good milch cow and calf, a Berkshire pig, a terrier, white mice, a monkey or paroquets, they are to be had in Wall-street. It is a strange spot. On Sunday or early in the morning during the week it is like the street of a deserted city. About ten o'clock it begins to show signs of extraordinary animation. Through the day the turmoil increases, people run to and fro, and literally "stagger like drunken men." Toward three o'clock the street appears undergoing a series of desperate throes. Men rush madly past each other with bank-books in their hands, uncurrent money, notes, drafts, checks, specie. Occasionally you may see an individual on the steps of a building, evidently waiting for something, with an air of forced calmness. From time to time he turns his eye anxiously to the great dial-plate which is displayed from the church, and then up and down the street. The minute-hand has worked five into the last quarter. In ten more minutes it will be three o'clock. Occasionally an acquaintance passes; the man attempts as he bows to smile pleasantly; he can't do it, he only makes a grimace. What is he waiting for?

That individual has a note to pay, or a check to make good before three. He has worked hard, but the fates have been against him. One friend is out of town, a second is short, the third can't use his paper: he has sent to the last possible place. Look! the young man is coming. Yes? No? He runs eagerly up, thrusts the welcome little slip, a check for the desired amount, into the hands of the now agitated principal; it is rapidly endorsed, and on flies the youth to the bank.

Our hero relieved—he has probably borrowed the money for a day only, and has to renew the attack the next morning—now prepares to leave his office, he lights a cigar, invites the first friend he meets to take a drink with him, and strolls leisurely up Broadway as unconcernedly as if he had not a care in the world. Perhaps he does not come off so luckily; perhaps his young man reports to him, while standing gloomily on the steps, that it is "no go;" then the fatal hand which points toward three, travels fast. He considers a moment; he sees it can't be done; he waits till he hears the chimes ring out the full hour, and then his "mind is easy." Your shrewd money-lender understands this perfectly. He knows how unsafe it is to let his victim pass the point unrelieved; for, once having gone to protest, he becomes demoralized, and in consequence indifferent. So, just before the hour, the money is generally "found."

I find I have unconsciously departed from my proposed plan, which is, to allow the reader to become acquainted with the particulars of Wall-street life, by what he can learn of it from my personal history. This I will now resume, and ask pardon for the digression.

CHAPTER II.

PERSONAL.

I HAD buried my wife, and removed with my three children up-town, and settled into a cheap habit of living. I had no credit at the grocer's, nor with the baker, butcher or milk-man. I did not ask any. I was known only as an elderly gentleman, who bought very sparingly, and paid away his money as if he had but little of it. My daughter Alice and I understood each other perfectly. She was my only companion—for while the two younger children were a great solace and happiness, they were not old enough for society for me.

When you undertake, reader, to pay as you go, and never to purchase a penny's worth on credit, you will become economical in spite of yourself. Carefully indeed did I dispense the little sum which still remained to me, and which with the most careful husbanding of resources, grew ominously less.

The time had arrived when I must decide what to undertake for a living—how to support my children. I have referred to the influence of family connection under such circumstances to sustain a broken-down man of business and provide him a means of support. There was no one to raise a finger for me. "Well," I exclaimed to myself, walking up and down the little parlor, "is there really any thing left of you? House and home and fortune gone. O Parkinson! you are a poor devil, with nobody to get up an insurance company for you to be the president of. Let me see; without a fine house, a fine carriage, fine horses and money, what do you amount to? That's the question. You have lived and worked hard many years, and failed. What have you to show for it? Lawrence, your classmate, is not worth a dollar in the world; yet what consideration he commands. He has *done* something. What have you done besides selling goods and looking carefully to the main chance?"

.   .   .   .

"Well, what is the cause of this heart-ache? Is it in consequence of living more meanly, faring on poorer food, keeping up no establishment? True, this may cause certain others to regard you in a different light, but why should *you* deem *yourself* thereby insignificant? If really, O Parkinson! your *position* was all there was of you, and in leaving it you became *per se* a nobody, having in times past done nothing and achieved nothing to entitle you to self-recognition and to recognition from the world, beyond the disbursing of so much money per annum—but is it so?"— Then returned the question, what had I really done beyond selling goods, etc.? Do we inquire, I asked myself, if certain persons who fill prominent places of honor and trustfulness are rich or not? Yet, to become rich had been too much the question with me.

How had I neglected my life!

The great thing now was, not to lose my self-respect; not to seem contemptible in my own eyes. Had I not the same brain, and heart, and soul as ever? Were I dismissed from

this world, these alone would stead me. Standing on the
other side of the river, I was perhaps superior to Russell.
Now, then, could I endure until the appointed time?

Merchants, business men of New York, hearken! I do
not accuse you of loving money too well, of being avaricious, covetous, miserly or grasping, but you devote your
entire energies too much to your occupation. You make it
the end and aim of your life instead of a means to comfort
and happiness. You work too hard; you enjoy too little;
you lose yourself in your employment. You rise early,
breakfast; taking time scarcely to greet your children, you
hasten to your place of business. Perhaps you only return
in the evening after the little ones have gone to rest; or if
to a late dinner, it amounts to the same thing. You manage
to read the newspapers going and returning, and you read
nothing else. On Sunday you endure a wretched, dyspep-
tic day; mind and body suddenly and entirely relaxed, the
reaction is too great; you do not know what to do. You
attend church; you stroll home; you yawn, smoke a cigar,
make a call; play a little with the children, who are not
more than half acquainted with you, and go to bed. You
rise next morning and find it "blue Monday," and it takes
you till Tuesday to get right. Why? Because you so
overtask yourself that a day's relaxation makes you sick!
Perhaps you accumulate a fortune, and you feel that you are
entitled to repose and relaxation, *but you dare not retire
from business for fear you will become imbecile or lunatic!*
and your fears are well grounded. You have so fitted yourself into the harness that you can never get out of it. You
are worse off than a poor man, for he is permitted to pre-

serve his faculty for enjoyment, while you lose yours. Your children grow up, marry and leave you alone—ah! how terribly alone.

Can't you change all this? I am not going to preach a sermon. But really it is a pitiable object to behold a man twist himself into a deformity. We read of prisoners so long confined in one position that the limbs refuse to do their office when they are set at liberty. So with you, who have no other thought but to merely buy and sell. Suppose you attempt to become interested in what is going on at home. Cultivate your children's affections, and thus enlarge your own. Then you will cease to be absent-minded or preoccupied while you caress them; then you will get rid of that nervous irritability which will not permit you to sit quietly half an hour with your family, because the time is up for you to be off, although you know your presence is not required at your place of business. In short, do not work so hard, but apply more intellect to what you do undertake. Recollect, nearly half that you do is done wrong or injudiciously by being done with too little reflection and too much precipitation. Think what a large portion of your time is spent in repairing damages, or in undoing what you have begun. So you cannot lose by following my advice; on the contrary, you are sure to be the gainer. Therefore, I say, take time to *enjoy*—I repeat, enjoy all you can; something of nature, the green of the meadow, the majesty of the full flowing river, the forest and the mountain; something of art—a picture, a statue, a fine building, an engraving; something of society—lay hold of persons who are genial, and create a world of pleasant intercourse, in which no taskmaster shall enter nor intermeddle; at all events, for HEAVEN's sake, make *some* effort to get out of the rut you are in at present. Do not look down as you walk along, but look up. How long is it since you have actually *regarded* the sky, the sun, moon and stars? Observe them now, and get back if you can some of your youth's romance. Or at the least let your eye rest on a church spire, or the façade of some fine building; or, failing that, look at the horses and carriages which fill the streets—*do*. If at last you fail in business—and you know what are the mathematical chances against your ultimate success—you have not lost all you are worth; on the contrary, you will be worth more than you have lost. There cannot exist a more unhappy spectacle than a man who has devoted his very life to "business," and who fails or "retires" toward the close of his career. Whether you are to fail or to retire, keep yourself from becoming a hideous ossification! These observations are the result of my reflections that morning as I paced up and down the little parlor, while I subjected myself to a searching analysis. That analysis was not altogether discouraging. In short, I felt that I *was* something outside of my occupations—not what I should have been, but still something; and then I discovered that *so far as one has the faculty to enjoy what is daily presented so far one is rich.*

7*

CHAPTER III.

WHAT IS TO BE DONE?

FOR two or three months I occupied myself in looking about me, endeavoring to hit on some means of supporting my family. Once in my life I recollected, in the course of a conversation, kindly criticising an acquaintance, who was leading apparently an idle life, while he remained quite dependent on some relations, when his health appeared good, and he was withal very competent. His answer I never forgot, and it came home to me with much force. "Mr. Parkinson," said he, "I am neither indolent, nor, I think, inefficient; but I am used up after I have passed the prime of life. GOD grant *you* may never know by experience the difficulty of getting any thing to do, which you *can* do at my age and in my circumstances. I am an experienced merchant, but no young man who is a principal in business wants to pay me for my advice. Faith, no young man would relish my advice anyhow. As to a clerkship, people prefer younger persons, and very properly. I am not suitable for a book-keeper, nor active enough for a salesman, nor strong enough for a porter. I am not on the right side of politics for a place in the Custom-House, and my friends cannot afford to *make* an employment for me."

I asked the man's pardon, and I felt now as if I wanted to go to him and ask it a second time. Carefully I surveyed the ground. It was that of the unfortunate individual whose experience had preceded mine.

" What can I do ?"

It happened that one of my mercantile acquaintances, with whom I had always been on agreeable terms, advised me to see what I could accomplish as a note-broker. At that time the present system of large offices, where a capitalist can go and select such notes as may please him, had not been organized. But one house of the kind was then in existence. There was much more favoritism at the banks than now ; in short, those who will look back to eighteen hundred and forty-eight will recognize an entire revolution in money transactions, and in doing business generally since then. At that time there was much less capital, and, consequently, much more credit in proportion. My adviser urged, that, with my experience of the various firms in the city, and with the kind feeling entertained toward me by the two banks where I had kept my account, I should have no difficulty in earning, by way of commission, what would make us at least comfortable. Besides, I might also take up various negotiations as occasion presented. I had myself thought of this plan, and on conversing with Mr. Norwood, I found he did not oppose it. I next undertook to ascertain what I might reasonably expect from the banks. At the Bank of the World, notwithstanding my experience of what a change of fortune would produce in the demeanor of people, I was perfectly taken aback by the extraordinary treatment of the president.

He was seated in his private room, giving directions to one of the book-keepers as I entered. He did not appear to notice me when I came in, so I remained standing while he talked to the clerk. After a while he was through; thereupon he raised his eyes, and looked at me much as he would at an apple-woman. "Good morning!" was all he said. Whereupon I sat down, and was commencing to tell him what I called for.

"I say, Willard," calling back the clerk, who was just outside the door. The man returned, and received another direction, and went away. Then Mr. President took up a piece of paper with some figures on it, and exclaimed, while he regarded it attentively: "Go on, Mr. Parkinson, I can hear just as well." I had only begun again when in stepped a customer, a favorite customer, who whispered a word to the president, produced two pieces of paper, on both of which the latter placed a small mark in pencil, and he was off. I attempted to continue, when in came the cashier, who had other questions to put. Not the least notice was taken of me meanwhile, and shortly he concluded. After that another acquaintance came in, and claimed attention. Each time I had opportunity to utter only half a sentence before I was interrupted. But it was not the interruptions; it was the contemptuous, supercilious manner toward me of this man in power, who evidently regarded me as wholly and absolutely insignificant. Twice I determined to walk out, and abandon the whole business, but I gulped down my pride, and managed by degrees to communicate what I had to say.

"Really, Mr. Parkinson, the bank can give no assurances to you; our regular customers take up all we have at present."

Just then I saw a well-known broker at the door, whom I knew did not keep an account with the Bank of the World, but between whom and the president pretty large operations were always going on.

"Walk in, Mr. Breeze," with a pleasant tone. "That's all I can say to you, Mr. Parkinson," with an air of contemptuous indifference.

I left the bank, boiling over with—what? not rage, nor hatred, nor envy, nor malice, nor chagrin alone, but with all these and every other wicked passion combined and concentrated. I ground my teeth savagely together. At that moment I could have turned burglar, and robbed the bank's vaults, or set fire to the building, or throttled the officers. Desperate violence was in my heart: what aroused it? Not the president's refusal to do business with me: that might have disappointed me, but nothing more.

"The sting of contempt," says the proverb, " will penetrate the back of a tortoise:" it was his insulting way of regarding me as beneath the slightest consideration, and as utterly insignificant, which cut me to the quick, and aroused passions and emotions I never before experienced. Tears of vexation actually filled my eyes when I thought how powerless I was to resent this despicable slight.

A very few minutes served to dissipate the force of the storm which was raging within. Soon it gave way to calmer feelings. Then I took a necessary, I may say a compulsory view of the matter, and while I still smarted under a keen sense of the man's treatment, I began to see how foolish it was to permit myself to become so disturbed by it. Indeed I could not but remember how I myself had formerly stepped into this very private office as a privileged person, and found some poor fellow waiting, humble and obsequious, whose interview *I* interrupted until *my* business was disposed of. Had I not left the bank on such occasions in a complacent mood, caused by the ready attention which my requests commanded from this same president? But why could he not have received me with at least a show of courtesy and declined my request in a civil manner?

The arrogant, self-sufficient tone and bearing assumed by so many who have control of capital, do much toward engendering hatred, bitterness, and often crime. It is this which helps to create radicals in society, which leads to the promulgation of doctrines that make the rich man turn pale sometimes as he hears audacious avowals from noisy, turbulent men, no respecters of his position, who talk of " equal distribution of property," " the right of every one to a home," and who openly denounce the abominations of a system which makes the "rich richer, the poor poorer." However, it is idle to indulge in such observations. As the devil was ever a liar from the beginning, so the rich have always been justly chargeable with oppression and contumely,* because it is the attribute of wealth to make people self-confident and overbearing. The evil must cure itself, but when—how?

Not disheartened altogether, I went to the Bank of Credit.

* It seems to us there is an unnatural bitterness in this observation of Mr. PARKIN-SON. It is not quite consistent with the general spirit and tone of the Memoirs. There is no sin in becoming rich or in inheriting wealth, but rather in too great *devotion* to mammon. We must say we think the remark too sweeping.

Mr. PARKINSON, who has just read this paragraph, desires us to refer to the prayer of AGUR: " Give me neither poverty nor riches," . . . "lest I be full and *deny thee, and say, Who is the Lord ?*" etc., and also the numerous and general denunciations of the rich throughout the Scriptures, Old and New.—EDITOR OF MEMOIRS.

I had·known the president less intimately than the president of the Bank of the World. The cashier, however, I was better acquainted with. Indeed I had been chiefly instrumental, through two of the directors, in procuring his appointment. Passing his room, I stopped to speak with him. He was civil in reply, but *changed*. No pleased alacrity of demeanor greeted the man to whom he owed so much. He appeared very busy—very much engrossed—had not time to converse. I went into the president's room. I am pleased to record the truth that he received me kindly, with a difference compared with his former demeanor, yet absolutely with kindness. Without committing himself, he listened to my plans, and suffered no one to interrupt me, and finally said that if I saw no other opportunity or means of employing myself, he would do what he could consistently, but really he would not advise me to undertake this sort of business. He assured me of his personal respect, however, and added, although the collaterals left with the bank would not make good the deficiency arising from the payments under the assignment, the board felt friendly toward me.

What more could I ask or expect? I took leave somewhat discouraged, however, by the tone in which the president advised me to seek if possible some other occupation; but I could think of no other; and on consulting further with several acquaintances, I decided to attempt this.

Meantime, the foreclosure suit had been brought to a termination, and the house advertised for sale. Just then real estate was " dull," but the sale brought a few capitalists together. Goulding was there, supported by Bulldog, though when on the spot he seemed averse to acknowledging the connection. Finally the property was struck down to a German by the name of Spink, for nineteen thousand three hundred and fifty dollars! A little short of twenty thousand dollars for what should have brought at least twenty-five thousand. The sum which I hoped would be derived from this house for the benefit of my children had dwindled to an insignificant amount. The mortgage was fifteen thousand; something over a year's interest, eleven or twelve hundred dollars more; add the costs of foreclosure, payment of the year's taxes, sheriff's fees, etc., and considerably less than three thousand dollars would remain, and even that was to be tied up under Bulldog's injunction, while he attacked the validity of the trust to my wife.

A piece of good fortune befell me about this time. It was the abandonment of his claims on the personal property by Bulldog, and his allowing judgments by default on the replevin suits. This was quite in accordance with his tactics. Bulldog was chiefly successful by making a sudden *coup*, whereby he sought to strike terror into the heart of his victim and compel immediate settlement. If stoutly resisted, he was too shrewd a knave to prolong an unsuccessful fight, and would acknowledge his adversary had been too "smart" for him with the same unblushing effrontery that he would manifest in the first attack. Indeed the day after the suits were disposed of, Bulldog went out of his way to pass me, when he exclaimed with an oath he liked my pluck, and admitted I had been too "damned knowing for him." "I shall give you a long pull, though, on the house money," he added; "besides, you have only bitten your own nose off, damned close to the face too." These refined observations were made to me, *nolens volens*, while Bulldog was passing on his way. I neither replied to nor noticed them; in fact, to have defeated Goulding put me in too pleasant a mood to be disturbed by any such comments.

Another agreeable episode was a little incident connected with my counsel, Mr. Norwood. When he drew up so hastily the assignment of my personal property, after putting down all the personal debts, he added also the claim against me by Norwood and Case for professional services. This bill he now proceeded to render, and to give at the same time an account of what he had done as assignee. The bill was made out in form, and with great minuteness, and reached a pretty large figure.

" I am sorry to say, my friend," said Mr. Norwood, " that after paying off the other claims, which were preferred by my express wish to that of Norwood and Case, there does not remain enough to satisfy us. However, we shall make those fellows pay a good bill of costs, and you must not feel distressed about it."

I did feel distressed. I hardly could tell why, but there was something in the tone which seemed very different from all Mr. Norwood had ever before said. I replied I was sorry, and endeavored to express my gratitude for what he had done for me, but the words stuck in my throat, and in the midst of it Mr. Norwood took his leave.

I learned shortly after, that he had deposited five hundred dollars in Alice's name in the savings bank, to be employed by her as a reserve fund in case the " house-money" should on any occasion happen to fail. Alice kept the secret from me just twenty-four hours; she could contain herself no longer. "Really, papa, I was thinking how charming it would be to surprise you some day when you had no money for the marketing. Just as you were beginning to shake your head, and to feel very bad, I would produce my purse, in which I should have ten dollars, only ten dollars, you know, so as not to excite your suspicion, and I would say: Look here, papa, do you see that! and then I should enjoy your surprise, and I would keep my secret, to enjoy it again and again. That was my plan, but I could not carry it out. To think of keeping any thing happy from you! Oh! no. I could not do it."

Do you not suppose, reader, that listening to my beloved child, I forgot every misfortune, and could even bless the severe and untoward destiny which had developed such filial tenderness? .

CHAPTER IV.

SOL DOWNER.

MANY years before, I had known a man in my old business, prior to 1837. Our stores were adjoining, and on one occasion we were passengers together in this same vessel, the packet ship "Roscoe," to Liverpool. This person failed, and disappeared from business circles. Later he could be found in Wall-street, and I used to meet him frequently, and sometimes stopped to speak with him, for my heart warmed toward the man, because we had been neighbors; and it brought back the recollection of my early business life, and of the prosperous days before my first failure, when nobody was poor, and almost every one was making a fortune—on paper. Besides, we both had broke. I recovered, he never did, but after a while found his way into Wall-street, where he turned his hand to any thing and every thing out of which a commission could be carved. His name was Downer—Solomon Downer—and he was known in the street familiarly as Old Sol. His reputation of late years had become considerably damaged, and the terms, "Old Rip," "Old Scamp," "Old Knave," were freely applied to him. I never could learn what Solomon Downer was guilty of. If you asked for particulars you would be answered only by a fresh application of epithets.

"Wouldn't trust him as far as I could swing a bull by the tail," said one.

"Why not?"

"Give him a note to sell, and you will find out."

"Did he ever swindle you?"

"Me! do you think I would give him a chance?"

"Or any of your friends?"

"My friends are not so green."

"So you do not *know* any thing about him?"

"I know enough to give him a wide berth."

Notwithstanding these severe observations, I continued to exchange friendly greetings with my old acquaintance, and frequently entered into conversation with him when occasion presented. He had a shrewd biting manner when he talked with you, not exactly bitter, but keen and sharp. One could see that the man lived a life of perpetual alertness; as if always under martial law, and in constant expectation of an attack. So all humanizing qualities were kept under, lest they should afford an exposed point to the enemy.

Some days after my conclusion to take an office in Wall-street, for the purpose of acting as a broker between parties who wished to sell notes and acceptances, and those who would buy, I met Solomon Downer on the north-east corner of Wall and William streets, standing near the entrance to the Bank of New York. He stepped down to the side-walk as I came up, and we shook hands. I thought he looked rather more gaunt than usual, and his face thinner. I asked him how he was. He said he had been ill for two or three days. "Must keep stirring, though," he continued; "hunger wont wait, though I have had to—a man promised to meet me here at two, to give me the money for a note: now it's ten minutes to three."

A person here ran up in great haste, and asked some questions. "Not yet," was the answer.

"But what shall I do? I *must* have the money."

"Wait a few minutes."

"Few minutes be damned! I tell you I shall be protested; you have deceived me; kept me waiting all day; said I was going to have the money. Where is my note?" It was handed to him. "Guess you wont get another of mine into your hands very soon;" and off he ran, muttering something which sounded like "old swindler."

Solomon Downer resumed his conversation with me, as if he had experienced no interruption. "Yes, I have waited for the man since two o'clock, and if he comes now he wont do me any good: not in luck to-day."

"How do you like Wall-street?" I asked.

"How do I LIKE it; how would you like HELL!" he exclaimed almost fiercely. "Oh! I like it well enough," he continued, just as if he had made no previous answer; "yes, well enough. We all get along; it don't make much difference where we are. Plessis came to me the other day with the horrors: folks will have them, you know. 'My God, Sol,' says he, 'what am I to do? distress-warrant served this morning at eleven; my furniture will be turned out by three o'clock if I don't raise the money for the landlord. Sol, I am weary of it; worn out; used up; it's no use; I can't go on any longer.'

"'Why, Plessis,' says I, 'don't be discouraged; you've *got to* go on. I never new a man stick yet; sure to be kept a moving—ha, ha, ha! Don't mind it. Take it quiet—ha, ha, ha" You see Plessis wasn't toughened to it as I have been."

Thereupon I rather bluntly announced to my companion that I myself entertained the idea of engaging in a Wallstreet business. Solomon Downer turned square upon me, and caught hold of my arm.

"'Taint so. I swear I don't believe it. I knew of your failure, but you have not come to *that.*"

I nodded.

"Parkinson," said Downer looking at me earnestly, "Parkinson, I say, do you remember how once in company we made a voyage to Liverpool; both of us young men; active; educated to business, and honest, I guess? Do you remember how we used to talk together, those long evenings; hopeful, fresh in feeling, eager in pursuit? bah! now look at *me.* Well, never mind, but do you recollect among other things we both said we never would stay in a place where we had hopelessly failed? We agreed it was the only way, to strike out somewhere, try a new field, and so forth. We did not either of us believe we *should* fail. Every thing was gold in color then, but we talked wisely about misfortune, nevertheless. We had pleasant times after we landed," he continued. "If I remember right your wife was with you. God forgive me—you look—have you lost her? Well, be thankful. I was about to say, *I* have broken the resolution we esteemed so judicious: beware *you* don't break it."

"You have been unfortunate here perhaps," I said, "and you look on the gloomy side."

"I do, for both sides are gloomy. I don't suppose you will change your decision for any thing I can say. Indeed, why should you? Folks call me a rascal, Parkinson," said Downer after a pause, and in a careless tone, in strange contrast with his previous manner; "I know they do: you know it too. I suppose I do a good many things which would not bear clerical criticism, but I adapt myself to the company I keep, and so must you, if you come among us, or be plucked bare, and no larceny committed either. Lewis don't get hauled up by the police because he keeps a man till five minutes before three, in order to squeeze an extra percentage out of him, before giving him the money he knows he is bound to have. Jones gets up a corner in stocks, and beggars Smith, a poor outsider, who just steps in to try a hand; but Jones is not sent to Blackwell's Island. Now I have fought beasts at Ephesus from self-defence, *because I can't get out of the den.* And you want the grating opened to let you in! Well, good luck to you!" and Sol Downer turned and started rapidly away.

His advice did not much affect me. I had already decided, and why should the words of a man soured with his destiny overturn a carefully considered plan— a plan recommended by judicious persons?

CHAPTER V.

CLOSE CALCULATIONS.

I TOOK a small single room for an office. I was fortunate in getting it in an excellent locality, and at a comparatively moderate rent, in consequence of its forming the smallest of a large suite, occupied by a new coal company, which having no use for this, gave it to me at a bargain. A neat "tin," on which my name was modestly printed in gilt letters, was placed in the centre of the door. A roll of carpeting, which remained over at the auction unclaimed, was nicely fitted to the floor. I added a desk and some chairs, and a small table; and thus I embarked my small shallop on the sea of Wall-street life. I was to put in the market my business experience, my aptitude in affairs, and my facilities for negotiation derived from a large acquaintance with the mercantile class. I felt confident I could earn by legitimate industry in this way enough to support myself and my children.

I had counted over and over the probable expenses of our establishment per annum, beginning with "Rent," three hundred and fifty dollars, and going through every item of household expenditure—grocer, butcher, market-man, bread, milk, fuel, gas, water, clothing, schooling, omnibus, pew-rent, one servant. Alice availed herself of each week's experience to make some improvement whereby we lived a little better on the same sum, or reduced the amount to be expended. With fifteen hundred dollars, calculating very closely, Alice and I concluded we could get along. That was about thirty dollars a week. Could I earn thirty dollars each and every week, besides paying the rent of the office ? To do it I should have to make five dollars per day, one day with another. No allowance here for "extras;" a new book, or a ride, or a week out of town, a bottle of wine or a cigar. No. The first struggle was to live, and live decently. This was what I undertook to compass, by making the most of my intelligence, and my acquaintance with business and business men.

Fifteen hundred dollars a year does not seem a great deal to you, does it, my young friend, who are just embarking in mercantile business, with some capital and a good credit? You are just married, and you have no idea of limiting your expenses to so insignificant a sum, have you? Yet, if you should be forced to bring your expenditures within your actual profits, who knows if you would exceed that sum? Actually embarked in affairs—buying, selling, receiving, paying—you are not apt to distinguish between what belongs to you and what to your creditors. You dip into the general deposit, and help yourself to a living : more than that, you have your pleasures and your luxuries to pay for, and your wife has hers, all to come out of the bills receivable, and without any great regard to the bills payable : nay, more, while on your part this is generally mere thoughtlessness, occasionally some of you—I have myself heard it —will say : "Never mind. If I succeed it will be all right; if I don't, a few hundred dollars wont make much differ-

8

ence in a dividend among so many, and I shall have had the good of it!" In the first case it is inexcusable improvidence, in the last dishonesty. To live within your *available* means is the most sacred of obligations, and three-fourths of all the troubles and cares of life are from a violation of it.

I was forced to the adoption of the rule: "Earn before you eat." I could have wished for a little leeway, but I had none. It was true Alice was the possessor of five hundred dollars, and the knowledge of it was a source of great satisfaction to me. It relieved me of a most unhappy apprehension of what might befall us should I be taken ill, and be for a time unable to earn any thing. Unfortunately I had when a young man neglected to insure my life, and at this advanced period I could not afford to pay the premium on a comparatively moderate sum. I strove therefore with energy to *not die.* I must not leave these three children unprotected.

It was with considerable confidence, then, that I girded myself to the task of earning five dollars a day, and officerent. Alice was so cheerful, the arrangements of our little house were so complete, owing entirely to her good taste and assiduity; we were all of us so happy in each other, shut out from the world, and making a blessed heaven of our home, that I began to yield to these precious influences, and to feel a courage which I expected never again to regain.

The spring had put forth its early blossoms and green leaves; summer had come with its rich flowers and foliage, and early fruits; with its usual heats, too, sending away from the city those who can afford the expense of the relaxation, while I was endeavoring to decide what I should betake myself to for a support. It was late in the month of September when I did determine, as already narrated, on going into Wall-street. The equinoctial storm had passed. The bracing, yet genial air of a New York autumn—how glorious it is!—welcomed the returning denizens of the town, and made the pulse beat with a renewed strength. The streets once more assumed the appearance of great animation. The effects of the past calamitous season were nearly effaced. Every thing pointed to a promising fall trade. There were various indications of considerable speculative action in the stock-market, and among mining and railroad companies. Once more the genius of the Yankee nation was beginning to display its restless activity.

"Parkinson, you have just hit it," said Lecount to me; "couldn't have chosen a better time. You'll make a fortune, sure, if you keep your eyes about you."

CHAPTER VI.

SPLENDID OFFERS.

WHEN it was understood that Charles E. Parkinson was "going into the street," as the phrase is, the impression at the same time generally gained ground that the said Parkinson had money at his command—that is, the outsiders thought so; people who were familiar with the name of our firm and its extensive operations, but who were not acquainted with particulars. There were a good many, too, who entertained the idea that my wife left a large property which I held. The schemes which in consequence were presented on making my appearance among the operators, surprised even me, who was presumed to be well up in all that was going on in the city. Each of these enterprises required but a little money to give it an effectual foothold, and if I would make the advance my fortune was assured. One man had a plan for fertilizing the vacant lands on Long Island, which he said could be bought up at ten dollars an acre, and in twelve months sold for at least five hundred dollars. Another owned a coal mine in Maryland, and required only a thousand dollars to enable him to float a company. Another had an improvement scheme at Hoboken, and a fourth brought me a prospectus for establishing a society for the manufacture of the choicest toilet soap out of common bar. This last man wanted but a hundred dollars, and if I would raise it I was to be an equal partner in the business, with a permanent profit insured to me for my share, of just ninety dollars a week. Very comfortable.

There were also projects on foot for bringing under cultivation the vast and unexplored regions of Western Virginia, where lands could be had for from three to five cents an acre—title from the state! California had begun that year to tempt adventurers, and there were many schemes presented for traffic there.

I was at first completely surrounded by these various applicants, who fastened on me as mosquitos in a southern clime are said to assail new-comers from the north. Persons at my age are inclined to philosophize, and the first conclusion I arrived at was, that the majority of these individuals were honest, well-meaning enthusiasts, and in no sense sharpers or knaves. They were in the main people who were anxious to make a fortune at a stroke, and who believed they certainly would do so, just as soon as their scheme was taken up. Sometimes I was inclined to envy them the brightness of their prospects, the buoyancy of their hopes, and the elasticity of their natures. No rebuff nor discomfiture affected their spirits; the good day was surely coming, and their eyes brightened and their faces gleamed when they spoke of it. They were sorry, all of them, that I could not see the thing as they did; it was in vain I told them I had no money, and besides, it was out of my line. They knew that I knew where money could be found, and what matter how I made a fortune if it were done honestly? one happy stroke, one single investment, and a comfortable independence would be secured to me for the remainder of my days. Happy men, who see a golden prospect in every thing they undertake, who are discouraged by no disasters, whose ardor is damped by no disappointment; who, just as one project fails, are put in possession of another much more promising, and who live on under the encouragement of expectations the most brilliant and results the most sure. Sometimes people of this class chance on a valuable thing, but they reap little benefit from it. The profits are all absorbed by the capitalists, while they just as eagerly as ever set about some newer enterprise.

But it was not the class of harmless visionaries alone who beset me. I have already mentioned that the room I occupied was one of a suit taken by a newly launched coal company. This company occupied three apartments, expensively fitted up, with every appliance for facilitating transactions in their stock. As you entered, the first object which met your eye was the "transfer desk," behind which stood a handsome young man, fashionably dressed, apparently occupied with the books. You passed on along a line of counters, until you reached room number two, in which the company held their meetings. On one side of this was a very neat office for the president; on the other side was the little room which had been rented to me. ·

The Concordia Valley Coal Company—such was its corporate name—was evidently preparing for large operations; certainly from appearances there could be no lack of subscriptions or of paid-up capital. It was therefore with some considerable surprise on the first morning after taking possession of my office, that I received an invitation from the president to step into his private room. Accordingly, I followed the gentleman into his special apartment, which I found admirably carpeted and fitted up. On one side was a handsome lounge covered with morocco, on the other an expensive desk, with an arm-chair to match, besides a full supply of smaller furniture displayed around the room. There was a handsome map of the Concordia coal region on the wall, and several smaller ones, showing with picturesque effect the practical workings of this particular company in the famous Concordia Valley. Here was presented a section of the remarkable mine itself, where were toiling hundreds of men, all visible to the naked eye, getting out coal. An expensive double-track railroad received the product of various tram-roads, and, as per map number two, conveyed it to several first-class steamers, all the property of the company, and which lay at a fine dock near by on an expansive sheet of water, with steam on, and only waiting for the balance of the freight, to proceed to New York and report to the accomplished gentleman in whose presence I was. The gentleman himself was in perfect keeping with these surroundings. He might have been five-and-thirty, very handsomely but not foppishly dressed, if I may except a rather prominent display of a heavy gold watch-chain. His manner was easy, frank, and off-hand. He was one of those who always seem to manifest a magnetic appreciation of the position of every person he is brought in contact with, and at the same time to enter with an active sympathy into the presumed cares and annoyances of each.

As we came into the room Mr. Tremaine closed the door very carefully, asked me to be seated on the lounge, wheeled his large chair, which worked on the rotary principle, close to me; crossed his legs, swayed himself gently once or twice about the segment of a quarter of a circle, then bringing himself to a stand-still, with an arm resting on each arm of the chair, he commenced the conversation.

"Excuse my laying hold of you thus early, Mr. Parkinson," he began; "but I wished to talk with you about the prospects of our company before you become interested in any other enterprise. To be perfectly frank with you, I instructed Sewall (he was the broker through whom I rented my office) to give you that little room at half price, because I wanted you near us, Mr. Parkinson. I wanted to reap some benefit from your great and varied business experience, and I am sure you will excuse the little stratagem, since it has given you a very cheap rent, and as I avow the truth so frankly, you can hardly fear the effect of so direct an attempt on you."

Mr. Tremaine paused, as if to give additional force to his air of sincerity. For myself, I could only bow a pleasant acquiescence to his statement and wait quietly for what was to come.

"Now, Mr. Parkinson," he continued, "you understand the difficulty in *starting* any valuable enterprise. We have got on thus far better even than could be expected. But we must now make an extraordinary effort, and it is on this point that I wish to bring you into our consultations. Of course, you will consider whatever is said as strictly confidential. I am sure I can rely on you."

It seemed to me as if this was a proper time to interrupt Mr. Tremaine's "confidential" communication. So I stopped him as he was about to proceed, and began to explain that in coming into Wall-street I had but one object in view, and proposed to myself but one way to compass it. I had determined to adhere to a single business; and since I had positively no money to invest in any enterprise, my time must be devoted to this one.

I was proceeding still further, when Mr. Tremaine in his turn interrupted me with: "Really, Mr. Parkinson, you quite mistake me. Do not suppose for an instant that I have the least idea of presenting any thing to you which shall take your money, or more of your time than you are quite willing to bestow. Do you think, even if I were disposed to draw in any human being, and God knows nothing is further from my thoughts, that I should begin with an old, experienced New York merchant? No, no, not quite that. So I am sure you will at least give me a hearing."

Thereupon Mr. Tremaine went on to explain how the Company had control of seven thousand acres of choice bituminous coal lands, located within three miles of navigable waters, to which by an easy and level access a railroad could be built at a small expense. The coal was of the best quality—so good that the Cunard Company was ready to enter into a contract to take their whole supply from the Concordia Valley Company as soon as it was ready to furnish it.

From further explanations of Mr. Tremaine, it appeared that the capital of the company was two millions of dollars. Of this, one million four hundred thousand dollars were represented by the seven thousand acres of land, which the proprietors generously put at the very low sum

S*

of two hundred dollars per acre. Three hundred thousand
dollars were appropriated as active capital for the building
of the railroad and a wharf, and opening the mine, and the
remaining three hundred thousand dollars were held for a
reserve fund.

It was further explained to me, in the strictest confidence
too, that the stock of the company was already quoted at
the board, through the influence of one of the members,
who was to be interested in the future operations, and that
as a matter of policy, considerable transactions were carried
on from time to time, and the stock allowed to fluctuate two
or three per cent. with the hope after a while of getting
outsiders to take hold of it. This Mr. Tremaine admitted
was rather expensive, since it would not do to let the small
brokers, who were intrusted with the purchases and sales,
into the secret, so every transaction cost the company at
least one-eighth per cent., and sometimes a quarter. Still, .
this was the only way. Indeed, could the company now
raise the trifling sum of fifty thousand dollars, the railroad
could be built, and coal actually sent to market! The moment traffic was reported, a dividend could be declared, if
necessary, out of the reserve stock, and sufficient of the two
millions launched on the street to make the company perfectly easy in its transactions, and the projectors rich men.

Up to this point it did not transpire what was to be my
own special agency in bringing about so pleasing a consum-
mation. But I was not long to remain in ignorance or sus-
pense, for Mr. Tremaine, after one of his impressive pauses,
continued in this wise:

"Now, Mr. Parkinson, I think I have succeeded in satis-

fying you that our enterprise is strictly a legitimate one—
that is, it can stand on its intrinsic merits, and on strict
commercial principles. The lands are worth all that is
claimed for them. The expense of transportation can be
calculated to a penny. We know just what it costs to deliver the coal on board the steamers, and what it will bring
in New York. And you must be convinced that when we
are in full operation we can readily divide from ten to fifteen
per cent. on our capital of two millions. Now, I repeat, my
object is to interest you in this great enterprise. Perhaps
you will say, if such are its advantages, why have not the
capitalists taken hold of it? My dear sir, do you think I
would present it to *them?* Why, I could raise what money
we required in half an hour, but they would insist on the
lion's share—you know it is so—and lick up all the profits,
and leave us just where we began. No, no, we can't quite
stand that; but we are willing to divide fairly with those
who help to raise the necessary funds; and my proposition
is, that I will issue to you a hundred thousand dollars of
our stock, for which you shall raise us ten thousand dollars
cash. In other words, you get your stock for ten cents on
the dollar. The company will guarantee that every dollar
of this money shall be employed for the building of the
road, and you must agree not to put your stock in the market except in conjunction with our own operations, *pro rata*,
the usual way, you know."

"But, my dear sir, I have just explained to you that I
have no money to invest ——"

"And I," interrupted Mr. Tremaine, "assured you that
we did not want *your* money. But you have a large circle

of influential friends, Mr. Parkinson, who will be only too happy to take a thousand or two dollars at par on your recommendation. Why, as money is now working, I have no doubt you can raise the whole sum in a week; and see what a brilliant stroke it will be for you. I know what you are thinking about," continued this frank and earnest-hearted man; "the affair strikes you as too good. I know it, but I can't help it—there it is. We have got the lands; that is the point, and we are willing to dispose of five hundred thousand dollars at ten per cent. rather than give up to the capitalists. We shall still retain the three hundred thousand dollars as a reserve fund. Now, you have it all in the strictest confidence—do not forget, Mr. Parkinson, in the strictest confidence."

Reader, there is something fascinating and most pleasantly bewildering in these charming schemes which promise so golden a future. As the weary and thirsty traveller in the desert is constantly allured to various quarters of the horizon by images of shady groves and cool fountains, so in the great desert which poverty creates, there is ever present the same wonderful mirage where the poor wretch sees again a happy home and the return of life's pleasurable luxuries, and enjoys in prospect his seasons of ease. We are tenacious in our memories of past good fortune, and are apt to be desperate in our attempts to regain it. The man who has lost his property walks moodily along of an afternoon, and sees his old acquaintances driving out for an airing on the avenues. The very posture which these people innocently enough adopt, annoys and irritates him. The quiet but very conscious *abandon* of mamma and her daughter, the

not easy but entirely self-satisfied air of papa, as he folds
his arms and looks with careless unconcern upon vacancy,
while the coachman, carriage and horses are in perfect keeping with the *pose* of master and mistress. Well, what
wonder that the unfortunate are willing to attempt much,
and venture much to regain their lost position? what wonder that they desperately grasp at the phantoms which al-
lure them with promises of renewed fortunes?

While the last tones of Mr. Tremaine fell on my ear, the
room seemed to dance round and round, and the maps of
the Concordia Valley Coal Company were converted into .
one grand, magnificent tableau, revolving swiftly, but growing larger and brighter each revolution. Ninety thousand
dollars of the stock! Ten per cent. dividend! A clear
rental of nine thousand dollars per annum! Why not?
The most successful enterprises are from small and difficult
beginnings. . . . . The bland tones of Mr. Tremaine
once more fell on my ear, and recalled me to myself. " I
perceive, Mr. Parkinson, that you are carefully considering
this matter. Don't let me press you to a decision : take
time and think the affair over, and if any question arises, or
any objections to the plan occur to you, let me hear them
frankly, and I am certain I can fully satisfy you."

I had recovered myself. Instead of the nine thousand
dollars a year dividends from coal stock, the more practical
and pressing requirement of five dollars a day rose up to
view. But while I had too much sagacity not to understand the absolutely chimerical nature of these propositions,
yet, so much do we love to cheat ourselves with some sweet
delusion, I did not decline his proposition : I even said I

would consider it; and I left Mr. Tremaine's office feeling
as if I was in some sort a man of substance, with an option
at my disposal, and a considerable stake in the valuable coal
regions of Concordia Valley.

CHAPTER VII.

THE USURER.

RETURNING home that afternoon, after my first day's trial, Alice ran to open the door.

"How much have you made, papa?" she exclaimed, in a confident tone.

I kissed her, and answered cheerfully as possible: "I declare, Alice, one would think it was little Anna talking, instead of a grown-up girl. Patience: it will take a week or two at least for me to get to work, and then you may expect to hear something."

"What a goose I am! I ought to have known that. But we have been talking so much about Wall-street that I suppose I was calculating on your picking up money there. Never mind, the best dinner you have had for a long time is ready this minute. It is in honor of your commencing business again. Ah! papa, how happy I am!" and humming a favorite air, she pushed me into the room, where I was seized by the two younger children, and dragged to the table. My felicity at that moment was supreme. I was honestly grateful to God who had so ordained it, that the wealth of the heart, like the riches of free grace, is open to all who choose to cultivate the treasure.

. . . .

What binds us to our children; what binds them so to

us ? It is, aside from instinctive attachment, which amounts to but little, because we regard each other always and invariably in the strong light of affection, which makes us alive to whatever is pleasing, and good, and charitable toward any thing which is the reverse in our conduct or dispositions. Now, could this be extended outside the circle of our homes, what a change would come over the form and habit of this old world! It would not be a bad state of things, would it, where every man regards his neighbor with kindness and good-will; always recognizing what is good in him, and always considerate toward what is reprehensible ? Would it not seem strange to see everybody turning short about, and trying to help everybody in every possible way ? Delane says it would'nt pay, but Delane is mistaken; it would pay in the long run, but selfish people can't be made to understand it.

. . . .

I soon found myself beset with a crowd of the smallest kind of note-brokers, or rather of runners, if I may use the term, who, believing that I could command more or less cash, attempted to palm off on me all sorts of worthless paper. Most of my readers are doubtless entirely ignorant of the various expedients employed to raise the wind, as it is called, by the unscrupulous and the desperate. Frequently, where a sale would be impossible, they attempt to borrow a comparatively small sum on a large amount of notes, or acceptances; the lender, unless very shrewd and experienced, being seduced by the great margin into the belief that the loan will certainly be taken up, and his heavy "shave" secured. But the auspicious day never arrives.

The operator having borrowed three or four hundred dollars on as many thousands of "collaterals," takes no further trouble about the loan, but immediately procures a fresh supply of "paper," for the signatures cost him nothing, being executed perhaps by some relation who is "under age," or some mythical personage so obscure that he may with impunity defy civil process.

Finding after repeated efforts that nothing was to be made out of me, these people let me alone. Meanwhile I had myself something to do besides beating off applicants for my supposed capital. I found after considerable observation, that what is called first and second class paper is readily disposed of at a current rate, while lower grades are difficult to negotiate, and depend on the brokers finding some person who happens to know the parties, and is satisfied of their position. There are, however, individuals in Wall-street who seldom purchase any thing better than third-class paper, taking pains to inform themselves specially about it. Such invariably charge two per cent. a month, and from that *up*, and thus accumulate large fortunes.

It may seem strange to you, reader, but it is nevertheless true, that there are men who spend their whole lives in Wall-street, and who do nothing else but buy notes. They come in early and go out late. Their time is occupied in making fresh inquiries, and in haggling about the rate per cent. You can to-day see these persons, if you will take the trouble to station yourself on the spot, and I predict you will behold what will deeply interest you. Wait a few moments near this corner, and you will not be disappointed. There he comes, passing thoughtfully along the street. He has the appearance of a man laden with many cares. Look at him! He is respectably encased in a moderately worn suit of black. His head inclines forward; his eye has become stony; his nose pointed; his chin angular; his cheeks rigid; his lips wooden; his mind—alas! he has no longer any mind, but in place of mind he possesses an instinct so subtle and acute that it will detect a piece of "made" paper in the very curl of the signature. As to his soul—ah! GOD, how rayless and emotionless it is!

Go to this man with something which does not exactly suit him, he will catechize you half an hour, putting questions which nothing but a great hope of ultimate success induces you to tolerate, when, just as you are expecting a check for the desired amount, he tells you quietly he does not want the paper. This person sympathizes with no human being. He has not a single human attribute left. "Does he never," you ask, "in some silent, solitary moment, perchance during some wakeful hour by night; does he *never* think of the time when he was a child, and learned to lisp his prayers, and repeat his little hymns; or later when he was at school, playing as other boys play; or when he married that tender young girl, to whom he promised so much before heaven, and whom he has since killed by his hard, stony nature?" No; he never does! Such terrible compensation does PROVIDENCE exact from this entire surrender to mammon.

If you wish to see more of this sort, go and take a seat for an hour or two in one of the many small note-brokers' offices, which abound, and watch the arrival of others of these paper-sharks. They come in hungry, eager, sharp, to hear and see what new offers. They have a large capital, perhaps hundreds of thousands of dollars, invested in notes, or represented by securities, which can be converted into cash in twenty-four hours, should it be required to buy more paper with. They are always mousing about to pick up the note of some good mechanic, who they know for certain reasons is hard-up, and who is willing to bleed freely rather than to fail in a contract. Thus they drain the life-blood of the industrious; and compounding their profits day after day, they work at their disreputable business till Death, who always wins in the end, overtakes them, and they are cut short in their cold-blooded and wicked work.

I am of opinion that money should command, like any other commodity, its market value, yet it is unlike any other; since it is the standard of value of all commodities, and cannot be the subject of sale, but only of hire; and the rules which control it depend on many contingencies, which prove unfortunate for the borrower. But it is not market value which the note-shaver takes advantage of. He detests a market. It interferes with his plans. For he speculates not out of the risk he runs, but out of his customers' necessities. It is an undeniable fact, the man who drives the *trade* of usurer has been branded as ignominious from the earliest history of civilized transactions to the present time.* There is no occupation which so darkens the soul, blunts the affections, shuts out all that is human, and retains all that is selfish and devilish, as that of the man who devotes himself to accumulating by usurious gains. I speak from what I have seen and known.

* "He that by usury and unjust gain increaseth his substance, he shall gather it for him that will pity the poor."—*Proverbs* xxviii., 8.

Pursuing my inquiries, I found it was the habit of many of our best merchants, whenever they had more money on hand than they had occasion for, to buy first-class paper as an investment; such merchants generally made their purchases through one broker, who regarded them as his constituents. Then there were capitalists who usually invested in stocks, or bonds and mortgages, yet who from time to time, as favorable opportunities presented, made large purchases of commercial paper. The banks too in easy seasons were bidders. But between the better grades of paper and the poorer a great gulf is fixed. The first, as I have said, goes at market value; the latter having no market value, affords rare chances for cut-throat rates.

CHAPTER VIII.

AN UNLOOKED FOR OCCURRENCE.

Such, then, was the sea on which I was to adventure; and Saturday morning, which would complete my first week in the street, found me without having made a single negotiation, or having earned a single dollar. During this week I had had no conversation with Sol Downer. It is true I met him several times, but I thought he rather avoided me. At any rate, I did not feel inclined to cultivate a greater intimacy with him, and perhaps he perceived it.

On this Saturday morning, coming into my office a little past eleven o'clock, after a few moments' absence, I found him standing in the centre of the room, as if impatient for my return. I don't know why, but I was annoyed at the sight of him. Perhaps I remembered our last conversation, and thought of my ill-success during the week. Perhaps I had formed some inchoate resolution to rather avoid Downer as an unlucky associate. Whatever it was, I repeat, I was annoyed at seeing him stand there, and I believe my countenance showed it. If it did, Solomon Downer took no notice of it, but approached me hurriedly as I entered, and placing a note in my hand, exclaimed: "Take that over to the Bank of Credit; they'll do it for you, and we will divide the commission."

I looked at the note, and found it was for over four thousand dollars. The makers I did not know, although I recognized the endorsers as highly respectable.

"Why do you hesitate?" said Downer, who saw I made no haste to carry out his suggestion.

"I do not know the paper," was my reply, "and——"

"Supposing you don't," said my visitor impatiently, "what the devil has that to do with it if the bank *does* know it?"

I suppose I colored at this rough answer, for Downer instantly added in a milder tone: "For heaven's sake make haste, Parkinson. I *must* make a little money to-day. I can keep this note just fifteen minutes and no longer. *I* know that the Bank of Credit has plenty of money. I know too that this is just such paper as they want. It is offered at seven per cent, and a quarter per cent. commission. That's but a trifle, but it's quick done."

By this time I fully understood the matter, and turning, started off immediately for the bank. Downer ran after me, and called out, as I got near the stairs: "Try them at six per cent; that's all money's worth, and this is A 1, and no mistake."

I walked rapidly along toward the bank, not quite satisfied I was going on a successful errand, since I was not acquainted with the names of the makers of the note, yet having a sort of confidence in the unqualified assertion of Downer. The president was fortunately in, I handed him the little "piece of paper," saying, I believed it would be acceptable. He looked at it, turned it over to regard the endorsement, and said quietly: "We will pass this for you, Mr. Parkinson."

"At six per cent.?"

"We will say six and a half."

Thereupon he rose, and stepped to the discount-clerk, said a word to him, came back, remarking, "He will tell you the amount in a few moments," and resumed his occupation, while I went round to the clerk's counter to wait for the computation.

We are weak creatures. I cannot describe the almost delirious happiness of that moment. The gratitude I felt toward the president was extravagant, unbounded. In truth, however, I had conferred a favor on the bank, as well as receiving one myself, by taking them a prime note when they had idle surplus funds. But I was too much elated to look at the affair in that light. I flattered myself that something of my old influence was left; at any rate, that the president regarded me with especial favor and kindness. I ought to have remembered that when money is abundant the faces of bank officers are wreathed in smiles, and they seem to be your fast friends forever-and-a-day. But when money is in demand, wonderful is their altered demeanor; strange how they forget you.

In ten minutes I was on my way back, with the money in my hand. I found Downer pacing up and down the room in a state of great excitement.

"Have you got it ?" he exclaimed.

"Yes."

"Good GOD! you don't say so ; but I knew they would jump at it. - Here, just give me the amount, less discount and commission. I have calculated it while you were gone, and I will come back presently, and we can then divide."

Thereupon I handed him the required sum, and he ran off at great speed.

Meanwhile, I sat down to count the treasure in hand, and which on Downer's return we were to share. How much larger this looked than the four thousand four hundred dollars, which I had surrendered! The quarter per cent. commission amounted to eleven dollars and ten cents. It was a four months note, and the difference between seven and six and a half per cent. was seven dollars and forty cents. Total, eighteen dollars and fifty cents. My half, nine dollars and a quarter.

I was in the midst of this pleasing computation when Sol Downer returned, still much excited, with the appearance of a man who had ventured on a great risk, and had had a narrow escape. I could not help feeling that there was some mystery about the affair. Considering poor Downer's unfortunate reputation, how did he come by a first-class note, one which any banker would be ready to take? Who would employ him on such a service? These thoughts were passing through my mind while I was busy ascertaining the profits of the transaction, and which his return interrupted, as I have just observed. He came in, sat down, took off his hat, and with his handkerchief wiped away the perspiration which stood thick on his forehead.

"I wonder what that famous house would say if they knew I had negotiated one of their notes? and he laughed significantly.

I made no reply.

"Wouldn't you like to know how I got hold of it?" he asked.

"Yes."

"Well, I had got desperate. It was Saturday, and I must take home four or five dollars, so I went in to Brest and Company's, and asked them if they had any big notes of A 1 houses, as I knew an individual who would like to invest four or five thousand dollars. I saw the list, and a young man who stood by gave me permission to look over the paper. I asked the best rate for the note I brought you, for I knew the Bank of Credit would discount it if offered by a respectable party, and found I could get a quarter per cent. out of it, besides legal interest. I told the young man I would return in fifteen minutes with the money, and to tell you the truth, Parkinson, I brought away the note without his knowing it."

"Good Heavens! it is not possible."

"Oh! it is very possible, and when *you* come to be driven from one corner to another, you will be surprised what expedients you will resort to, to keep from starving. Yes, a man will venture a good deal before he will let— *women and children go hungry.*"

"But finish your story."

"Certainly. You know what took place with you. We did make first-rate work of it. I was absent from Brest and Company's just twenty minutes. Wasn't there a storm brewing up there? Fortunately they had discovered the note was missing only five minutes before. Every thing was in confusion. Of course I was the vagabond who had abstracted it. The young man was saying he gave me no permission even to look at the paper; only at the list. Another minute a police-officer would have been on my

9

track. I stepped coolly in with the money in my hand. Cash has a scothing influence. I marched up boldly to the desk of the principal. 'I promised,' said I, 'to return in fifteen minutes. I am five minutes behind my time. Here is a statement of the discount and commission (I had prepared it while you were at the bank, you know), and here is the money.' Old Brest is too shrewd a man to get up a row when there is nothing to quarrel about, and no harm done. So, without saying one word, he took the money and the statement, compared the latter with his own memorandum, and after two or three minutes growled out, 'All right,' and I quit. Close shaving though; wouldn't like to try it again."

"But tell me why did you do such a thing? You committed a criminal act."

"Ay! that's the talk," exclaimed Downer, "of you respectable people. Criminal offence! Do you suppose, had I missed seeing you, I would have failed to run back with the note? And having got the money, did I not hasten to hand it over? Wait a little, and see if you will tread always on velvet scruples. Don't I know Old Brest? Don't I know how he made a smash-up ten years ago, and how he got started in this business, in which he's coining money? Oh! yes, it's all correct with him, but I am a damned scoundrel, of course."

I saw that Downer was getting into his old strain of bitterness, and I endeavored to say what would soothe him. In this I partially succeeded. And then I showed him the exact amount I had, and handed him nine dollars and a quarter as his share. Sol Downer would not take it.

"What I want," he said, "is five dollars and fifty-five cents. I have nothing to do with what you have made by getting the note done at a better rate. My offer was, discount at seven per cent. and divide commission with you. Won't take it," he persisted. "This serves me for to-day. If it didn't, I would not mind, under the circumstances, borrowing a couple of dollars of you." So saying, he left the room, leaving the balance of the money on the table.

In this way my share was increased to twelve dollars and ninety-five cents. How *good* it looked as I counted it over and over. Reader, do you think I was beside myself? I, who all my business life was dealing in thousands and tens of thousands, yes, hundreds of thousands, to be thus carried away by the sight of twelve dollars and ninety-five cents in . hand? If you do you know little of the "uses of adversity."

Never did money seem so sweet as that. I had *earned* it—the very first gains since my great break-down. In former business operations, when I made large profits, they went into the general account, and were, to be sure, so much to the credit of our concern. But this twelve dollars and ninety-five cents I could touch, I could handle. I could calculate what it would pay, how far it would go. I thought how pleased Alice would be—for she had delicately forborne to question me after that first day when I led her not to expect any thing for a week or two. Then my thoughts ran back to the operation of the morning. It struck me it would be dangerous to have any more business with Downer. Yet had it not been for him I should not now be rejoicing. Had he not acted honorably, nay, gen-

erously with me ? Was not his condition rather that of an
unfortunate wretch at bay, with the odds against him ?

After a while I took my hat, went into the street, and
talked pleasantly with several acquaintances about affairs.
Then I walked back to my office, ate the lunch which Alice
always prepared for me, and determined to give myself a
holiday for the remainder of the afternoon. Descending, I
indulged in a glass of ale. I purchased a few figs for Charlie,
some raisins for Anna, and a bunch of grapes to "divide."
For Alice I bought a pair of small side-combs, which I knew
she wanted very much. Thus equipped, I turned into Broadway, and joined the crowd of human beings which throng
this extraordinary thoroughfare. It has since occurred to
me how entirely we are carried away with what is immediately present. The fortunate circumstance of making a
small sum after a week of fruitless exertion, seemed for the
moment to dispel all anxiety for the future. I felt very
comfortable, and returned the salutations of my acquaintances with a feeling of quiet assurance. Thus I strolled
along until I came opposite my old house. I stopped and
looked at it a moment, and went on. I had triumphed. I
had no regrets. I felt in my soul that what I had passed
through, and what I was to encounter in the future, would
give to me a moral strength, and truer ideas of life and its
purposes. So I went away from the spot where I had enjoyed so much of this world's good, and continuing my
walk, at length turned the corner near my house. The two
younger children were playing on the steps, there being no
school on Saturday. They ran joyfully to greet my unexpected arrival. Going in, I summoned Alice, who was

assisting in preparation for the dinner. Sitting down near the table, I produced my little store. "Papa has treated himself," I said, "to a part of a holiday, and there is something to show that he has not forgotten the children." Alice received the combs as a token of good fortune, the rest went quietly to work with the fruit.

"You have made some money, I know you have by your looks, papa; and it's only a week!"

CHAPTER IX.

THE ACTUAL.

THOSE who, attracted by the title of these papers, have taken them up with the expectation of reading "startling developments," "wonderful disclosures," "remarkable confessions," or fancied in the various descriptions they would be able to see through the gauze covering which should lightly mask a battery of satire upon certain notabilities of various grades, have ere this laid the *undercurrents* aside, disappointed, and probably in disgust. For, in presenting a narrative of some periods of my life, I have no animosity to gratify, no wounded pride to revenge, no shaft of ridicule to launch, and indeed nothing but the simple truth to record. Whoever shall recognize me through the name I have assumed, and happen to recall any of the incidents I now publish, will bear witness that I write with no malice and without exaggeration. We are all jogging along together. The various circumstances which now serve for daily excitement will soon pass and be forgotten; but the relations of one man to another, and of one set of men to another set of men, extend through generations, affecting our whole social life. What we want now, it seems to me, is to be introduced to the actual. What lies as substratum? What is the original necessity, and what the conventional? The various classes of mankind are all occupied. What are they about? To find out is the present fascination.

One man drives to his office in Wall-street in a handsome carriage. How did he get that carriage, or rather, how was the money acquired that paid for it? He spends a few hours there, signs his name to several bits of paper, which put in motion various pieces of machinery, which produce for him certain valuable results. Satisfied with these results, and very complacent with the day's operation, he goes back to his house, dines sumptuously, drinks his wine, smokes his cigars, attends the opera; and this is the history of that man's life, from one year to another, and the man himself is one of a species.

Another trudges to Wall-street a poor, unfortunate wretch with a family, in circumstances the most straitened. He is a better educated man than the first, has a more cultivated taste, is honester—worth more for soul and brain anywhere. Standing side by side before GOD, this is so. Looking at both, away from so dread a tribunal, we see one clad in garments originally expensive, but carefully brushed till they are threadbare. We behold a face exhibiting traces of much mental suffering. We observe in the lines which mark it evidences of the struggles of the man as he resisted, step by step, the fate which was in store for him. We all remember the story of the prisoner who fancied one morning, as he awoke, that the walls of the lofty apartment in which he was confined did not seem as high as usual. Regarding the number of apertures in his grated window, he discovered the next morning one less. Another had disappeared the following day, and while he was reflecting on the singular circumstance, the terrible truth burst on him, that by the slow but sure action of the machinery which controlled the movable iron ceiling, he was to meet his death. Day by day it descended nearer and nearer. There was no escape—no hope of an escape. The man we are looking at is in the same sort of prison-house. His fate is just as certain, the machinery which is to crush him just as effectual. And he knows it. That is the meaning of those lines over the countenance and that despairing expression.

But the other man? The man who signs bits of papers, who moves fortunes by the employment of his name; whose face, without any lines of care or disappointment, shows that he is at ease in Bank as well as in Zion? This person, by a long and successful career of good fortune, is so well grounded in his own esteem, that his self-complacency is at times painful to witness. How patronizing he is, how jocose, how pleasingly familiar, how hard and overbearing, as by turns he comes in contact with different classes and conditions! What does such a man understand about the great objects and purposes of life? What have his operations in the stock-market, his transactions in bills of exchange, his advances on good security, taught him about the first question in the catechism: "What is the chief end of man?" By the light he lives and works by, how would he answer it?

Now let us have an introduction to these people with fortunes and habits so different. Put the novelists and romance-writers aside. We do not want any hot-house developments, any big, horrid villains, any sweet, charming bread-and-butter saints. Away with caricatures and exaggerations!

Let us look at Harris and Williams, and Brown and Johnson, and Jones and Smith, and see what they do ; how, as types of their class, they get a living. For the fellow who works with those aforesaid pieces of paper claims in a sense to get a living, to make money, whereby he lives and pays for houses and horses and opera-boxes, and his—pleasures.

These investigations will serve to bring the fortunate and the unfortunate nearer each other ; as it is, there is a great abyss between them. If we could bridge it over and mix them up a little, it would not do any harm. It might do some good. After these "Undercurrents" of mine are concluded, I propose to present a volume to several of our well-known philanthropists : that class of philanthropists who, born with a silver spoon in their mouth, and without much masculinity, and having been educated by good pious parents and left with large fortunes, are persuaded they have a mission to perform here below before they are translated into heaven. These distinguished persons are life-members of the Bible Society, the Home Missionary Society, the Foreign Missionary Society, the Tract Society, and the Colonization Society. They preside at meetings, they head subscription-lists, they occupy prominent positions in the church ; and, notwithstanding these important engagements, they do not know what to do with their time or their money. They are moral, and wont spend either in the pleasures of this life, for this sort of things don't suit their temperament. So they take to courses more sedate, and which will give them an enviable prominence before the world.

Now, as I have just said, I intend to attempt to interest these worthy people in the situation of Wall-street. I am

9*

persuaded they can do more there than with the Five Points Mission. Why will they not try? Perhaps they will.

Again, a very genuine philanthropist as I believe, Mr. Horace Greeley, has made public his plan, and a good one it is, for the relief of the overcrowded streets of New York. "Flee from the city," he exclaims. "Go to the country. Return to first principles. Cultivate the soil." But how to do it? Grant that it was an unwise step that fixed the individual *in* the city, how is he to escape now? Of what use to tell the sufferer, who has a family dependent on him, and who barely manages to keep them alive: "Friend, leave this place; you are not working out your proper destiny here. Go into the rural districts; to the far West, if you prefer, where lands are cheap, and begin anew." Why, this man can by no possibility get five dollars ahead. His furniture would not bring at auction two hundred, and it is mortgaged besides to some kind friend who lent him money in a pressing emergency. I repeat, this man is chained down, held fast; he can't escape, and Mr. Greeley's plan don't help him.

We once read of a banker's safe so cunningly contrived, that when a burglar attempts the lock, he disturbs a secret spring, and suddenly iron arms are protruded, which clutch the terrified wretch, and hold him in a fatal embrace. It is so with the miserable man who ventures to tamper with that great money-safe—Wall-street. He is seized and held secure, and sentenced to perpetual imprisonment, with hard labor, in the service of the proprietors. Will not Mr. Greeley aid in getting up a society for the relief of those unfortunate persons who want to quit the spot and cannot? For my part, had

I a hundred thousand dollars to dispose of to-day, I would select twenty or thirty sufferers, whom I have known in the street for twenty-five years, and make them happy. Some theoretical individuals would object to this because the proposed course lacks "plan and system," and is not grounded on "principle." It would only do a few people a great good, but would confirm no favorite theory, and would be carried out without the aid of the complicated machinery of any society!

CHAPTER X.

HARLEY.

AFTER a while I began to get reconciled to the peculiarities of my Wall-street life! Indeed the excitement of it was not without its charm. The sharp necessity of realizing a certain sum, disappointment in one quarter, success in another, the hour's uncertainty, the petty crisis—to me not petty—repeated day after day, not only accustomed me to these fluctuations, but they became in some sort agreeable ; that is, in the sense that all stirring sensations are so. This was, however, while I was achieving a species of success. And I was thus taught that there is rarely an occupation disagreeable to man by which he makes money. My desires were very humble. I wanted only to earn a living. After a few weeks, by much industry and painstaking, I learned the condition of the note-market; and by the aid of my reputation for strict integrity, I acquired the confidence of various parties, and was thus enabled frequently to exceed the moderate sum necessary for our support. Meantime I looked with feelings of pity on the poor wretches wandering about the street, eager to seize on some chance to clear a few dollars.

Since the operation with the four thousand dollar note, I endeavored quietly to avoid Downer. I cannot say he made any effort to prevent it. At any rate, he never came again to my office. One Saturday, I had been more than usually successful; I stood in the door of one of the banks, with a roll of bills in my hands; turning around, I saw Downer looking at me from the corner. He started off immediately on seeing that I noticed him. My heart smote me, I know not why, and I took a few steps in his direction, with a view to offer him a part of my store if he stood in need of it; but a selfish prudence overcame the benevolent intent, and I stopped short, none the better at heart for not keeping on.

About this time I made a new acquaintance. I had laid by, over and above the sum set apart for our support, two hundred and fifty dollars. This I gave to Alice, who kept it carefully in a private drawer. The possession of this sum made me feel like a different creature. Never in my palmiest days did the heaviest balance in bank so exhilarate me as this two hundred and fifty dollars. Five hundred dollars in the savings bank for Alice; two hundred and fifty dollars in her escritoire; business good, and new channels opening. Besides, that law-suit with Bulldog is sure to go in our favor. Norwood says so. Well, well, the world is not so bad after all. People who *will* make mistakes must suffer accordingly, but the prudent——

I was saying, about this time I made a new acquaintance. It happened in this wise. One afternoon, about two o'clock, while I was seated in my office, after having made one or two very good negotiations, a gentleman entered, and exhibited a note for nearly a thousand dollars, which he asked if I could get discounted. I recollect the figures now. They were all odd numbers—$979\frac{37}{100}$, three months to run. I never fancied odd numbers, and the style of the note did

not please me.* Seeing me hesitate, the person remarked:
"Excuse me, I perceive I am not known to you. My name
is Harley. Our mutual friend Alworthy (one of the makers
of the note) advised me to come directly to you, and gave
me permission to use his name. 'Since the note is in the
market,' he said, 'I recommend you to my friend Mr. Parkinson, who will get it done for you without hawking it
about the street.'"

I tried to call to mind how intimate my acquaintance was
with Mr. Alworthy. I knew him as the senior partner in an
extensive commission house, whose transactions were generally large, and whose operations were very bold. There
was no intimacy between us, and his sending to me seemed
a little apocryphal. Still the paper would sell, and why
should I trouble my head further about it? I had two
places where I thought I could dispose of it. I paused a
moment to consider which I should first try, and then innocently enough asked: "Have you any more of this?" My
visitor colored, and for an instant appeared to lose the tranquil and imperturbable manner which had hitherto distinguished him. It was for an instant. He recovered with so
much ingenuousness, and put himself at once so confidentially in relation with me, that I was charmed with him.

"I will be truthful with you, sir!" he exclaimed. "The
fact is, I have a pretty large amount of this paper. I did

* There is a great difference in the appearance of commercial paper. It is frequently
remarked of a man, that he makes a "good signature;" that is, a signature which in-
spires confidence. There are some who really judge a good deal by the "looks" of a
note or acceptance. "I don't like it; think 'twas 'got up,'" said an experienced note-
shaver once to me, apropos of a piece of paper I offered him. This might have been
mere caprice, but it was useless opposing it. Again I know many who delight in
"odd numbers," who think there is "luck" in them; and others whose fancy runs the
other way.

not intend to offer you any more, however. But since you have inquired, I shall tell you precisely. You will perceive that this note is indorsed by Pollock, Pemberton, Hollis and Company. Perhaps you know the house?"

I confessed I did not.

" Well, that is not to be wondered at, since it was established only last May. They are old personal friends of mine. Very enterprising, ample capital, and will do a very large commission business. By the way, I should like you to know them; the acquaintance might prove mutually beneficial. Such a house is always taking a large amount of marketable paper, and it would be well to have them as customers; for you know the banks will only do about so much."

While Mr. Harley was laying this benevolent plan for my advantage, I had leisure to observe him more carefully. He was apparently thirty years old, of medium height, possibly a little below, stout, but not corpulent, handsomely dressed, yet not in a manner indicating any special attention. He had clear, intelligent blue eyes, a pleasing face, open and ingenuous, without any of that affectation of sincerity which one could detect in Mr. Tremaine. In fact, I was insensibly drawn toward the man, and the suggestions he was making for my benefit seemed so natural, that I forgot I had never seen him before, and now for only ten minutes.

" But," continued Mr. Harley, as if recollecting himself, " we were talking of how much paper I could offer you of this description. I have about nine thousand dollars, and really, I do not see why you cannot manage the whole of it—quietly, you know, so as not to hurt the credit of the parties."

Just then the question occurred to me : " What interest or agency have you, Mr. Harley, in this business ?" I had scarcely thought thus much, when I found my new friend was about to give me an opportunity to touch the point.

" Yes, I am sure it is best to do these things through one person ; and, as I was saying, Alworthy knowing of course that a portion of the notes must go in the market, said: ' Call on my friend Parkinson.' And since I am quite out of the way of such transactions, I shall only be too glad to put it all in your hands."

" Are you not in business here ?" I asked.

" Oh ! yes. I call New York my home ; my family resides here ; but I am engaged in some important enterprises, which take me frequently to Europe, so I am obliged to be absent a good deal. Since the first of May I have kept my office at Pollock, Pemberton, Hollis and Company's."

He handed me his card—James Algernon Harley—with his business address at the aforesaid firm in Water-street. Soon we entered into general conversation. I found Mr. Harley knew many of my old friends abroad, and could give late intelligence of several. After a while we came to speak of ourselves. Before I knew it I was telling him something of my life, and then I listened to a short history from him. He was from Boston ; he knew all about my own family in Providence. He was unfortunate in business a few years before, but had paid all up—a hundred cents on the dollar and interest—but this had swept him clean. He came to New York with his family, a wife and one child, and was now living at the Gloria Hotel.

In this way the rest of the business day was spent. Mr.

Harley suddenly started, looked at his watch, exclaimed: "I declare I don't know what has become of the time; but it is pleasant to forget affairs once in a while, especially if we make a friend, and I cannot but feel I have done so. I will call to-morrow, and we will then talk further about the negotiation of these notes." Mr. Harley took leave of me, and I proceeded on my customary route toward home.

The interview with Harley produced a happy effect on me. Since I lost sight of my old associates, I had become very solitary in my habits, confining myself entirely to the society of my children. I know it may seem strange to many, that at my age—past fifty—having spent nearly my whole life in New York, having made a great many acquaintances, and I may say friends, and enjoying intercourse with a large social circle, that I should not have secured some who were proof against adversity, that I should find myself so entirely forsaken, left to one side—high and dry.

Well, it may appear strange, but such was the fact. And now it strikes me that I might refer to still stranger cases: instances in the same family. [Stop and think a moment, reader, and say if you are not yourself familiar with some.] One sister marries a rich man, another a poor one. They live both in this very city. The rich man is a banker, and resides in one of the finest avenues. The poor man is a clerk in the Custom-House, and lives somewhere above Fiftieth-street. I cannot say those sisters don't love each other; but they are so separated by circumstances that there is no room for any exhibition of affection. Their daily associations and habits and necessities are so different, that there seems to be no longer any sympathy between them. So they exchange visits three or four times a year: the rich sister sends presents sometimes to the children of the poor sister, and perhaps to the sister herself. And so living different lives—ah! how different—the offspring of the same parents, who sat around the same table at home, attended the same schools, played the same plays, and shared the same bed, became absolutely like strangers, except that a sense of duty sometimes compels a certain recognition, too often sparingly bestowed.

And after all, we must not be too severe with such cases. Circumstances have generally more influence than principle or natural affection, and there are few who do not yield to their force. I declare I never indulged in any bitterness of feeling, because when I lost my property I lost the society of those who still kept theirs. It was only when I was treated with contumely or contempt that my spirit rebelled. I never resisted nor questioned the truth of the announcement: "Wealth maketh many friends, but the poor is separated from his neighbor." Yes, the poor is separated from his (former) neighbor, but the poor soon erect a new neighborhood among themselves. They go to each other for sympathy, and they find it.

I was remarking, that having confined myself entirely to the society of my children, this pleasant conversation with a person who manifested so much interest in me had an agreeable influence, and served to bring back my feelings into their natural channel.

CHAPTER XI.

AN EXTENSIVE OPERATION.

I THOUGHT a good deal about my affair with Mr. Harley. The next morning my enthusiasm had somewhat cooled. It occurred to me it would not be an unwise precaution to make some inquiry about him. I did so quietly of persons I thought most apt to be informed, but nobody could give me any information. I then asked as to Pollock, Pemberton, Hollis and Company, and could learn little or nothing about them. The firm was not composed of well-known business men. It had suddenly sprung into existence. No one appeared to know any thing against them, nor for that matter, in their favor. Finally I strolled leisurely past their place in Water-street. It was a fine large store, running through to Front-street, with an immense gilt sign extending across the entire front. On the stone columns, at each side of the door, the several names of the firm were neatly inscribed. Evidently all was above-board.

To be sure, the appearance of things struck one as a little too new and fresh to be substantial; yet it was a very fair and shining outside, and it was only the outside I could see that morning.

As I turned back into Wall-street, I met Mr. Harley. "I have just come from your place," he remarked, as he cordially shook my hand, " and will go back with you, if you please."

" Certainly," was my reply.

" Perhaps you have been to call on me ?"

" Oh! no, I expected you by appointment."

" I suppose," continued Mr. Harley, " you have hardly had time to ascertain what you can do with the Alworthy paper."

" I did not think best to make any attempt till we had conferred about it."

" Very judicious—very judicious," was the reply, and we mounted the steps to my office.

" How soon is the money wanted ?" I asked.

" Oh! there is no pressing haste. I would like a couple of thousand negotiated in a day or two, and the balance as opportunity serves."

" And the rate ?"

" Well, as to that, it must depend on what you can do," said Harley, with candor. " I will not at the very commencement of our acquaintance say any thing which even by implication is not frank and above-board ; and I may as well tell you, and if you do not now know it, you will discover it on inquiry, that Alworthy's paper will not sell at the best rates. You can dispose of it, but it will very likely be at some sacrifice. No doubt you will do the best you can. I will leave you the whole batch, and will only say, manage the affair after your own judgment, so as to make the best sales with the least injury to the parties. I will look in at two o'clock. Good morning. By the way," looking back, " it is best not to offer too much in one place, you know."

This was charming. Such a constituent did not turn up every day. I examined the paper. There were eleven notes, all told, carefully divided so as not to fall due too near together, averaging not quite a thousand dollars a piece. I selected the notes which I would offer to Loomis, and those to Finch. One I would take to the bank, two I would try at Brest and Company's. The first man I called on was Finch. I said: "I have some of Alworthy's paper; will you take it?"

"Don't want it."

"Nothing wrong, I hope."

"Oh! no, only I have got enough of it; rather sell than buy."

"At what rate will you sell? perhaps I can find a customer."

"At one per cent.; and if he don't like that, I wont say I wont take one and a-half."

So much for gruff old Finch. I went next to Loomis. I had better luck there. He was just as well "up" with regard to Alworthy as Finch; but he had more confidence in him than the other.

"Well, I have bought a great deal of their paper," he said, "and *have* a great deal of it, perhaps more than will pay. How much have you got, Mr. Parkinson, to offer? Perhaps I will make one transaction of it."

I hesitated slightly. I had at first determined to offer him three of the notes—should I say four? However, I stuck to my original decision, and answered: "Not quite three thousand dollars," and laid the notes before him.

He looked them over, then at the indorsement. "Who

the devil," he exclaimed, " are Pollock, Pemberton, Hollis and Company," drawling out the names; " whew!"

"You are behind the age," I said, "and have not made the acquaintance of a new but very extensive commission-house in Water-street."

"Mr. Parkinson," said Loomis, turning quickly on me, " is there any more paper out with this indorsement?"

"Not that I am aware of."

.   .   .   .

I had uttered a deliberate falsehood, uttered it almost before I knew what I was saying. Some keen devil instinct whispered to me that even the twenty-nine hundred dollars was rather more than Loomis wanted, and quite as much as he would regard as a legitimate transaction for Alworthy to make with this new house. Yes, the falsehood was uttered, and there I stood, with a life-long reputation for honesty and truth—a liar! Loomis supposed me incapable of deceiving him, and so he put the question, and I had answered it.

. My reply was satisfactory, for after a short pause he said : " I will take the whole at one and a half."

I endeavored to lower his terms. He only replied : " The best I will do ; all I will do. I know it's a high rate, but it is not salable paper. To be sure, I think it good, but there are more who don't."

The affair was closed, and I received a check for the money. A little after two Mr. Harley came in. I reported the transaction, and showed him a statement in which I had charged him a quarter per cent. commission.

He drew his pen across it. " This will never do. Leave the matter of commission to me. By the way, you may give me two thousand dollars net; it is all I want at present; it wont hurt your bank account to let the rest lay. If you can employ it for a few days, do so and welcome."

"I was overpowered with so much kindness, and could not but show I was sensibly affected by it.

"Arrange your deposit," said Mr. Harley, "and let us lunch together."

I did not decline, and after a little we proceeded to Delmonico's, and partook of a nice steak and a bottle of excellent claret. As we came out, my new friend asked me to step with him one moment to his office. It was directly over the counting-room of Pollock, Pemberton, Hollis and Company; and as we entered, I was introduced to Mr. Hollis, one of the firm. I was any thing but favorably impressed with him. He was a very young man, and exhibited neither wit nor intelligence; he spoke in monosyllables, and only in answer to some observations of mine. Indeed I thought his countenance very stolid. I saw Mr. Harley, meanwhile, giving the porter some special directions; then returning, we went up-stairs for a few moments, when he seemed inclined to apologize for the appearance of Hollis. "A mere youth, but his father puts in the capital for him, and really he is an excellent book-keeper." I could appreciate this, and so I said; and after some pleasant chat, I took leave. Glancing through the lofty store, I discovered very few goods. Some baskets of champagne were piled up in the centre, and several hogsheads and quarter casks were on one side, and a good many cases of wine opposite, but no other merchandise. However, I was not in a scrutinizing mood, and I did not think twice of the matter.

At the usual hour I reached home for dinner. A carman was just leaving my house. Alice stood at the door directing the stout Irish girl. There I saw a basket of champagne, a case of claret, another of Madeira, and a demijohn of brandy, each with a card attached—"C. E. Parkinson, Esq. From Pollock, Pemberton, Hollis and Company."

When Alice perceived me, she exclaimed, "O dear papa! this seems like old times," and she threw her arms about my neck in very joy. "But you don't look happy yourself, papa; are you ill?"

CHAPTER XII.

THE LIE.

"You don't look happy yourself, papa; are you ill?"

Yes, I was ill—sin-struck, conscience-struck. There I stood facing my innocent child—a liar; a mean liar, who had thrown away his birthright, a life-long character for probity, for a quarter of one per cent. commission on twenty-nine hundred dollars; seven dollars and twenty-five cents. No, it was not that, it was not for the money. Had I been suffering from hunger, and this crime would procure me food, there might be some excuse. But I did not lie for the seven dollars and twenty-five cents. I never thought of my commission. I told that apt and ready falsehood in order to carry my object, to succeed in my negotiation, to show Mr. Harley that I was a capable agent, a shrewd man of business. In doing this, I deceived one who had entire confidence in me and who in this particular case had trusted implicitly to my word. Such were the thoughts which passed swiftly through my brain.

Again Alice repeated: "Dear papa, what is the matter?"

I put my arms gently around her and kissed her forehead. "Not ill, at all, but much fatigued," I said. This seemed to assure her, and she ran in gayly before me. She was overjoyed to see the boxes of wine: she knew, she

10

said, that every thing would turn out happy again. Her father would soon recover his position—she was certain of it.

I was accustomed to talk over with my daughter every evening the various incidents of the day. She was the only being in the world who sympathized entirely with every effort of mine and every emotion. She would sit looking earnestly at me, expressing joy or regret as my narration was favorable or the reverse. Indeed, she appeared to be my guardian angel, placed there for my consolation after my wife had gone. On this occasion, however, I did not feel disposed to speak of the day's business. I did think at one moment that I would give Alice a full account of it. Should I tell *all?* I was tempted to do so, but I reconsidered the matter, postponed it rather, for dinner was coming in, and with dinner was placed on the table, a bottle of the wine from Pollock, Pemberton, Hollis and Company. It was of the best quality, and I partook freely of it. Then I was in a better humor with myself; I saw things in a mellower and more charitable light. "Be not righteous over-much," rose aptly to my lips. "Morbid too from great seclusion," and so forth.

The scene at the table became quite gay: children are so magnetic and appreciative, so ready to enjoy! The evening passed pleasantly, and I went to bed almost longing for the next day in which to push my enterprises; and, filled with pleasant visions and cheering hopes, I fell asleep.

Reader, do you not pity me in your heart? Like Samson, I knew not that I was shorn of my strength, but was ready to exclaim as he did: "I will go out, as at other times before, and shake myself." Do you not pity me, that after entering on the declining years of life, with loss of fortune and friends and social position, I should now make shipwreck of a good name? Or are you one of the free-and-easy sort who will exclaim: "LORD bless the man, what's the matter with him? What has he done more than is done every day by merchant, doctor, lawyer, priest? What business had Loomis to ask him such a question. Answered him right enough. Sorry Parkinson is going to turn out such a milk-and-water fellow. Shall lose all sympathy for him."

Perhaps so. But the mass of mankind are honest in their instincts, and the mass will understand the mortal wound inflicted on myself that day.

The next morning I went early to my office. I felt a certain sense of diminution as I walked up the stairs and entered it. It appeared to me that all of a sudden I had ceased to respect myself; that I was merely floating about with no fixed principle, attempting to pick up a few dollars like poor Downer or certain others whom I knew. While I was indulging in these reflections, Harley came in. His arrival had a pleasant, soothing effect on me. Every thing seemed all right the moment he entered. He shook hands with me, not as one would say, cordially, or with friendly emphasis, or hearty good-will, but with a serious warmth, as if he meant by it: "How happy for both that we have met; we are destined to be of great service to each other; at any rate, you can confide in and command me from this time forward."

"I called," said he, "to give you some seasonable information about Alworthy and Company. They have just gone into an extensive operation, which will throw a large amount of their paper on the market. Although we are in no haste for the money, you had better place the notes you have before these others get into the street. In fact, just resolve to make a day of it and the thing is done. They are bold fellows," he continued, " and are coining money by their operations in cotton, but so much paper will raise the rate : so sell to-day. Don't you say so ?"

Of course I agreed with him. The question was, where it was best to offer the notes, and in that connection I found myself narrating to Harley what I had concealed from my child, to wit, how, as it were without knowing it, I had told Loomis I was not aware of there being more paper of that sort afloat.

" I see, I see," said my new friend. " I am sorry. You should have avoided the question, and now you may be hurt with a valuable customer. My advice is to go direct to him, take the bull by the horns——"

" And tell him the plain truth," interrupted I; " that's just what I was thinking of doing."

" Tell him no such thing," rejoined Harley. " The truth is not to be spoken at all times. Not that I counsel falsehood, never ; but having unfortunately *committed* yourself, let us see what is the next best thing to do. Loomis is a coarse, unfeeling man ; I know him well. He could never appreciate your delicate and sensitive nature. No ; my advice is, to call on him at once and say you find there are more of those notes in market—that you have them to negotiate, and name exactly the amount and ask him to take them.

To be sure, he wont buy any more, but it will be turning your mistake to the best account."

What shall I say of Harley's influence over me? How explain it? I do solemnly aver that while he detailed to me this plan for repairing damages, I saw no great evil in it, nothing very objectionable or calculated to do violence to my moral sense. The plausibility of the statement, its likeness to the truth, its not containing any rough, angular contradiction, together with the happy result to be achieved, completely lulled my conscience.

Perceiving that I was quite lost in thought, Harley continued : "Mind, Mr. Parkinson, I don't say this plan, standing by itself, is strictly right, but I repeat, considering what has already occurred, I see nothing dishonorable in my suggestion ; nothing which can by any possibility harm Loomis or any one."

Strange how thoroughly we began to be acquainted ; strange how this man began to exercise a species of magnetic power over me. Do not be incredulous. Upon my honor I am recording the simple truth. I took the notes, went to Loomis, made my announcement, and offered him more of the paper.

"And how did he receive it ?" you ask.

Without moving a muscle, as a keen, sharp-witted man receives unsatisfactory information. There was, however, a calculating expression in his eye, as if he were weighing what I was saying, not with reference to the altered value of the paper, but of the truth of my statement ; at least, so I fancied. He did not want to purchase farther, he said. He asked me if I knew the indorsers. I told him I had

seen one of the partners after negotiating the notes with
him yesterday, but could give no information about the
house. I took my leave, and will remark here that I never
sold that man another note. He formed his judgment off-
hand, and acted accordingly.

By very active exertion I succeeded in selling the remainder of Alworthy's notes. It was hard work, and I had to
submit to high rates; but Harley said: "Better place all
to-day," and before three o'clock it was done, regardless of
the sacrifice. Then we sat down in my office, where I gave
him a statement of the whole transaction. When he had
examined it and counted the cash, he laid aside two hundred and fifty dollars, and handed it to me, saying: "I
hope this will be a slight compensation for the trouble you
have been at in this business."

I was astounded, and knew not what to reply. While I
was hesitating, Harley continued:

"If you please, not one word; you are entitled to this,
and I can afford to pay it; if I could not, I would not offer
it, I assure you. It is only bringing you in to share a portion of the profits of a legitimate commercial transaction.
One of these days I may ask you to do something without
any commission; and I promise, if necessary, I will not hesitate to call on you."

This explanation was very comforting and satisfactory.
My heart was full. It seemed that PROVIDENCE, after a
bitter ordeal, had furnished me a genuine friend. At last,
Fortune was beginning to relent. Was it possible? I had
now five hundred dollars ahead! The *bitterness* of poverty
was past. I could breathe with a kind of freedom. And

there sat the kind-hearted man who had done so much, and was preparing, I was certain, to do still more for me. How pliant all this appeared when viewed in the light of his accommodating nature. Every thing seemed so plain and easy of accomplishment, and so long as I was with him it was impossible even to invent a difficulty.

"My friend," said Harley, addressing me with an air of deep interest, "permit me to tell you what you are suffering from. You have encountered a series of disasters, which, with the loss of your wife, has broken your courage, and reduced your moral status to below par. You have foolishly decided to accept your fate instead of battling against it. In this you show weakness, not natural in you, but induced by the untoward circumstances you have encountered.— Now, there is no reason you should confine yourself to the treadmill work of selling notes for a paltry commission. At present there are various enterprises in which, as negotiator, you could come in for a share of the profits without having to advance, or indeed risk any money. And you owe it as a duty to your family not to permit them to fall in the scale of social life. Believe me, my friend, you have a grave responsibility in that quarter."

Had I been dreaming? or was I now dreaming? Could any thing be more self-evident than what Harley was urging on me? [Yes, I had lost my courage, become humble, was ready to hew wood and draw water, if necessary, to gain a living. But O reader! I was meanwhile an honest man. How much that means none can fully understand who has not fallen from the high estate.] I replied to him, assenting to what he said, but remarked he little knew the difficulty of a fresh start after being so completely prostrated as I had been.

"Courage, courage," he replied; "all depends on courage. You will dine with me to-day. The children will let you off for once. I shall introduce you to my wife, and I hope we may make an hour or two pass cheerfully."

I accepted Harley's invitation, and he proceeded to send his boy (who was waiting in my office) with a note from me to let Alice know that I should not be home as usual. "Now," continued Harley, "It is not always I have money over, but just at present I happen not to be short. Let the balance on the other transaction (it was between seven and eight hundred dollars) stand to your credit in the bank for a while; and, as I said, if you can employ it in the mean time, you are welcome to do so. It will give you more strength, and what is better, it will add, I hope, to your confidence. I must now go to my office, but I shall see you at five."

After Harley left, I put the two hundred and fifty dollars, which was lying on the table, carefully in my pocket, and starting to my feet, I walked briskly up and down the room, rubbing my hands together with a species of glee; and thus I celebrated the success of the day. I had still something on hand to do. One or two small notes to get through for very respectable parties; and although it was after three, I knew I could find several money-lenders still at their posts. So I descended to the street.

Reaching the pavement, I saw a few persons congregated on the corner. Walking in that direction, I perceived Sol Downer in charge of a police-officer. They were evidently waiting for something. But the official was impatient, and seemed disposed to proceed on his way.

"For God's sake," I heard Downer exclaim in a low tone, as I came up, "step into my office, for a few minutes, till my lawyer can come. At any rate, give me a chance to send home."

The officer had doubtless received a charge to make quick work with the arrest; indeed, I saw a young man whom I recognized as a clerk in a most respectable banking-house, whispering to the police official. Whereupon the fellow became still more peremptory, and said he could wait no longer. I am happy to say, my better feelings prevailed over the selfish ones. I walked up to Downer, and asked him if I could be of any service.

He was sensibly affected. "Thank you," he whispered in a hoarse, unnatural tone—he put me in mind of a wild beast hunted to his lair, and desperate. "I wanted to see Storms, my lawyer, but this humble servant of justice can't wait; oh! no, because the almighty house of Strauss, Bevins and Company says, 'Proceed,' I must go to the Tombs in double-quick time."

"And what is it?" I asked in a low tone.

"Why, what turns out to be a forged note on a good house was put into my hands by a stranger to sell; I did sell it to them, paid over the money, and received my commission, and on my soul, that's all I know about it. Yet I am to be made the scape-goat." The policeman here interposed, and said they must be off.

"What can I do for you? Do you require any money?" I asked.

10*

"No, thank you, but will you call on Storms, and tell him where I am, and ask him to come to me as soon as possible, and—and——" his voice became tremulous—"will you please stop at my house, and tell my folks that I am obliged unexpectedly to go out of town to-night; mind you say out of town, to be back to-morrow; put this in an envelope, and seal it, and give it to my wife." He handed me a three-dollar bill, and the next moment was on his way up Nassau-street, toward the Tombs.

This affair depressed me greatly, I hardly knew why. I proceeded at once to Mr. Storms's office, where I waited half an hour before he came in. Then I repeated what I knew as to the charge against Downer and delivered his message. I was gratified at the lively interest that gentleman, who was a counsellor of high respectability, manifested in the case. "Poor fellow!" he exclaimed, "I will go at once. Whatever the charge is, I know Downer has intended nothing wrong."

CHAPTER XIII.

THE GLORIA HOTEL.

It was now too late to attend to any other business, and quite time for me to meet my appointment with Harley, at the Gloria Hotel, then the latest built, and in consequence the most fashionable house in the city. I found him occupying a handsome private parlor, where he introduced me to his wife (he had no children), who was a pale, stylish-looking young woman, dressed after the latest mode, a good deal affected, and rather inclined, as the phrase is, to put on airs. However, she received me politely, and during the few moments before dinner, managed to give me a very tolerable idea of the miseries and inconveniences attending living at a hotel. It was the ordinary, commonplace talk, very prettily rehearsed. I ventured to suggest keeping house.

"Oh! not for the world, not for ten worlds," exclaimed Mrs. Harley. "Heaven knows I have care enough now; nothing on earth would ever induce me to venture on housekeeping.

We were just then summoned to dinner, and the interesting conversation was interrupted. I soon discovered, by the extraordinary deference Harley paid his wife, that he was under a species of discipline while in her presence. In fact, he appeared like a different person. Not a word did he utter that he did not watch, with a kind of solicitude, its effect on her. During dinner, Mrs. Harley, who, delicate as she seemed, I found possessed an excellent appetite, made frequent inquiries if I knew this or that person or family. I could very often answer in the affirmative, which seemed to increase the lady's respect for me.

"Oh! well," she said, "I wish Algernon was not so engrossed in business as to neglect social life. I think it a shame, Mr. Parkinson, and so I tell him."

Mr. Harley here joined in the conversation, admitted the truth of the charge, filled my glass from a fresh bottle of wine; "women can't appreciate," said he, "all we have to contend against."

"Appreciate!" interrupted the lady. "If an incessant clamor about it would make us do so, I think we might. No; I *don't* appreciate it, I confess. You men love the excitement of business, and you don't stop to think your wives love the excitement of fashion, society, and so forth, and you are a selfish set, all of you."

I did not deny this, but helped Mrs. Harley to a sweetbread, and some preserved peas, which for a time seemed to quiet her resentment. Meanwhile, as dinner proceeded, and the wine began to circulate, my host grew even more friendly and communicative.

"Do you know," he said in a low tone, "we are about entering on a magnificent period for speculation? I mean legitimate speculation; there is much to be done, I assure you, and *we*—you and I—must take advantage of fortune at the flood. For myself, I am a sanguine man, perhaps too sanguine; I need just such a friend as you to counsel and advise with, and sometimes to hold me back. Do not think me too disinterested or too benevolent. I am sure your friendship will be as valuable to me, as I hope mine may be to you. It is when benefits are mutual that co-operation is really of value. By the by, you must taste this new brand of champagne. Pemberton has just secured the agency. Do not forget to recommend it when you have a chance, that is, if you are yourself satisfied. I have introduced it at the Gloria splendidly: got half a dozen friends to call for it on the same day. The next, down came an order for a dozen baskets, and it goes off now like hot cakes. I tell you, my friend, every thing has to be puffed into notice; and if what you offer is a good thing, and no honest man" (this said with great *empressement*) "will ever offer what is not good, why, the more you try to introduce it the better for the world at large, and yourself in particular."

"I really think it is downright rudeness in you, Algernon" (Mrs. Harley had finished her sweetbread and preserved peas), "to be monopolizing Mr. Parkinson in that way; talking about business too. I declare it is shameful."

"I agree with you," I hastened to reply, and so cover my friend, "but permit me to say, it grew very naturally out of your husband's offering me a new brand of wine."

"Oh! I am disgusted with all that sort of thing; managing, managing, the whole time; I am sick of management, I hate management. If I were a man, and a business-man, and could not get along without it, I would——"

"Yes, tell us what you would do," interrupted Mr. Harley, with a winning smile.

"Well, I know I could do without it, and I *would* do without it; that's all."

We both laughed, and Mrs. Harley continued much in the same strain till the dessert was brought in, when her attention was turned in its former direction. Dinner over, I escorted the lady into the grand hall, where several persons of both sexes came up to speak with her, and at this particular juncture her husband remarked : "Mr. Parkinson and I are going to smoke a cigar, my dear : shall we leave you here?" The lady bowed a careless assent, and we turned our steps toward the smoking-room.

We spent the time there in earnest conversation, in which I was principally a listener, and which assumed on the part of Mr. Harley a most confidential tone. He gave me an account of his past fortunes, the checks and reverses he had experienced, and his present cheering prospects. He was soon to leave for England, and should carry out with him several notable schemes, sure to attract the attention of the capitalists on the other side of the water. He produced some of his papers, and gave me a brief account of the various enterprises he had at command. Among these I distinctly recollect the following :

Three California gold mines.

One Virginia ditto, in working order.

One on the Isthmus.

Two magnificent Lake Superior copper mines.

One Tennessee copper mine.

Charter from the state of Virginia for a land company.

Ditto from the state of Georgia for a timber company.

Plan for purchasing live-oak lands in Florida.

Invention (already patented) for making paper out of the bark of certain trees.

Ditto for smelting ores, with little or no fuel.

Ditto for generating steam, ditto, ditto.

Plan for manufacture of French brandy at Paris, out of whiskey, to be imported from America, and returned properly flavored and colored, and sold in bond in New York.

Invention for making steel out of coarse pig-iron, at a trifling expense. Together with various little affairs, which Harley called playthings, out of which he "could always make a few thousand pounds."

"You see," he continued, "I have my hands full. I know what I am about. I have made every preparation in London. I left there only three months ago. I have secured Larry, Buxton, Westneath and Hope for my solicitors, the first men in their line in the city; very rich connections; had a letter from them yesterday. Glynn and the London and Westminster Bank will act as my bankers. I shall get off as soon as possible. Now, you see, Mr. Parkinson, why I want a reliable man to represent this side, while I am on the other. We can join forces, and in less than a twelvemonth I will promise you half a dozen fortunes, if one wont satisfy you."

It was with such hopeful conversation that the evening was beguiled. Although I could not be blind to the fact that Harley was a speculator, ready to embark in any scheme that should promise well, I knew at the same time that there were opportunities for making money out of such matters, and that not unfrequently they did turn out well when in clever hands. Now, Harley was already acquainted in London, and had laid the foundation for what he was to do. Why, out of all these enterprises might not one turn out a prize? I must say that while his ingenuous avowals rather lowered my previous standard of the man, I felt as kindly toward him as ever, and, I believe quite as much under his magnetic, I was about to say magical, influence.

During a slight pause in the conversation, I looked at my watch. It was after ten o'clock. Suddenly I thought of Downer, and my promise to visit his family. What would they not suffer all this evening from the unexplained absence! I started up and declared I must leave. Mr. Harley would have detained me, but he saw I was urgent. So we mounted again to his parlor, where I had left my overcoat, to say good evening to madam. She was seated languidly in one of the rocking-chairs.

"This is always the way," she said, "Algernon invites a guest. Immediately after dinner, on the plea of wishing to smoke a cigar, he disappears with him to the regions below, whence he emerges toward midnight, and where he talks business, business, business."

"Forgive me," I exclaimed, "I think I am the offender this time, not your husband, for permitting myself to become so interested in what he has been saying. I will promise better behavior in future."

The lady smiled, Harley smiled, and I came away.

CHAPTER XIV.

DOWNER'S FAMILY.

WHEN I descended to the side-walk, I found a driving, blinding snow-storm had set in, for it was now the first week in December, one of those storms peculiar to New-York. The wind blew half a hurricane through the streets, carrying the snow along laterally, and with a fury almost irresistible, into the face and eyes of pedestrians, turning umbrellas inside out, encasing the lamps with a thick crust, confusing the omnibus-drivers, and making every kind of locomotion nearly impossible. Sol Downer's residence happened to be quite as far up town as mine, but unfortunately on the other side of the city. I managed to get into an omnibus going near his home, but from which I would be forced to walk all the way to mine.

It was eleven o'clock before I rang at Mr. Downer's door. It was opened almost instantly by a tall elderly lady, neatly dressed in black, of a most prepossessing appearance, who exclaimed, on seeing me: "Oh! how relieved I am; I feared something had happened to you."

As I stepped into the hall, she discovered her mistake, and her terror was extreme. Her lips became bloodless and her eyes wild, as she seized my arm and uttered in a faint tone, " Where is my husband ?"

With a word I reassured her. " He is perfectly well.

Just as I was leaving my office he asked me to call and say he was obliged to go out of town, to return to-morrow." At the same time I put the envelope which covered the three dollars into her hand.

It was hard absolutely to convince her; that is, instinctively she felt something *had* gone wrong, but she was measurably relieved, and asked me into the parlor. As I was suffering from cold, after a slow, tedious ride in the omnibus, I accepted the invitation, and entered a room very inexpensively but prettily furnished, where around a table were seated two young ladies of really charming appearance, and a youth of fifteen or sixteen. The whole arrangements produced a subdued but pleasant impression. No one could mistake the quiet and unpretentious air which pervaded the apartment. I hastened to repeat my message and to explain still farther, that I had myself been detained late by a previous appointment.

"Yet, how much we thank you for coming," said the lady; "we were all in such distress. Mr. Downer applies himself so hard, and is so frequently subject to ill turns, that I am always very nervous when he is out a little over his time; but to-night, oh! it was dreadful, and in this terrible storm."

As I cast my eyes round the room, and saw the evidences there of a refined and gentle spirit; saw the order of the household; saw well-educated and well-regulated children; saw what should make a person happy in his home, I thought of the hard-pushed and desperate man, who was toiling, sweating, agonizing to keep that family together. I could fancy Downer coming in from his degrading labors, casting off the slough with which his encounter with rogues and knaves, sharpers and misers had besmeared him, and enjoying the lovely influence of that home scene. Yes, now I understood what he was battling for—to keep *these* safe, and screened from misery. Poor fellow ! and my heart reproached me for what my heart had felt toward him of late.

In the course of conversation I mentioned that Mr. Downer and I were old acquaintances, and repeated my name. Mrs. Downer recollected, she said, but she made no allusion to former times, and our remarks turned wholly on present topics. In a few minutes I took my leave, preparing to encounter the fury of the storm on foot.

CHAPTER XV.

AN ADVENTURE.

It proved to be a night of adventure.

I had four avenues to traverse, and the storm coming from the north-east, drove violently in my teeth. I buttoned my overcoat about my ears, settled my hat close over my face, and presenting my head combatively to the tempest I pushed on. I had in this way crossed from the Eighth to the Sixth Avenue, scarcely conscious of the progress made, when I struck against an object in the middle of the side-walk, and was saluted by the exclamation: "Stop!"

Whatever alarm I experienced was immediately dissipated when I raised my head and got sight of the person who stood in my way. It was a girl bare-headed, without cloak or shawl; perhaps fourteen years old.

Before I could question her, she exclaimed: "Mother is dying. Wont you come quick?"

Without a word being said, for she hurried me on too rapidly for conversation, I followed down the avenue to the next street, and turning into it, went perhaps half a block, when my companion entered a two-story wooden house, and ran rapidly up the stairs to the front room. Here on a bed lay a woman moaning and gasping, and exhibiting symptoms resembling epilepsy.

"Don't be frightened," I said, "your mother is not dying —is not going to die."

"Are you sure of that?" said the girl.

Something in the sound of her voice strange and startling · —a masculine vigor, coupled with an extraordinary maturity, caused me to turn and regard her. Large black eyes were fixed on me with a firm but unsatisfied look, as if they would say: "Do not amuse me: I am no child. Tell me the truth."

To these imaginary observations, rather than to the direct questions I replied: "I repeat, your mother is not dying, but evidently has had a fit of some kind. Is she subject to such attacks?"

"No!"

She looked at me almost defiantly.

I was at a loss what to say or do when I was relieved by hearing the poor woman, who had regained her consciousness, exclaim, "Matilda."

She went to the bed-side of her mother, who asked what was the matter.

I replied that I believed she had been taken suddenly ill, and her daughter in alarm ran out for aid and met me. "And now that I am here," I continued, "I shall be happy if I can do any thing to relieve you."

"Give the gentleman a chair, my daughter," said the sick woman, for although I had shaken the snow from my hat and coat, I was still standing.

She obeyed, and I sat down. Meanwhile I had glanced about the room and taken a closer look at its inmates. The appearance was that of biting poverty without squalidness

or misery. The girl was very handsome and well formed,
but exhibited in her demeanor no softness, indeed, little that
was feminine. When I sat down, she seated herself at the
window and looked out on the storm. There was something
in the expression of her eyes which brought back some old
association, but what I could not tell. The mother was evidently a lady and possessed of natural refinement and delicacy. She explained to me that she had been very closely
at work all day with the needle, and as she was getting into
bed she had been seized in a most alarming manner, and
was for the time insensible. When she recovered she saw
me standing over her.

It was the old tale of destitution, hard work, and a final
breaking down of a naturally strong constitution. Yes, the
familiar story, so much so that the novel-reader who has
persevered thus far, in the belief that some extraordinary
incident would yet turn up, will exclaim: "Pshaw! how
very stale and common-place this meeting a girl in the street
and being conducted up a pair of stairs to a sick-room, and
so-forth and so-forth. To be sure, all this is very common—
would it were otherwise, but GOD permits one class of his
creatures to fare sumptuously every day, while another class
starves, and the mystery of this we may not undertake to
fathom.

The poor lady seemed so nearly recovered that there was
nothing to be done for her. I asked if I could render her
any assistance, and if she was suffering from any pressing
want. She answered no, and regretted that I should have
been taken out of my way.

There was no reason why I should stay longer, yet I felt

irresistibly impelled to speak to the young girl, who maintained her seat by the window, looking fixedly out of it. As I rose to depart, I said, turning to her:

"You see I was right, your mother will be quite well by morning."

She assented by a nod.

"Where were you going when I met you?" I asked.

"I thought mother was dying, and I started to find some body to come to her. I did not dare stay to see her die." And she looked again with that expression which had touched me, and which called up a strange feeling, like the memory of a half-forgotten dream.

"I think I must call and see you to-morrow," I said to the lady, "for we are in the midst of a heavy storm. I reside not far from here, and I shall see if I can't be of some use to you. Pray, may I inquire your name?"

"Mrs. Hitchcock."

"And your husband?"

"Has been dead for a long time."

"He was —— "

"A physician; Dr. Ralph Hitchcock."

"Who graduated at Yale College, thirty years ago?"

"Yes."

"Who resided in Cincinnati, and died there?"

"The same."

"And you are Ralph Hitchcock's widow?"

"I am."

"And this young person?"

"His daughter. The only surviving of five children."

The room swam round. Ralph Hitchcock, my class-mate,

my room-mate in college, my beloved friend, my cherished correspondent, so long as he lived, cut off in the flower of his life; while already acquiring fame, and laying the foundation for a grand success, death had snatched him away.

I stood oppressed with these thoughts, not speaking, not moving. Mrs. Hitchcock lay waiting calmly for some explanation. She had been too long schooled by trouble to become easily excited. Not so the daughter; she rose from her chair, came into the middle of the room, and burst into a hysterical sobbing, which was so violent that it alarmed me. I had made no explanation, but my questions showed I was well acquainted with the one whose decease had caused such a revolution in their fortunes.

After a short pause, I said: "My dear lady, I knew your husband well; more than that, we were the best of friends. It is now late, you are just recovering from this sudden attack. I shall be sure to see you to-morrow. GOD bless you both! And I came away.

Desperate as my own affairs had been, here were circumstances much more discouraging. Reader, if you yourself are unfortunately borne down by the weight of what seems a calamitous destiny, cast about for some more afflicted, and take on you the office of aid and adviser. Assume a part of their burdens, it will help to lighten your own. You will be surprised what strength you will gain beside. It is so. For thus marvellously has GOD established the paradox: "There is that maketh himself poor, yet hath great riches."

I reached home about midnight. Alice was waiting for me, and had a cheerful fire, which glowed in happy contrast with the night out of doors. I recounted to my daughter this last adventure, and she was eager to undertake any thing which could serve to aid my new acquaintances. She exhibited an especial sympathy for the young girl, and evidently appreciated her character better than I did. After many plans advanced, rejected and approved, we concluded to wait till I saw Mrs. Hitchcock again before deciding on any.

11

CHAPTER XVI.

DOWNER BEFORE THE MAGISTRATE.

Sol Downer was discharged the next day, on his examination before the magistrate. Mr. Storms, his counsel,
having carefully investigated the case, and examined the
papers, came before the judge, indignantly denouncing the
men who could swear to such affidavits as those on which
the warrant was granted. These affidavits were made by
the head-clerk of Strauss, Bevins and Company, and by
Mr. Strauss, the senior partner. To be sure, the paper
which Downer sold to the house was forged, and the house·
had purchased it. These were the only truths stated by
them.

The head-clerk had transacted the business, and although
he had not transcended the line of his duty, felt it necessary, or at least thought it would be highly praiseworthy,
to fix the responsibility somewhere by criminating somebody. As Downer's reputation was a good deal below par,
he felt it would be safe to strain a point against him. The
chances were (so he reasoned) that "Old Sol" knew something about it, and an arrest might frighten the truth out
of him. This was the logical conclusion arrived at by Mr.
Tompkins, head man of the highly respectable and well-to-
do banking-house of Strauss, Bevins and Company. Thereupon he visited the counsel of that establishment, who

taking the tale as it was told him, prepared some affidavits to suit the case *as stated*. The head man, after considerable reflection, decided in his own mind that Downer told him, in answer to a question, that the makers of the note *had* assured him (Downer) that it was all right. Of course the makers had done no such thing, and swore they had not, neither had Downer said so. What he did say was, as the note was a large one, that if it was thought best he could call and get the makers to say all right, and so forth; and since the head-clerk had thought it unnecessary, he felt the more aggravated by the swindle, as people always do when they neglect any simple precaution which would have made all clear, and saved loss and trouble.

Mr. Strauss and Mr. Bevins were good men in their way, that is, for millionaires. The former was a vestryman in the most fashionable church in the city; the latter a leading elder in a church of much greater wealth, but of a different persuasion, and of less worldly pretensions. Both those gentlemen were honest, straightforward business people, quite above trick or chicanery. Neither one would hardly commit a wilful perjury to save the half of his fortune. But Mr. Strauss reposed great trust in his confidential clerk. He had seen Downer before the desk, probably heard a word or two drop in relation to the transaction, and that was all. But the dignity of the house had been assailed by a miserable fellow without any character. What right had he to select them for his victims, for Tompkins could not be mistaken, and Tompkins said so? He felt willing to make any proper statement which should bring the man to punishment, and clear the street of rogues;

and after reading the affidavit of his clerk, the principal remarked that it seemed quite correct.

The result was, the drawing up of another affidavit by the counsel, by which Mr. Strauss, being duly sworn, deposed and said, that he was present on the occasion of Solomon Downer's coming to their establishment to offer a certain note, etc., etc., as set forth in the affidavit of his clerk (naming him); that he heard a portion of the conversation between said Downer and said clerk, that he had read the affidavit of the said Tompkins, and *that the facts therein stated were true.*

By which it really appeared that two respectable witnesses swore that Downer said he was told by the makers the note was all right; when the fact was, Mr. Strauss knew nothing about it! Certainly a strong case for suspicion against the poor fellow, and likely to bring him into serious difficulty, defenceless as he was, without even the shield of good character to interpose against the oath and influence of one of the most respectable bankers in New York.

But mark the sequel. Mr. Storms, an independent, quick-witted lawyer, had, fortunately, known Downer and his family for many years, known and sympathized with them in their misfortunes. He started, therefore, with the absolute conviction of the innocence of his client, a tower of strength always to a professional man. He had, too, in common with the better class of advocates, very little veneration for men simply on account of their position.

I was myself so much interested in the case, that I determined to be present, and accordingly was already on the spot at ten o'clock the next morning, when Mr. Strauss and

Mr. Tompkins presented themselves, for it was too late the night before to go into an examination. Tompkins evidently began to feel fidgety, to say the least, when he saw his paper case was to be subjected to a critical examination, and he along with it. He had not calculated on any thing of the kind. Supposed the statement he had sworn to would just do the business, and bring the culprit to light. Doubtless he really believed Downer was implicated, but how cruel and how wanton to endeavor to consign him to perpetual infamy on mere suspicion!

As I have said, Tompkins became nervous and fidgety. Not so Mr. Strauss, who took his seat in a patronizing manner, not far from the magistrate, with the air of a man who in leaving his business was making a sacrifice for the purpose of upholding the law. Mr. Tompkins was called on.

At this juncture, Mr. Storms said he had a special reason for requesting Mr. Strauss to withdraw during the examination of his clerk.

"Me, sir!" said the banker, in astonishment.

"You, sir," replied Mr. Storms, quietly.

"Can you suppose, sir, that my confidential clerk or myself can have any object to serve in this affair beyond the furtherance of justice."

"Certainly not," answered Mr. Storms; "and it is simply to further justice that I must ask the magistrate to request your retiring a few moments."

The magistrate assented to the demand. Mr. Strauss, taking up his hat, walked away into the next room. A little of the starch was already taken out of him.

Tompkins, meantime, had somewhat recovered; he felt

that the best way for him was to fortify against the anticipated onslaught, by making himself up "hard," as the
phrase is. So he stood up with a bold and rather audacious
outside, which said plainly: "Now, sir, come on, you will
find I am ready for you!"

Mr. Storms, however, was too good a tactician to assail
the enemy at a point where he was expected. On the contrary, he commenced in a mild and insinuating tone; he indulged most amiably in the merest commonplace questions.
He sought for information about unimportant details. The
amount of the note, how long to run, if the house had lately
purchased much of the paper, and so on, until the examination assumed a conversational shape. In fact, one would
suppose Mr. Storms was actually helping along the case.

Mr. Tompkins was finally put quite at his ease. He was
neither fidgety nor defiant.

"By the way, Mr. Tompkins" (this was run along in the
examination in a most unsuspicious manner), "how came
you first to suspect Downer?"

"Why, because he brought us the note."

"Of course, of course; nothing more natural. Still, you
would not suspect every body who should bring what turned out to be forged paper."

"Certainly not, if they were respectable parties; but you
know a man's character will tell against him."

"I know it. That is very true. If Downer had been
differently situated, no doubt you would not have thought
of him as the guilty party."

"Why, no, sir. We don't suspect men of character, of
course; why should we?"

" Well, we shouldn't."

" This gentleman's testimony," said Mr. Storms, " is very clear, very honest, and explicit, such as becomes the respectable house he serves. I think that is all."

Mr. Tompkins was delighted ; the " bitterness" of the scene was past, he had come off with flying colors, and with a compliment from the man he deemed his enemy. He was about leaving, to ask Mr. Strauss to step in, when Mr. Storms exclaimed :

" By the way, just one word more. I don't know as it's of much consequence, but I think you stated in your affidavit that Downer said the makers of that note *had* told him it was all right. Is there not a trifling error here? Did he not tell you the makers doubtless *would* say it was all right ? *Think a moment !*"

The whole demeanor of Mr. Storms had changed with the words, "Think a moment." These were not uttered in a loud, severe or bullying tone; on the contrary, in a low voice, as if it were a private matter between the witness and the examiner, with a look, an action which said: " I know all about it, and you had better tell the truth." I found myself unconsciously holding my breath.

" Very possible, sir, that was the expression," answered Tompkins, a little crest-fallen; " but that makes no difference, for it shows just as conclusively his determination to mislead me."

" Precisely. I have nothing more to ask."

Mr. Strauss was then ushered in. Mr. Storms's manner toward the banker was entirely different from that toward the clerk. It was severe and curt and off-hand.

" You are the senior partner of the house of Strauss, Bevins and Company ?"

" Yes."

" You purchased of the prisoner such a note ?" (describing it.)

" It was purchased by Mr. Tompkins, with my knowledge and assent."

" And you were present, and heard all that passed between the prisoner and Tompkins in relation to the note ?"

" No, indeed, I heard very little."

" But you were present ?"

" I suppose I can say I was. The prisoner was at the counter, and I was passing up and down from my own room to the middle office, in which he stood."

" Can you recollect a single intelligible remark the prisoner made ?"

" No. I paid no attention to what was going on."

" But, Mr. Strauss, you have sworn in your affidavit that the prisoner told Tompkins that the makers said the note was all right."

" I beg your pardon, I have sworn to no such thing; although I do say I believe he did."

" Never mind what you believe. You have sworn that the facts stated in Tompkins's affidavit are true."

" And so they are, as I honestly and conscientiously believe."

" Now, Mr. Strauss, do you know, of your own knowledge, *any thing* about this case beyond what you have just stated ? Mind, I say, of your own knowledge ?"

" Sir, I have never professed to know any thing about the

case, except through Mr. Tompkins, who, permit me to say, has the entire confidence of our firm, and on whose statement I most implicitly rely."

"And that was all you meant by swearing his affidavit is true?"

"All, sir."

The case was at an end. The banker did not "see it," but the court did. The former was consequently astounded when the magistrate announced that he did not wish to examine the prisoner, not feeling willing to detain him another moment, adding that it was highly culpable to swear so carelessly to affidavits.

"I do not know, Mr. Strauss," said Mr. Storms, addressing the banker, "what course my client will take; but if he follows my advice, he will commence an action for false imprisonment against you without delay."

Mr. Strauss deigned no reply, but looked highly indignant. And thereupon all parties separated.

I walked down from the "Tombs" with Downer and his counsel. The latter expressed his opinion in no measured terms about the affair. "These men should be punished," he said. "They are as much to blame for their carelessness in taking an oath as if they had intentionally committed perjury. I am speaking about Strauss. Tompkins knew he was lying. But in Strauss's case, carelessness is criminality. You must make him pay for this," he continued, turning to Downer.

"Not I," replied his client. "I am too old for that sort of thing. When I was a young man, I was ready to play give and take any day, although I never was revengeful.

11*

Now, I would not cross the street to do a harm to my worst enemy. It is unprofitable business seeking how to injure another. Never shall undertake it."

"I declare," said Mr. Storms pleasantly, "I think a week's sojourn in the Tombs would do you good—at least it might take some of this nonsense out of you."

"Don't believe it would," responded Downer, "but I don't want a trial, though. I am content with my present experience."

"By the way," I remarked, "I feared you were going to let Tompkins off without bringing him to the point."

"Oh! no," said Mr. Storms, "I had no such idea. But the fellow was on his guard, and I had to work cautiously. I once cross-examined a witness more than half an hour, and actually put the only question I wanted to ask by carelessly stopping him after I told him he might go, and when he had actually opened the door and was leaving the room. I did not even request him to come back to the witness-stand. I gained my end, and got the truth out of him. A dishonest witness dislikes amazingly to return to the stand, especially after he has received a thorough overhauling. His nerves are relaxed as he steps away, and it is some effort to brace them up again. A single response he reasons, can't turn the scale, and so he answers right in order to prevent more questions.

Downer did not appear greatly interested in the conversation, and on reaching Wall-street, Mr. Storms said, "Good morning!" and went to his own office. I told Downer that I had called at his house as he requested, and prevented any alarm there. He thanked me. "I have lost half a day," he said; "I must try and make it up." And away he darted in the direction of his own place.

I have carefully described this affair of Sol Downer, because it is what happens too frequently. Besides, my object in these papers is not only to record some prominent events in my own life, but also to endeavor to show what is going on in a locality where I spent ten years of it. I have often heard respectable lawyers remark about a peculiar habit prevalent in our business community, namely, that individuals otherwise straightforward and honorable, do not stop much to examine an affidavit they are about to make when a debt is in danger, or they have already been swindled out of it. In this way many improper arrests are made, and great injustice done, and actually *perjury committed.*

The response of a large wholesale merchant in Water-street to his attorney, who was engaged preparing his client's affidavit in an important case, unfortunately is characteristic of too many. The merchant had called on the attorney, and told him what he wanted, to wit, to arrest a certain person. As the attorney proceeded to draw up the document, he kept asking his client if he could swear to this, if he could swear to that, and so forth.

The merchant got out of patience; the questions annoyed him: "Look here," said he, "just draw the affidavit like a lawyer, and I will swear to it like a man!"

He might have said, "like a knave."

CHAPTER XVII.

THE CLASS SPECULATIVE.

THE events of the previous night and the incidents of the morning had quite driven Harley and his speculative schemes out of my head. When on reaching my office I did think of them, it was with a strange repugnance. While I was engaged in what called out the true and just emotions of my nature, I felt like myself; the moment I recalled my transactions with my new acquaintance I felt unnaturally—that is the word, unnaturally. I was either cast down under a sense of a certain humiliation or buoyed up with the glit-. tering idea of suddenly acquired wealth. My habits as a merchant had been so legitimate ; my theory of acquisition was so completely associated with industry and application, that I could not, at my age, reconcile myself to a speculative career. It was in vain I argued to myself, if I am fortunately possessed of a share in a valuable property or charter. or privilege, and it can be disposed of so as to bring me a large return, why is that not a perfectly correct and business-like transaction ? I could not say it was not; but my conscience, or rather the severe habit of a long and correct business life, said, keep clear of all this sort of things.

And here I may as well speak of a class who form one element and a considerable one of the " street" I have undertaken to depict. I do not mean the class of visionaries already alluded to, nor any kind of broker, nor yet the adventurer who from time to time appears and disappears upon the stage to suit the occasion, but *par excellence* to the class speculative, to which belong Mr. Tremaine and Mr. James Algernon Harley. If the reader will run over his list of acquaintances, he will, I am sure, recognize some of this class among them. They are persons who, having failed in business, ordinarily twice or thrice, have become disgusted with trade, and are determined to take a short cut to wealth. They have generally good connections, socially and otherwise. Their wives spend a good deal of money, and do not know but that it is as easy for their husbands to furnish it as it was when they were in the wholesale business. These people are very respectable. They are in the best society. It is true a few of them were disappointed in getting tickets to the Prince's ball last year, but it was because things were not managed in the usual way, and their cards were disposed of to the presidents, cashiers and tellers of the larger banks. But generally, no such injustice is rendered to the class aforesaid. A portion confine themselves to the "home consumption;" they watch an opportunity when a piece of property goes for half price, and by getting an advance from a wealthy friend, manage to control it long enough to sell it again for something near its value, and so realize a handsome profit from it. Or they encounter the owner of a coal-bed in Pennsylvania or Maryland, and, like Tremaine, start a company out of nothing and work off the shares; or they meet a man with a good invention, and getting the control of it, find parties who will take it up, advance what money is necessary, and allow a handsome sum from its earnings.

The operations of the other portion are more extended; they vibrate generally between London, Paris and New York; they follow the run of the money market, and "put up" where it is most plentiful. From 1849 to 1854 it was a perpetual gala day for the travelled class abroad. From the quieting of the railway crisis in England, in 1847, to the breaking out of the Russian war, in 1854, London was the favorite arena for the American speculator. No lesson of experience can teach John Bull. He is an incurable schemer. No person is so easily gulled if you will but lay the scene a good way off. He is used to distances—India and Australia, for example. And he was completely gorged during the years just mentioned with all sorts of schemes, inventions, grants, charters, mines and patent-rights from over the water. This gave brisk employment to the class to which Mr. James Algernon Harley belonged.

The gentlemen who compose this class are really gentlemen. To be sure the regular man of business, who has a sure and reliable occupation, turns up his nose at them. Would not take their notes for eighteen-pence, and sneers at the idea of their ever paying their debts. Herein great injustice is done them. It is true this class are generally so situated that an execution against their goods and chattels would probably reach nothing of consequence. They board at a first-class hotel, and have nothing to move when they change their lodgings, but their luggage. Still these people are not dishonorable or dishonest. Sometimes, but not often, for they seldom take risks, they get swamped in

a large transaction ; but if they do, it is not the petty creditor who suffers. At times they are hard pressed for money,
driven nearly to the wall ; but something turns up to relieve them, and just as you expect to see one die out absolutely, you find him rearrayed in fresh plumage, on the top
of a new and successful adventure. I repeat, these people
are generally agreeable, kind-hearted, over-plausible, it is
true, but well-connected, and in good society.

Reader, I confess, in the character I here endeavor to depict, I have some difficulty in drawing the line between
what is honest, and right, and true, and its opposite. I
confess that while I have a strong conviction, that the life
these people live is not the life to lead, and is such a life as
I would not lead, yet there is another set of men who are to
me much more repulsive. Do not start—I mean the hard-
visaged, sharp-cut, angular, mathematically honest man !
You know such a person, and perhaps you dread his companionship as much as I. Perhaps you don't. Perhaps
you are the identical man himself ! A man honest not from
principle, but from a cold temperament, and a right-angled
conformation. A man who never violated a moral rule ;
who, in the language of his friends, can be trusted with un-
told gold. Who performs and exacts to the uttermost far-
thing. Who could not cheat you in accounts, because it
would disturb the proportions of his ledger. Who is without an impulse, an emotion, a desire. Every thing with
him is by scale and measure, this or that ; all justice, no
mercy ; all requirement, no allowance.

Such men are always rich men, because they are eminent-
ly selfish. Selfish and successful (as the world calls suc-

cess) being true alliterations. To these persons the Eastern
proverb applies : "The extreme of right is the extreme of
wrong."

To return to the class speculative. The persons of this
class are pleasant companions, and generous in their expenditure while their money lasts. If bachelors, they occupy
in the favorite hotel a seat next the host,* and are surrounded by good fellows at least five deep. The best wines
are called for without stint, and the dinner is prolonged
always into the evening. If married, a similar scale is indulged in, but in a different way. There are parties to attend, an opera-box, and possibly a carriage (if matters have
gone right) to provide for. When things go adversely, the
scene changes, an economical scale is submitted to, and
they wait for another turn of the wheel. And so they
manage to preserve a great deal of this life's romance,
which is the true essence of life, after all, and which the
treadmill man of business loses completely and forever by
his iron course of existence.

The fascination which attends the labors of the class speculative is easily understood. There is a great charm in a
pursuit where room is left for the imagination to have full
sway. What cannot be reduced to a certainty, but is entirely subject to the calculations of a sanguine temperament,
is sure to afford extraordinary pleasure and gratification;
and while, after various experiences, I would avoid the

* It is proper to state, for the benefit of the reader who resides out of New York,
that in some of the fashionable hotels (Anglice taverns) of this city, the proprietor
(Anglice landlord) is accustomed to sit at the head of the bachelors' table, and by patronizing smiles and gestures manifest his approbation of those of his "guests" who
spend money most freely—decorous and praiseworthy habit this.

career of these people, I still admit an extraordinary sympathy with them.

I beg to be distinctly understood, that in the classification I have made I do *not* include another species of the genũs speculator, which also figures conspicuously in the annals of the "street." Those I have just described are respectable. Those I am about to describe are not. There are, by the way, other speculators, whom it is unnecessary to notice in this connection, whose transactions are ordinary and commonplace. Among them is the real estate operator, who spends his time in changing city property into country, and then back into city, rarely touching any money, but always getting an excellent trade! the dealer in wild lands; the individuals who speculate at auctions, and so forth, and who are well-meaning people in their way. The class I now refer to is the counterfeit of the first class; a counterfeit so admirably got up that it is sure to deceive on first inspection. The appearance and habits of both are alike, so also the associates and the associations. The man of this class affects the same transactions, and boards at the same hotels. He, too, visits London and Paris, and is mixed with various schemes and adventures; but there is one grand distinction between the two. The counterfeit has not a particle of honesty in his composition, and he never pays his debts. To be sure, he is full of talk about honor and honorable men, he himself, according to his own showing, *is* an honorable man. If any one presumes to doubt it he shall insist on an explanation. I said this sort of person never pays his debts. I am wrong; he does sometimes pay, but it is only when he thinks he can double his indebtedness in the same quarter by doing so. When he comes to town, he decides what hotel he will patronize, and generally manages to bring, or appear to bring, by arriving in their company, several respectable persons along with him, and thus at the start put the landlord under obligations to him. Once established, he calls for very expensive wines, and thus induces others to do the same. He frequently sends to the office for ten dollars, and tells the people to put it in the bill. He takes occasion to make a confidant of the landlord—invites him to his room, shows him thousands and tens of thousands of dollars of fresh, alluring, bright-looking certificates of stock in a dozen different companies *about to be* launched, and explains, of course, *apropos de rien*, how it takes all one's spare cash to start so many valuable enterprises, any one of which, when started, is going to give him all he wants, and he confesses himself, in consequence, hard-up for ready money, and really so interests the good-natured host that he feels it would be cruel to pester his guest with weekly bills, as is customary. In short, he makes up his mind, since it is sure to be paid in the end—oh! yes, for gentlemen always pay their hotel bills—he can afford to wait on so good a fellow, who talks so ingenuously about his situation; besides, the landlord reasons, he really is of great advantage to the house, so let him stay.

This man belongs to a set of what I term picturesque rascals, who never present a straight line or plane surface, but who deal always in the curvilinear; and so far as there are grace and elegance in curves, these fellows are essentially graceful, versatile, and what I call picturesque. What is wonderful, they make few enemies. When our friend thinks

it time to leave the hotel, it is because his various enterprises take him elsewhere. These enterprises have not quite
yet culminated, so he gives the landlord a note at ninety
days for the sum due, insists on leaving four times that
amount in good stocks, and quits the house as a gentleman
should, all right. In the same way he arranges with his
tailor and his boot-maker. He manages so to put every
one of these people under some species of obligation to
him, through his zeal in recommending customers, or by
doing them some little favor, that they can't for the life
of them, abuse him. Now, if our gentleman was really a
sanguine, enthusiastic man, who expected to succeed, and
who really hoped to pay one day, one could have some charity for him; but this is not so. He is a cool, calculating,
adroit knave; his blood is cetaceous, not a warm impulse
beats in his heart. He makes up his mind not only that the
"world owes him a living," but it also owes him champagne,
oyster suppers, a fast horse, good dinners, the best Otard
brandy and Havana cigars; a good seat at the opera and
theatre, *and so forth*—a great deal being contained in that
" and so forth." Since the world owes him these he helps
himself to them; and since the world is wide, and metro-
politan cities large, with an ever-shifting population, he, with
his nice discriminating qualities, collects his dues judiciously,
and manages his various expedients as the Scotchman is
said to get drunk—soberly and with discretion.

CHAPTER XVIII.

WAS I RELIGIOUS?

I AM about to touch on another topic. I was for a time undecided whether or not to carry it along with my narrative, but as it is intimately associated with my reverse of fortune, and as I desire this reverse and its consequences to be fully presented, I determine to do so. I refer to my religious feelings.

I have already mentioned that I was subject, to a considerable degree, to what I believed to be a kind of sentimental piety, springing from a desolate sense of my misfortunes and an instinctive desire to find a safe shelter from them. My good sense rejected all this as not genuine. So that I finally discarded it when it appeared, as a make-believe—a mock sentimentality born out of mere weakness under the pressure of surrounding troubles. After I had become established in my humble abode, and my mind was more calm, I began to reflect. The sacred lessons of my childhood were not lost on me; they now came up with full force. As I have already remarked, I was not what is called "religious." My wife was a member of the church, exemplary and good, if mortal ever was. I myself was a believer in the truths of our holy religion. But I had never felt the need of its "saving influence," which clergymen tell us must be experienced in order to secure a change of heart.

After I had become domesticated in our new abode, it seemed as if GOD was nearer to me than in the handsome house in Broadway. I frequently felt the desire to pray to HIM. But I repressed it. I could not escape from the conviction that it was a mockery to supplicate my MAKER *now*, when I had neglected to do so in the days of my prosperity. Yet I frequently felt in that little quiet home, shut out from the world and so forgotten by the world, a wish to commune with GOD, a desire to rise to the height of true piety, to be a good man. But, I say, I could not act on this. I dare not undertake it as a genuine performance. Place me suddenly back, with hundreds of thousands at my command, and what would become of the religious instinct? where would go those pious aspirations?

> "When the devil was sick,
> The devil a monk would be;
> When the devil got well,
> The devil a monk was he!"

I repeated frequently to myself as I asked the question.

You see, reader, I could not afford, poor as I was and almost starving, to become a hypocrite or even a self-deceiver. I did not *dare* to trifle with subjects which concerned the GREAT future. But I did feel that PROVIDENCE would sooner or later work out in me HIS own purposes.

There is nothing to compare with the grand Calvinistic doctrine of INDIVIDUALITY, which admits the idea that every human being is the direct and immediate subject of GOD's watchful regard, working heroism out of the egotism of mortal man. In no such strong degree did I feel faith or courage. Yet I did believe out of these stormy trials I should by-and-by come, purified as by fire. So I daily asked myself the question : "If you were restored to wealth, how would you feel? what would you do ?" And so long as I could not answer it, except to say I should become as I was in the former days, I knew I could not take credit for any change of feeling or purpose.

At length I began, as I thought, to gain fairer and clearer views of "duty," and to enjoy more of that calm spirit which is so comforting, when my acquaintance with Harley commenced. Its effect on these religious developments was unfriendly and chilling. The thoughts and emotions I was attempting to cultivate, and which were, as I was convinced, to afford me happiness and tranquillity, now gave place to feverish and disturbed ideas, until the former got to be distasteful. I asked myself why this change? Was there any thing about Harley, or what he proposed, which should in any way conflict with my sense of right and honesty; if not, why should I not yield to some of the pleasurable sensations which his presence always produced? Might it not, on the other hand, be possible that the feelings I was endeavoring to cherish were sombre, morbid, unnatural, not the result of a manly effort to do right, but developed, as I have hinted, by the depressing circumstances which encompassed me?

I shall not here answer the question, but leave the reader to trace out the response to it as the narrative proceeds.

CHAPTER XIX.

ALWORTHY AND COMPANY.

ALWORTHY and Company failed just three weeks after my negotiation of their paper. It turned out that for several months previous they were in the habit of putting their own notes on the market, for the purpose of raising money. They had also exchanged acceptances largely with other houses, for the same object, and their speculations turning out badly, they broke.

There was considerable sensation in the street at the announcement. As is usual in such instances, the assets were nil, after protecting the "confidential." In fact, the concern was at the time of stopping payment a mere shell. There was also a good deal of fluttering among the houses who were really solvent, and who had exchanged notes with Alworthy, in the belief that he was so. With others it proved an even thing, since both were worthless. Among these last, I fear, might be classed our new friends Pollock, Pemberton, Hollis and Company. They had given Alworthy about ten thousand dollars of their promises to pay, and had received a like amount from him. As these last were negotiated with their indorsement, both amounts would come against them. Now-a-days they manage these matters better, by having notes drawn to the order of the makers, and indorsed only by them; and if they will sell as "single-name paper," all responsibility is avoided. Except in a great crisis, which carries down business-men suddenly, and in battalions, the knowing ones soon discover signs of probable disaster in a firm, which is evidenced by a gradual rise in the rate at which their notes can be disposed of, till they become unsalable. Still there is a class of shrewd but greedy money-lenders, who are tempted by high prices to purchase paper of this sort, and who sometimes meet with a heavy loss, but always charge enormous rates.

I was a good deal exercised when I learned early one morning of the failure, for fear it would prove calamitous to Harley. He came in my office shortly after, and put me quite at ease on the subject.

"Have you heard the news about Alworthy?" he said.

I told him I had.

"I confess I have had my suspicions ever since that second batch of paper, which I knew nothing of when I offered you the first. However, my name is not mixed up with them, thank fortune."

"But I thought you were interested with Pollock, Pemberton, Hollis and Company?"

"Interested? not to the amount of a penny. It is true I have known Pollock for a long time, a first-rate fellow; and as I wanted an office for a few months, I took the furnished one directly over theirs. I had, besides, a little operation with them, by which I received the most of the Alworthy paper, and paid them a certain amount in cash, and the balance in real estate. I am quite satisfied with the bargain. They tried unsuccessfully in several quarters to sell the notes, and this fact helped me in the trade. So you see I am more obliged to you than you supposed for negotiating them."

" But I understood you to say they had abundant capital."

" So they had, for their regular business. You see Hollis is a little wild by turns, and his father, who is a rich man, put in ten thousand dollars for the sake of establishing his son. But they got to be too ambitious, and struck out right and left. At last they fell in with Alworthy, who is as smooth and keen as a razor, and he put very expansive notions in their heads."

" I declare," I exclaimed with some warmth, " had I known all this, I would not have offered the notes."

" And had I known it," replied Harley, " I should not have taken them. Now, pray, don't put such a long face on the matter," he continued, seeing I looked grave. " You remind me of the Englishman who was miserable all his life for fear his country would never be able to pay the national debt. The loss in this case falls just where it ought to fall, on the note-shavers. They take the risk, and charge accordingly, and they must accept the fortune of war. Had Alworthy's speculations in cotton turned out differently, all would be right."

" True," I remarked, " but Alworthy was reckless. His transactions were not legitimate. He was a gambler, and nothing else."

" My good friend," replied Harley, " I am sorry to see a man of your excellent sense misled by that humbug word ' legitimate.' As to Alworthy's being a gambler, I can only say, all trade is but gambling; a bold bet against Providence,

12

that there will be such and such a market, and such and such a supply, on which depend such and such risks, and such and such profits. Yes, a merchant is not only a gambler, but the most unfortunate and most miserable of the whole gambling class. He never knows, like the man who risks on the red or the black, just where he stands. His results cannot be calculated speedily like those of the stock gambler, but he is forced to take hazard after hazard before any one of his ventures is determined. His fate, too, is dependent on the good or bad management of others, and is so mixed up with incidents and occurrences beyond his control, that I repeat, I pronounce him the most unfortunate gambler of them all. I have been fifteen years in business, have failed twice, went through the horrors of those in purgatory. I don't mean to gamble any more in trade. So, pray, don't talk to me so sanctimoniously about 'legitimate transactions.'"

I perceived that I had touched a delicate point, and I did not debate the subject. Indeed, there was matter for reflection in Harley's observations.

"Come," he said cheerfully, after a little pause, "let us speak of something else. I must get ready for the other side, and you must make yourself master of all the particulars of my various enterprises, for much will have to be done here. Soon you will retrieve your fortunes, and you shall confess how much more satisfactory our labors are than any you have heretofore undertaken."

I was as usual lifted up above ordinary events by the seductive language of this man. We sat down to examine his several projects. I was surprised to see with what order and precision all his documents were prepared. Certified copies of charters ; original patents ; searches of title ; powers of attorney, which were always " full" powers in the largest extent ; accurate descriptions of property, and so forth, and so forth. It was amazing to witness the readiness and the versatility which Harley displayed in explaining his plans for each particular scheme. This would be brought out by a company under the limited responsibility act. That, he was certain a well-known broker would take up. Another would engage the attention of his solicitors, who would manage all the details. Harley's head-quarters would be at Morley's, then the resort for the majority of Americans in London.

The day was consumed in these various examinations. When I rose to go home, I was myself so much elated that I forgot I had quite neglected some important business for a valuable constituent, and that it was now too late to attend to it. Indeed, I had begun to taste the intoxicating sweets which are a part of the luxuries of the class speculative ; my former operations seemed so insignificant compared with what now lay before me. As I walked up Broadway, I looked with some sort of pity on the hard workers pushing homeward.

What a glorious hallucination ! What an ecstatic state of brilliant hopes and joys !

CHAPTER XX.

THE STORY OF RALPH HITCHCOCK.

RALPH HITCHCOCK was my classmate in college, and I was perhaps more intimate with him than with any other student. He was an orphan, and was adopted at the age of fourteen, and educated by his uncle, who was rich. This uncle had sent Ralph to Europe. On his return, he took up his residence in Cincinnati, and shortly after married a young lady from New York. He occasionally visited this city, and when he did was invariably my guest. He rose rapidly in his profession, for he was a man of brilliant genius, but his life was clouded by a great misfortune—the loss of his children. When I saw him last, in 1838, the eldest and only remaining of four, a daughter, had just been snatched away. She was a lovely child, about ten years old. I never saw him dispirited before.

"My friend," he said, "they are all gone, and I do not want to live any longer." He returned to his home more gloomy than when he left it; and in the autumn was seized with a bilious fever of a malignant type, and died. I was acquainted with no particulars, but supposed my friend's circumstances were prosperous, for so he had in general led me to believe. And, putting away in my heart the recollection of our early and later intercourse, as one of the happiest and saddest of my memories, I little thought another scene out of that drama was still to be presented.

I called on Mrs. Hitchcock the day following the night-scene which I have already described. I found her apparently pretty well, and quietly engaged with her needle. She received me politely, but without a particle of alacrity or enthusiasm. She exhibited the spectacle of a refined and gentle nature, so broken by a hard destiny as to lose all sympathy with this world's currents, while she calmly awaited the termination of her fate. Even when I stated my intimate relations with her husband, I could not perceive that her eye quickened, or that her countenance gave any sign of increased interest. Still she conversed freely with me, and gave a clear but condensed account of what had transpired since her husband's death.

It appeared the young doctor had offended his uncle, by going to the West to commence practice, instead of settling in New York. Ralph was of an impatient and an ambitious nature, and believed he could rise more rapidly in that fresh and growing region than in an older place. He was not obstinate, but high-strung. His uncle reproached him for his ingratitude. His reply was, "Whoever reminds one of an obligation cancels it;" and uncle and nephew parted, and never met again. He went at once to Cincinnati, and, as I already knew, married soon after an interesting girl from New York, and set to work to conquer a position. He succeeded. Year after year he sent to his uncle, without word or comment, a certain sum, until he had, according to a liberal calculation, reimbursed the old gentleman, principal and interest, for every possible expenditure incurred on his account. Here was the fault of my friend's nature, half noble, half evil in its origin; a deep and perpetual recollection of a taunt or unjust reproach. Much as we had conferred together by letter and otherwise, and intimate as we had been, Ralph never alluded to any disagreement with his uncle, and I now heard of it for the first time.

Affairs went happily with Ralph until his children began to die. He bore up against the repeated blows till, as I have before stated, his eldest was taken. Then it was the world first knew what a sensitive and impressible nature the rapid, energetic medical man carried about under the brusque outside. His heart-strings snapped. In vain his wife, herself in the depths of affliction, sought to console him. It had no effect. And so the fever found him a most favorable subject, without any nervous resistance, or apparently vital energy. He left but little property besides his furniture and medical library, horses and carriage. For he had lived generously, and, like too many professional men, had not counted on what "after death befalls" the family who are left behind.

The widow struggled on for a while, assisted by the usual resource, boarders. "Matilda" came into the world nearly six months after the death of her husband. She was emphatically the child of sorrow. Unlike the other children, she resembled her father; and from infancy manifested great maturity of mind. With this she exhibited to an unhappy degree the peculiar sensitiveness which was in him so striking a characteristic. She was full of every generous and tender emotion, affectionate and pitiful in the extreme, but proud, quick, violent, and impatient; very passionate,

too, on occasions ; neither obstinate nor wilful, but wayward
and fitful as the wind. Mrs. Hitchcock, unfortunately, had
yielded to her imperious temper; the more so, as she could
see her husband in every burst and outbreak; exaggerated,
it is true, but the more striking because exaggerated.

After several years of hard work in Cincinnati, the furniture needed replenishing, the rent of the house was increased, two of her best boarders had gone away, and Mrs.
Hitchcock was in despair. About this time she received a
letter from a cousin in New York, an estimable lady, as the
world esteems people. That is, she was rich; she was a
church-member. She contributed largely to several of the
city benevolent societies. She was president*ess* of one, and
a directress in half-a-dozen. She was, in fact, one of a large
class, who, like the Pharisee of old, thank GOD they are not
like other people. This lady had married rather late in life,
had been blessed with one child, a daughter; and, as it happened, just the age, within a few days, of the pet lamb of
the widow Hitchcock. With all her cold philanthropy, her
formal religion, her tiresome deed-work, her labored charities, there was a spot in this woman's heart not quite covered by the armor of self-righteousness and formality. She
loved her child. That single, simple outlet from an arid,
unproductive heart, betrayed the existence of a vital point.
Her cousin, Mrs. Hitchcock, and she were girls together,
were at school together. Then, the latter was in a far better position than the now wife of a rich merchant, and was
looked up to accordingly. But things had changed. Mary
Anne, then a bold and showy girl, had made a "good
match," and finding nothing to love in a leather-hearted

man, twenty years her senior, had, fortunately for herself (for she might have laid hold of the other extreme, and disgraced her family), taken to piety for occupation of her leisure hours, ambitiously aspiring to lead the feminine portion of the congregation. Her cousin married, too, and left for Cincinnati. Shortly after, Mrs. Hitchcock's father, who was a lawyer, departed this life, and like most lawyers, who are said to "work hard, live well, and die poor," left little for his widow, who went to take up her abode with her only child, and survived her husband but a few years.

Mrs. Lemuel Dings, for some reason or other, always kept up a correspondence with her cousin, Mrs. Hitchcock. Perhaps she thought, after all, that the old uncle would relent, and at the last moment leave his fortune to the Hitchcocks. Perhaps the deference the family paid to her better position in society, still had a certain influence with her. At any rate, when the really worldly-minded but professedly pious Mrs. Dings found a visitor which she had talked a great deal about, preached and prayed a great deal about, and professed to have no sort of fear of, suddenly an inmate of her house, lodged in her own apartments, close to what was left of her heart; when DEATH in actual presence presented himself, and took—not her husband, but her child; this poor woman was desolate. After the funeral she went about the house very sad. She found no consolation in those precious promises of Scripture which she used to make such parade of.

After a time she remembered the child of her cousin, how handsome it was when she last saw it, only the year before, during a tour West with her husband. Then she contemplated the idea of adopting that child for her own. It never occurred to her, that her unfortunate cousin would herself be bereft of her only source of happiness, should she succeed in stealing away her daughter. It never occurred to her to let her charities flow in the direction to relieve that cousin, and make her happy with her child. Oh! no, not for a moment. But she feared to write, and propose bluntly to receive Matilda and adopt her as her own. So she wrote, proposing that Mrs. Hitchcock should remove from Cincinnati to New York. She explained how easy it would be, with the influence she, Mrs. Dings, could exert, for her cousin to live very pleasantly, and support herself very comfortably there. This letter came at a time when Mrs. Hitchcock was perplexing herself about more furniture and how to pay a higher rent. The poor woman began to be very weary of life, as she had found it since her husband's decease, and she welcomed the idea of getting back to her native city. So, after some correspondence on the subject, but without settling any details, she decided to come. The few effects remaining to her were sold out, and Mrs. Hitchcock, with Matilda, took leave of Cincinnati.

Arrived at New York, Mrs. Dings received her at the steamboat landing, and conveyed her, not to her own handsome mansion in Fourteenth-street, but to comfortable apartments in what in New York is called a "tenement-house," in the Sixth Avenue. Justice to Mrs. Dings compels me to say that the building was new, and of the better description of that class of edifices. It belonged to Mr. Dings, who, it was to be hoped, would not prove a severe landlord. The fact was, Mrs. Dings, considering the situa-

12*

tion of her cousin, and the very slender means at her disposal, had really calculated judiciously for her—judiciously, but out of a very cold heart. Without indulging in any generous impulse, she had come to the icy decision as to just what was best for such a person (that is, any such person, "cousin" out of the question), in just that reduced situation. She intended, not because she indulged in any kind emotion, but in order to "live up to a sense of duty," to throw sufficient needle-work in her cousin's way to enable her to support herself. Then, in due time, she would broach the subject of adopting Matilda. Mrs. Hitchcock, though wounded by the course pursued by the charitable Mrs. Dings, had good sense enough to make the best of her situation.

Matters ran along for nearly a twelvemonth. Matilda was growing very fast; her mother began to feel how necessary education was for her. Mrs. Dings, who had watched the progress of events, finally made her proposition, at, as she considered, just the right juncture. The widow could not listen to it. But poverty is a great persuader. Ought she, at length she asked herself, to stand in the way of her child's advancement? She decided she ought not. But how to prevail on Matilda, for her love for her mother was unbounded, and her passionate nature would resist. At length she persuaded her to make the experiment. The child was not insensible to the allurements of a fine house filled with servants, a handsome carriage, in which she was to ride, and a large variety of pretty dresses. Her mother dared not tell her she would see her but seldom, and that Mrs. Dings would have in the future

entire control over her actions in her place. Well, the
change was made. Mrs. Hitchcock kissed her child, and
gave her up to the woman who had coveted her so much.
She previously had a long and earnest conversation with
Matilda, in which she enjoined her, by the memory of her
father, and by a mother's love, to curb her impatient nature,
and restrain her violence of temper. Matilda's promises
were interrupted by tears and hysteric sobs.

Three days passed without incident. Mrs. Hitchcock was
very lonely, and was beginning to feel she could not endure
the separation, when late in the afternoon Matilda rushed
into the room, and threw herself into her arms, exclaiming:
" I will never go back, I will never go back. The woman
wants me to call her 'mother.' She says I *must* call her
'mother.' I will not do it, I will not. You are my mother.
I will call no one mother but you !"

This was the *denouement* of the selfish scheme of Mrs.
Dings to rob the poor widow of her only child. I am forced
to record that with its failure she ceased to take any interest
in her cousin's affairs, and soon managed to lose sight of her
altogether.

Mrs. Hitchcock did her best to support herself and daughter. The latter had become skilful with the needle, and
though impatient of restraint, worked industriously for her
mother's sake, yet always manifesting evidences of a proud,
haughty, self-willed nature. She would not humbly submit
to her destiny; she revolted against it. She became more
and more bitter toward the world, and looked with almost
hatred on the rich. She delighted at times to go into the
streets, dressed like a pauper, and watch with feelings al-

most of malignity the carriages as they rolled along.   At
thirteen she had acquired nearly the stature of a woman,
and her poor mother was sadly exercised about her, since her
expanding beauty already attracted the attention of all who
encountered her.

Such was the story which I gathered from the widow,
and from facts which afterward came to my knowledge.
It appeared Mrs. Hitchcock had never, before that stormy
night, been attacked in such a manner.   I found she was not
in actual want of the necessaries of life, but it was evident
her constitution was fast breaking down, and that her days
were numbered.   After gleaning this history, I repeated it
to Alice, who the next day paid Mrs. Hitchcock and her
daughter a visit.   What resulted from it, the reader shall
learn in due time.

CHAPTER XXI.

DAY-DREAMS.

A GREAT change came over the appearance of my office. From a quiet, retired room, with few visitors, it was transferred into a bustling, active place, filled with people from morning till night, very agreeable people too. They were generally the parties originally interested in the schemes which Harley had undertaken. For, since the Alworthy failure, my friend had thought best to remove his office from Pollock's, especially as he had concluded not to engage with that firm, as he at first intended, in shipping pure spirits to Bordeaux and have it returned a first-rate article of French brandy, to be sold in bond. The consequence was, since Harley expected to leave in a few weeks for Europe, and I was to be so closely interested with him, we thought it best he should remove to my office, which, by the ready adaptation of a large screen, we easily converted into two rooms.

I now became fully acquainted with the class ycleped "non-industrial" by severe and rigid people. I recollect being most interested in a gentleman who wished to call attention to the harbor of Brunswick in Georgia, a neglected position, and claimed to be one of the best havens on the whole line of coast. It was proposed to erect a city there in place of the few scattering houses, and make it the *entrepôt* for Georgia pine betwixt the interior and England.

This man was very sanguine of becoming a millionaire and of making Harley a millionaire also. He was a liberal, whole-souled fellow, who was possessed of a large landed property in Georgia, and was desirous to avail himself of Harley's genius to make it available. He lived well: ate good dinners, drank good wines, and waited with patient good-nature for the auspicious day when English capital should cross the water, guided by the extraordinary talent of his friend (to whom he had given a written contract to share equally), and proceed to develop the resources of his native state in a manner serviceable to all parties.

It is quite unnecessary to make mention of the many schemes presented to Harley, which were at once rejected as altogether too visionary or impracticable. One, however, I will allude to, and hope an old acquaintance will pardon me for recalling an instance when his usual good sense and shrewdness so far forsook him that he actually lent a serious ear and a good deal of money toward the construction of a flying-machine. This was first offered to Harley, who rejected it on the spot, but as it promised so much—the ocean could be traversed in a few hours with ease and without danger—it so far found favor in Wall-street as to induce the gentleman just mentioned to put in sufficient money to build one. Delicacy forbids my going into particulars, and telling what became of the machine.

I repeat, my office was now filled with individuals who were about to realize fortunes. The tone of conversation was always cheerful and encouraging; in fact, we had it all our own way. But unfortunately, reader, the more my office became frequented by these sanguine gentlemen of the future, the greater was my distaste for my daily occupation. Listening continually to remarks where no sums under tens of thousands were spoken of, and from these numerals as a minimum up to fabulous amounts, it is not to be wondered at that I became disgusted with the petty labors of a note-broker, wherein my first ambition had been to make five dollars a day. To run about all the morning without success, or if successful, to secure but three or four dollars as the fruit of my industry, became very irksome in view of the large sums I was certain of realizing in the course of a few months. Harley thought it very ridiculous of me to be still digging away at what he called my break-back work.

Without exactly withdrawing from it, I found myself taking less and less interest in what I had to do. This was soon perceived by my constituents, and the result can be readily divined. By degrees my business fell off. I was too much occupied to think about it. Indeed, it was not long before I was engrossed heart and soul in the various schemes which Harley had under preparation. Possibly the reader will wonder at this avowal. *I* wonder when I now look back on what I was doing. I had experience. I was fully enlightened on the subject. I may say I knew just what I was about. But for all that, a certain hallucination had possession of me. I can compare its effects only to what is produced by the extraordinary stimulus of wine or tobacco. The conversation of men about every-day affairs became insipid. I lived in a world shared only by my companions in exaltation, and if occasionally I permitted any foreboding of the issue, or any distrust of the results to cross my mind, I had only to cheer myself by conversing with some of my friends, who were fully competent to reassure me. Harley had not yet called on me for the seven hundred and odd dollars which he had desired me to retain. He finally said he should not require it till he left for Europe. I was exceedingly prudent, taking care to invest on "call," on perfect security. But the control of the money made me feel richer than I really was, and helped to heighten the day-dream which entranced me.

One thing proved a source of constant embarrassment. I have observed that I was in the habit of informing my daughter of my daily plans and various business details, · interesting to her in consequence of her intense sympathy with every thing which concerned me. Now, I could not explain to her just what I was doing, and hoped to achieve. Why couldn't I? That was the question. Did I not fear that to her clear and unsophisticated sense, child as she was, my hopes and expectations would seem visionary and delusive, especially as I was losing the substance—a sure support from day to day—while I grasped at what *might* turn out but shadow? That was it. And while in a general way I gave Alice to understand that I had undertaken several business matters which promised largely, I no longer talked over affairs with her as heretofore. I grew silent and *distrait*. I spent less time at the house with the children, and even when at home, began to feel a nervous restlessness to get back to the scene of so much promise, where I could talk over our plans with Harley, and find in his ever-cheerful companionship a solace against any fear or foreboding.

I said my business diminished. It is remarkable how

soon the world discovers when a man is not in earnest in what he is about, and deals with him accordingly. Of all occupations, the one I had selected required perhaps the most assiduous attention. The reader will not be surprised to learn that before Harley got ready to sail for Liverpool I had quite abandoned the occupation of note-broker, or rather, it had abandoned me. And why? I have already explained. Not that my time was really entirely taken up in the new schemes, but because attention to them absolutely unfitted me for any steady occupation, so that I could not endure the tranquil uniformity of ordinary life. But how was I to live, meantime? Even so serious a question did not embarrass me, did not present itself in force or seriously. Oh! in all these various projects, a few thousands must come under any circumstances. I have already five hundred dollars ahead, besides the five hundred dollars of Alice's. I can at any time draw for what is necessary on Harley, so he says; and we shall yet have between two and three thousand dollars out of the proceeds of the sale of the old house.

At the same time, I insensibly adopted a more generous style of living, so that I was soon spending at the rate of two thousand dollars a year instead of fifteen hundred. My friends perceived the agreeable change in my appearance, and congratulated me on my doing so well. Even Mr. Norwood was deceived. He was not familiar with what I was about from day to day, and did not know, and I did not tell him I had abandoned my original occupation. But his congratulations embarrassed me. It seemed as if I were deceiving him by receiving them. However, things went on pleasantly during the heyday of that speculative dream. I saw I was considered to be in a prosperous way, and I really fancied myself so. If called on for the reason why, I should have waived the subject, for I could not give any.

I took, however, some precautions, although Harley had repeatedly intimated I could rely on him for any thing. I seized an opportunity to explain to him that my embarking in these various affairs quite prevented attention to any regular business. His reply was every way satisfactory. He fully comprehended it, he said, and supposed from what he had already told me, that I distinctly understood he was aware my business would be sacrificed, and he intended to relieve my mind on that head by authorizing me to draw on him, pending negotiations, for what was necessary for the support of myself and family. If the reader could have witnessed the kind manner and appreciative tone of Harley while making this communication, he would not wonder at the effect it produced on me. Nothing could have been more generous, and such confidence did this man inspire by his extraordinary address, that the failure of any one of his plans seemed impossible—that is the word, impossible. I now felt at ease with respect to the future. My days at home were happy again. I was no longer absent-minded or *distrait*. Oh! how I did enjoy that period of repose from anxiety and apprehension.

CHAPTER XXII.

HARLEY ABROAD.

IT was not till February of the new year (1849) that Harley was quite ready to sail for Europe. His determination to have all his documents in unexceptionable shape before presenting them to the capitalists over the water, led to the delay. But at length every paper was in order. Exemplifications of public documents, certified copies from public records, elaborately-drawn powers of attorney duly executed and acknowledged, and properly authenticated both by the English and French consuls ("for," said Harley, "I may decide to operate in Paris as well as London"), filled a large, substantial, iron-bound box, to us the true philosopher's stone, the real elixir for transmuting into gold.

Prior to Harley's departure, I refunded him the money which he had left in my charge and which I knew he relied on for immediate expenses. He would take no interest, although I had received not only interest, but several commissions, from its employment. He even apologized for touching the money at all. "You know," he observed, "it will never do for me to go out to London in any other character than that of a man of wealth. A poor devil is John Bull's special abhorrence. Notwithstanding his severe hits in America, he still believes it is the place to realize fortunes. And on account of his own prudent habits, he can't understand why if we live *like* nabobs, we should not be as rich *as* nabobs. So I shall take my wife with me to London; hire a handsome furnished house; open spacious offices in the city: set up my brougham with a spruce tiger in livery, and drive into town at precisely the same moment of time every morning, and leave just as precisely every afternoon. This will show several things; that I am a very independent fellow; that I am very punctual as well as punctilious, and therefore a thorough man of business. You shall see," he added after a pause, in which it seemed as if he were contemplating himself descending from his carriage in the neighborhood of the bank, and marching with an easy, much-at-home air into his office, " you shall see, my friend," he repeated, nodding complacently, " and that very soon."

Harley actually left the country to carry out his various plans, including the play of rich man by setting up an establishment, brougham and all, with less than a thousand dollars at command, and with no resources beyond what could be derived from the contents of the aforementioned large iron-bound box.

I know the regular business man will sneer at the ventures of my good friend. For he regards such people as pests in the community, because they live so much at their ease, and act so charmingly the part of capitalists without having a dollar of capital. And yet this same regular man of business looks at the man of speculation with a species of envy akin to that with which your severely virtuous woman regards the free-and-easy manners of some stylish lady who, her reputation having become a little questionable, independently places herself just outside the limits of severe propriety.

Knowing just what I did about Harley, would you not suppose I trembled for the result of certain drafts I was to draw on him to defray immediate expenses? Yet the subject gave me no uneasiness whatever. Indeed, so fully did I believe in his ability to accomplish his objects, that I forbore to ask him for about two hundred dollars, which I had already expended out of the five hundred laid aside, because I perceived how important the money would be to him at the start.

Harley was particular to put our understanding in writing before he left. By it I was to receive one-fourth part of the net profits to be derived from the various schemes he had undertaken or should undertake in connection with his present trip to Europe. Perhaps it may occur to the reader to inquire how I was to be of use to Harley, at least to such an extent that he should be ready to let me into so considerable a share of the results of his enterprises. I was myself at first a little at loss on the subject, but in getting to be thoroughly informed of all his plans, I saw how important it was for him to have a reliable coadjutor on this side. Besides, I still retained some valuable correspondents there, and I could materially aid Harley in establishing himself.

. . . .

It was precisely at noon, Wednesday, that the Cunard steamer "Hibernia" left her dock, with Harley and his wife among the passengers. Mrs. Harley was especially delighted at the idea of "going to Europe." For she had not accompanied her husband on his previous trip. My whole family went with me to the steamer to see our friends off; we had become very well acquainted during the winter. The children were much delighted at every thing they beheld, and Alice played the matron astonishingly well. As I bid Harley adieu, it seemed as if I had been well acquainted with him all my life. His cordial, whole-souled " GOD bless you!" struck into my heart. We watched the steamer for some time as she worked slowly down into the bay, Harley waving his handkerchief at intervals, all of us returning his signals. At last he was no longer to be seen, and with a parting glance at the ship, we took our way homeward.

I expected to feel lonely after his departure. Indeed, the next morning I found myself quite below par in spirits. On reaching my office, however, some of our friends who were interested in one or the other of the enterprises Harley had in charge, came in, and the day was spent discussing various points relating to them. In the course of the week one or two gentlemen, hearing I was concerned in such negotiations, came to introduce new projects to me, so that my time was quite occupied with examining these and others which now fell in my way.

I have stated that I gradually increased my daily expenditures. Strange, you will say, since I, had thus far made nothing at all out of any of these schemes, but on the contrary, had already spent two hundred dollars of what I called my principal. But the future was to be my paymaster, and I trusted to it implicitly. I adopted, therefore, Harley's advice to occasionally invite to dinner some of the persons who were interested in the most valuable enterprises. This threw a cheerful air over our house, and made Alice especially happy because she believed it a sign of renewed prosperity. In return, many were the charming dinners I was invited to at several fashionable hotels of the city.

I well remember one given at the Gloria Hotel by the Georgia gentleman, who was proposing to develop the capabilities of the port of Brunswick. It was a very delightful set-down—ten covers. The bill of fare was printed on satin, commencing with "Saddle-Rock oysters on the half-shell," and followed by all the delicacies New York could afford. The wines and *liquors* were superb. At that dinner was the agent of a British capitalist, who had come at Harley's suggestion to examine and report generally about the property, and also the facilities for cutting and transporting the pine timber on it; also the depth of water at the port of Brunswick. This person was an engineer by profession, not in the permanent employ of the capitalist, but selected for the occasion. Of course it was for the interest of the Georgia gentleman to produce from first to last a good impression. He therefore opened the campaign with the dinner at the Gloria Hotel. This was followed by other agreeable attentions, until both took their departure for the famous harbor. For our friend was too sagacious to allow the agent to proceed by himself, not that there were any untruthful representations made respecting the enterprise; but the fear was, that other parties, jealous of his good fortune, might get the ear of the Englishman and underbid their neighbor in the price of pine timber lands, of which this particular person certainly had not the monopoly in that district.

In just one month I received a letter from Harley. He had arrived safely with his wife. Had already had a most encouraging interview with his solicitors. Every thing looked prosperous. Would write fully next steamer.

From that time forward Harley proved a most regular correspondent. He was a voluminous letter-writer. The least measure of success, and every shadow of adverse prospects, were vividly daguerreotyped. But there was very little shadow to a man of Harley's temperament, so his epistles were generally inspiriting. He was remarkably clear and methodical; to each particular scheme was devoted a certain space, and headed accordingly. Under each head were his remarks, requests, or instructions. Sometimes fresh documents were required for this; more information to be forwarded about that; a new set of papers for a third, and so on.

It was not long before something definite appeared to be gradually working out of the innumerable matters in hand. To be sure John Bull was not to be hurried. Yet Harley understood his character so well, that he lost no time. At length a company was formed under the auspices of his enterprising solicitors, for working the Tennessee Copper Mine, " provisionally," it was true, based on the report of a scientific man, to be sent immediately forward. So far so good. Again, a wealthy broker of Austen Friars had consented to send an agent to Lake Superior, to investigate the value of the property which Harley had offered for exploitation. The California mines promised still better; for all London, Harley wrote, was crazy after them.

Those were bright days, indeed, when each successive

steamer brought some favorable tidings. Harley had been successful in procuring a delightful house, in which he was installed, and his plans were all working to a charm. At the end of two months I drew on him for one hundred pounds, to cover, according to agreement, my personal expenses, and also certain disbursements made in the course of business. The bill was duly honored, and it is impossible to describe my transports on experiencing this first evidence of success. *There* was something tangible. To be sure only amounting to what I had disbursed, but it included a livelihood.

Harley, meanwhile, was careful to explain that it must necessarily be some time before profits could be realized. He managed, he said, in his various operations, to arrange for a small sum to be raised on the provisional shares, or on the various conventions he entered into. These provided for the cost of examining property, and other incidental matters, which Harley took good care should cover his expenses and my own. In this way the brougham and tiger were sustained, and a very nice time generally inaugurated for Mrs. Harley, while my own drafts, which gradually increased in amount, were promptly met.

It was not long before Mr. and Mrs. Harley were presented at court, and soon found their way into society which, had they been born in England, they could never have entered. But, as wealthy Americans, residing abroad, whose position was assured by their ambassador, and who stood well financially with their bankers, the *entrée* to fashionable circles was easy and felicitous. There, for the present, we may leave them.

13

CHAPTER XXIII.

THE CHOLERA.

IN the summer of 1849 the cholera visited New York. It did not interfere much with rich people. There were certain startling exceptions, sudden and sharp, which made the luxurious sensitive as to their hold on life, and induced a general hegira from the town to the mountains or sea-shore. It was the poor, however, who were forced to take the principal burden of the epidemic, as they have to carry other burdens grievous to be borne, but which Providence has decreed they *must* endure so long as they live.

By the middle of July, the deaths by cholera alone reached one hundred daily. This account soon ran up to two hundred. I felt no great apprehension for myself, but children have an instinctive terror of pestilence, and I began to fear for them. So, early in July, I took pleasant lodgings at a small town in the interior of Connecticut, and remained there until the middle of September. I was happy to be able to aid Mrs. Hitchcock and her daughter to accompany us. In this quiet but delightful retreat I spent two months very pleasantly. I devoted myself to the young people, and glimpses of happier days shone in on me. Matilda appeared more natural than I ever saw her ; only she had a nervous fear of the contagion, which was at times melancholy to witness. I received my letters from Harley regularly, and although my absence from New York necessarily delayed some matters, I became each day more and more sanguine of satisfactory results.

. . . .

When we all came back in September, the city had resumed its wonted aspect. Congratulations passed among friends and acquaintances, as they met and found on inquiry each others' families with unbroken numbers. Sometimes condolences were tendered instead. But the pestilence had now left us, that was certain, and the inhabitants returned to their business or their pleasures with undiminished zest ; indeed, rather with a heightened ardor, caused by a natural reaction.

As I gathered my little family safe around me the first evening of our arrival, I felt grateful to God for permitting us all to live. I called to mind how two years before we had come in from Newport, so suddenly to encounter that calamitous reverse. I could not prevent some severe pangs as I thought over the occurrences of that year ; recalled the scenes in my house in Broadway, scenes in which my wife was always in the foreground. I thought of the stormy night, when I came home drenched with rain, to find her waiting for me, a ready, active, sympathizing spirit. How vividly I saw her, with her hand resting on my shoulder, looking anxiously into my face, asking what troubled me. Then the scene changed to the last, sad parting ; the melancholy termination of our united life. Oh ! the rich, unbounded resources of her woman's heart ! Where was she now ? And I ! What had I still to do here ?

I looked up, and my glance fell on Alice. I was impressed

for the first time with the fact that she was now a young lady. For the first time I comprehended the entire sacrifice she was making of herself to promote her father's happiness. She was at an age when young girls are fondest of society; when its pleasures are fresh, and its enjoyments genial and innocent. But Alice lived without any of these. Her time was devoted to the younger children and to me. It is true she had received invitations from some of our old friends, but she refused them all. For a time Miss Stevenson visited her, and endeavored to bring her out of the seclusion she had chosen; she called several times to ask her to ride. It was of no avail, and the visits were at length discontinued. Alice, evidently, had come to a decision as to her course, and was firm in abiding by it.

I say that I regarded her at that moment in a new light. It struck me that I was very unjust to permit her to go on in this manner.

"Alice," I said.

She looked up.

"Come here, my child."

She came, and seated herself by my side.

"Do you know what I am thinking of, Alice; do you remember two years ago?"

"How can I forget it, papa; the time when you were so unhappy?"

"I know, Alice; but I was not thinking of that. I was thinking of the time when *you* had so much to make you gay. You were just beginning to enjoy society—still a school-girl, but old enough to appreciate what you saw at home. Now, when you ought to mix with young people of your own age, you are shut up here, and are nothing but a drudge."

"How can you say so, papa; do I seem so stupid and drudge-like to you?"

"No, indeed; but, my child, you are no longer a little girl. You have become, almost without my perceiving it, a young lady, and it is very wrong for me to permit you to be confined in the way you are."

"My dear father," said Alice, seriously, "I know what you mean; and knowing it, let me entreat you not to bestow one moment of uneasiness about me. For I assure you I think I never was so happy in my life—no" (she paused as if to consider), "not even when dear mamma was alive. It seems as if I had so much to live for; to make things pleasant for you, and to look after Charley and Anna. Oh! so much depends on me, papa—at least I make myself believe so—that I am very, very happy."

"Besides, papa," she continued, "do not think I neglect myself. I read a great deal, you know, for you select the books. I practise my music, and you often tell me how much I improve. We have, too, some very agreeable neighbors; not wealthy people, I admit, but who are really refined and intelligent, whom I frequently see, and have pleasant chats with. And now can you not understand why I should be content?"

"GOD bless you, my child; GOD bless you." It was all I could say. I kissed her tenderly, and rose, and walked out till I could subdue my emotion. Then I came back to the parlor, tea was brought in, after that we were musical—and so the evening wore away.

.   .   .   .

The cholera had not passed me by altogether. The next day, as I was going to my office, I learned what was to me very distressing intelligence. Mr. Norwood had fallen a victim to the terrible scourge. He owned a pleasant summer residence near New Rochelle, and, although there was a good deal of sickness in the vicinity, he did not think it necessary to go elsewhere. He was taken suddenly one evening on returning from town, and in twenty-four hours was a corpse. I suppose I was selfish in my grief at the loss of my only steadfast and disinterested friend. The suddenness of the attack, and the swiftness of the result, appalled me. How full of life was this man! Literally he had been taken away in the midst of his days. I did not know how much I really depended on him till he was lost to me. So it is with us. We cannot appreciate the various props and supports which surround and sustain us till one after another is struck away, and we are left defenceless. Mr. Norwood dead! was I never more to be cheered by his encouraging smile, nor buoyed up by his kind assurances? No, never again.

I sat an hour in my office thinking over events connected with my intimacy with this high-minded, honest advocate.

Unable longer to bear the sad thoughts which overcame me, I descended to the street. The first person I met was Downer. We shook hands. I never felt so cordially disposed toward him as at that moment. His countenance indicated a good deal of recent suffering.

"Have you been in the city all summer?" I asked.

"To be sure I have. How could a poor devil like me get out of it? I sent my wife and children into Delaware county, among the woods, where they could live cheaper than here, but I had to stay and make something to support them. Thank GOD I have lived through it. Never had a dispute with my wife before. This time I was determined to have my own way. She insisted on not leaving me; I declared she should. I brought the children into the argument, and that helped to carry the day. The fact is, I knew I shouldn't die. But I came pretty near it, though. Was taken one night all alone in my house. Well, I lived, and here we are."

Since I had seen Downer's family, I entertained very different sentiments toward him. I could fully understand, I thought, his struggles, and the feelings which actuated him. Little did he care for the smooth conventionalities of society when those he loved were ready to perish.

"So," he remarked, after a pause, "you are out of it?"

"Out of what, pray?"

"Why, out of this hell-begotten business. I knew you wouldn't stand it long. I knew you couldn't."

"Oh! I perceive your meaning now," I replied. "It is true I have taken up other matters, which I thought promised better. But not because I was disgusted with what I was doing, I assure you. On the contrary, I sometimes have doubts as to the expediency of leaving a business I think I could have made a comfortable living in."

"Well, you were doing pretty fair, that's a fact. But you started at a good time, and hadn't been through one of our hard scrabbles. Then, I tell you, there must some go to the wall. It is the hardest fend off. So, thank HEAVEN that you are well out of it."

"If I am *well* out of it, I will. Good morning."

I turned to depart. Downer called me back. He hesitated a moment, and then bluntly said: "Can you lend me five dollars ?"

"With much pleasure," I exclaimed, and I handed him the desired sum.

"Doubtful if you ever see it again," he said, with an attempt to be jocose, and walked rapidly away.

．　　　．　　　．　　　．　　　．　　　．　　　．

I found I had a good deal on my hands in bringing up various matters which had to be neglected during my sojourn in the country. My former *confrères* soon gathered around me, and I was presently engaged, busily as ever, with Harley's instructions, with receiving and getting off the agents who were coming out, in laying hold of some new projects, and attending generally to the details of our various enterprises. My mind was buoyed up with a feeling which sure prospect of success invariably produces.

The reader, who has thus far followed me, as I have endeavored truthfully to recount some occurrences of my life, must not make up his mind too hastily, that I was altogether without decision of character, or fixedness of purpose. It is a dreadful thing to become unsettled after one has passed fifty, and a most difficult thing to recover again. Indeed, it seems to be just a hazard, and nothing more.

You meet a man, for example, you have not encountered for many years. You had lost sight of him altogether. He was formerly an active, enterprising citizen, occupying a prominent position; now he is a complete wreck: that is very evident. But what stress of weather has brought him to this condition? His ship has gone down, perhaps, in very sight of port. From position and influence of a certain kind, having missed his footing, perhaps by no fault of his own, he has fallen clear into the other extreme. Reader, do not forget this class. Try, if it be possible, to do something to relieve those who belong to it. Remember, if you find in them any thing to censure and carp at, that great have been their trials and misfortunes, and your charity must be proportionably great.

You meet another man whom you had also lost sight of. When you last saw him his coat was threadbare; he was struggling with difficulties; pressed down, harassed; borrowing money to-day, so as to return what he owed for yesterday's debt; jumping from bog to bog, very soon it seemed he would be engulfed. Now, how quiet and complacent he is; how unembarrassed and quite at ease! He has grown stouter and taller and broader. His face is fuller, and his complexion finer. You no longer see any restlessness of the eye, any perturbation in the countenance. He wears gloves, and he takes one off with unction as he shakes your hand. The first individual avoided you, this one evidently courts a recognition. It is plain he has weathered the storm, and got safe into harbor. But it might have been the other man who weathered it, and this who went down. Rejoice, therefore, with the one who is snug and safe in a fair haven, and lend a helping hand, if you can, to the one struggling among the breakers.

13*

It is comparatively easy to write the history of our lives, but oh! who shall write the history of the lives we do *not* lead? I mean the lives which our youthful aspirations, our tastes, and our hopes mark out for us. The lives, perhaps, which we are just ready to enter on, when a cruel destiny overtakes us. Ah! who shall dare to write that history!

END OF PART SECOND.

UNDERCURRENTS OF WALL-STREET.

PART THE LAST.

"To plunge and perish, or with patient mind
To suffer and to live. The sufferer's part
At length I chose, and resolute survived."

CHAPTER I.

THE RETROSPECT.

THIS narrative is resumed at a period nearly two years and a half subsequent to the date referred to in the preceding chapter. It brings us to the spring of 1852. The lapse of time we will bridge over by a brief epitome of what occurred during those thirty months. It would be easy to fill a volume with details, but it would contain many repetitions, and would not serve the purpose I have in view.

Two years and a half, after we are fifty-two, cannot well be spared. At that age every year counts. It is not pleasant to be reminded in the midst of our labors, especially when a family at home is entirely dependent on them; it is not agreeable, I say, to be reminded by some incipient debility or tell-tale weakness that the infirmities of age are beginning to hover around us. All of a sudden we dis-

cover we have not the same suppleness of joint, the same
elasticity of limb, the same general activity of body as before. We put it down to a cold, a touch of rheumatism, or
a slight visitation of neuralgia—to any thing but what it
really is, the advance-guard of dissolution. After a while
we give it up. The cold is not cured, the rheumatism and
neuralgia do not mend, and we submit to the inevitable
destiny which says: "Grow old or die!"

It is then we grudge the years which bring us no returns,
which leave us no better than they found us. For men, as
they advance in life, feel a saddening disappointment when
they think how meagre of results it has been to them. So
true is it, that there is implanted in the breasts of us all a
consciousness that we ought not to live in vain.

Two years and a half, reader, and we meet again.

There is an end to my numerous speculations; and without my being made rich or comfortable, or having one
penny laid aside. I have an impression that most of my
readers imagine that Harley had undertaken to lay some
snare for me, that I was about to become his victim, or
dupe, or be unfortunately involved by his practices, or
something of the sort.

I have no such experience to record. Harley proved to
be just what he appeared. During those two and a half
years he worked indefatigably. He crossed the ocean several times. His perseverance was marvellous; his hope
always large and encouraging. On the whole, I cannot say
I have any reason to complain of him. I must give, therefore, a brief explanation why I find myself in this unpleas-
ant situation.

It will be remembered that I was to have one-quarter of the net profits of the various enterprises connected with America, which Harley should engage in. At the same time, I was to draw on him for my necessary expenses. The result of each separate undertaking may be briefly summed up as follows:

Of the three California gold-mines, but one turned out to have a title which would pass. It took a year to get satisfactory evidence of that, and a great expense. By that time far better placers were offered. In fact, London was flooded with auriferous projects, from the Mariposa mines of Fremont to the mere "show" of the California squatter, represented only by an attractive lump of gold. So Harley thought best to sell our mine, for five thousand pounds (twenty-five thousand dollars), cash. It had simply cost the owner the trouble of prospecting it, and of going through the usual squatter-law form of taking possession, nothing more.

From this twenty-five thousand dollars had to be deducted, by the terms of sale, the various charges and expenses of the solicitors, for examining titles, attending meetings, etc., etc., etc., which amounted in round numbers to seven thousand dollars. Mem.: The solicitors who received these large fees had influenced their clients to make this purchase, and had to be paid accordingly.

Of the seventeen thousand five hundred which remained, the owner got one-half, and I a fourth of the balance. I had no reason to complain certainly.

The Virginia gold-mine promised very well. Here were some improvements, and a quantity of ore already excavated. A geologist of respectability was sent out to examine it. His report was flavored with the choice viands and fine wines of the Old Dominion; and on the strength of it a company was brought out, nominally in Paris, under the French law of *en commandite.* The shares were really owned in London by some speculators, who to avoid all responsibility prevailed on a Frenchman in their employ to act as *gerant.* These people soon began to speculate in the stock, having got it on the mining list, and paid not the slightest attention to working the mine itself. The proprietor did receive in cash the amount of his improvements; for the rest he obtained a certain amount of the shares, and Harley and I took our proportion, but we had to engage not to offer them in the market for the space of one year. Harley also received a pretty large sum under the disbursement account, of which my part was about a thousand dollars. After a while, the stock began to fall; those in the scheme had worked off their shares on the simple ones who were outside, and the whole broke down. To be sure they violated their contract as to working the mine; the fact is, they never intended to work it, only to use the company for stock operations, which they were enabled the better to do, because the mine was in working order. Harley threatened law proceedings and various other measures, but the affair subsided as such affairs generally do. He was too busy to prosecute; it might not have been judicious, and so the whole matter dropped. Certain shareholders to this day curse Harley as a swindler, when it was the Englishmen who swindled their brother Englishmen in the business.

An interesting book might be written about the mine on the Isthmus. Here every thing was right. The ore was very rich and abundant. The grants perfect. The conveyances *en regle.* In due course a company was formed in London, a *bona-fide* company, to exploit this really valuable gold-mine. It was on this enterprise that Harley principally depended for the realization of his grand ideas of fortune. And there seemed nothing in the way to prevent. The directors were not only respectable, but embraced some of the best men in London. The plans were good; the subscriptions promptly paid; Harley's share in the contract was so large that with a moderate success, wealth was insured to us both. He had agreed (he could not well do otherwise if he wished to exhibit confidence in the scheme, and he certainly had confidence in it) to receive a certain portion of paid-up stock after the company should raise the requisite amount of working capital.

This company sent out a splendid lot of machinery, a first-rate engineer, a geologist, practical miners to work the mines, a large quantity of provisions, including pork, beef, flour, together with *a generous quota of spirits.* Harley had repeatedly warned the manager that it was absolutely essential for the success of the expedition that no liquor be allowed to the men. He had carefully investigated this subject as connected with the Isthmus, but the advice was disregarded. The people arrived. Before the machinery was erected the fever broke out among them. Nearly all died, or suffered the entire loss of health. Only those who practised total abstinence were saved, and they were few. By this time over one hundred and twenty thousand dollars

had actually been expended, or rather wasted. A fresh call
was made, for Englishmen will not readily give up an affair
they have put their money into. Another hundred thousand
was raised. Harley had to contribute on his stock, although
they were paid-up shares, or lose it, for the company had
raised all the working capital they agreed to. Another expedition started. Strange to say, rum in large quantities
was again permitted to be sent, although under the control
of the manager there. The men, unused to the climate,
clamored for spirits. The manager yielded. In fact, he
thought it would do them good. The result was a repetition of the same unhappy scenes as before. This consumed
more than two years. Still the company would not give up.
But Harley could no longer respond to the tax on his shares.
He had already managed to sell some, although the stock
was not on the market, but now nobody would buy. Other
matters not going to his mind, he was unable to pay the
considerable sum called for, and so his stock was forfeited.
I will remark here, that after two more discouraging experiments, the company were entirely successful, and their shares
are worth at this day, on the London mining board, nearly
one hundred per cent. premium! Thus we just escaped
realizing an immense fortune!

I have already mentioned an agent had been sent out to
report as to the value of the two Lake Superior copper-
mines. These were two separate properties. Unfortunately,
the title to one was in litigation. Harley was promised by
his principal that all difficulties relating to it should be
settled before an agent could arrive out. It proved to be
impossible, and that was an end of the matter. The other

property was very valuable, and promised largely. The owner was a 'cute down-easter, who, seeing the advantages to be reaped from the enterprise, came back with the agent to London. These two had put their heads together on the voyage to cheat Harley out of the benefits he was to derive; he had a written contract for one-half the profits, as usual, and this now seemed to the owner beyond all reason. The result was, he intrigued with the London broker, told stories to Harley's prejudice, employed a solicitor to look into the contract, who decided Harley had not complied with every particular, and in his judgment it could not be enforced. In short, Harley saw clearly what was going on, and determined to have no litigation or scandal. He therefore permitted the owner to buy out his interest for five thousand dollars, which was paid to him in cash, and the parties remained apparently on the best terms. For it was a principle with Harley never to quarrel with any body.

The company for the working of the Tennessee copper-mine went forward very well. But it was subject to the fate of every English undertaking; that is, it was badly managed at first, and a large amount of money wasted. After two or three misadventures it began to produce something, but Harley was in no position to wait for dividends, which, to the great joy of these Englishmen, promised to be very regular in four or five years! So he sold out our interest on the best terms possible.

The Virginia land-company charter amounted to just nothing at all. The titles were involved in such inextricable confusion, "lapping over" each other sometimes five or six deep, that although, as the solicitor said, the lands were doubtless there, and enough of them, it required more professional skill than he was capable of, to disentangle the snarl.

The Georgia affair might have turned out well could we have kept our secret. But the appearance of a British agent, whom it was soon rumored was a special messenger from the Bank of England, (!) and whose every word and gesture were watched and reported, threw the whole region into a state of excitement. When it came to the mysterious business of taking soundings in and around the harbor, and making minute inquiries on various subjects connected with the resources of the country, the excitement was complete. The agent, despite the endeavors of our Georgia friend to keep him close, was surrounded by hosts of pine-land people, who were ready to sell at any price, cash down. It is but fair to say, the agent remained true to his convivial pledges; he had come out, he said to all inquirers, for a certain purpose, and he had nothing whatever to do outside of his instructions. This only added fuel to the flame. In vain our Southern friend endeavored to quiet it. He became the object of envy to the surrounding country, so that in less than a fortnight after the return of the agent to London, there followed him three individuals from that region, each with plenipotentiary power to sell at least a hundred thousand acres of land at ONE QUARTER of what Harley asked for his! The next steamer brought out two more Georgians, on whom these three, who acted in concert, had stolen a march, and who offered other large tracts at still lower prices. The result was, the whole scheme was knocked in the head; although Harley had the pleasure, if pleasure it was, to see the five " representative men," after spending six months in London, and quarrelling with each other, return home with loss of money, time, and reputation, only to be abused by their constituents, on whom they had drawn largely for expenses.

But the live-oak lands of Florida—there was an opportunity ! The price of the land was understood and settled on. The titles beyond question. The quality of the oak timber undisputed. All the expenses calculated, and what a fortune!—on paper. Alas! there was one screw loose. The little item of *transportation* had been overlooked ; or rather at the last moment it was ascertained that the speculation turned on the completion of about one hundred miles of railway, on which trains were already running but twenty-five miles !

The invention for making paper out of the bark of certain trees, although patented in America, Harley found to be an old French discovery, which had already been unsuccessfully experimented with.

The plans for smelting ores with little or no fuel, and for generating steam with equal economy, turned out mere chimeras of the brain of some half-crazed mechanical genius.

The French brandy scheme, I have already said, was abandoned.

The invention for making steel out of coarse pig-iron promised a great deal. The inventor was a poor man, who could advance no money for testing it. So he gave Harley three-fourths of the profits, on condition that he would furnish all expenses. It cost quite a sum to patent it all over Europe, and still more to erect a small shop for experiments.

It can scarcely be said that these experiments failed, but while the theory of the process was successfully demonstrated, practically it would not pay, except on a large scale; and no Englishman could be found ready to embark so much money in a new process, when the old served very well. Here was a considerable loss, but there was no help for it.

The other "little matters" turned out little. A few pounds were, from time to time, realized, but there were no important advantages.

Thus, in brief, I give the reader the result of over three years' work, counting from the time I first engaged with Harley, to the period referred to in the commencement of this chapter. During that period, I repeat, that Harley was indefatigable. He worked very hard, and with a marvellous energy. Nothing could exceed the tact, and activity, and adroitness which he displayed. Had it not been for these, we should have realized nothing.

As it was, the account current stood about as follows:

California gold-mine	$8,750
Virginia do., received for expenses	3,800
Sales of Isthmus gold-mine stock	13,800
Received from same as expenses	4,000
Lake Superior property	5,000
Sale of interest in Tennessee mine	10,000
Other receipts	5,000———
	$50,350

Per contra.

Paid assessment on Isthmus shares	$4,300
Loss on experiments with pig-iron	4,200
Various small losses	2,000———
	$10,500
	10,500———
	$39,850

In round numbers, forty thousand dollars in net cash was the result of our labors from say the first of January, 1849, to May, 1852.

Of this Harley made a scrupulous division, although the expenses of his office, compared with mine, were more than three to one; still he simplified the whole by crediting me with just one-fourth of that net amount, to wit, with ten thousand dollars, less a mere trifle. After all, not a bad business for something over three years' work. How, then, am I to explain the condition you find me in at the end of the time? I can do so very easily. I confess I was much surprised when Harley sent me his account current, in which I stood credited with the above-mentioned sum, and charged with my drafts on him, which amounted to nearly five hundred dollars *more* than the sum to my credit! On looking over the account, I found it was quite correct. Was it possible that I had drawn at the rate of three thousand dollars a year? I could not believe it, yet it was so. There were the figures, and the figures were correct. The fact is, my household expenses, under the agreeable system of drawing for what I wanted, insensibly increased. Not by Alice's consent; but I had, as already explained, undertaken to show some hospitality to our speculative friends, and all house-keepers understand the extra expense entailed even by a small dinner. Then this involved a larger outlay in Alice's wardrobe. Besides, I sent the younger children to a more expensive school, and Alice had taken music-lessons from a first-class teacher. Considering these various circumstances, it is not to be wondered at that my expenses were so much increased. Indeed, had it not been for Alice's careful management, they would have been a great deal heavier. She, be it understood, having full faith in her father's judgment, believed we were on the road to renewed prosperity. Money seemed to come so easy, things were never so charming in that respect, that she was entirely deceived. During the last year, however, I began to have my misgivings. I saw that Harley, having done his utmost with what he had in hand, was not the man to pursue failing schemes forever, but would certainly lay hold of new projects, in which I might or might not be called to share. Not that he was in the least dissatisfied with my exertions. But after residing so long abroad, and being brought in contact with the very best class of speculators there, he might take up some project, and cut loose from American operations.

The dreaded blow fell at last. I received a long letter from Harley, in which he assured me he did not think any more could at present be realized out of the matters in hand ; he spoke of certain prospective advantages, of which I should certainly receive my share ; he said his own expenses were large, necessarily so from the position he was forced to maintain ; and he had availed himself of a very excellent opportunity to embark in a scheme for an Italian railway, under the direct patronage of the pope, which promised more than well. That if the hoped-for success should crown his efforts he should not forget me—no, assuredly not. Many were the kind wishes expressed for us all ; as to the little balance of one hundred pounds in his favor, it was of no consequence whatever.

When I received and read this letter, my heart sunk within me. I felt like a sailor alone on a desolate island, abandoned by his shipmates, who have left him by accident or design. My first impulse was to feel bitterly toward Harley. Yet why? Had he deceived me in any respect? No. Had he not lived honestly up to his contract? Yes. Of what had I to complain? Alas! of nothing, save my own folly.

Reader, here was the loose screw, here the leak in the ship, here the break in the axle; ponder it well, and let the moral teach you something. Harley when we first met was thirty-five. I was *fifty-two*. Harley was of an age still to embark in a speculative career; I was not. He pursued it consistently as a business. I struck into it hoping to make a fortune rapidly and quit. Now he, as a matter of policy, having spent each year all he had earned (at least ten thousand dollars per annum), had acquired position and a reputation for wealth, and was just ready to embark in something more promising than gold-mines, patent-rights, or land-charters; but I, having spent all *I* had earned, had nothing to go on with, or fall back upon, while poverty, more hard and unendurable than ever, stared me grimly in the face.

I sat holding in my hand the letter of Harley. A cold sweat broke out all over me. It stood on my forehead, it suffused my eyelids. I could feel it on my body, and my limbs. I experienced a painful sensation at my heart; I breathed with difficulty, and was forced to open my mouth, literally gasping for breath. "Oh! what am I to do? who shall comfort me?" I exclaimed aloud. Then it was I thought of my daughter—of Alice. I could talk with her. I could tell her all. And she would forgive her father; we would plan together what was to be done. She should be my *confidante*, my sympathizer. In a more humble manner than ever before we would endeavor still to have a happy home.

At that moment the door opened, and Alice herself entered. It was an occasional practice for her to ride "downtown," about the time I was ready to leave, and accompany me home. Now she came in with a fine flow of spirits, and ran gayly up to me.

Her lively demonstration was suddenly checked, and she exclaimed, "What is the matter, papa, what has happened?"

"Nothing, my child, nothing has happened; but I fear there is an end of all my hopes in Europe."

"Indeed."

"Yes. I have been fearing it for a long time; and now I am thrown back on what I can do here."

I found it difficult to explain to her just the exact state of things. For she could not readily conceive of so sudden a turn in affairs, nor why I should be so distressed, since, as she supposed, I had still occupation here.

At last she seemed to take the whole, as it were, on trust, and to appreciate that once more I had anxiously to cast about for a few dollars each day on which to live. Then came my recompense, my consolation. She was so much older and stronger, she said, and understood so much more than formerly how to economize, and how to make things pleasant for me. I must not be worried a bit! Why, she could each, she could do ever so many things, if necessary. She kissed me, and called me by endearing names, brought me my hat and coat, forced me away from the office, and I was made to feel cheerful in spite of myself.

I went home with my child; led home, I may say, by her.

I spent the night thinking what I should do. Speculation was at that time rife, why not undertake various local schemes? My acquaintance was large among the speculative class. I rejected this plan because it was necessary for me to be in the way of earning some money forthwith. It was two months since I had received any thing from Harley, and his letter came just in time to prevent further drawing. Besides, my eyes were suddenly opened, and I sickened at the idea of such hope-deferred business. Could it be possible? Where was my reason, my common sense? Had I been mad for the last three years?

Twice I awoke during the night with that dreadful sensation at my heart, which is only understood by those who are at times tortured by what is termed the " horrors." Why had this come so suddenly on me? Why for the last six months did I not make some preparations for what, had I not been an idiot, I might have known *would* come? For six months affairs had promised just this termination. Yet I kept on hoping and hoping, and drawing on Harley.

At last I did fall asleep, and slumbered long into the morning. When I opened my eyes, Alice was standing by me. She smiled when she saw I was awake, and exclaimed, "For once you have overslept yourself. Breakfast has been ready an hour." The fact was, I had been exhausted by the severity of my mental sufferings, and nature had come to my aid. I rose considerably refreshed, determined to cast about with activity and with prudence.

14

CHAPTER II.

FRESH STRENGTH.

1 FOUND I had neither the hope nor the energy which I possessed when I embarked in speculation three years before. The habit of those three years had nearly spoiled me for any regular pursuit. How hard to come down to the level of ordinary industry! Besides, how mortifying was my situation. My acquaintances were beginning once more to consider me a man of wealth. The very day I received *that* letter I had been congratulated on my fortunate operations. So my last state was worse than the first.

Again came the old question, renewed with triple force, what was I to do? I thought of attempting business as a stock-broker, as produce-broker, of trying what I could do in real estate There were objections to all these. A stock-broker required some capital, or at least a good credit. I had neither. I was no longer active enough for operations in merchandise, nor had I sufficient experience in the business for real estate. So I resolved to go back to what I first undertook. I would begin once more the labors of a note-broker, and work industriously.

Never till about this time did I have any just conception of human life, nor of God's design in the announcement: "In the sweat of thy face shalt thou eat bread." No,

never till now; and it happened in this wise. As I was
preparing to resume my task of hard daily labor, under
circumstances the most depressing and disheartening, and
when it seemed as if I could not sustain myself under this
last disappointment, a new light suddenly broke in on me.
I always look back to it with a feeling of profound gratitude. Up to that moment the object of all my efforts, my
anxieties, my active exertions, was to get back to where I
stood before, to recover my position, or at least, to support
my family comfortably. So, when I failed in one quarter,
or met with disappointments in another, I suffered to a
great degree. Sometimes I was irritable, sometimes complaining, and often bitter and defiant. I repeat, in all this
I looked solely at what was immediately before me. If I
gained somewhat, I was pleased; if I lost, I was depressed.
In fact, my existence was rounded by mere occurrences.
Even my moralizing—and I did moralize a great deal—had
reference solely to these. It did not strike deep. To be
uncomfortable was an evil [instead of an inconvenience];
the reverse, a blessing.

What I am about to recount may seem extraordinary,
but it is true. On the day I decided with a heavy heart to
commence again my disagreeable labors, hope had apparently entirely deserted me. I rose in the morning miserable. It seemed as if I could not go through with what
lay before me. Borne down by the weight of sad thoughts,
I prepared to descend to the breakfast-room. My suffering
was unendurable, and growing every moment more intense
Suddenly something whispered to me audibly: "How have
you been mistaken! There is a worse thing than misfor-

tune and misery, a better thing than wealth. All that happens to you shall develop and enrich your character!"

I turned and saw my wife smiling on me.

The weight was lifted off my heart. I threw the door open and walked from the room untrammelled, free. I knew something trying awaited me, else why such new strength? From that moment I learned to regard every thing which took place as a part of the experience which was to make of me, Charles Parkinson, something better and more deserving than I then was. All things were clear to me. Now I could see—not with that narrow and circumscribed vision which enabled me in a keen, shrewd way to understand my error in joining Harley, but with a sight which, regarding the whole circumference of my being, carefully surveyed the whole, instead of a meagre portion of it.

The reader must understand this extraordinary and sudden change was not what is termed of a religious character, except so far as that enters into and forms a part of our very natures. In other words, I did not think any thing about God, nor what the priest would call "the concerns of my soul." It was the divine element, breathed into man with the breath of life, which was evoked by the utter desperateness of my condition. Sinking almost to despair, carried down to the point of lowest abasement, the divinity which stirs within came to the rescue; just as that strange physical power, vitality, is said sometimes to display its efficacy in the chamber of the sick, restoring to health, after the physician has given up the case and gone away. In this change there was neither a sullen submission nor a daring resistance to God's providence. Prometheus, when chained by Jupiter to the rock, while a vulture was perpetually tearing his vitals, defied the god, exclaiming: "Do thy worst, tyrant. My fortitude shall be as eternal as thy revenge!" I had no such defiance in my heart; on the contrary, I regarded Providence as my friend, persuaded the severity of my fate would serve to perfect my character and rescue my moral nature from the degradation which during the past three years had threatened it.

CHAPTER III.

NEW ARRANGEMENTS.

I TOLD my daughter every thing. I could not start fairly if any thing was concealed or kept back from her. I even repeated how I had uttered a falsehood when I negotiated the Alworthy paper. I explained in a way she could understand my operations with Harley, and why affairs now looked so discouraging. I presume many will think this was quite an unnecessary humiliation, as they may call it, serving to lower me in the estimation of my child. But I was right. And however for the moment Alice's feelings might have partaken of a painful pity, I know she reverenced her father for these honest avowals, while her filial affection was strengthened by this display of confidence and regard.

We entered at once on plans for retrenchment. I was now very glad I had not taken a more expensive house, which at one time I was tempted to do, and indeed should have done had I not been deterred by the large outlay necessary for additional furniture. Anna's quarter would end the following week, and Charley's in a fortnight. They must go in future to the public school, and Alice would teach Anna music. We now had two servants. When the " month" would be up they should leave, and we could go back to a single domestic, who would do " general house-work." Ah! there was vigorous planning to keep out the old enemy, wolf! No heart-pangs, no whining about a hard destiny, no wry faces nor expressions of suffering and injury, and the like, but a manly, I will say, a heroic determination to make the best of my condition.

The reader may remember, I had already five hundred dollars ahead when I began with Harley, besides the five hundred of Alice. I spent, however, two hundred before Harley left, and although I drew the amount from him which I have put down, still I never made this sum good to myself. But the remaining three hundred had not been touched. It was placed in the savings bank and was drawing five per cent. interest. I had not however kept up my practice of cash payments since I began to receive money from Harley. Indeed I had insensibly relaxed all my habits of strict economy; it was so easy to run up an account (for it was soon understood that I was worthy of credit at the shops and stores), so easy, when time for payment arrived, to draw on Harley, that I became quite unconcerned, not to say careless, in these matters. When I came to get in all our bills, I found I should have barely money enough to provide for them by drawing the three hundred dollars and interest. A serious business, but I must look it in the face. Fortunately the quarter's rent had just been paid. After the first year, the landlord, seeing I was a punctual tenant, had not required the security of Mr. Norwood, so that the death of my friend had not forced me to look elsewhere.

Well, my debts were paid, our children withdrawn from the seminary and sent to the public school, our two excellent servants given up and the general house-work maid substituted in their place, and I once more launched on the street.

On looking about me the first day or two, I was struck more forcibly than ever with a fact I had often observed before, to wit, how rapidly business firms change in the city of New York. On inquiring for the various houses which did business in Wall-street four years before, I found at least one-third had disappeared and new ones were in their places. One large money and exchange broker had suddenly disappeared and never been heard of. It turned out that his assets would not pay two cents on the dollar. Yet the man was called a millionaire, and had credit to any amount. Another, a very rich stock-broker, had, in the midst of his operations, been stricken with paralysis, was carried home, lived three months, and died. This man insisted a fortnight before his decease, helpless and half imbecile as he was, on being driven in his carriage to Wall-street, where he essayed to undertake his ordinary business transactions. For three or four days he continued his ghastly career. But he had engaged in a contest in which the odds were against him and where there was no discharge. Death claimed him; death was victorious, and Wall-street saw him no more forever. Other individuals had retired on their fortunes, most of them to mope out the remainder of their lives in idiotic inactivity. Some had been used up, had left the street, and taken to agriculture with great good-nature, and had changed very much for the better.

I ought to say here, that during this very spring culminated and burst the bubble of the Concordia Valley Coal

Company, of which the worthy Mr. Tremaine was the first president. That company met with a splendid success. Its shares ran up to about par. Tremaine managed its affairs, or rather his own in connection with it, with great cleverness. He sold out his stock in trade and interest in the company the very first year to a set of unprincipled scamps, who could, however, control the market, and who had their own designs to further. He received in payment very little money and a large amount of shares, which he managed to "feed out" very adroitly, and which the parties in interest continued to buy in the most unsuspecting manner; in fact, it was diamond cut diamond. Tremaine kept on till he had disposed of considerably over one hundred thousand dollars, at about eighty, when he retired, purchased a villa near Florence, and for aught I know, lives there with his family at this day. The parties discovered the sell too late, but they were not discouraged. They had entire sway in the street. The stock went up and down. It was a great favorite, and just the thing to play with. Issues, then double and treble *over*-issues were resorted to. By great industry, perseverance, and rascality, the shares were widely circulated, and then, as I have said, the bubble burst and the public suffered.

Among the "curb-stone brokers" many familiar faces were missing, and their places filled by fresh subjects, who are generally broken-down merchants and financiers. It is rather a habit with the curb-stone operator when he gets severely winged, to go into the cigar business, which, by the way, furnishes a living for a great many dilapidated worthies. This is but temporary. After a while they

14*

recuperate, and you find them again at work on the pavement.

Since I had abandoned the note business, two extensive establishments had been started, for the purpose of affording greater facilities to the capitalist for purchasing paper. This interfered greatly with the business of the small note-broker, throwing into his hands only the poorer descriptions. My old friend, the president of the Bank of Credit, had resigned, and his place was filled by the former cashier, who was, as I have already intimated, indebted mainly to me for his promotion in the bank. In looking about to discover where to commence, I saw much to dispirit and little to encourage me. There was not the same sympathy to be excited as for Charles Parkinson, the honorable merchant whom misfortune had struck down by a sudden and unlooked-for blow, and who was endeavoring industriously to earn a livelihood. Now (for the truth leaks out betimes) it was Charles Parkinson the operator, the speculator, who was resorting to another expedient for subsistence, after living quite at his ease, regardless of his creditors, for so long a time. The public had discovered my matters had not turned out well, and I was lowered at once in the public's estimation.

I was a good deal discouraged. After some reflection, I concluded to consult Downer. Of all my acquaintances, there was not one at that moment toward whom I entertained such genial, kindly feelings as toward him. At the same time, I always felt reproached when I thought of the uncharitable opinion of him which I indulged in at one time. It was not long before I encountered Downer in the street, for he had no office, only a place where he kept a slate, on which persons who desired to do so could make appointments with him. I asked him to come with me to my office, and we proceeded thither together. When we were seated, I gave him a brief history of my situation. I explained how my various schemes had failed, and I was forced back upon my former plans.

After I had finished, Downer remained silent for some time. At last he said: "Mr. Parkinson, I am sorry for you. And to be sorry for any body, is what I have not been for a long time. Tell me," he continued, musingly, " would we have believed when we were 'leading men' among the importers, that it could ever have come to this? It seems kind of human-like, though, for you and me to be sitting together, consulting how, when the evil days are on us, they can best be weathered. It does me good, Parkinson, it does me good to have you give me your confidence and ask my advice."

There was a sensible yielding of the hard tone in which Downer usually spoke. And his voice sounded natural as he proceeded.

"I hardly know what to say," he said. "If you can't manage to buy a little place in the country, of course you must stay in New York. Most people would tell you there were fifty things you could turn to. I, who have tried it, know better. Yet, for you to stay in this street, I can't bear to think of it. I suppose you find a great many changes since you quit. Some of your best customers are gone, and some of your friends; changes, too, at your bank. Twynam is out of the business. Loomis, I hear, is prejudiced against you. Don't explain," he added, quickly, perceiving I was about to speak; "I am sure through no fault of yours" (it was, though; the reader may remember the sale of the Alworthy paper), "but whosesoever fault it is, it makes no difference. However, nothing like trying, and there's nothing like luck. You were in luck before, and you may be again. As to me, I have had bad luck ever since I failed. I know what sort of a character I bear in the street. You know. Do you think I am insensible to it? Remembering me as I used to be, do you suppose, after experiencing the success I did, and enjoying position as a first-class merchant, and having my own ambitious hopes and anticipations like other people, I say, do you suppose I look with indifference on blighted prospects, or think calmly on a blighted reputation? God, no!" he almost hissed out; but immediately repressing his emotion, he continued: "It is all over with me. You understand, I live to take care of the folks. What I was going to say is, that it was bad luck only which destroyed my character. Something like my arrest two or three years ago by Strauss, Bevins and Company, a matter where I was in every respect innocent. Once a bad name, however, always a bad name. Therefore, I say, in every thing you attempt be more than careful. You can't come back now with the same chances you had just after you failed; still you have a good name. You have reputation, and it is just so much capital. Besides, poor as I am, I think I can be of service; I think I can do for you what I could not do for myself. I will try. And there's another thing, Parkinson. Come in and see us. We don't entertain any company, but let us be pleasant with each other. Something tells me we are going to have hard times. Let the young people get acquainted; we shall feel a little stronger in this social way. But recollect, *here* you must avoid all intimacy with me. I am a fire-ship, and you must keep clear. I can help just the same. Ah! well it is strange, the idea of my aiding any body; but two are better than one, no matter how impotent the second is."

Downer here changed the subject, and proceeded to offer valuable hints and suggestions as to the situation of affairs. He gave me the names of persons who had money, which they employed in buying paper, or lending on collaterals, and yet who were not generally known in the street. He told me how he thought I could reach such a one, who, if I gained his confidence, would be a valuable acquaintance, and how to approach another.

The great point, I may explain here, for a person who undertakes the business I was engaged in is, if possible, to secure the confidence of some moneyed men. If they are not *habitues* of the street, all the better. If, after many trials they find they can depend on you, and so place reliance on what you say, you have at once certain facilities for doing business which are invaluable. Poor Downer had none of these. By a series of misfortunes he had lost the confidence of every body in the street. A note was looked on with suspicion, simply because he had it in his possession. But his keen wits, his extensive knowledge of parties and his familiarity with the business, enabled him to render essential outside service to other note-brokers, by which he managed to pick up enough to support his family.

Downer's observations, when he set about carefully to advise me, were clear and sagacious, untempered with any bitterness of expression or misanthropical views. He gave me a correct idea of the situation of the street, the changes which had taken place, and many little alterations in the way of doing business. Then he rose, shook my hand and withdrew.

CHAPTER IV.

A CONSULTATION.

I SET to work without delay. I called on many old acquaintances, who received me kindly, and heard my statement of what I proposed to do. It was very evident, however, they no longer entertained that good opinion of my mercantile ability which they had before my embarking in a speculative career. Their treatment of me, to all appearance, was the same as ever, but a species of magnetism told me I had lost the sympathetic hold on them I had before. I was prepared for this, it was the natural result, and I had no right to complain. I did not complain. One of the gentlemen to whom Downer referred me as employing his funds in the street, proved to be on intimate terms with Goulding. This latter personage had kept watch of me all the time during the past four years. On one occasion he had even employed a lawyer to take out "subsequent proceedings" against me on the judgment he had recovered in Bulldog's name,* and put me under examination with reference to any property I might have acquired since my assignment. Mr.

---

* I learned from good authority that GOULDING applied to BULLDOG to proceed against me on this judgment, and that BULLDOG answered with an oath that he wouldn't do it, swearing that PARKINSON was too hard a nut to crack, because he was fool enough to let his feelings run away with his judgment, and couldn't be reasoned nor compromised with.

He never forgot my turning him out of my house. It increased his respect for me marvellously.   C. E. P.

Norwood, kind, considerate man that he was, had guarded
me against this. By his account, I was still indebted to
Alice for certain articles given to her by her mother, which
on the sale I had, with her consent, received the money for.
This more than disposed of the five hundred dollars placed
in her hands. I was, therefore, quite prepared for Goulding's action. He did not push his investigations beyond a
single examination, and he never meddled with me after that.
But he continued my persistent enemy. I found I could not
enter into business transactions with any one it was possible
for him to influence, and it is very easy to influence where
money or credit is concerned.

In calling on another gentleman recommended by Downer,
I encountered Loomis, and although the man nourished no
vindictive feeling against me, still he had received an un-
favorable impression in the Alworthy affair, and did not
hesitate to express it when inquired of. This I deserved,
but the acts of Goulding were persecution. I submitted to
both as part of what I had to go through. One taught me
how we are forced to bear the consequences of doing
wrong, even when we repent of the wrong; the other added
to my strength, for the conviction that we suffer unjustly is
an extraordinary element of endurance.

I soon discovered I must take up with a lower department in the business, and deal with a poorer class of
paper. The rent of my office had been raised after Tremaine left the coal company, and I decided I must take another, by which I could save fifty dollars a year. My new
room was smaller than the old one, and not in so good a lo-
cation; but it was unobjectionable, and I took some pains,

or rather Alice did, to make it look cheerful and pleasant.
It was a great happiness to see her busy arranging this little
office, changing the furniture from one place to another, till
it exactly suited her. And I said to myself, as I stood regarding her : " No, I am not to be discouraged with such a
treasure ; a child so watchful and considerate, so loving and
devoted." Yet how my heart had sunk within me before,
when I first adventured in Wall-street, when I had so much
more to encourage me than now ! Then I had the active
sympathy of business men, recently excited by my misfortunes. I was four years younger; I was buoyed up by a
certain hope that things might still take a turn for the better. Yet I did not feel the strength I now felt, advanced in
life, with no hope of any improved condition, and nobody
to encourage me but Downer.

Before, I did not experience, to any great extent, the
power of the human spirit. For I did not place myself in
the way to receive its aid. I ought to have done so. I had
read a hundred times that " The spirit of man will sustain
his infirmity," but I do not think I ever considered what it
meant. I now saw that if I would have the immortal part
come to the support of the mortal and finite, I must be
genuine. It was not enough to be an honest merchant,
honest in all affairs ; honest in social life, but I must be an
honest MAN. So long as what I was striving for, however
laudable or proper, was not the great end *for which* to
strive ; in other words, if I was striving right, but for a
wrong reason, the spirit would not sustain me under discomfiture. For example, I needed to be sustained in my
failure, in my subsequent trials, when I lost my wife. In a

measure, I was so. But it was rather by a strength derived from a fine physical energy, from great resolution and a determined purpose, than through any support from the soul. I do not know if I make myself understood. If I fail to do so, I shall fail in one of the objects of this narrative. For it is in this view of myself that I hope to interest the reader. However insignificant the perusal of this history may appear, the history of the workings of the human spirit cannot be regarded with indifference, and teaches a profound lesson.

Let me repeat, then : when I failed in 1847, and in all my struggles and efforts and experiences afterward, I enjoyed no unwavering and consistent support. My wife could comfort me; my children could make me happy ; various circumstances, from time to time, produced an agreeable but temporary state of exaltation ; but I enjoyed nothing of that calm, that tranquillity which belong to him who understands what life is made for, and whom the spirit labors unremittingly to sustain. Now I was about to start afresh under circumstances still more disheartening, but with the conscious *me* supporting the active, stirring, every-day individual. The house was no longer divided against itself. What was the result of this union of forces, we shall presently see.

CHAPTER V.

AN UNFORTUNATE CLASS.

DEALING in a poorer quality of paper, I was brought in contact with an entirely different class of people. This led me to observe how completely one's occupation is apt to control the character. In a previous chapter, in giving a description of Wall-street, I spoke of the different grades of notes and bills offered in the market, and explained how, after getting below a certain quality, the rate rules enormously high, and holders have to submit to great sacrifices. The important point then is, to find some person who knows the paper. But such a person is sure to take advantage of his knowledge in making the purchase. That, of course, the broker expects, only too glad to sell at any price.

It was distressing to see the nervous, anxious people who had to raise money from day to day. Such persons form a class, and this class is perpetuated, from year to year, out of the individuals struggling to maintain a respectable front.

It seems miraculous how this class can endure such a never-ending state of bondage. Some of these are fashionable, their connections are of the first distinction, their associations most desirable. They keep up handsome establishments; they earn by their pursuits four thousand dollars a year, and spend five thousand. They always anticipate what is due them, and are always harassed for ready money. They are honorable fellows, and would not plead usury under circumstances the most aggravating. They make notes, and get a broker to sell them. This broker, understanding their antecedents, and who they are most intimate with, goes probably to some rich friend of the particular "party" wanting a loan, who is thoroughly acquainted with the "case," and who knows that the note will be paid when due, although at the sacrifice of putting a new one on the market, and getting it shaved elsewhere. So he cashes it at a fearful rate, puts the broker under an oath of secrecy not to reveal where he got the money, which oath it is for the broker's interest to keep, and our fashionable acquaintance is relieved. He hurries home in time for the opera or a dinner-out, and. meeting several duns in the hall, he pays them off and sets about his evening's enjoyment.

There are others who, having secured an excellent government contract, either "general," "state," or "corporation," need friends to help them through with it. They can afford to pay well and they do pay well for cash accommodations. In fact the street is full of persons *about* to realize, who want money a little in advance of the period, and who are ready to pay a large bonus for it. The result is, they do all the work, and the money-lender gets nearly all the profits. Sometimes this latter personage mistakes his investment and makes a loss. But he can well afford it. And he never quarrels with the man who has been so unfortunate as to "let him in." He knows he can't do without such people, so he nurses them along when it is necessary. He treats them with as much care as a planter treats

a valuable negro who has been taken ill, and for precisely
the same reason.

Among those who habitually want money are builders
with little capital, who, having taken a contract, find they
must raise more cash than they anticipated to go through
with it. When their necessities are discovered, they have
to bleed freely. Often the capitalist who has engaged these
men to erect a row of buildings for him is the very person
to shave their notes, at the rate of four per cent. a month,
or cash their checks, dated a few days ahead, at the moderate charge of cent. per cent. Very safe operation this,
since the money has already been laid out by the builder,
though perhaps not quite due under the contract, or it may
be it is withheld through some quibble, in order to make
these very operations. Now, reader, you must understand
that such delicate little matters are managed through the
intervention of third parties. The builder, foolish man, fancies he is keeping up his credit because he meets his obligations at such fearful sacrifice.* He does not wish the
wealthy proprietor to know how hard-up he is, for fear he
may not think him reliable for another contract. So he employs a broker, who takes care to be thoroughly posted in
all his affairs, and who goes straight to the man, of all
others, the poor builder wishes to avoid.

* I shall never forget with what gusto a wealthy acquaintance once pointed out to
me a block of buildings he had just erected, remarking: "There is a row of what I
call honest-built houses. Not a thing slighted, from cellar to roof. Drew the contract
myself; one must build two or three times to learn how. I don't leave any loop-hole
for extras. I tell you, the fellow who did that work lost a heap of money by it. I
was afraid he would break down when he saw how it was going, materials rose so fast,
but he stuck it out like a trump.'
Yes, this rich man actually chuckled over the idea that an honest, high-minded mechanic had lost a couple of thousand dollars and a whole season besides, in manfully
carrying out his agreement. "Honest-built houses" indeed!—c. ĸ. ᴘ.

To this inferior class of paper belongs, as I have said, an inferior class of brokers. Men who are willing to wait on a set of supercilious, avaricious, mean creatures ; to follow their suggestions; to run back and forward to carry out their plans of low cunning for getting high rates and triple security. I say who are " willing" to wait—rather who are *forced* to do so. For only a dire necessity compels such an allegiance.

I was disappointed in the kind of people these brokers proved to be. I had associated them with whatever was tricky and dishonest. I did them great injustice. While there are of course a good many unprincipled persons among them, the majority are simply unfortunate. Men who have been driven into this business by stress of weather. They are a poor, hard-working, and *sympathizing* set. For I know of no misery so despairing that it does not "love company," or which avoids association. And I believe the wretched slave of the nabob and usurer, griper and money-knave of Wall-street may hereafter find a place in the kingdom of heaven, when these latter miscreants are " thrust out." I can truly record that, with some special exceptions, which should only prove the rule, I was treated with more kindness and congeniality by the individuals just alluded to, than I had ever before experienced from any class. They are really sorry if you are in trouble; they exhibit genuine regret if you meet with a disappointment; and they will take pains to remove an obstacle from your path, whenever they can do so.

CHAPTER VI.

DEATH OF MRS. HITCHCOCK.

ABOUT this time Mrs. Hitchcock was taken sick and died.

Soon after our first acquaintance, I procured for her the third story of a small house, quite near our own, which was occupied by a worthy family, who, desiring to economize, concluded to rent a part. This was easily arranged for housekeeping, and afforded the widow an agreeable home at a low price. She had an abundance of needle-work, and by close economy, mother and daughter managed to support themselves. Matilda was a constant visitor at our house. She was as unlike Alice as possible, and perhaps for that reason the two girls became attached to each other. It was not always easy to remain on intimate terms with her. She was so sensitive, and consequently so quick to take offence, so proud, so passionate, and at times so unreasonable, that I used to wonder how Alice managed to keep up the intimacy. On the other hand, she manifested so many noble and generous traits, she was so kind-hearted, so disinterested, so truthful, so affectionate, that she attached one to her in an extraordinary degree, despite her faults. Her character showed ever-varying phases of cloud and sunshine, of storm and pleasant weather. After all, such natures attract more powerfully than any other.

Of these two, if Matilda appeared to be the controlling

spirit, being the readier and more demonstrative, it was Alice's influence, after all, which led. Not through any contest or competition, but by acquiescence of her companion as something natural, and as a matter of course. The result was, they became firm and devoted friends. Matilda was about three years the younger, yet she had an extraordinary maturity of mind and body. So that, really, the two appeared to be of the same age.

Matilda Hitchcock had one great fault, which it was impossible to correct, scarcely to modify. She would not submit to circumstances. On the contrary, she perpetually deplored and resisted what she called her miserable destiny.

"Why did God make me so?" she would exclaim; "why have I such a love for every thing rare and expensive, and such a disgust for whatever is common and coarse, when I was born in poverty, and when I am destined forever to suffer in poverty? I am fond of gayety. I love society. I should enjoy life in the world; my tastes are expensive; my ideas unsuited to my position; I cannot help it. I was made so, but why? Does it not seem unjust? You need not look shocked. I didn't make myself. I didn't make my tastes. I didn't make my condition. I can't control my fate. I hate every thing and every body, and I wish I were dead!"

Such was the occasional strain indulged in by this singular girl. Alice, shocked by expressions bordering, as she considered, on the blasphemous, would attempt to reply, to argue and explain. It was never of the least use. The dark hour, however, would presently pass, and not a trace of all this bitterness remain. It was sure to return, sometimes at brief intervals. For whenever Matilda went in sight of the gay world, where she could witness the display of the rich and fashionable, and see the parade made by fine equipages, fine dresses, and so forth, she gave way to the same freedom of speech, unrestrained by remonstrance or entreaty.

I have mentioned a strange habit of hers, when a child: to be sure she could no longer indulge in such extraordinary exhibitions, but she made it up in the violence and extravagance of her observations. It served no purpose to contradict, or attempt to silence her. The only course was to wait, and let the paroxysm pass. Then it would be all sunshine, and you would witness such tokens of a rich and affluent and noble nature, that those unhappy characteristics would be lost sight of; thought of no more, and no more remembered, till some disturbing causes again brought them to the surface.

I have already spoken of Matilda's beauty. At sixteen this came to be marvellous. She herself was perfectly sensible of it, without exhibiting a disagreeable consciousness on the subject. A latent fondness for admiration gradually developed itself, I thought; not striking; perhaps not more than the majority of girls manifest. Yet, in her position, it was a dangerous quality. She knew it very well, and it lent an additional argument to her discourse, when the "fit" seized her. Sometimes she would be subject to the impertinence of men, or annoyed by their meddling curiosity in attempting to discover where she resided. Then she would curse the day in which she was born, and find fault with her MAKER in the manner I· have already explained.

15

Alice's influence on Matilda was admirable. The latter had an impressible nature. The two were much together; and, as I have said, the mild but decided bearing of my daughter, always consistent, and always the same, had great influence with her companion. Charley and Anna were also very fond of her, so she was always welcome at our house.

Returning home one afternoon, I found Alice absent, and a message for me to follow her to Mrs. Hitchcock's.

I hastened to her residence, where I found her just reviving from a very severe attack; similar indeed to the one she was seized with the evening I first met her. I was struck with the extraordinary pallor of her countenance. In it an experienced eye could not fail to recognize the finger of death.

The widow was quite conscious of her situation. When I came in, she motioned Matilda and Alice out of the room. Her daughter left with reluctance, but Alice quietly drew her away.

Mrs. Hitchcock pointed to a seat, and said: "My time is very short. I shall die with a heavy load at my heart if you cannot accede to what I am about to request." . . .

She paused to take breath. She was fast failing. . . .

"Matilda—my child," she continued, as it were to herself, "oh! what days and nights of anxiety have I passed for you! how can I leave you exposed to—to—— Promise to adopt her as your child," she said suddenly, and with startling energy. "*Promise!*"

The widow's hands were clasped in supplication. She looked in my face with eyes supernaturally brilliant and piercing.

I dared not hesitate an instant.   I took her clasped hands in mine, and said : " I do promise."

" Call her," she gasped.

The two girls came back together. Up to this moment Matilda had been in no great alarm. She thought the worst of the attack was over,

" Matilda," said Mrs. Hitchcock.

" Yes, mother."

" You will go home with Mr. Parkinson. He accepts you as one of his children."

" What does this mean ?" exclaimed Matilda, turning indignantly toward me.

I made no reply, but pointed toward the bed.

On it already a corpse was extended.

CHAPTER VII.

MORALIZING.

THE reader has already perceived, if he have devoted ordinary attention to the topic, as he ran over these pages, that one object which I have in view is, to attract notice to a class in Wall-street (using that as a representative locality) who suffer and die in harness. That while I do not ignore the claims of the "lower classes" (about whom it is now so fashionable to write tales and romances, whose chief merit frequently consists in the ingenuity with which broken . English is manufactured for their use, such certainly as they never themselves employ), I have a design to present in a single volume the claims of those who are precipitated from a certain point of prosperity into a wretchedness almost indescribable; who suffer beyond any human conception; and who at last miserably disappear.

Yes, I wish to print such a book, and ask philanthropists to read it; people who honestly seek a field for their active benevolence to work in. Did they know the aching *hearts* concealed under a most respectable exterior, which are to be encountered, and which present much stronger appeals than those suffering bodily want, it seems to me they would endeavor to devise some plan for their relief.

Is there, after all, to be no radical change, which shall cure some of these evils? Probably not. Our SAVIOUR said: "Ye have the poor always with you." Doubtless, we shall have the miserable also. Still, we attempt to assist the poor; let us try to relieve the heavy-hearted. Just now will not people be apt to consider? May it not be, that out of the general calamity which encompasses us, there will spring an increased regard for the condition of our neighbor?

I do not know.

It is with a species of awe that I see a man who feels that his destiny in this world is *settled*, who understands that he is sunk into a state of chronic misfortune, encounter face to face an arrogant rich man, who considers his own position secure beyond contingency. How the countenance of each describes what each has experienced, *is* experiencing! There they stand together. How superciliously the sleek, amply dressed, complacent man of wealth regards the hard-featured, iron-marked man of adversity!

" I am lord paramount, you a poor devil;" you can read it as plain as if it were printed.

" I know it." That is the reply—printed deep too.

Now, I say, if the man of misfortune is not possessed of a high moral sense, which teaches him to regard this world as a part of a comprehensive and compensating whole, he will not only feel bitterly toward that rich man, but he will be very apt to reason himself into the belief, that it is very unjust that such an insolent, overbearing creature should be in possession of all his heart's desire, while he is ground down in misery. Then he may reason, that what can be got out of such a man, in any way, will be a just depletion. So, insensibly he may be led into crime, and thereupon suffers the " penalty of the law."

This is right, of course; but how much of this crime is morally chargeable to the other? I should not be surprised, if some time in the long future, he should be called on to answer the question. . . . . .

A few weeks after the receipt of the Harley letter, the suit about the Bond-street house was brought to a final decision, in the Court of Appeals. That decision was in my favor, or rather in favor of my children. So Goulding not only gained nothing, but had a large bill of costs to pay, besides heavy counsel fees. The victory was dearly bought. The expenses on my side were very large. In this I felt sensibly the difference between Mr. Norwood and a strange lawyer, who took no personal interest in my family. After paying all that was chargeable in the suit, and then deducting the bill of Norwood and Case, now represented by Mr. Case, against the estate, scarcely two thousand dollars remained! Of this two-thirds were decreed to be invested for the benefit of the two younger children. Alice's portion was retained in court, on suggestion of counsel, that she would in a few months be twenty-one, and could then receive it in person. I experienced some degree of despondency when I beheld what I once considered a sure resource for my children, to the amount of at least five thousand dollars, diminished to so small a sum. But I checked the feeling. I would not permit such an enemy to enter when of right I ought to be content, since a litigation, uncertain as every litigation is, had terminated in our favor. Besides, had I not resolved to turn whatever came to pass to my advantage? Walking on a pleasant errand is easy. Laboring for a rich result gratifying. I was now to labor always for a rich result!

CHAPTER VIII.

MATILDA.

THERE was one thing inexplicable in Matilda Hitchcock. She did not exhibit the least feeling at the loss of her mother. Except that she was more reserved than before, no one could perceive the slightest difference in her demeanor. The fact that she was now to be an inmate of my house, and, as it would seem, dependent on me, appeared to irritate her. So far from manifesting any gratitude, a stranger would suppose she was suffering daily some wrong at my hands. At length I spoke to Alice about her singular conduct, and suggested that my daughter should talk with her. Alice, however, advised me not to notice these strange exhibitions. She said it would only make matters worse should we pay any attention to them. "She is so different from other girls, papa. If we let her alone, her good sense will triumph; if we attempt to interfere, we shall go from bad to worse."

I thought of Matilda's father, my classmate, and could see in the daughter, magnified and distorted, the same characteristics which had given force to the man's career; yet the same qualities led him to quarrel with his uncle at the expense of his birthright. And my heart grew soft, and I told Alice she should have her own way with her friend.

A week passed—Matilda had been with us a month—

when one morning after breakfast she desired to speak with me.

When we were alone together she said: "I want to thank you for affording me food and shelter so long. I am now going to leave."

I was astonished. "Where are you going, my child?"

"I do not know; where I can support myself."

"Ah! you think my circumstances so straitened that you are an additional burden. Is it not so?"

"No, indeed, it is not. Had you been rich, I would not have staid one week. It is because I know you are not rich that I have been able to remain so long."

"I scarcely understand you."

"I do not know if I understand myself," exclaimed Matilda passionately; "but yes, you can, you do understand how in the family of a person of wealth I should feel all the time as if I were the object of their complacent charity. In your house I have no such feeling, because I know you are struggling hard yourself and cannot feel the rich man's contempt for the poor. I can't explain myself," she added with impatience; "I only can repeat what I have said."

"Then, why can't you remain with us."

"Because I am not willing to be dependent. I wont be dependent on any body. Mother fretted her life away, indebted daily to the patronizing charity of religious hypocrites, who claim to confer favors by giving her work to do at half-price. She is dead and gone. I am glad—yes, glad her weary life is over. For me, I will never be dependent on human being, no, not for the slightest aid."

I looked earnestly at the girl. She seemed almost to defy me. My first impulse was to show becoming indignation, and with all proper severity of manner to read her a sound moral lecture on the folly, the wickedness of such feelings, to austerely explain how we all are, and must be dependent: first on GOD, then on each other, and so forth. My mouth was open with an important dignity to go through with these trite truisms. But I paused ere I spoke the first word of my discourse, for something told me that the girl's destiny would turn on my treatment of her that morning. There she sat, self-willed and imperious. Her manner, too, was provoking and tantalizing. Strange, what a marvellous beauty she displayed in this exhibition. There was no affectation in the scene, not a bit. She was thoroughly genuine.

Her decided, independent bearing, coupled with expressions which certainly showed a wrong state of feeling, and were very censurable, prompted me to the moral harangue aforesaid; the interest excited by displays of so extraordinary a nature, the recollection of her orphan condition, the thought of how weak and powerless she really was, while she bore herself so bravely, touched me aright, and the idea of the moral lecture vanished. A natural view of the situation came in its place.

"You are not so far out of the way, Matilda, as some persons might suppose," I said. "You are too old for me to manage as I would Anna, and therefore, I think, old enough to be reasonable. Now then, as you have no plan except to avoid a state of dependence, which is intolerable to you, and as I know you love Alice and the children, and used to like to come here, I propose that you pay into the common treasury what really, on a fair computation, we shall decide it actually costs us extra for your being here. For the present, your needle can easily provide that, without any appeals to the 'benevolent' people you detest so much, and we will hope something better in the future. Beyond this, I am sure you wont insist on my making money out of you as a boarder."

I smiled The tears came into Matilda's eyes, and she walked hastily out of the room. From that day it was all right. Alice and she fixed the rate of the weekly stipend; in short, the latter interested herself at once in our daily routine, and, through my daughter, soon came to know as much of my own daily affairs as Alice herself. I do not mean to say that her infirmities of temper were cured: by no means. But she felt at home in our house, and appeared to take the same interest in what occurred as if she was one of my own children; and I believe, from that time she had for me feelings similar to, if not as strong, as those she would have had for her own father. The fact was, Matilda required from her infancy a firm but reasonable and consistent government. When I got better acquainted with her, I discovered she relished the rule of a strong hand, provided it really *was* strong and always right. Her mother had not undertaken to restrain her. She knew, indeed, how to touch her feelings, and unfortunately, used to strike the string too often. Indeed, to the weakness of her mother's management could be attributed a great share of the daughter's faults.

．　　．　　．　　．　　．　　．　　．

Long as I had lived in the house I now occupied (over

four years), I had made no acquaintance with any of the
neighbors. For the first season after leaving Bond-street, I
attended service at our old church, where I owned a pew,
and where I had paid the regular assessment for the year.
After that expired, I was in the habit for a time of going to
different churches .Sunday mornings as inclination dictated.
Sometimes I staid at home, sometimes I went with the children. For Alice had herself selected a church near by,
because she was so much pleased with the minister—a good
old man of the Baptist persuasion.

Now, I determined to look about me, discover what sort
of human beings dwelt in my immediate neighborhood, and
interest myself in whatever should prove of interest around
me. I would bring myself back within the pale of human
sympathies, and form a part of the world within my reach,
instead of merely vegetating in it while I was hoping for
better times. My daughter, I repeat, had selected the
church she preferred to attend, and where Anna and Charley
went regularly to the Sunday-school. Besides, she knew
several of the neighbors, and felt the very interest in some
of them that I was myself disposed to cultivate. Now that
I was to be pressed every moment by anxious cares, and
tortured lest I might not earn enough for our daily wants, it
seemed to me all at once that life was very rich, if I could
only stay by the way and enjoy it. Many were the beautiful thoughts which had floated through my brain in the
years I had lived—thoughts of a higher life, of exquisite
happiness, of the changing, the joyous, and the free in this
world and out of it—beyond it ; had these all vanished and
forever ? Was a time yet to be when these should come

back and become once more enjoyable, when I could call them mine?

Recollect, reader, I had lost my companion, and it was natural, at times, that a deep melancholy should steal over me. But it was only on occasions. Deciding I ought to humanize myself by taking part in what went on around me, I told Alice I should hereafter go every Sunday morning to the church with her. I made inquiries about the persons who lived near us. I ascertained that a book-keeper in one of the banks, by the name of Austin, resided next door, on our right. Opposite lived the proprietor of a livery stable; next to him, a ship-carpenter; on our left, a clerk in a large wholesale dry-goods house. This last family had two boarders, which helped to support one of their children at an expensive school. The Austins were refined people; the husband, a quiet, sensible, unambitious man; the wife, intelligent and well-bred. They had no children, and lived very pleasantly together. The other family had harder work to make the year meet, for they had a large family; but the wife managed well, and the husband was kind and good-tempered, and laughed when many would have made sour faces.

Now, reader, don't think I mean to impose on you by attempting to make you believe I am to enjoy the surroundings of these people as well as I did those of the circle of congenial friends I had left, and who brought around them every thing wealth could bring to make life pleasant and delightful. Other people may talk such cant to you. I will not. But what I could compass was this. I could find out —I did soon find out—that there were honest hearts and refined natures in every condition. That these do not *depend* on wealth, while wealth lends to these additional charms, and frequently smooths the rough and disagreeable qualities of very coarse people. I could, with an appreciative spirit, seek for the good and true around me, and whenever I found it, I would enjoy and honor it. So I listened to the benevolent white-haired old minister, as he preached on Sunday, and exchanged words of greeting with various members of the congregation. With some this widened into an acquaintance, so that I began to take an interest in the church society. We had our poor to look after, our various interests to foster, and our general charities to bestow. I began to form a strong attachment for Mr. Selleck, for he seemed to have no idea but how to serve the spiritual interests of his people. How independent of soul he must have been who had not the slightest thought of self-interest, and cared only to do good! I could not help contrasting him with the fashionable clergymen who dispense religion *à la mode* to admiring audiences, who quit the presence with the complacent feeling that the path to heaven has been made very comfortable for them. I was thus gradually coming to an appreciation of what was honest and real, and an abhorrence for the counterfeit in life.

Matilda did not enter with any relish into Alice's Sunday occupation. She did not like to attend church, she said; the building was hideous, the congregation dressed in bad taste, and altogether a vulgar-looking set. Besides, the clergyman had a habit of snuffing.

Now, many will hold up their hands in horror, at such an irreligious demonstration in one so young. What a mistake!

The simple truth was, that Matilda's senses were so delicate and her appreciation so nice, that certain sights and sounds shocked her eyes and ears, which would produce no effect on ordinary organizations ; just as a person with a fine musical ear detects a discord where another perceives only harmony. This was the secret source of the greater part of her miseries, and to this most of her faults were chargeable. This same subtle sense made her dislike common clothing, and admire whatever was rich, so that her tastes were expensive ; it gave her a love for the refinements of wealth, and a disgust for poverty. Failing to possess what she appreciated so fully, and forced daily to take up with what was repugnant to her, she displayed at times an irritability of temper, coupled with many passionate demonstrations, which made her character appear in a very unhappy light. Yet the poor girl could not help this extraordinary temperament, neither was she to blame for it. Unfortunately, nothing had been done when she was a child to moderate its intensity, and now it was quite too late to effect a change. However, Matilda did go to church, but I doubt if she derived much benefit from what she heard.

In and about the house she was charming. Competent as Alice herself, with a more demonstrative energy and resolution, she accomplished whatever she undertook in the most successful manner. Thus she really helped to lighten the load which I had to carry, which was destined to become more and more heavy as the years rolled by.

CHAPTER IX.

FRINK.

To be obliged to spend five dollars a day, and be able to earn but three dollars, gives one a gloomy look into the future. To a person accustomed to "doing business" on a large scale, it would seem a very petty affair to secure five dollars per diem—so I used to think. But when one is ousted from one's position and divorced from one's circumstances, it is not easy to lay hold of a new opportunity. Charles the footman, in becoming livery, giving complete satisfaction to his employer, at twenty-five dollars a month, is quite a different person from Charles discharged—in disgrace—walking about in very plain clothes, not earning a dollar, and eating into his last month's wages very fast. You would not know it was the same person. Indeed it is doubtful if Charles recognizes himself.

Now, stop one moment, reader. In imagination, separate yourself from *your* position. Think how it would be with you. Cut off, this instant, your business, your income, your old associations—all. Turn yourself (thank GOD that it is *only* imagination) loose into the street, and be told to *earn* five dollars a day. Ay, let it be understood you and your children will STARVE if you don't earn it, and try and fancy how to do it! Beat your head against the dead wall. There is no door there which opens as doors used to open to you. You strive, you agonize. You have had enough of it. You implore to have the spell dissolved, and you returned to your friendly associations.

With me, it was not fancy work, but fact.

It seemed at first as if I should never get started. The first money I made on this return to business was three dollars on a hundred-dollar note, and this was through the agency of Downer. For there was but one man in the street who would buy the paper, and his name was Frink. He occupied a small hole, literally seven by nine, up two pair of stairs, in a side-street leading out of Wall. Downer directed me to him. I found a man apparently about sixty-five years old. He was at work at his check-book when I entered. He did not even look up, but continued his addition. I sat down. In about five minutes he paused from his labors and peered at me over his spectacles.

"Will you take this note?" I said, at the same time placing it in his hand.

Thereupon the following dialogue ensued:

"What's your name?"

"Parkinson."

"Don't recollect seeing you before."

"Perhaps not."

"Parkinson" (repeating to himself). "Wasn't you in the silk business in '37?"

"Yes."

"I was in the dry-goods business myself. Went out of it the year before; thought I remembered the name."

Another pause.

"You in the note business?"

" Yes."

" Haven't been in it long ?"

" No, not long."

" Do you know this man ?" looking at the note.

" I don't know the maker."

" What was it given for ?"

" I believe for castings."

" You know this other man ?" meaning the endorser.

" I have seen him two or three times."

" Did you get the note from him yourself ?"

" I did."

" What do you expect for it ?"

" You can have it at two per cent. a month." I had been told it was idle to offer less.

Honest Mr. Frink paid no attention to my reply, but proceeded to fill out a check. When it was signed he handed it to me, saying : "That's the best I take his notes at."

I saw on glancing at the amount that the old bloodsucker had deducted three per cent. a month. As it did not exceed my instructions, and as I saw Mr. Frink meant what he said, I pocketed the check and came away. By this transaction I made three dollars—the voluntary offering of my man, who had given up all hope of getting the note cashed, and was delighted to get the money at any sacrifice.

This Frink, let me tell the reader, was worth over half a million of dollars. He had no family, no relatives, as I was told. He resided in New Jersey to avoid being taxed in New York ; and for abundant caution, was careful to keep his name out of the city directory. He was never known to bestow a cent in charity, or to do any human being a kindness. He took great pains to make himself acquainted with second and third and even fourth-rate paper, and was exceedingly shrewd in his judgments about it.

" What will become of this man ?" said I to Downer as he finished a pretty long story about him, which it is unnecessary to repeat here.

" What will become of him ?" repeated he; " Why, some time or other he'll swallow a dollar the wrong way and die."

I could not help smiling at the practical and very literal character of Downer's response, but forebore to follow it up by inquiring as to any speculations my friend might entertain concerning Frink's destiny *after* the dollar was swallowed. I thought a good deal nevertheless, about this man. He excited in my breast a profound feeling of compassion. As I walked homeward, I asked myself, " Is he never to change ? *must* he go on so *always ?* What would induce you to take his place ?"

A shudder passed over me at the bare idea. I drew a long breath, experiencing a sense of relief, in being assured of my own identity. " What does it matter," I said, " how poor I am, how hard I am pressed, so long as I *feel* as I do ?" I was very rich at that moment, in all my emotions ; and I was happier, I do believe, as I walked along, than ever I was before.

CHAPTER X.

THE PAWNBROKER.

Do the best I could, it was impossible for me to meet our necessary expenditures. I had a good many notes to sell, but the men who would purchase drove such hard bargains, that the commissions were necessarily small. It was astonishing how close they all calculated. On one occasion, I was asked what commission I expected to charge on the transaction; I answered frankly, when the griping wretch insisted on my allowing him that before he would give me the money.

" You must make your man pay you," was all I could get from him.

As I was limited by the owner, and knowing the note would be sold elsewhere by other brokers, I preferred to close the matter, and do the whole for nothing to losing a customer. Very different business indeed from the ready, off-hand work of disposing of first-class paper.

At the end of three months, I was decidedly behind-hand. We owed the servant two months' wages. The grocer a two-weeks' bill. The butcher also for two weeks. The children all required new shoes; some summer dresses were necessary. I myself should at least have a new hat. I could not bear the idea of disturbing Alice's treasure, so carefully placed in the savings bank. What had I best do?

Up to that time I had never visited a pawnbroker's shop. It seemed as if it were a species of humiliation to enter one. Disappointed in receiving a small sum I had that day counted on, and knowing I must not go home without some money, I determined to make the trial. I had in my pocket a valuable watch, of an approved maker. It had cost me two hundred dollars. I looked at it. Never did it seem so much of a companion as at that moment. I strolled slowly along Nassau-street, till I reached the Park, and stood quite undecided. It was here that Downer, on his way home, came up with me.

"What are you waiting for?"

I told him.

"It's of no use," he replied, "to pawn any thing. You will lose it, that's all; and you will be just as bad off afterward. If you have any thing to part with, *sell* it; for you will keep on paying twenty-five per cent. per annum for two or three years, perhaps, and it goes in the end."

"That may be," I said, "but there is no help for it; I must have the money to-night."

"Hold on, Parkinson," said Downer, as I started to cross the street. "Let me go, I have been through with it, just as lief as not, I tell you."

I was on the point of assenting, and had partly raised my hand to my pocket, when I looked in his face, and saw his harsh, repulsive features betraying the strongest feeling. He seemed actually as if he were in pain on my account. Had I been a child, about exposing myself to some great peril, he could not have appeared more apprehensive or considerate.

"No, my friend!" I exclaimed, "I will go through it too; better now than at any other time."

"Mind, you ask for as much again as you want," he said.

I nodded, and crossed over to where Simpson displays three golden balls, the arms of the Lombard merchants, who were the first in old times to lend money on pledge of chattel securities.

My heart beat violently as I entered. I would not thrust myself in one of the coffin-like stalls, but walked straight up to the counter, where a man was already engaged, attempting precisely what I proposed to do, to wit: to get a loan on his watch.

He had just handed it in. Behind the counter stood not a black-eyed, long-bearded, sharp-visaged Jew, as my imagination had pictured, but an intelligent, business-like looking individual, who carelessly opened one side of the watch, and shutting it again, without the least examination, said: "How much do you want?"

"Twenty-five dollars," replied the man.

"Will give you ten."

"Can't you give fifteen?"

"Only ten."

"Well, take it."

It was now my turn. My hand trembled as I drew out my watch. The fate of my predecessor augured poorly for me.

The watch was speedily transferred to the hand of the pawnbroker. The same careless examination was passed, just a springing of one of the sides, as if by habit, and then the monotonous, "How much do you want?"

"I must have fifty dollars on it."

"'Tis good for that," was the answer, "but we are not loaning now over twenty-five dollars on any watch. The demand is so great, and we must give our small customers the preference."

"I suppose so, but really I *must* have this money, and I beg you to accommodate me."

There was a moment's hesitation; then he turned around, and took up two pieces of paper.

"What name?" he inquired.

"Parkinson."

In just a minute a ticket was handed to me (the name written on it looked more like Frogson, than any thing else). Fifty dollars were placed in my hands, and the transaction was closed. A new-comer took my place, and.I marched away triumphant. I felt very grateful to the man behind the counter. I hardly knew why, but I stepped out on the pavement, with a happy appreciation of the institution of pawnbrokers, since it could thus so suddenly bring relief to the suffering. Just then I cast my eyes up at the dial-plate on the City Hall, and was surprised that it was so late, and unconsciously I undertook to compare the time with my own. My hand took its usual course to my watch-guard, but it grasped vacancy; a slight pang, and it was over. After all, my friend of the three balls had a very perfect security, and an excellent rate of interest.

"Well! all right?" It was Downer's voice.

"All right."

"Mind, I say, you have been very foolish. Such a thing as a watch gets to be a part of yourself. You shouldn't

have parted with it. You should have imagined you had
no watch, and then you would have managed some way to
" raise the wind" without it. I tell you, it's so. What
are you going to do when you have pledged every thing ?"

" God knows."

Downer shook his head, and we separated, each on his
way home.

When I came to pay off the petty debts which had accumulated, I found I had but eighteen dollars left, with which
to purchase shoes and summer dresses ! How the fifty dollars had melted away ! Never mind. I must keep at work.
I gave Alice no opportunity to ask questions that night.
The next day, I went early to the office. I thought I
should escape unobserved, but I did not. I heard nothing
about it, though, for several days. One evening, after dinner, I was seated, reading the newspaper, when a ring at
the door was followed by the girl bringing in a small box,
carefully done up, and directed to me. I proceeded to open
it. The young ladies raised their eyes with a very natural air of inquiry. I found a neat morocco watch-case, in
which, on opening, I discovered my own handsome lever !
I was amazed. I hardly knew what to say or do. I imagine I looked a little foolish, too, for the young ladies kept
eying me, and I fancied, with an air of ill-suppressed mirth.
But when I proceeded, with a kind of vacant deliberation,
to put on the watch, both the girls burst out in screams
of laughter. They jumped up and stood before me, and
laughed and laughed, till I assumed to be angry, and told
them, half-smiling all the time, to have done with such nonsense. I asked them what there was to laugh at, when a

gentleman received his watch back from the jeweller's clean?"

"Oh! nothing, nothing," and away they went again, half-crazy, one would suppose.

You know, reader, I enjoyed the scene very much; but I enjoyed, also, affecting to be vexed over it. I could get no explanation from either of the conspirators. So I put on my watch, and never parted with it again, and I wear it now as I write.* . . . .

It was utterly impossible for me to earn a living for myself and family, but I did all I could. I gladly made three dollars, two, even one dollar. I kept on, however, extending my acquaintance, and gaining, from day to day, an insight into matters I knew little of before. Had I permitted myself to do as many persons around me did, and taken advantage of the situation of people who were thrown in my hands; had I chosen to lie, and deceive, and cheat, I could have squeezed out dollars enough to support us. But this I never did, I never could do. I acted honestly, and with conscience. Alice knew precisely how we were situated. She knew I was falling behind hand every month. She exerted herself to the utmost to economize. I could see this in so many little things, which she thought escaped my observation. Matilda was not one whit behind Alice. She took occasion, however, to abuse the world liberally, and declared often, she could see no justice in my being exposed to so much distress, while knaves had every thing their own way.

---

* I learned some time after, that it was MATILDA who first discovered I did not carry my watch as usual. Thereupon, its whereabouts was suspected, and the pawn-ticket filched from my pocket. Then the two girls actually sold some of their trinkets, to raise the money to redeem the watch.—c. R. P.

Meanwhile, my petty debts accumulated in spite of me. For the first time, too, since my wife died, I was obliged to employ a physician. Charley got wet through and through in a soaking rain one Saturday, while enjoying his holiday. He came home chilled, and went to bed with a high fever. The next day, he was seized with inflammation of the lungs, and for a time his life was despaired of.

Thus, to the burden of poverty was added the sickness of my child, and with it, a serious apprehension as to the result.

16

CHAPTER XI.

VARIOUS MATTERS.

CHARLEY recovered after several weeks' illness. But not to enjoy again his usual health. One of his lungs was permanently affected, so that any overexertion or exposure confined him within doors. I cannot express how sad I was to witness this. I was not aware before how much I was depending on the future of my boy. He was nearly thirteen, and could I hold out a few years longer, what might not *he* accomplish for us? After a little, my new-found strength came to my support, and I worked resolutely on. I could see compensation, even in this last misfortune. His delicate health refined and elevated Charley's nature. It made Anna very considerate of him, and threw an additional softness over the demeanor of the whole family. Still Matilda took frequent occasion to arraign PROVIDENCE for thus afflicting me. I did not attempt to argue with her, that was impossible, for it would only excite and irritate her. So I would make no reply, except to say pleasantly, "Read the ninth and tenth verses of the second chapter of Job," which sometimes had the effect to silence, if not to convince her.

Meantime, I continued to run behind-hand. The summer was over, and we had to provide again for winter. There was but one way to do, and that was, to endeavor to get an advance on Alice's share in the house fund, which would be paid to her when she was twenty-one. Despite my utmost exertions, I was forced to make petty debts, and thus lived in perpetual purgatory. Through Mr. Case, I obtained an advance of three hundred and fifty dollars, out of the six hundred and fifty which my daughter was to receive in about three months. Alice entered into an agreement, by which she assigned sufficient of that sum to pay the advance, and which obligation contained a careful statement that the money was for her support, clothing, and general maintenance. This was an extraordinary relief, yet it was consuming the little capital which remained to us. Never mind, we will work on!

And we did work on, through the year, through the winter, through the spring, into another summer; a new summer, when the trees were covered with foliage, and nature was everywhere in bloom, rich, prodigal, joyous. No way impeded by man's distresses, the sun, the moon, the stars, the earth, rejoiced together.

Meanwhile, what passions were busy, what plans, what plots were devising, what efforts making by people to circumvent and overreach each other!

How much better had they all been honest! During this last year I made some progress. I got into a routine of petty business, where I earned small sums. But with all my exertions, I could not make enough to support my family. So by the succeeding autumn, Alice's fund, which had been paid over to her in the spring, but from which was deducted the sum already advanced, was entirely exhausted. It seemed as if there was no possible way of increasing my receipts. I earned just about so much, and fell about so much behind.

It was true, Alice had still five hundred dollars and the interest, still untouched in the savings bank. But to commence on that deposit conveyed the dreadful thought, that our last hope was failing, and destitution was absolutely staring us in the face. Notwithstanding the severe portraiture I have drawn of Mr. Frink, it was through that singular personage that I realized the larger portion of my little commissions. Penurious as he was, he was not so despicably mean as many with whom I was brought in contact. Neither did he ever desire me to do any thing dishonest. Such and such notes he would take at such and such rates— hard enough, to be sure; if the parties did not want to close with him, they could let it alone, that was all.

I had kept my account open all the time in the Bank of Credit, with the hope that I might ultimately get the control of such paper as the bank would be willing to discount. One day Downer brought me a man who had an acceptance of a firm which he said was known there, and whose paper had been frequently discounted. I hurried with it to the president (formerly the cashier, as I have already mentioned), and asked him to pass it for me. This man, who was indebted in the first instance to my influence for promotion, was civil, but barely so; he said he did not know the names, indeed had never seen them before, but he would offer the acceptance at the board, which met that day, at twelve, and if it was favorably known to any of the directors, it would be passed for me. I left the bank, with the pleasant expectation of making a handsome commission out of the day's work. I returned at one. The president handed me back the paper, with the remark, that not one of the directors (and it was a full board) knew it. I expressed my disappointment.

"You know, Mr. Parkinson," continued the official with some severity, "that the Bank of Credit never has, and, I venture to say, never will discount a piece of paper not known to some one of its directors." There was no gainsaying so good a banking rule, and I said so. I took the acceptance, and came away. I returned it to the owner, and stated what had occurred. The next day, however, he brought me five pretty large notes of the same makers, discounted at the Bank of Credit, and duly paid. I was indignant. I asked for the possession of the notes a few moments, and stepped to the bank, and, without saying a word, exhibited them to the president.

He turned red with anger. Glancing at the indorsements, he said: "These notes were offered, sir, at separate times, by a firm worth a million of dollars; offered doubtless in a batch of tens of thousands. You don't suppose we would stop to scrutinize one little note indorsed by such men, when we were satisfied with the respectability of the lot?"

"No. I don't; or at least I should not, had you not told me *every* note was specially passed on—that's all."

This was the end of my operations with the old bank, where I had done business for so many, many years. I was foolish to give way to any exhibition of feeling; but it is difficult always to repress it.

. . . .

There were times when I thought seriously of attempting some other plan for a livelihood. Again I endeavored to devise a way to increase my earnings, by attending to some matters outside of my daily occupation. It was in vain. My old acquaintances were fast disappearing from the business world, while I was fast becoming *fixed* in the miserable work I had undertaken. Oh! if I could but gain enough for a bare support! What toil, what privation, what mortification would I not endure to be able just to pay my way! The privilege to work, and live by my work, was all I asked—*all*. These reflections did not always afflict me. On the contrary, I preserved my cheerfulness well, and it was only on occasions that I had some despairing moments. Even then I felt persuaded that whatever happened it was all right.

One morning before I was up, I involuntarily exclaimed aloud: "If I only could find out what the ALMIGHTY wants of me, I would try and do it!"

I started at the sound of my own voice, and, thus brought to myself, smiled at my own soliloquy.

. . . .

One day I had been running about for several hours, hoping to find a purchaser for a note which had been placed in my hands. The owner was in great distress for the money, and I could encounter no one who would take it. Finally, I sought information of Downer, as I always did when in a quandary. He directed me to a stock-broker, named Sidney, who, he said, knew the party well; and who, he thought, would buy the note. This broker was a gay, rollicking, good-hearted fellow, who was generally fortunate in his operations, and sometimes invested in business paper. So I called on him at his office, and presented what I had to offer.

"I have half a mind to take that," he said.

"I hope you will," was my reply.

" I suppose you will say two per cent. ?"

I was about to acquiesce, when at that moment one came in, and whispered in his ear. "Yes, yes, immediately," he said. "On the whole, I think I wont buy this; fact is, cannot stop now," and off he went in a twinkling. I felt very sorry for the poor fellow who was expecting his money, and who manifested a keen disappointment. I was sorry too on my own account.

" Do you want me to tell you what to do ?" said Downer, to whom I communicated the result.

" Certainly."

" Well, Sidney dines every day at five, with several of his set, at the 'Shadow,' in Broadway. Go there about half-past six, and tell him what distress the man is in, and you will get the money."

I hesitated about going; finally I concluded I would go, as much for the adventure, and for the sake of the novelty, as any thing. I waited, therefore, till the appointed time, and then proceeded to the place of entertainment, ycleped the "Shadow," and asked one of the waiters for Mr. Sidney, stating I had business with him. The man conducted me through several passages, where I could hear sounds of bois-terous mirth, long before we reached the door of the private room. When arrived there, the waiter knocked, but no one heard him, and I checked a further advance, while I listened to the following, sung in a fine deep voice, by one of the company, while all joined in the chorus:

> "Wine cures the gout, boys, the colic and the phthisic,
> Wine cures the gout, boys, the colic and the phthisic,
> And it is allowed by all,

And it is allowed by all,
And it is allowed by all,
To be the best of physic."

At this juncture, the waiter opened the door, and asked for Mr. Sidney. That personage, thus appealed to, rose, brushed the ash from his cigar, tightened his pantaloons, and came to the door, amid cries of "Stop him; no running away," etc., mingled with voices shouting:

" For to-night we'll merry, merry be,
For to-night we'll merry, merry be,
For to-night we'll merry, merry be,
To-morrow we'll get sober."

I hastened to explain my presence there, by saying I thought he did not positively decide not to take the note I had offered. That the owner of it was in great distress for the money, and I was thus induced to intrude on him. I concluded by saying, that the man was now waiting in the public room, trembling for the success of my mission.

The broker's face exhibited at first some chagrin, but before I was through it was serene again.

"A devilish queer time," he said, "to shave a note—a queer place too; but if, as you say, the poor devil is *in extremis*—how shall we calculate? never mind—you have the statement all ready, I see. Don't know as I have cash enough by me."

Thereupon he thrust his hand into his vest pocket, and drew out a roll of bills. "Phillips, I say, got a hundred dollars—all right. There, I perceive, you understand my weak side. Don't try it again though; please don't. Good evening."

I could hear the merry voices joining in—

"Come, landlord, fill your flowing bowl!"

as I wound my way back to the public room, where I delighted my constituent with the sight of the money. I received myself, a handsome commission, and went home all the more cheerful, instead of the more morose, for having encountered a set of "jolly good fellows."

To speak truthfully, I did not moralize on the sin of extravagance in eating and drinking, or the wickedness of being jovial. I did not even congratulate myself that these men, who were singing so merrily, were on the high road to perdition, while I perchance was happily bound in the other direction. Nor did I feel the slightest pang of jealousy that Sidney had his pocket full of cash, while I was penniless.

16*

CHAPTER XII.

A NEW-COMER.

BUT I did enjoy returning to my home that evening, and being met with affectionate greetings and demonstrations.

How different the Charles E. Parkinson within those doors, and the Charles E. Parkinson walking wearily up and down the street, visiting Frink and his coadjutors! In my house, GOD be praised, I forgot all the deformities of my life—all. For there my existence flowed naturally and free. It is true, I knew I was losing ground, in a pecuniary sense, still I could do no more than my best, and that done, I was content to let GOD work out His will.

I labored on incessantly. From the fund belonging to Charley and Anna, invested by the court, I received, as their guardian, about ninety dollars a year. This was something. It served to pay one quarter's rent.

.   .   .   .

The following season we had a new-comer in our neighborhood. Among the boarders at Mr. Ellis's (the name of the family next door), was a young man, three or four and twenty, of a prepossessing appearance, who, I learned, was a law-student in the office of a respectable counsellor down town. I became interested in this young man before I was aware of it. He came and went with great regularity, and invariably walked each way. We thus frequently encountered each other, and often went along together. His name was Warren. He was a native of New-Hampshire, and a graduate, he told me, of Dartmouth College. After we had seen more of each other, he gave me some further account of himself. His father was a farmer, with a large family, and quite too poor to aid his boy to attain his heart's desire—an education. Still he did toward it what little lay in his power, so that at last the youth was imperfectly fitted for college. He succeeded in passing his examination, and was admitted. By dint of teaching a district-school in the winter, working out at haying and harvesting during the four weeks of his summer vacation, at a dollar a day, together with some trifling aid from his father, he managed to pay his way, and graduated one of the "first four" in his class. Then he set to work teaching, till he accumulated enough to support him a year in New York, after which he was promised at least sufficient to pay for his board and lodging. Mr. Ellis was originally from the same town, and knew the young man's family. It was thus he came to take up his abode in his house. This brief account, told with simplicity, and not as in any respect an unusual story, greatly attached me to Robert Warren. Intellectually, he was no common person. I saw that no ordinary impediments would ever retard him. He had begun at the rough end of life, and was mastering a destiny for himself. And now how close and calculating he was, while his nature was generous, and his heart open! I asked Warren to my house. He did not give himself much time for visiting, but he dropped in often on us, and, according to my request, without ceremony. Alice liked him very much. So did

Matilda—after a while. At first she sneered a little at
Warren's appearance; he dressed in wretched taste, and
was horribly countrified; but his qualities of head and
heart soon threw dress, and a slight provincial manner, into
the background, and Matilda confessed she liked the clown-
ish fellow amazingly. Warren really was no clown. It
was astonishing how rapidly he improved in every way.
Matilda claimed great credit on this score, and, I think, deserved it. For she pounced on every peculiarity, and dealt
mercilessly with every little fault of conduct or character.
Warren took all in good part, and never neglected a fair hit
or a sensible criticism. Before many months entire confidence had sprung up between us all, so that he was familiar
with our whole history, while we were equally so with his.
There arose a very strong sympathy between this young
man and myself, from the fact, perhaps, of our both having
to work hard, and calculate very closely from day to day.
In fact, Warren was never unwelcome among us. He
would run in during the evening, and tell us about some
new case which he was examining; or listen to an account
of what I had been doing. He would bring books for the
girls to read, or he would sit and chat with them, or listen
to the music when they played. Thus, while scarcely sensible of it, we had virtually added another member to our
family, and had greatly enlarged our sources of happiness.

CHAPTER XIII.

THE LAST EFFORT OF DOWNER.

It was a very stormy day in the month of November. The rain drove in torrents from the direction of the river up Wall-street, till it beat against the front of Trinity, or was carried by the changing gusts of wind fiercely around the corners of the streets. Those who were obliged to be out and brave the fury of the tempest, dashed wildly forward, now darting in and out of the banks and brokers' offices, and then rushing on to the places they had to visit. Umbrella-peddlers abounded with wares to suit customers and the times. Groups of men stood in the door-ways, ready to take advantage of any cessation of the flood, while occasionally a carriage would drive rapidly along. As I stood myself on the steps of the building where I kept my office, I saw Downer plunging through the wet, as careless as if it had been one of the pleasantest days of the year. He seemed to be poorly protected against the weather, and the water dripped from his shoulders as he stepped up to where I was standing.

"You are soaked through," I said. "Come into my office and dry yourself; I have a good fire."

"Not I," said Downer; "I prefer to stay here. I love a storm—God! how I love a storm. It makes me feel on an equality with every body. How it pelts a nabob and poor devil just alike. Look! look quick, Parkinson! there's

your friend Goulding. See how he has to run ; no umbrella
—left his own at his house, too mean to buy another. See
what devilish cavalier usage the elements treat him to."
And Downer laughed so very loud that it attracted Goulding's notice in passing. In looking up, his foot slid on the
slippery pavement and he fell flat. " Good, good !" continued Downer. " I swear I never saw any thing done so
well. A north-easter is no respecter of persons. That's
why I love to be out in one—we all fare the same. It
would not do for me to lay that man on his back, although—
damn him!—he deserves it at my hands ; but the old nor'-
easter has done it, and it's all right."

There was something wild and unnatural about Downer's
manner that alarmed me. I took him gently by the arm
and made him come up-stairs to my office. Then I almost
forced him to lay off his coat and attempt to dry himself.
He was shivering with the wet and cold, and now fell into
a moody silence. After he was more comfortable, I persuaded him to get into an omnibus and go home.

A few days after he sent me word: he was ill and requested me to attend to some business for him. I did so.
A week more, and I was about calling to see him, when
one morning early he entered my office. It was very cold,
and he wore a heavy surtout, and over it an immense cloak,
which nearly concealed his features, so that on entering I
did not recognize him. When I did so, the change in his
countenance frightened me. His usual gaunt face was now
so shrunk and emaciated that it appeared as if nothing
remained but the skin drawn tightly over the bones of his
cheeks. He came in rapidly and dropped into a chair.

" Have you got fifty dollars ?"

" I am sorry to say I have no such sum."

" Then you must get it for me," he exclaimed, and he handed me a paper, which I perceived was a life insurance policy. "The quarterly payment is due to-day. The premium must be paid, Parkinson, and you *must* get this money for me. I can't run a step further. Do you understand? That policy is worth to-day to my family at least fourteen thousand dollars (it was originally for ten thousand). Now, go, go quick and bring the money."

A man in earnest, who *must* carry a certain point or perish, *will* carry it. He exhales a certain Odic force; he is surrounded with a magnetic *vis*, which compels others to do his bidding. Certain men have this on occasions; certain others always possess it, and these last are the really great ones of the earth.

At this moment Downer was irresistible. I took up my hat and started mechanically to do what he demanded, without thinking where or for what I was going. When I recovered a little, I tried to decide where I should go to borrow fifty dollars. I stood some time, not being able to think of any body to apply to. At length I proceeded to the office of Mr. Case. He had done a great deal of business for my firm and me, which had proved lucrative. To be sure, I knew him perhaps still less, on account of my intimacy with Mr. Norwood, but I resolved to try him. He received me after some delay. I told him an unexpected occurrence presented itself, when I was compelled immediately to have fifty dollars more than I could command, and

I wished him to lend it to me for a few days. He complied, though not without hesitation.

I carried the money joyfully to Downer. He showed no particular sign of gratification. "I knew, old friend, you would get it," he said. "Take this policy and step to the office; make the payment; have it properly indorsed, and get me a duplicate receipt."

It was but a few minutes before this was done.

"Now let me have your arm till I can get into an omnibus. I must hurry home. My wife don't know I am out of the house. I sent her away on an errand. The doctor forbid my leaving my bed."

The omnibus stopped and I helped Downer in. It was then he seized my hand and pressed it tight. "Good-by!" He looked me cheerfully in the face. His countenance had changed wonderfully. It wore an expression of rest and repose. "Good-by!"

It was all he uttered. I never saw him again alive. He died the next day.

I attended Sol Downer's funeral. I gazed on his features as he lay in his coffin, and the tears flowed freely as I took a last leave of this unfortunate man. I never knew a husband or a father so much beloved as he. The sorrow of his family was indescribable. For myself, I felt desolate the next day when I went into the street; and when a vulgar, low-lived man of money remarked to me in a coarse tone, "So Old Sol has kicked the bucket," I could have throttled him, for speaking thus of one whose nature he was incapable of understanding, and whose soul was as noble as the soul of the other was base and mean.

CHAPTER XIV.

MRS. FREDERICK AUGUSTUS HAVENS.

RETURNING home one day, Alice showed me an envelope containing wedding-cards. The parties were Miss Henrietta Stevenson and Mr. Frederick Augustus Havens. The latter was now an "exquisite" of the first water. His father having died, he came in possession of a few thousand dollars, which was nearly spent when he succeeded in his suit with the heiress. This young person I introduced to the reader in the early part of my history. I had not altogether lost sight of her. The influences of wealth— she enjoyed about twelve thousand a year—were gradually having their customary effect, and she was becoming by degrees more worldly and selfish. Her marriage with Havens surprised me. However, Miss Stevenson was now at least twenty-five. She had refused innumerable offers, and perhaps began to perceive that it was possible to decline once too often.

This incident gave rise to considerable conversation. Matilda sat unusually silent. At last Alice appealed to her on some point.

"Don't speak to me," was the petulant reply; "I have nothing to say about it."

"Why, Matilda, what is the matter?" I asked.

"Nothing."

"Oh! but it is something," cried Alice. "Tell me what."

"Just nothing at all, only I hate that girl."

"Hate her! why?"

"For robbing me of my own."

"What *do* you mean?" re-echoed Alice.

"I tell you I mean nothing but what I have said. Can't you understand English?"

"Yes, but there is something connected with it which we don't understand," replied Alice, "and you don't choose to enlighten us."

"Well, in a word, Uncle Walden disinherited pa, and left all his property to this girl's father, who was about his sixtieth cousin. I have hated her all my life, and I always shall hate her."

"My dear Matilda, why have you never told me this? How I should have liked to bring you two together."

"Bring us together," returned Matilda. "I suppose you take it as a matter of course that I should be only too happy to humiliate myself before her: only you happen to be very much mistaken," and her eyes flashed with anger.

"Now, don't be vexed, and you shall have every thing your own way," said Alice good-naturedly. "You know I didn't mean to annoy you."

"I know you didn't; but please never mention that person's name to me again. Mother once, when I was very young, wrote to the girl, and got no answer. Poor mother!"

Matilda rose and went to the piano and began playing a lively air. I knew she was endeavoring to subdue her emotion. Suddenly I recollected the little girl I saw on the pavement when handing Miss Stevenson to her carriage. I turned and looked at Matilda. The features were the same. "It is she," I said to myself; "not a doubt of it!"

.   .   .   .

Two or three weeks after Downer's death, his widow sent to me to request I would call at her house. I had previously offered my services to do any thing she might require, and she promised to avail herself of them if necessary. I went immediately to her. She had regained a certain degree of composure, but it was evident she had received an irreparable shock in the loss of her best friend.

"I have a command to carry out and a letter to deliver," she said, after the greeting was over. "The company has already paid me the amount of my husband's life insurance. He has left minute directions how to invest it, so that I need have no care nor anxiety. A small sum he directed me to lose no time in giving to you in token of his friendship and affection."

Mrs. Downer here handed me a bank-note' for one thousand dollars.

I was at first so deeply affected I could not speak. "It was like him, madam, like him and like nobody else," at length I cried. "What can I say? my heart is full. I must not take this. I am made happy by his remembrance of me. It is all I want, all I can accept."

I forced the money into her hand, and walked up and down the room under the pressure of the strongest excitement.

When Mrs. Downer perceived I was firm in my resolu-

tion not to take this last gift of my friend, she forbore to
press me further, but at my request, proceeded to tell me
what her plans were. She would purchase a small place;
it had previously been selected by her husband, near New
York, which would be a home for the children. It was
near enough for her son to come in and out daily, while he
attended to his duties in the city. He had lately secured a
situation in an excellent mercantile house. Her husband's
affairs required really no attention. He owed literally nothing, and he left no estate to be settled. She had only to
invest according to his directions the fourteen or fifteen
thousand dollars now paid to her, and nothing else remained to look after; so careful and so provident had been
this considerate husband and father.

I went directly from Mrs. Downer's to my own house,
and to my room. I opened the letter. It was as follows:

"Dear Friend: I am going first. These last few days,
at home with my wife and children, without any care or
anxiety, waiting to die, have been the happiest of my life.
It is a great thing to be able to rest. Well, we shall not
meet any more in the street, shall we? You will miss me,
I know. I fear your life will be hard enough; but you
don't need any advice. I want to help you, though, if I
can. There are three or four men for whom I did a great
deal of hard work for small yet sure pay, who will, I think,
employ you. I mean Allison, Forbes, Baker and Yard.
You know who they are and their places. It is better to
work for them than let your folks starve. Call on them all,
and say you are ready to take my place as their broker.

Say how you came to call. And now one word more. Never believe I have been a dishonest man. Never mind what you hear people say; don't believe *that*. I have done things which seemed unscrupulous, not compatible with red-tape morality, but never what would wrong any body. I have borne much. I need not tell you; you know enough about it. Good-by. s. d.

"P. S. My wife will hand you the fifty dollars."

Not a word about the thousand dollars. He had too much delicacy to allude to it.

And here I take leave of one who lived and toiled in the "street," enjoying there the sympathy of no human being, except myself; who gained a reputation for dishonesty, while incapable of wronging any body; whose life was one bitter struggle—so bitter that death was welcome. By his foresight in securing an insurance, he was able, dying, to provide for those he loved. Farewell, my friend. In re-calling these scenes, I have to part with you afresh. Fare-well!

CHAPTER XV.

HEART-BROKEN.

ALLISON, Forbes, Baker and Yard, the four individuals
to whom I was referred as just mentioned, belonged to a
nondescript class, who are possessed of considerable cash
in hand, and who are constantly on the watch for an opportunity to double their money. Such men rarely buy notes;
they can't make enough by the operation. But if a gentleman is hard up and wants to pledge his silver or his wife's
jewels, and is sensitive about its being known, these people
will accommodate him, through a third party, with a reasonable advance at enormous rates; or they sometimes
find a piece of property going at auction by accident at
half-price, and they step in and buy. Occasionally they bid
off a lot of goods at the lower end of Wall-street, and
clear fifty per cent. without moving them. They will make
advances on government contracts at the rate of cent. per
cent. In short, they are ready to turn their honest penny
in any transaction which will pay. Such men generally
have a kind of satellite revolving around them, always on
the hunt for chances, who is enabled to earn a small pit-
tance as a reward for his persevering industry.

Reader, I was now so hard pushed that I was thankful
for an introduction to these four men. I lost no time in
calling on each. I was received by all of them pretty

much in the same manner. They had no idea I was half as smart as Old Sol; still, I might go ahead and see what I could do. I was treated by these people, I don't say unkindly, but with coarse indifference, precisely as if I belonged to them. I was ordered here, sent there; told to do this, and to be careful not to do that. And what meagre compensation! sometimes a few shillings, sometimes one, two or three dollars. I soon found I must give up my office. I could not afford the respectability of having one all to myself. So I engaged what is termed "desk-room" in a pretty large basement-office, already occupied by three other persons. For this I paid at the rate of one hundred dollars a year. There was this advantage, that I did not have to mount any stairs; for I began to feel the exercise severely. Besides, in what I was now working at, it was important I should be as accessible as possible. So I moved my desk and two of my chairs to the new place, and sent the rest of the furniture, including the carpet, to auction. I felt rather badly when I thought what pains Alice had taken to arrange it, but, after all, what did it matter? The proceeds, small as they were, proved very acceptable. I continued to make something from time to time through Mr. Frink and one or two other usurers, but it seemed as if they grew daily more and more griping. However, I kept manfully at work. I would not permit myself to be much disturbed by the vexations to which I was constantly subjected during the day, and at night I came back to the happy world of home, grateful that it still remained to me.

   .   .   .   .

I come now to the most important occurrence of my life.

I have taken some pains to make the reader understand how of late I had been fortified by an extraordinary self-reliance, coupled with a sense of the power of the human spirit to enable one to rise superior to misfortune. In this way I came to feel that I was more than a match for whatever could happen. I am now going to narrate how I was mistaken. There was a man in the street by the name of Horace P. Devine, who was a sort of general broker, but with whom I had no more than a bowing acquaintance. Downer used to dislike him, and often cautioned me to have nothing to do with him. The warning appeared unnecessary, for we never met in any business transaction. For several weeks, however, Devine had managed to put himself in my way, and by degrees we entered into conversation. His address was pleasing, and his air ingenuous. He spoke of the difficulties of getting on without capital, stated with an air of candor that he was not worth a cent in the world, and that sometimes he was perplexed to know what to do for five dollars. I began to think Downer had conceived an antipathy to this man, and for once, that his usual good sense had yielded to his prejudices. By degrees my acquaintance with Devine became more intimate. He told me he should have left New York long since and gone to the West, where active industry was more available, but he had a mother and two sisters dependent on him, which tied him down here. On one occasion Devine came in and asked me if I had any use for fifty dollars until the next day, as he happened to have that amount over for the twenty-four hours. I replied I had no use for the money, but thanked him for his kindness in offering it. It seemed to me very considerate. Devine by degrees ingratiated himself in my favor. He would consult me confidentially about his private affairs; was a most respectful listener whenever I gave my opinions, and treated me with a deference which was both agreeable and flattering. He never asked any favor at my hands, but, on the contrary, frequently undertook to do me some trifling service, which I received as a mark of respect to my age, and perhaps as some return for the advice I gave him.

One day a gentleman, for whom I had already done some business, brought me a note for six hundred and fifty dollars. It was just before three o'clock. The owner wanted one hundred dollars at once, but was in no haste for the balance, and was willing I should take three or four days if I could sell the note to any better advantage. As it was a respectable piece of paper, I felt anxious to secure it, although I had but a few minutes to raise what was wanted. Now, Devine was in the room when the man came in with the note, and although he rose at once to leave, he heard the request made for the hundred dollars. When I came out on the sidewalk with the note in my hand, Devine was standing by the door.

"If you have no place in particular," he said, "where you expect to get the money, I feel sure I can find a purchaser who will take the note in a day or two, and who will, meanwhile, advance what is wanted upon it."

"Very well," I replied; "if you can bring me a hundred dollars immediately, and are certain that you can sell the note well, you can take it, and I will divide the commission with you."

"My dear sir," cried Devine, "I hope you don't think I

17

made this offer for the sake of securing a part of your commission, which, permit me to say, I shall not touch. I happen to know where the money can be had, and I thought I could save you from running after it."

This was very kind. I handed the paper to Devine, who promised to be back in five minutes with the money. I think he returned in three, and, quite breathless, placed a hundred-dollar bill in my hand. This I handed to my constituent, with the remark that the note would be speedily discounted, and he left much pleased with my promptness.

The following day, and the next, and the next, I saw Devine as usual. He spoke of the note, and said it would be done within the promised time.

On the fourth day Devine did not appear, but my constituent did, with the expectation of getting his money. I went immediately to the place where Devine had a desk, and saw a paper pinned upon it, on which was written : " Will be back in half an hour." Persons in the room, of whom I inquired how long Devine had been out, were unable to give me any information. After waiting without success the half hour indicated, I hurried to my office, hoping to find him there. I was destined to be disappointed, and was obliged to make the only excuse I could to the owner, which was, that I was unable to see the person that day from whom I was to receive the money. Of course, he was disappointed, but he left with the assurance that I would have every thing all right for him the next day.

I hastened back to find Devine, but he had not returned. According to the piece of paper, he was still coming " in half an hour !" I waited till it was nearly time to close the office, but he did not arrive. I inquired of the people there where Devine lived. They could not tell me. I consulted a directory. It contained only his place of business—no residence.

I started home with very uneasy sensations. Yet, when I reflected a moment, my fears would seem groundless. After all, was it any thing extraordinary that a person, and that person a broker, should leave his office, expecting to return, and be detained beyond his time? I endeavored to quiet my apprehensions, but so much anxiety did I feel that, contrary to my habit, I carried it home with me that evening. The girls perceived it, and tried to make me tell what was the matter.

The next morning I was early at my office. I was scarcely seated at my desk before Devine entered.

"You were at my place yesterday," he said. "I'm sorry I was out. I was subpœnaed as a witness. They said they wouldn't detain me ten minutes, and kept me all day. What makes it worse, I've just been round to see the man who is to discount that note, and find that he went to Philadelphia yesterday, and will not be back till to-morrow afternoon. I fear this will disappoint you sadly, but I declare I don't know what can be done."

I felt so much relieved by the early visit of Devine and his prompt explanation, that I spoke of the delay as of little consequence, but requested him, as the next day was Saturday, to be sure and see punctually to the matter Monday morning, so that it could be positively closed on that day. He promised very faithfully, and took his leave. I hastened to anticipate the visit of my man by calling on him. He received my explanation with rather a bad grace, but as there was no help for the delay, as he himself said, he could but wait till Monday.

Monday came. Devine came, but his man had been detained over Sunday in Philadelphia. He was expected back, however, at two o'clock. Of course, I had to put off my constituent again. He was very much dissatisfied, and it was very clear that he suspected me of dishonest practice. The affair now began to be threatening. The "party" could not stay in Philadelphia forever, and so about Wednesday, according to Devine, he returned. But having had some very large transactions in his absence, he had drawn his bank account down so low that he would not be able to discount the note for two or three days. By this time I was fully roused to the danger of my position. I began to see just what kind of man this Devine was. I did not wish to alarm him, however, by my suspicions. Still I begged him to tell me the exact truth, and if he had used the note, to say so. His reply was simply a repetition on his honor that he *had* told me the truth, and that the money would certainly be forthcoming. Meantime, my man was enraged. He insisted on knowing to whom I had given the note, and as Devine had already evaded the question on my putting it to him, there was nothing left for me but to tell the owner the precise facts.

At the mention of Devine's name, his manner, which had been before simply angry and splenetic, became insulting in the extreme. "I know all I want to know," he said, and left me. He returned soon with a witness, and tendered me the hundred dollars advanced to him, and demanded his note. Of course, I did not have it to give him. My distress of mind was indescribable. I did not know what to do. I went again to see Devine, but he had left, and after waiting a long time, I came away.

The next morning, as I was about entering my office, I was addressed by a person outside, who appeared to be waiting for me. On ascertaining I was Mr. Parkinson, he told me he was under the necessity of taking me into custody.

I asked him on what charge.

He answered: " On a charge of conspiring with a man named Devine to swindle a party out of five hundred and fifty dollars."

I could not help assuring the officer of my innocence, although I knew it was nothing to him.

The only reply he made was: "Better settle it, I guess. It is no use my finding Devine, he's a slippery fellow, there is nothing to be made out of him; but if you say it will be settled, I tell you I will be accommodating."

"But how *can* a criminal charge be settled?" I asked; "you have no right to let me go, have you, even if I should make all right, as you call it?"

"I don't say I have, but, don't you see, if you fix it straight with the man who has entered the charge, he'll tell the judge it was all a mistake, and wont appear against you? I tell you it's so; it's done 'most every day."

During this brief conversation, I was deliberating what was best to do. I had no time to feel unhappy about it. I told the officer I wished to see the owner of the note. "That you can do very easy," replied he, "for he is at his lawyer's, next door, waiting to hear from you. We will go in there, if you like."

I did not care to go in, but said I preferred to speak with

him outside. We went accordingly to the place, and he was called out.

"If I manage to raise the money which is due you," I said, "is it understood that you will not appear against me?"

"Mr. Parkinson," replied the other, "I have no wish to do you an injury. I was pained to have to take this course to protect myself. If you can manage to return me the note, or to pay me the money, I shall not hesitate to say to the judge, that there has been a misapprehension on my part, and shall decline to appear against you."

This was enough. I asked the officer if he would accompany me to my house. He assented, and we rode up together.

Arriving there, we both went in. I left the officer in the parlor, and proceeded in search of Alice. I found her in her room.

"Why, papa," she said, joyfully, "how early you've come home to-day."

"Alice!"

"What, papa?"

"I want you to go to the savings bank, and draw out the money you have there."

There was a look of mingled anxiety and terror, as her eye inquiringly met mine, while she uttered faintly: "All, papa?"

"All."

She went at once to her drawer, for the bank book. Rapidly she prepared herself to go out. After the door was half open, she turned and said: "We could save six months' interest, papa, by waiting two days."

"We cannot wait; you must be sure to bring the money immediately to my office." Another moment and she had hurried away.

On the staircase I encountered Matilda. " Who is that knavish-looking fellow in the parlor ?" she said.

" A man that came up with me."

"Something has happened, I know: I am sorry," and she passed on.

It was two hours before Alice reached Wall-street, but she brought the money. She had some difficulty in obtaining it at first, as the rules required her to leave the book to be written up.; but she stated her case so strongly, that she succeeded in having this done at once. From this sum I immediately paid the balance of the note, and, accompanied by the owner, we proceeded to the Tombs. There the judge was assured by the merchant that the charge had been made under a mistaken view of the circumstances, and that he proposed to withdraw it. He submitted to a slight reprimand for his precipitancy, and I was thereupon set at liberty. I had previously paid ten dollars to my companion of the day, for his kindness in riding up town and back with me.

Although the business-day was nearly over, I returned mechanically to my desk. There were two or three letters lying on it from parties I was at work for. I did not heed them. I sat for over an hour, anxious about nothing, thinking of nothing, dumbfounded, paralyzed. At last, mechanically I arose, shut up my desk, and walked out. I paused on the corner of Wall and William, on the very spot where several years before I met the President of the Bank of

Credit, and talked with him about the failure of Wise and Company. Vacantly I gazed up and down the street. A rich broker was in the act of getting into his carriage, in which his wife was waiting to drive him home. I thought how Florence, in the days of my prosperity, used sometimes to come for me.

The people were fast leaving the street, while I stood idly looking on. My attention was at that moment excited by hearing my name pronounced, in a conversation between two or three gentlemen, who stood on the steps near where I was. Suspicious and sensitive, it seemed as if my hearing was doubly acute.

"What a damned old scoundrel he's got to be!" said one.

"That's a fact," said another.

"Dear me, dear me, I can't think it possible," added a third; "he was always considered such an honorable man.

"I can't help that," said the first voice. "Loomis says he's been in the Tombs all the morning—he and Devine, for swindling; and when he found he had to be put through, the old knave planked down the cash in less than no time."

Two of the voices were familiar to me. I thought especially that I recognized that of the gentleman who ventured a word in my favor, but I had no desire to satisfy myself. I did not turn round, but started swiftly for my house.

I saw nothing, heard nothing, noticed nothing. Arriving at home, I brushed past Alice, ran up-stairs to my chamber, locked and bolted the door, threw myself on the bed, and cried—cried piteously as children cry.

CHAPTER XVI.

THE SOLUTION.

THE next day was Sunday. I rose, dressed myself mechanically, and went down to breakfast. I was suffering from no sharp sensations. A dull, heavy, muffled pang, at regular intervals, took the place of the usual nervous, energetic action of the heart. Literally *it* seemed to be broken.

So much were Alice and Matilda impressed by the change in me, that neither ventured to ask for an explanation. The younger children shared magnetically in the feeling. What a silent table! How different from our usual cheerfulness!

At the proper hour, we all started for church. I thought the placid face of the old clergyman looked more benevolent and tranquil than ever. "He is at rest, at rest," I said to myself. "Shall *I* ever be at rest?"

The services did not attract my attention, until the text was announced. It was as follows:

"The spirit of a man will sustain his infirmity; but a wounded spirit who can bear?"

"My friends," said the old minister, "the translation of a part of this verse from the Hebrew is not felicitous. Let me improve it by another rendering. 'The spirit of a man will sustain his infirmity; but a wounded spirit—what shall

17*

sustain *it?*' That is the question I propose to answer this morning.

"The spirit of a man will sustain his infirmity! What a statement of the power, and might, and pride of the human race! Ah! yes; the spirit will sustain against all infirmity; it will carry man resolute and undaunted through fire and sword; in perils by land and by water; through misfortunes and calamities; through contests, troubles, and dangers; 'midst disease and pestilence; and it may even nerve him to meet death itself with dignity and composure.

"But if man's *spirit* falters; if the day comes when the *keepers* of the house shall tremble, if a wound is inflicted *here*" (he laid his hand on his heart), "what is to be done? The form of the question in the text implies that there can be no help from within. Physically, a man cannot support himself by his own weight. Neither can the spirit receive support through its own power."

The venerable man went on to show how only the "FATHER of our spirits" can heal the wounds of the spirit. That it is not until man is brought into direct communion with his MAKER, that he is armed at all points, and proof against whatever may happen.

I have no design to give even an abstract of the discourse, but only to convey the leading paramount idea. I listened entranced. Every word seemed prepared for me, directed toward me.

By degrees, as he proceeded, I felt a sense of relief steal over me. The action of the heart resumed its healthful pulsation. By a sort of instinctive effort, I ejaculated in a low tone, "GOD help me!"

.   .   .   .

I went out with the rest of the congregation, a happy, cheerful man. The children felt the change, they were cheerful too. But no explanation was asked. All seemed more than content that I was myself again.

.   .   .   .

Monday morning I resumed my labors in the street, as if nothing had happened to disturb my serenity. Not one of the four worthies whom I have mentioned cared a jot whether I was honest or not. Neither would Frink ever stop to inquire the character of a man who brought him a note to shave. I knew, however, that my reputation had been greatly injured by the report of my arrest. It had the effect to ostracize me to a certain extent, but it did not interfere with my every-day drudgery.

In a few days I told Alice and Matilda what had become of the savings bank money. I narrated the whole story. My daughter was only happy that the money had been kept for this very emergency, and tears stood in her eyes at the thought of what I had undergone. Matilda was in a rage. She declared she would not have paid the man a cent, the sordid, contemptible creature; she would lie in prison all her life first. Why did I allow the scoundrel to frighten me? As to Devine, he ought to be hung—he would be hung. She wondered I could have been so misled; why did I have any thing to do with such a knave?

In the midst of all this Warren came in.

"Tell him about it, Alice," said Matilda.

Alice looked a little confused. She glanced at Warren, then at me.

"Yes, tell him," cried Warren, smiling.

"I think *I* can repeat the story better than Alice," said I.

So I told the whole over again. Warren listened attentively. "I have heard of this Devine," he said. "He is an arrant knave, very ingenious and adroit. If you attempt to arrest him, he would be ready with straw bail, and would swear you out of it in the end. But we will do one thing—stop the payment of the note. This may drive the scoundrel into a compromise before it falls due."

During this conversation, I observed what I had never before noticed, a certain degree of confidence between Alice and Warren. I thought a moment. Why did not Matilda, who was usually impulsive and ready, open the note subject? Why did she call on Alice?

I experienced a feeling of satisfaction at the thought that the two were becoming interested in each other. Warren had now been admitted to the bar, and was struggling with might and main to get into practice. I had no fears for his success, as I looked at his resolute countenance, and ample forehead, and thought what he had already achieved for himself, and how. What a happiness, could I see Alice, dutiful, self-sacrificing Alice, married to such a man! What a contrast to that puny, insignificant Havens! Charley, too, who, as his health was delicate, became the more nice in his appreciation, was greatly attached to Warren. Anna liked him. Matilda liked him.

.   .   .   .

So the months sped away. I continued at my servile work in Wall-street, drudging, toiling, slaving on. I made very few new acquaintances, while occasionally old ones died or disappeared. I thus became more and more isolated. As years passed, the inconveniences of age increased. I was now the oldest man in the street who employed himself in just my business. I seemed to have taken poor Downer's place, and presume I was called "Old Parkinson," as he was called "Old Sol." I began to find that I could not run about as readily as in former years. In ascending a flight of stairs, I had to stop at the top and take breath. In going up and down town, I was frequently forced to ride.

Two or three young men had latterly introduced themselves to my constituents, and threatened by their superior activity, and by being very unscrupulous, to supplant me. All this told very hard on me. But I nevertheless worked cheerfully on, grateful for life and health, happy if I might only support those who were dependent on me.

CHAPTER XVII.

CRISIS.

IN August, 1857, came the monster "*Crisis.*" Unlike the monster "*Cholera*," "Crisis" sprang fiercely at the rich, seizing them by the throat, tapping the jugular, making instant depletion of wealth. This time it came suddenly. Bankers, and brokers, and merchants at Newport, and Saratoga, and Sharon, and Cape May, were telegraphed to fly home and save themselves. They did fly home, to find themselves not worth saving. What a fluttering! what a commotion! After that what changes! Those who occupied first seats moving down to the lowest benches. The old tale again, with renewed severity. I looked on. Twice I had been through similar scenes. Now I was impregnable. I had no friend or relative whose fortune was about to be lost. The storm swept high. The humble, who had little to be anxious about, suffered no apprehensions. I was glad that Warren was not in any pursuit where crisis could visit him. But a great many of my old acquaintances went down. Among these was the man who refused to credit my explanation about the note, and caused my arrest. He was swept completely away. Screwtight and Company, and Gripeall, both went by the board. I am almost sorry to say, so did Oilnut. This bland creature had speculated largely in certain manufactures, which adverse affairs knocked completely in the head. He made a bad failure. *My* people were of a different stamp. It is true they lost a great deal of money, but then they had it to lose. From all I could learn, Frink sunk about fifty thousand dollars, not a large sum considering the amount he had invested, an evidence of the caution with which he operated. I will say one thing for Frink, I never saw a man lose money with such perfect *nonchalance.* He would work an hour with real concern to save or make a sixpence; and he would bear the loss of ten thousand dollars with entire equanimity.

Bank stock made a terrific tumble. Some fell over thirty per cent. Here was a rare chance for those who had money, for in a year the broken paper would be tinkered up, or in some way patched together, and the stock go back to the old figure.*

It seemed strange enough to me to be standing by, looking at all these changes. Even as I had been obliged to sell our house and furniture, so they who were lately so rich, some of them old acquaintances, others comparatively new men, were obliged to sell theirs. Some of these individuals exhibited remarkable cordiality toward me. They would stop and shake hands, and affect much candor in speaking of their failure, as if they would say, " We are now one of you, and we may as well talk it all over."

* Our banks could not go into a general liquidation at any time, and return more than half their capital to the stockholders. This is of little consequence, since such an occurrence will never happen, for it presupposes a general liquidation of the whole mercantile community. Occasionally a bank gets a black eye, is forced to settle up, and rarely pays over fifty cents on a dollar, often much less. The fact is, the banks represent the commercial interests. They are really special partners in the business of each one of their customers, and suffer accordingly.

Meanwhile, my own special work went on as usual, with the difference that I had to run longer and later, and for less pay. By degrees my rent got in arrear. The landlord, by virtue of my punctuality for so many years, was lenient, but I could not expect him to wait forever. Petty debts began to accumulate, incurred as a matter of necessity, with the hope that some fortunate day's work might sweep them off. But the fortunate days grew more and more infrequent, and the petty debts larger. I earned and paid as fast as I could, but it was evident that sooner or later I must go down. I was like a man struggling for life against a strong current, and gradually weakened by its force. Still I managed to go through that winter. As I look back to it, I can hardly say how. I sold one or two valuable articles from my house, and some choice books from my library, and so we kept on.

CHAPTER XVIII.

THE GIRL ON THE SIDEWALK.

It was a pleasant day in the month of September, 1858. I am brought to this period after encountering the same wretched routine which I have already described too often. Two quarters' rent remain due upon my house, and we are running into the third. The landlord has kindly but decidedly announced that we must prepare to vacate the premises in time for the fall demand. There is no help for it, we must go. My own health begins to fail. This incessant, ever-present, never-ending anxiety, coupled with too much hard work, tells severely on me. But my spirit is tranquil, my mind serene, my heart strong.

It was a pleasant day in the month of September. I had started somewhat earlier than usual, thinking to walk the entire way home. I proceeded slowly up Broadway to its junction with the Fifth avenue, and thence along that street of palaces. Not a trace of the last year's disasters could be noticed. It seemed to me that the carriages were more numerous than ever, the liveries more gaudy. This part of the town had been built up since I moved from my old home. In fact, we began to find ourselves almost within the fashionable precincts. Expensive houses had gone up in the adjacent streets, and several near us in our own. Indeed, our landlord had more than once spoken of taking down the simple structure in which we lived and the two adjoining ones, and erecting buildings more in accordance with the present surroundings.

While I pursued my walk along the avenue, a barouche drove by and stopped a little beyond me. Just as I reached it, Henrietta Stevenson—now Mrs. Havens—descended, followed by a fashionably dressed young woman, very affected, who put on a great variety of airs as she shook her dress into shape after reaching the sidewalk.

Mrs. Havens stopped short on seeing me; offering her hand, she exclaimed: "Why, Mr. Parkinson, is it possible this is you? What a long time since we have met. Don't wait for me, Maria," to the supercilious article who stood by her. "Do you know, Mr. Parkinson, I have been thinking of you all the morning? You never can guess why. Wont you come in a moment, I want to speak with you?"

She led the way into her fine house, purchased since her marriage, and newly furnished. Entering the front parlor, she asked me to be seated.

"Now," she said, assuming a confidential tone, "I am going to tell you something strange. Do you remember—oh! years ago, so many years ago it seems to me—one day, after calling at your house in Broadway, that you put me in the carriage, and just as I was driving off I saw a strange-looking little girl staring so fiercely at me that it nearly took my breath away? No, you don't know that; but do you not recollect I asked you to speak to her and find out if she wanted any thing; and do you remember how she looked, and how saucily she answered?"

I began to feel not a little curious to know what was coming, but I replied, quietly: "Yes, I recollect it."

"Now, will you believe it, Mr. Parkinson, I saw that same girl yesterday."

"Well." -

"The same girl, grown up into a young lady, a beautiful young lady."

"But is there any thing surprising in that?"

"Wait till you hear me through. Yes, grown up into a very, *very* beautiful young lady; only the eyes were just the same, just as fierce, just as cruel, and she looked at me so."

Mrs. Havens here nearly gave way to hysterics, but somehow, I could not feel any great alarm on her account. I sat calmly waiting to hear if she had any thing more to add.

At that moment a pretty little child, just beginning to walk, toddled into the room, followed by its nurse.

"The dear little creature. That's my Hetty, Mr. Parkinson," exclaimed Mrs. Havens, rising. "She is a little angel. What could I do without her?" and she caressed the child. "Now you can take her, nurse."

"The fact is," she continued, "I was so nervous I did not sleep a wink all night."

"But really I am at a loss to discover the reason of so much excitement."

"I cannot tell, and that's what distresses me so. It *has* excited me—I *am* excited, and I cannot help it," and she began to cry.

It seemed very extraordinary, that scene. Of course I was now certain that it was Matilda Hitchcock whom Mrs.

Havens had encountered. But how extraordinary the effect on her!

"I do not know, my dear Mr. Parkinson," she continued, "what is the matter with me. I never shall be as happy as I was in old times. You have no idea how miserable I am —indeed, you have not."

I was desirous to avoid any confidential communication, but I began to suspect that Mrs. Havens was not so happy in her domestic relations as she had anticipated; that, coupled with some such misfortune, she was experiencing the usual heart vacancy which her wealth, and consequent inactivity of mind and body, sensibly increased. In this way I accounted for her fits of nervous depression and susceptibility. In one of these moods she had seen Matilda and recognized her. That was a little extraordinary to be sure, but I had myself discovered the identity, which was just as remarkable. The fact is, it was not easy, after seeing Matilda once, to forget her. On this particular occasion she had, doubtless, thrown the whole force of her passionate nature into the look she gave to the fashionable denizen of the avenue, and this seemed to me a natural explanation of the matter.

Mrs. Havens rallied. "Excuse me, Mr. Parkinson, but you seem to be such an old friend—such a good friend—that I feel relieved to tell you about this. I see so little of you. Why doesn't Alice come and see me. Anna has grown up now, I suppose. Charley, my little favorite, is almost a man by this time?"

She ran on in this style a few minutes, until I rose to leave. I really did not know what to say to her. Fortunately, she talked so fast it was not necessary for me to say any thing.

Just as I was going, she rang the bell.

"Not quite yet, Mr. Parkinson. You will taste a glass of sherry. I recollect Madeira used to be your favorite, but Frederick says Madeira is a myth now, and I can only offer you sherry."

I stopped and drank wine with this spoiled child of fortune, this nervous, fidgety, handsome woman. Glad to make my escape, I murmured a few words about not permitting herself to be excited. I could see nothing to cause alarm, and so forth. The atmosphere inside sickened and oppressed me. Outside I breathed freely, and hurried on my way, grateful that Alice and Anna had not grown up like Mrs. Havens. Yet wealth, or a foolish application of it, *would* have made them like her.

CHAPTER XIX.

WHAT DOES IT MEAN?

We were all seated that same evening around our large table. I was reading the paper. Charley sat occupied with a book, Matilda was sewing, Alice was at the piano, and Anna teasing Warren, who was turning over the leaves of a volume which he was not permitted to read. Presently he laid it aside.

"There, now," said Anna, "you need not take it up any more. I don't want you to read when you come here; I want you to talk."

It was evident that Robert Warren was preoccupied, for he only smiled in an absent manner, without saying a word.

Presently he looked up and said: "Matilda Hitchcock."

"Well, sir."

"Do you know what was the Christian name of Mr. Walden, your father's uncle?"

"James."

"How long ago did he die?

"He died about six months before I was born; I suppose you know how old I am?"

"He died after your father?"

"The week after. He never heard of pa's death."

"What did you ever learn about his will?"

"Nothing, except that he left all his property to a distant relation."

" What more did you hear?"

" Now, Robert Warren, please don't be a fool. What more did I hear, you ask. I've just said all this happened before I was born."

" Oh! I thought your mother might have told you something about it."

" Well, that was all there was to tell. Uncle died and left us nothing."

"So your mother told you?"

" So my mother told me."

" And you were born six months afterward."

" I was born six months afterward. My mother told me that, too."

" You are sure his name was James?"

" If by 'his' you mean my father's uncle, Mr. Walden, I am sure his name was James."

" Very strange."

" What, the name?"

" Oh! no."

" Strange that he should be called James?"

" Nonsense."

" Now, Robert Warren, tell me why you ask these questions?"

" Oh! nothing; just to satisfy my curiosity."

" About what?"

" Why, about the matter generally."

" Well, I hope it is satisfied."

"Not altogether; but I suppose I have got all that I can out of you."

"What *do* you mean?" chimed in Anna.

Warren smiled.

"Make him tell, papa," said Anna.

I confess I was wondering quite as much as she. I smiled, too, and said nothing.

"Come here, Alice, and make him explain," cried Anna.

"Oh! he's only rehearsing," cried Matilda; "pray let him alone. If the fellow thinks he can learn how to examine and cross-examine a witness by practising on me, I am quite willing he should."

This provoked no reply from Warren. He continued silent and abstracted, and in a little while took his leave.

"Really, what can it mean?" continued Anna, as Warren left the room.

"How can I tell," said Matilda, pettishly, "unless it means he's a fool?"

"Well, I shall not give it up so. I will have it out of him next time he comes, and Alice shall help me. Charley, don't you feel interested?"

"Oh! yes," said Charley, looking up from his book; "but then, you know I am not quite so excitable as you are, and I am willing to wait."

"Bravo! Charlie," cried Matilda. "There's a philosopher for you."

CHAPTER XX.

THE TURNING-POINT

ANOTHER month passed. We now come to the middle of October. Within a few days, several persons had called to see the house. I had paid the landlord forty-five dollars on account of the rent. It was the semi-annual interest on the fund of the two younger children, invested by the court. There was still more than two quarters due, and the proprietor said he could not let it run on any longer in arrear. Every day I expected to hear that the house had been let, and we must go. Go where? The little debts due in the neighborhood began to annoy me. By that species of prescience, which creditors so often exhibit, it was now very generally understood I was reduced to extremities.

It was Saturday morning, and several little sums had to be paid that afternoon, or we must go without our Sunday's marketing. As I was leaving the house, Alice told me that the servant-girl wanted a part of her month's wages. I hurried to my office. I hoped I should find some calls already on my desk. There were none. I went to half a dozen different places where I thought I should be most apt to find something to do, but no one just then required my services. The sky seemed made of brass. Never had I been in such utter perplexity.

As the day began to wear away, my anxiety increased

18

At length this idea came into my head. I would go to Mr. Frink, and ask him to lend me five dollars! I had rendered him many little services, for which I received no compensation. Besides, he always appeared friendly. It was not unusual for me to go and spend a few minutes with him, even if I had no note to take in, for he sometimes gave me valuable information about paper. So I clambered up to his little room to try the experiment.

Mr. Frink was in, engaged as usual with his check-book. After a few minutes he looked up at me over his spectacles, and said: "How do you do?"

Thereupon a rather pleasant conversation ensued; for Mr. Frink, when he had nothing else to do, was fond of hearing himself talk, especially as his listeners were very sure to agree with him, whatever he said.

The usurer had no commands for me on the present occasion, and as the longer he talked the more unready I felt to broach my subject, I determined to do so abruptly.

Taking advantage of a pause in his remarks, I said: "Mr. Frink, I have been unfortunate to-day in my attempts to make a little money, and I want you to lend me five dollars."

Mr. Frink immediately commenced again at his check-book, saying at the same time, in his ordinary monotonous tone: "I never go into any such transactions."

"I know you do not," I replied; "but I thought, under the circumstances, you might possibly accommodate me with this small sum."

"Oh! it's out of my line; I don't do any of that sort of business."

"I suppose not. Good morning."

I went back to my desk. Alice was standing by it as I entered.

"Papa," she whispered, "Mr. Hoyt has sent in word that he has rented the house, and will want possession on Monday."

"Very well, I will see to it. Now go right home again, my child."

She departed, and I sank into a chair stunned and helpless. After a few minutes I rose, and proceeded with uncertain steps as far as Broadway. I then turned and walked slowly the whole length of Wall-street to the river. There I entered a ferry-boat, crossed and recrossed, while I stood against the railing where I might be exposed to the full sweep of the air. Landing, I retraced my steps, entered my office again, and sat down, leaning my head upon my hand.

It was past three o'clock. All the other inmates of the office had left for home. Suddenly the door opened with a jerk.

"Charles E. Parkinson!"

I looked up. It was the postman, already standing near me.

"Two cents."

He left a letter, received the money, and was off in a twinkling.

I took the letter in my hand, and looked at it carefully. The postmark was illegible, the handwriting unfamiliar. I suppose I held it five minutes before I opened it. Then, not without some tremor, I broke the seal.

CHAPTER XXI.

THE LETTER.

THE envelope covered a short note and another letter.
The note read as follows :

"CANANDAIGUA, *October* 15*th*, 1858.

" MR. CHARLES E. PARKINSON, New York.

" DEAR SIR : It is my melancholy duty to inform you of
the decease of William Moulton, Esq., who died of consumption yesterday morning at eleven o'clock. In accordance with his last injunctions, I send you the enclosed.
When the will of the deceased shall be submitted for pro-
bate, I will communicate with you further.

" Respectfully yours,

" O. L. FARLEY."

I tore open and read the letter.

"TUESDAY EVENING.

" DEAR CHARLES :

" It is many years since a letter has passed between us.
I sometimes think how strange it is that two, whose sympathies were so much in common, should ever lose sight of
each other. Do you remember how in college we declared
our fortunes should be inseparable, that success for one
should be success 'for both ? I reproach myself now for
not communicating with you during my long sojourn in
Europe. But the time ran by, I hardly know how, and

my health becoming more and more precarious, I gave up the idea of indulging in correspondence. For the last two years, I have kept myself alive only by the exercise of the greatest care and prudence. When the physicians told me I could not live three months, I felt an irresistible desire to return and die in my own country. I came back to our old home. Perhaps you were not aware my wife died in 1853. We had no children, but we adopted one of my nieces and brought her up as our own daughter. She is married and I am now with her.

"My first thought on reaching here two weeks ago, was to inquire about you. It happened our old classmate, Allen, who you recollect used to know about every body and every thing, called to see me on his way to Cincinnati, and he told me you were suffering pecuniary distress. I was anxious to dispatch a letter to you at once, but I had many things to arrange and I feared my strength would fail. For a day or two I have experienced a great rallying of the system, with an increase of strength and spirits. I believe it to be the forerunner of death.

"And now about your own affairs. You remember the five thousand dollars you insisted on returning to me. When that was sent back, I said to myself, who knows but he may want it again? I resolved to put the sum apart and to treat it as your property. With this idea I purchased some real estate in 1845, at a very low price, and paid for it with your five thousand dollars. Had I been taken away at any time, this property by my will would have gone to you. It is now worth at least thirty thousand dollars. To prevent delay in affording immediate relief, I

have altered my will so as to leave to you that sum
in cash, or rather to your children, the income to you
during your life. I put it in this shape from prudential motives. I know it will be just as acceptable. I en-
close in this letter five hundred dollars. It is a little token
of my affection and in remembrance of old college times.
Those times come back to me very vividly. I lay awake
all last night and thought of you and Ralph. Do you remember old *Pater Omnium?* Baker, who had his leg
broken playing football, I saw in Nice last winter. Do
you recollect his helping us that cold night turn the bell
and pour water into it, so that there would be no ringing
up for prayers next morning? and how your hands got
frozen to the bell so tight that you had to slip them out of
your gloves, which you left behind?

"Dear friend, just as I must die my youth comes back to
me. Every feeling of my heart is young to-night. But I am
ready to die, I am indeed. For many years I have endeavored to place my whole trust in Christ. I trust in him now.

"Dear Charles, how relieved you will feel when you receive this. Think of it as coming direct from ' Will,' and
think of ' Will,' as in old times, on his way with you to
Rhode Island, to spend the summer vacation. Don't stop
to be a little melancholy when you read this, but, if you love
me, give a happy laugh and say, ' Good fellow.' Adieu,

"Affectionately yours,

"WILLIAM MOULTON."

A small piece of paper fell on the floor. I picked it up.
It was a bank draft for the five hundred dollars.

I sat very still for a little while for fear something would disturb the dream, and bring back the old reality. There was the letter—there the bank draft. I looked around the room. My vision was accurate. I counted three desks besides my own, six chairs, the windows and the doors.

Then I looked again at what was in my hand. Could there be any mistake? No, there was no mistake. I gazed at the writing, I handled the draft. I read and reread the last page of the letter. He says I must laugh and say, " Good fellow." Dear Will—ha, ha, goo-goo-good fel-fellow, ha, ha, goo-goo-good fellow.

Choking—eyes blinded by tears—nerves relaxed, it was too much for me.

.   .   .   .

Gradually I recovered. Slowly my senses returned. I drew a long breath, folded the draft and placed it inside the letter; folded the letter and placed it inside the envelope; folded Mr. Farley's note and placed all inside his envelope, and put it carefully in the breast-pocket of my coat. I rose and opened the door into the street; stopped and looked back into the room; turned and closed the door after me and walked away, into Broadway, along Broadway past Canal-street, further up Broadway, walking slowly on. Presently I put my hand to my pocket, drew out the package, examined it to see if the letter and draft were there—all right—and I went on.

I reached home. The children and Matilda were in the back parlor. They were sad, and Matilda angry. She was in a rage with the landlord. They all looked at me inquiringly as I entered. I stood and regarded them a moment.

Then I drew the package from my pocket, and laying it on the table, said, " Read that."

Alice took it up.

" Aloud."

The scene which ensued restored me to myself. Such a scene though. Each manifesting feeling in the way most natural. Laughing, crying; quietly, hysterically; joy, tears, pensiveness, mirth.

I shall not attempt to describe it.

.   .   .   .

In the evening Warren came as usual. I hardly know who was permitted first to tell the good news. If I recollect right the whole family had a share in it. Warren was, of course, delighted, but not to the extent to satisfy Matilda. She was vexed with him for not showing more feeling, and told him so. It seemed to me Warren appeared a little absent. He would look at Matilda vacantly, and make no reply to her accusations.

After a while I went out in order to call on my landlord, with the hope of being able still to retain the house. In this I was successful. When I told him I was ready to pay up the back rent, and also the next quarter in advance, if he desired, he appeared to be rejoiced on my account.

" I can get rid of the new tenant, Mr. Parkinson," he said, " and I will do so. I am very glad you are able to keep the house, more than glad, I assure you," and he shook my hand cordially.

When I got home Warren had already gone. He left a message that he wanted to see me in the morning, and would call before going down town.

CHAPTER XXII.

A STRANGE REVELATION.

WHILE we were seated at the table the next morning, Warren entered. He had already breakfasted. So he sat chatting with us until we had finished, apparently recovered from his previous abstraction.

When we were all through, he said : "Now, Mr. Parkinson, I want you to exert your authority, and order these young people out of the room, so that we may hold a specially private consultation."

"Bless the man," cried Matilda, "we are only too glad of an excuse to escape from his stupid society," and off they all ran, Charley bringing up the rear.

"I have," said Warren, advancing his chair nearer to mine, and speaking deliberately, "I have a strange revelation to make—a very strange revelation."

"Pray what is it ?"

"I would not speak even to you before I was sure. Now I am so ; it is settled beyond all doubt or cavil."

"What, pray ?"

"That Matilda is entitled to the whole Walden property."

"Heavens, you don't say so !"

"I do, indeed. I will tell you all about it. Some time ago, in the course of my business, I had occasion to look over the record books of wills in the surrogate's office, when,

18*

as I was turning a leaf, my eye fell on the words, 'Doctor Ralph Hitchcock.' They arrested my attention, for I knew that was the name of Matilda's father. I looked to see whose will it was. It was the will of James Walden. I read it. Can you imagine my surprise on finding that the testator, after making a few trifling legacies, devised and bequeathed the whole of his property to the children of his nephew, Doctor Ralph Hitchcock of Cincinnati; this failing, to Thomas Stevenson of the city of New York.

"I was thunderstruck. It was as simple as plain English could make it. I looked over the proceedings before the surrogate, when the will was proved. The citation had been duly served on "Mrs. Hitchcock, widow of Ralph Hitchcock." She did not attend. It was proved that Dr. Hitchcock died childless. I questioned Matilda, and found she was born about six months after her father's death. In the midst of her grief, at the loss of her husband, the widow, doubtless, never thought of getting a copy of the will. She was probably told that all the property went to Mr. Stevenson. She would not be disappointed, for she did not expect any part of it. Living so far away, she was afterward entirely lost sight of. That was my explanation of the matter. Next I called on Thaddeus Littleton, who was executor of James Walden, and also of Thomas Stevenson. You know what a careful, accurate man he is. I explained the object of my visit. He was a good deal excited at my communication.

"There was no doubt, he said, that Dr. Hitchcock's child, if in existence, would be entitled to the property; but he declared he did not believe any was living; that I must be mistaken or had been imposed on. He said he had made proper inquiries after Mr. Walden died, and was satisfied, at the time, that the doctor left no issue.

"I explained all, very particularly, in detail. I need not repeat to you. He was staggered; and it was agreed he should quietly investigate the subject before any thing was said to either side. That is what he has been doing. He is satisfied there was a child born; that Mrs. Hitchcock removed with it to New York, and it now only remains to prove Matilda's identity. For that purpose I want you to call on Mr. Littleton this morning, and tell him what you know on the subject. In fact I have made an appointment for you to meet him at ten o'clock at his office. Can you go?"

"Certainly, if I can recover from the amazement I am in at present."

"I don't wonder at that," replied Warren. "The fact is, it has seemed as if I were dreaming from the time I first came across the record of that will. Now, however, I feel sure. Come, it is time for us to be going—not a syllable to Matilda yet."

I nodded; went and put on my coat, and off we started for Mr. Littleton's.

As I walked along, the ground seemed to dance under me. I appeared to be in some strange delirium. Was I the same Charles Parkinson who walked down town twenty-four hours before? Oh, my GOD! is it possible—*can* it be possible? Am I free at last? Is such a tremendous change in store for Matilda?

My brain teeming with these thoughts, we reached Mr. Littleton's office. That gentleman received us very politely.

"Mr. Parkinson, I recollect you perfectly; although it is many years since we used to meet. We had a mutual friend in Mr. Alton. Dear me, dear me, what about this dreadful business. I say dreadful, when thinking of poor Mrs. Havens. Well, well, who could have believed it? Pray tell me all you know of this young person."

My statement was very direct, and to the point. I could not only certify myself as to Matilda's identity, but I could name many others who could testify to the same point.

Mr. Littleton heard me in silence.

When I had concluded, he exclaimed: "I see, I see. It is very clear; but how extraordinary! and yet how simple the mistake. It is very easily explained. You must know Mr. Walden's will was made two or three years before his death, and while Dr. Hitchcock had children living. After Mr. Walden died, I wrote to inquire if the doctor left any issue, and was told he had not. I did not communicate the contents of the will to the widow, because I thought it would only be aggravating to her feelings."

"Just my own explanation of the matter," I said.

"But what is to become of the poor woman?" continued Mr. Littleton, "what *is* to become of her? By the way, what kind of person is this young lady?"

"One who will not be a discredit to her new position," I answered.

"I am glad of that. She will step into a pretty property, a good deal larger, too, than people think for. It had got to be a clean fifteen thousand a year before Miss Stevenson married, and it was so tied up that her husband could not meddle with the principal. Nice little demand for arrears,

if there was any body to respond. I have a very disagreeable
business on my hands," continued he; "I don't see how I
am to get through with it. Just think of my being obliged
to go in and tell Mrs. Havens that she must vacate those
premises and surrender her whole fortune; in short that she
is a beggar. But I have got to do it. It is fit and proper
that I should be the person. As executor of her father this
painful task devolves on me. Old as I am, I would rather receive thirty-nine lashes, well laid on, than perform it. If her
husband were half a man I should not feel so distressed about
it; as it is, GOD only knows what is to become of her."

After some further conversation, I took leave of Mr. Littleton, with the understanding that he should open the subject to Mrs. Havens that evening, and communicate with me
in a day or two. I returned to speak with Matilda.

Reaching home again, I found Anna practising at the
piano. I sent her up-stairs to ask Matilda to come down.

When she entered, I led the way into the back parlor,
and stopping short, I said: "Matilda, you must summon all
your philosophy. I have a very extraordinary communication to make to you."

"Well, what is it?"

"Are you ready for it? Mind, I tell you, it will give you
a shock."

"I am ready."

"It turns out you are entitled to all your uncle Walden's
property."

"What!"

"It turns out you are entitled to all your uncle Walden's
property."

" Is that so truly ?"

" It is ;" and I told her all about it.

It was a scene for the painter. We were both standing, and while I related the story, her eyes dilated, and her countenance became rigid. Sunshine and shadow flitted across her face. Pain, terror, hope.

" And all this is certain beyond a question—beyond the possibility of a question ?" she asked.

" It is."

She stood a moment, her eyes fixed on vacancy.

" What a wicked wretch I have been all my life," she exclaimed, and rushed out of the room.

CHAPTER XXIII.

THE INTERVIEW.

A FEW days served to settle the whole matter. It was too plain for the lawyers to raise any question about. Mr. Littleton himself, one of the most acute of his profession, decided that it was a clear case, and nothing was left but to put the whole matter in proper legal shape. This, too, was soon arranged.

Then it was that Matilda asked me to go with her one morning to see Mrs. Havens. Since the first burst of feeling, she had preserved in every respect her ordinary demeanor. She was perhaps more quiet and thoughtful, yet quite natural.

We walked along together, neither speaking a word. As we mounted the steps of Mrs. Havens' (now Matilda's) house, she said: "You will introduce me." We were ushered in, and presently Mrs. Havens made her appearance. Poor woman, how she had changed since I saw her last, only a few weeks before. I was afraid she was about to give way to another fit of hysterics, but a real trouble had improved her nerves, and she preserved a decent composure. I introduced them to each other and we took seats.

"Mrs. Havens," said Matilda in a subdued tone, which I thought required some effort to make firm; "Mrs. Havens, I have come to ask you a single question. Several years ago my mother wrote you a letter, and sent it to your house. I have called to ask if you ever received it."

"Never, so help me Heaven, never," replied Mrs. Havens earnestly. "I declare to you I did not know your mother resided in the city, or that she had a daughter living."

"I am satisfied," said Matilda, rising to go.

"Stay," continued Mrs. Havens. "I think I can recall the circumstance. One day I was quite ill, so ill that I remained all the morning in bed. My maid brought in a letter, and as I was suffering from a severe headache, I bade her open it. She did so, remarking that it was a communication from some poor person, who wished for aid. I asked her if any one was waiting for an answer. She said there was not. I bade her put the letter safely aside, that I might examine it when I felt better. The next day I asked her for it, and she said it had been thrown into the fire by accident. Possibly it was the letter you speak of, but I solemnly declare I did not know from whom it came."

A flashing of the eyes, a swelling of the veins of the forehead, a dilation of the nostrils, a close compression of the lips, while Mrs. Havens was giving an account of the fate of her mother's letter, led me to fear some passionate outbreak on the part of Matilda. But she controlled herself, and only bowed when the former finished.

Turning to leave the room, she said : "Mr. Parkinson will call on you in a few days. I assure you I am much relieved by your explanation."

We walked back to my house as we came—in silence.

CHAPTER XXIV.

THE CONCLUSION.

"It is now my turn to ask that the room be cleared of all idle people, triflers and useless folks. I suppose Alice will come next and demurely ask an interview with "papa," to settle certain little preliminary arrangements about—don't look so frightened, young lady, I am not going to betray you—I only ask at the present moment that the supernumeraries vacate this apartment, and give me an opportunity to talk with the 'head of the family.' Oh! Charley, I beg your pardon; I did not observe you had not finished your coffee. Take your time. We are in no hurry."

The reader doubtless will recognize Matilda in the above speech.

We were speedily alone together.

"Don't you want to know what I am going to do?"

"Yes."

"Let me tell you. In the first place I shall sell the house Mrs. Havens now occupies. I cannot afford such an establishment. She may remain in it till May; will you tell her so? The furniture I shall not touch, she is at liberty to do what she pleases with it. Tell her that too. Further, I shall set apart two thousand dollars a year for her especial use. Will you communicate all this as kindly as you choose?

I do not think I wish to see her again. We have not a thought or a sympathy in common.

"Now for my plans. I shall purchase a nice house pleasantly situated. It must be commodious and neatly finished. The best room in it is for you. The next Alice and I will draw lots for. We will all have our own apartments, prettily furnished too; there shall be special arrangements for Charley, who is ill sometimes. I know Alice is soon to be married. That will make no difference, for the fellow is here now, all the time he is not at his office. For myself"—she stopped an instant, and proceeded with an air of solemnity—"GOD ought to strike me dead if, after complaining of HIM all my life, I dare to do as other rich people do. I shall limit myself to a reasonable sum. No horses, no carriages, no extravagancies. I don't know but I will have a saddle-horse, it has been the dream of my life to possess one; but no ostentation, no display. We will live together happy, as we have lived, and I will begin and try to do some good. Just think what I can do with all this money rolling in every month. I shall not require a quarter of it. I shall try to make some hearts glad, without putting them under an everlasting burning sense of disgrace and dependence.

She walked up and down the room, a good deal excited. I knew she was thinking of her mother.

"Well, what do you say?" she asked, turning and looking at me. "Will you be ready to move?"

"What can I say, my dear child, to such a generous suggestion? But, really, I must not accede to it. You have no idea how inconvenient it will prove for you."

"Mr. Parkinson," replied Matilda, "you are too old for me to manage as I would Warren, and therefore, I think, old enough to be reasonable. Now then, as I know Alice and Anna and Charley, are fond of me, and you used to like me sometimes, and as I wish you to preserve your feeling of independence, I propose you pay into the common treasury what really, on a fair computation, it actually costs extra for your being in the house. I am sure you wont insist on my making money out of you, as boarders."

I laughed at perceiving the very words I once employed to persuade Matilda to live with us, so ingeniously turned on me.

"I give it up," I said. "As usual, you must have things your own way."

"Thanks," cried Matilda, warmly.

"But stop a moment!"

"What now?"

"You will get married one of these days."

"One of these days perhaps I shall. When the time comes we will talk about it. Now, once more, is all settled?"

"All settled."

"Bravo! Let us announce our programme."

. . . .

Reader, we part here. I have become so accustomed to recount to you my doleful experiences, that I find myself quite incompetent to proceed in a new strain; and as nothing miserable is left for me to record, I must stop.

One word, however, in your ear—one word strictly confidential. I have exposed to you many of my weaknesses.

I will conclude by betraying one more. I confess I have never returned to look after my desk and my two chairs, in that basement office in Wall-street. For aught I know, those articles still remain there, and should any one have the least curiosity on the subject, he is at liberty to satisfy it by visiting the premises.

THE END